I0825082

Devils We Know

Also by L.T. Thompson

Devils Like Us

Devils We Know

L. T. THOMPSON

BLOOMSBURY
NEW YORK LONDON OXFORD NEW DELHI SYDNEY

BLOOMSBURY YA
Bloomsbury Publishing Inc., part of Bloomsbury Publishing Plc
1359 Broadway, New York, NY 10018
50 Bedford Square, London, WC1B 3DP, UK
Bloomsbury Publishing Ireland Limited, 29 Earlsfort Terrace, Dublin 2, D02 AY28, Ireland

First published in the United States of America June 2026 by Bloomsbury YA

Library of Congress Cataloging-in-Publication Data
Names: Thompson, L. T. author
Title: Devils we know / by L.T. Thompson.
Description: New York : Bloomsbury, 2026. | Series: Devils like us ; 2 |
Summary: Three queer teens make a bargain with death in order to save
one of their own, as they sail the seas on the run from a secret society
pursuing Cas's prophetic powers.
Identifiers: LCCN 2026012656 (print) | LCCN 2026012657 (ebook) |
ISBN 978-1-5476-1523-0 (hardcover) | ISBN 978-1-5476-1524-7 (e-book)
Subjects: CYAC: Magic | Supernatural | Death | Sailing | LGBTQ+ people |
LCGFT: Fantasy fiction | Novels
Classification: LCC PZ7.1.T46793 Df 2026 (print) | LCC PZ7.1.T46793 (ebook)
LC record available at https://lccn.loc.gov/2026012656
LC ebook record available at https://lccn.loc.gov/2026012657

Book design by Jeanette Levy
Typesetting by Six Red Marbles India
Printed in the United States by Lakeside Book Company
2 4 6 8 10 9 7 5 3 1

For Cara

Devils We Know

I.
FINN

When she was twelve years old, Finn Robinson summoned a demon.

She didn't summon the demon *well*. She played a bit fast and loose with the instructions from the old grimoire, although in her defense, the instructions were absurdly and impossibly specific. How on earth was Finn supposed to acquire "a girdle of lion's skin three inches broad"? Or "the blood of a white cockerel that never trode hen"? The Pendleton farm on the edge of town kept chickens, but there was only one rooster in the coop, and its feathers were brown. Finn wasn't quite sure what "trode hen" meant, and she didn't much want to find out.

It didn't matter. She wouldn't have had the stomach to slit the poor creature's throat anyway.

She made substitutions for the materials where she could. The spell book told her to hold a sword during the ritual, so Finn brought an old, iron fire poker from the house where she worked as a maid. The book told her to wear a "miter or cap"; her threadbare knit hat would have to do. For the "annointing oil to annoint thy temples and thine eyes with," she stole a scoop of lard from the kitchen, which turned sticky as it melted and made her hands smell like bacon.

She bundled all the materials into a sack. Then, a little before midnight, she broke into the old feed barn on the Pendleton farm. The barn was rarely used anymore, and its floor had plenty of space for Finn to draw the summoning circle, copying out the shapes from the spell book by dragging a stick through the dirt. This would be the main circle, here. She sketched a snake around the outer edge of it, though her snake was a wobbly, clumsy thing compared to the one in the book. Here, two feet beyond the circle's easternmost point, would be the demon's triangle. Supposedly, the triangle would force the demon to take a human form, and keep the demon contained. Finn was careful not to scuff the lines after she'd drawn them.

If she was being honest with herself, she didn't really expect a demon to appear that night. Even as she lit the stubby candles and placed them at the edges, it all felt like a game. An unholy play. The actions of a desperate, terrible girl, with terrible things in her heart. It wasn't that she was a skeptic, exactly; it wasn't that Finn didn't believe in demons. She'd been raised on stories of both Catholic miracles and Irish fairy folk. Though she hadn't yet witnessed anything supernatural with her own eyes, the existence of demons seemed plausible enough.

But she knew, deep down, that a demon wouldn't appear for *her*. The rituals in this old grimoire were meant for other people—the same sorts of powerful men who'd written such books in the first place. Men with influence and wealth that Finn couldn't even imagine. Men who could obtain their girdle of lion's skin by paying a butler to pay a merchant to slay a lion abroad and have its skin shipped back home.

These rituals weren't meant for girls like Finn, who had to steal supplies from the servants' quarters and break into other people's barns.

Even the spell book itself was stolen. Finn had nabbed it from her employer's study six days ago, after her brother had become too weak to get out of bed anymore. Kieran's sleep was fitful and feverish, and he was still coughing that terrible cough that made Finn's own chest ache in commiseration. Doctor Gregory told Finn in solemn tones that the consumption had progressed too far. The end was near. All the doctor could do for Kieran now was try to keep him comfortable.

Doctor Gregory was a useless man.

Still, Finn had called him back to Kieran's bedside that day, mere hours before she planned to attempt the ritual. The grimoire she'd stolen contained a list of seventy-two demons, along with the various gifts and abilities each might offer to those who summoned them. Each demon had a specific seal that was to be cast in a specific metal.

Finn had scoured the list three times over before she'd settled on the demon who would best suit her need: Marbas. He was a President of Hell, which meant that his seal should be cast in pure mercury.

That afternoon, Finn paced circles around Kieran's little apartment while the doctor did his examination. The prognosis hadn't changed. If anything, Kieran's condition was worse. Doctor Gregory patted Finn on the head and told her that he knew this was difficult, but he couldn't work miracles. Finn nodded and thanked him and said she understood.

When he was packing up, she stole the thermometer from his bag. Doctor Gregory was useful for one thing after all.

As the distant church bells began to chime for midnight, Finn knelt in the center of her summoning circle. She'd etched Marbas's seal into a small plate, scratching the lines to form deep grooves in the clay. Now, she snapped the glass thermometer in half and poured its contents into the mold, careful not to spill a single drop of the precious mercury. Slowly, the metal flowed to fill the shape.

She rubbed the lard on her temples. She held her fire poker. She opened her stolen spell book, and she began the recitation in Latin.

And she knew, all the while, that no demon would appear. Perhaps this was why Finn hadn't fussed too much over finding the proper materials. Perhaps, after this, when she staggered home crying like the wretched thing she was, it would soothe her to be able to blame her own substitutions. To know that she'd done something wrong. This was *her* fault. *Her* failure. If she'd only followed the instructions correctly, if she'd only performed the spell better, if she'd *been* better, then perhaps Kieran would live. She was pathetic. The Latin words sounded ridiculous in her mouth. Why was she even bothering? You didn't change every ingredient in a recipe and still expect it to turn out a decent cake.

She knew the summoning ritual wouldn't work, but she tried it anyway. And this, apparently, was the key.

"Do you really think I care about lions' skins or rooster blood?" the demon asked when he did, in fact, appear. He was standing inside the triangle in the dirt, just as the book had promised. "I've seen far too many pampered men of fortune follow a spell book to the letter. But they don't put any real *fire* behind it. So what's even the damn point?"

The demon had arrived as a column of smoke at first, then formed into the shape of a lion, then formed into something like a man. Finn couldn't look directly at the man's eyes, though she could feel his burning gaze as he studied her.

"But you have fire aplenty, don't you?" the demon said after a moment. "You're desperate."

In the end, it wasn't the lard on her temples, or the botched Latin recitations, or the seal cast in mercury that had persuaded Marbas to answer her call. It was her desperation.

"Are you frightened?" the demon asked her.

"Not of you," Finn said. It wasn't even a lie. However frightening this demon might be, it was nothing compared to the future she was facing otherwise: Kieran in an early grave and Finn somehow expected to live the rest of her life without him. Kieran, who was her last remaining family. Kieran, who was four years her elder but gentler, softer. Kieran, who Finn was meant to protect.

"Tell me what you seek," the demon said.

The grimoire had described several abilities of the demon Marbas, including this: *He causeth Diseases, and he cureth them.* This was why Finn had chosen this particular demon from the list of seventy-two. There was a Disease she needed cureth-ed.

After she'd laid out her cause in a shaking voice, the demon said, "All right. Easy."

Finn wasn't sure how to reply to this. "Is it?"

"Of course. I can remove the illness from your brother and allow him to live a long, happy life. But it will cost you. Dearly."

"I thought you said it was easy," Finn said.

"It *is* easy. It isn't free."

Finn thought the demon would take her that night, at the moment she signed the contract. He didn't. When the deal was finished, Marbas only smiled, though the smile didn't touch those burning eyes.

"We'll see you again soon," he said, and he was gone.

After Finn had hastily cleaned up all the evidence of her deed and closed up the Pendletons' barn, she raced across town. She let herself into Kieran's apartment. Kieran was sitting up in bed, breathing deeply for the first time in weeks. His cheeks were pink, but this wasn't the flush of fever. This was the flush of *life*.

The next morning, Doctor Gregory called his recovery a miracle. Perhaps it was, but not one from God. Only Finn knew how her brother had really been cured.

And for six years now, she's been waiting to pay the price for it. Biding her time. Drifting through her life. Trying not to form attachments, trying not to care too much, because what was the point when the demon might drag her off to hell at any moment? But the days stretched on, and the years stretched on, and she's still drifting, still waiting for the end.

It's almost funny, Finn thinks, that she, Remy, and Cas have found themselves aboard a ship called the *Memento Mori*. All humans should remember they will die, but Finn is more acutely aware than most. And Cas Sterling—with his prophetic visions of deaths that are to come—can surely never forget it.

Cas has foreseen Finn's death twice now, which means the death is coming soon. Finn tries to convince the others she's made peace with her fate, but they don't believe her. She's not sure she believes it herself. She tries to convince them all anyway.

It's better this way, safer, to keep them at a remove. This is what she tells herself. This is what she wants to be true.

When the time comes for Finn to die, she won't drag her friends down with her.

All morning, they've waited for the fog to lift, and all morning, it's only grown denser. By noon, the *Memento Mori* is sailing slowly through a heavy white cloud, a veil blocking out the rest of the world. Nearly the entire crew is on watch. The watches typically alternate, so that only half the sailors are working at any given time. Those on duty will handle any number of shipboard tasks: taking in sails, washing the decks, coiling up loose rigging.

Today, they've been tasked with *only* watching. All hands are stationed aloft or at the ship's rails, peering off into the mist, eyes peeled for . . . something.

Finn doesn't say it, but she doubts they're going to find their mark when they can barely see a dozen yards in any direction. The *Mori* has been sailing slow circles in this region for nearly three days with nothing to show for it. The mood is bleak.

"We're wasting time," Remy mutters, as she's been muttering all day. "Smith had these coordinates for god knows how long before *we* got ahold of them. His men have probably already come and gone. We need to be getting ahead of him—not chasing down leads he discovered weeks ago."

She and Finn are posted near the ship's bow. Finn is squinting out at the fog, just as she's been ordered. But Remy is sitting with her back against the rail, research journal open in her lap, scribbling angry marks in the margins of her own notes. The damp air has left her hair curlier than ever, dark ringlets that seem to escape no matter how tightly Remy tries to tie them out of her face.

"What other leads do we have to chase?" Finn asks her.

"I'm . . . working on some theories," Remy says, which means she doesn't have any leads at all. "But I can't do much when we don't have any new information. And we're not going to *get* new information by drifting around in the middle of nowhere. The coordinates were a fine idea, sure—but I'd say we've hit a dead end."

Seven days ago, when Finn and the others had broken into—and then out of—the Eden Theological Seminary, Finn had copied down the set of coordinates from inside a summoning circle in the Reverend John Smith's office. She had no idea what they might point to—only that the Order of Lazarus had gone to great lengths to acquire them. When she, Remy, and Cas sat down with the captain afterward and presented him with the numbers, the captain set an immediate course.

But plotting the coordinates on a map is one thing. Sailing to their precise location on the open sea turns out to be a different beast altogether. The coordinates are somewhere over Georges Bank, an area more than a hundred miles east of Cape Cod where the seafloor is only a few dozen fathoms down. There are no other landmarks here. Finn knows very little about nautical navigation, and the process is tedious. It involves a sextant, a chronometer, and a procedure called "shooting the sun." It involves Captain Hobbes and his first mate, Kit, arguing over a dog-eared copy of Nathaniel Bowditch's *New American Practical Navigator*. It involves a lot of complicated math that seems to baffle even Remy, which means Finn doesn't have a hope in hell of following it.

Kit insists they're narrowing in on their target. But she can't "shoot the sun" if she can't *see* the sun, so the impermeable fog has tipped her navigation into guesswork. And it doesn't help that they still don't even know what they're out here looking for.

"We ought to be heading back toward shore," Remy is saying. "At this point, we're only putting off the inevitable. I don't see why the captain won't give this up."

Finn startles as a figure swings down from the ladder of rigging beside her.

"You're going to get strung up for mutiny, talking like that,"

Immortal Gabe says as he balances on the rail. With his stocky build and long, windswept hair, he might cut an imposing figure, but Finn knows he's a sentimental sap at heart.

Remy frowns up at him. "Has the captain really strung people up for mutiny before?"

"Of course not," Gabe says. "Have you met the man? He'd probably invite the mutineers for a stern talking-to and have them begging for forgiveness by the end." He jumps down from the railing, narrowly missing Remy's knee when he lands on the deck. "Aren't you meant to be looking out like the rest of us?"

Remy gives an irritated huff and closes her journal. Her cheeks are flushed pink. "I'm not asking for *mutiny*," she says as she stands and faces the water. "I'm just asking that he recognize the urgency of the situation. His partner may be able to hide out forever while we figure out what to do about the Order. But some of us don't have that time."

"We've only been out here a few days," Gabe points out. "What's so urgent?"

Finn is very, very careful to keep her face blank, though she can feel Remy staring at her. The silence stretches. Finn wishes Cas were here to break it. But he's belowdecks somewhere with Striker, practicing meditation, of all things.

"Remy's just eager to get home to her mother," Finn says.

"Well, damn," Gabe says. "Can't fault you for that, I suppose. First lesson of seafaring life: Never trust the winds to get you home by curfew." He goes on for a few minutes about the whims of nature, and promises Remy they can send a letter to her mother when they next make port.

After Gabe wanders away, Remy rounds on Finn. "We'll have to tell them at some point."

"No," Finn says. "We won't."

"We need their help! *You* need—"

"There is no *help*," Finn hisses, voice low. She can't shake the sense of too many ears around them. "Don't start this again, please."

"What harm is there in asking?" Remy hisses back.

"What *harm*?"

"Yes! What do you have to lose?"

"Maybe I just don't want the rest of them looking at me like—*that*"—she sees Remy try to scrub the pity from her own face, but it's too late—"when they find out I sold my soul to a bloody demon."

"Ah, the bloody demon. My monthly nemesis," Cas says, and Remy and Finn both whirl to find him standing just behind them.

"In this case, we're talking about a literal demon," Remy says.

"Hmm." Cas wedges himself between them and props his elbows on the rail. "Could we argue that menstruation *is* a literal demon, though?"

"No," Remy says. "No, we could not argue that. What are you doing up here, anyway? I thought you were working with Striker."

"She gave me the afternoon off."

Remy and Finn exchange a wary look. "Because you're making such good progress?" Remy asks.

"No, because I asked too many questions, apparently, and she got testy and kicked a box."

"Jesus," Finn murmurs.

"Not *at* me," Cas clarifies. "She just kicked it. Can't really blame her. I was about ready to kick something as well."

He says this lightly, as if it's a joke, but Finn suspects his frustration is perfectly real. She squints at him. Same easy expression, same emphatically arched eyebrows, but there's something odd about his face that Finn can't place.

"Why were you asking so many questions?" Remy asks.

"I'm just trying to get it right! Striker keeps describing what it's supposed to feel like, and it *doesn't* feel like that, and I don't know what I'm doing wrong."

"I don't know that you can meditate *wrong*," Remy tells him.

"Clearly you can!" Cas throws up his hands; the easy expression was indeed a sham. "And nothing we've tried is working, because I still can't talk to Death, or tap into our *shared spiritual channel*, or whatever Kit called it—"

"You just have to keep practicing," Remy cuts in. She probably thinks she's being encouraging, though Finn can hear the edge to her voice. "No one expects you to be an expert immediately. Do you want me to come sit with you below while you keep working?"

"No. I want to claw my brain out of my own skull and throw it in the ocean."

He sighs and rubs a hand over his face, wincing a little as it brushes the half-healed scar running down one side of it. The wound left by Smith's knife back at Eden stretches from brow to cheekbone. Cas has been styling his cropped chestnut hair in a way that casts the scar mostly in shadow, but it's still conspicuous, a puckered red line against his fair skin.

"Sorry," Cas says. "I'm fine. You're right. I'll keep practicing. I just need a break for a while."

He does look exhausted. Finn isn't sure how much he's been sleeping these days—or *if* he's been sleeping. He's rarely in the fo'c'sle when Finn retires for the night, and he's rarely there when she wakes in the morning, either.

She realizes suddenly what's different about his face.

"Your stitches are out," Finn says.

"Oh. Right." Cas rubs absently at the wound. "Leo took them out this morning. It wasn't nearly as bad as getting them put in, but it was still pretty bad. I don't recommend it. Never get stabbed."

Finn snorts. "Decent advice."

"I've had a thought," Cas says, clearly eager to shift subjects. "Maybe a bad thought. But the captain said there's a whole slew of Deaths out there, right? His Death is only one of them. We think my visions come from a connection with *a* reaper, sure. But how do we know it's the right reaper?"

This seems to give Remy pause. Her lips purse in a way that brings out the dimples in the centers of her round cheeks. "That . . . is a very good question," she says in a tone that means she's annoyed she hadn't thought of it first.

She isn't looking at Cas, though. She's turned to where Captain Hobbes has been making his rounds, shoulders back, eyes keen. Finn hadn't been certain the captain was listening to their conversation, but he pauses now, considering. The eerie mist has left a sheen on his deep brown skin.

"When you've witnessed these deaths in your visions," Captain Hobbes asks Cas slowly, "where have the deaths taken place?"

Cas has straightened a little. "Near Windover, mostly. Or the towns around it. Except for—"

His gaze flicks to Finn. She presents him with a warning glare before he can tell the captain about his most recent vision, which took place on Mount Desert Island and showed the demon killing Finn. Again.

"That's it," Cas amends. "Just around Windover."

"And where is Windover?" the captain asks.

"Massachusetts, on the North Shore," Remy says. "Near the Lynn Woods."

In his usual measured tone, the captain says, "The reaper with whom you're connected is my partner."

He states it as fact—like this only confirms something he already suspected was true. He walks away before they can ask how he's so certain. Finn wonders at the captain's stoic veneer. This has to be strange for him: His partner of nearly two decades is missing, and the only person who might be able to find him is a jittery youth who stowed away on his ship a week ago and never left. Whatever frustration Remy might be feeling about Cas's lack of progress in contacting Death, it's surely nothing compared to the captain's.

Captain Hobbes's composure is impressive. If Remy were missing, even for a day, Finn would be losing her mind.

They all watch the captain's retreating back as he resumes his rounds.

"I guess that settles that," Cas says. He turns to look out at the sea around them. "Have we found anything yet?"

Remy gives a peevish sigh. "Don't you think we would've said if we had? We can't see anything in this damned fog."

"Maybe the fog itself is what the coordinates are supposed to lead to," Cas says. "Maybe we've already found it."

"Why would Smith want coordinates that lead to a patch of fog?" Remy asks.

The wall of white around them is disorienting; Finn has been staring at it for too long. Her vision has started to go spotty, flecked with red.

"I don't know," Cas is saying. "I was hoping *you'd* know. But this weather feels strange, doesn't it? Not natural. Or maybe the fog is . . . I don't know . . . hiding whatever it is we're supposed to find."

"It's certainly doing that," Remy says.

That speck of red isn't a trick of Finn's eyes.

"Do you see that?" she breathes.

It's flashing in and out of view, appearing and disappearing as the waves overtake it. But there it is again, right at the surface of the water, barely visible through the white. Finn keeps her eyes fixed on the spot as Remy and Cas both race to tell the captain and the others. She's terrified that if she looks away, the single spot of color will vanish forever.

A tattered flag, dangling limply on its staff. If the mast holding it were two feet shorter, or if the tides were higher, the flag would be hidden completely underwater.

The coordinates have led them to a shipwreck.

II.

CAS

Life at sea, Cas is learning, comes with a long list of petty discomforts. The food is mostly hardtack. There are cockroaches in the galley, and sometimes mice, and the ship's cat doesn't seem to have much interest in catching them. The constant wind abovedeck has left Cas's face scrubbed raw, and there's a permanent layer of salt in his hair that makes his scalp itch. And he can never quite shake the damp or the cold. Just when his clothes seem like they might finally dry out, a rainstorm hits, or a wave breaches the main deck. Or this damned fog settles in for days and leaves them all chilled to the bone.

Captain Hobbes orders the *Mori* as close to the wreck as they can get without hitting the sunken vessel's masts. Cas tries to be helpful as the crew takes in the sails and drops the anchor. Striker has come abovedeck, and Remy and Finn both move to join her, but Cas decides not to press his luck. Instead he trails along after Mita, the ship's carpenter, who doesn't seem to mind his constant questions, and who probably won't kick boxes over them.

"Captain says we can ride at just one anchor for now," Immortal Gabe tells Mita as she readies the windlass. "The winds are light enough."

"Is there a *second* anchor?" Cas asks.

Gabe lets out a snort. "Yes, there's a second anchor. Taken you a full week to notice that, has it?"

"I don't know," Cas says. "When would that have come up?"

"Literally any time we moor."

"Ignore him," Mita says, waving Gabe off.

She beckons Cas to the windlass and shows him how to lay out the heavy hemp cable on the deck beside it, so it can uncoil without snagging as the anchor lowers.

"Typically, we'd drop two anchors," Mita explains as they work. "If the sea is rough, you can't use just one—the ship would go spinning round it, like . . ." She twirls a finger in the air. "So you lower an anchor on either side, then pull the cables tight and fix the *Mori* between them. Two points of connection are steadier than one. Here, bring that buoy rope, would you?"

She holds the rope in place while Cas attaches the block of wood they've been using as a buoy. Mita checks his knot. She gives an approving nod.

"You're getting the hang of this," she says, adjusting the knot, but only slightly.

Even with the damp clothes and the cockroaches and the grubby layer of salt forever caked onto his skin, Cas would rather be here—aboard this ship, with this crew—than anywhere else in the world.

Cas had figured they'd be celebrating once they found the coordinates' location. But there's no air of victory here. Not with the bones of a broken ship scattering the seafloor beneath them. The water is too dark to make out much of the vessel, but Cas can trace the lines of the masts—at least two of them, somehow still intact and still mostly vertical. The rest of the sunken ship is just a shadow in the deep. Already, the red flag Finn had spotted at the top of the mainmast is disappearing back under the ocean's surface as the tide rises around it.

"Are our divers ready?" the captain asks.

Striker and Immortal Gabe are tying back their dark hair, their boots and jackets left in a pile on the deck. Gabe has rolled up his shirtsleeves, showing off his impressively muscled golden-brown arms. Striker's arms are nearly as impressive. They both look perfectly calm, though Cas's palms are sweating at the very thought of what they're about to do. Better them than him. He buries his hands in the pockets of his peacoat. The longer he stares down into the murky depths of the sea, the more harrowing their plan feels.

He should probably stop staring down into the murky depths of the sea.

Even Remy seems to be having doubts, though. "This water has to be at least twenty fathoms deep," she says.

"Twenty-three, if the charts are accurate," Striker tells her.

"Don't you need equipment for that? The pressure alone—"

"We've got the best equipment you can buy," Gabe cuts in, nodding at a rusted coffee tin that Kit has produced. Kit holds out the tin, and Gabe takes something from it that definitely isn't coffee—a small, waxy ball about the size of a chestnut.

Remy is already bringing her research journal back out. "What are those?"

"A perk of the captain's involvement with the occult market," Gabe says. "There's a witch in Portsmouth who makes these. I think there's whale feces involved. Or ambergris. Or both."

"We call them whale balls," Striker says as she, too, takes one from Kit's tin.

Kit looks appalled. "We do *not* call them *whale balls.*"

Striker shrugs. "Well, some of us do."

"It smells like an armpit," Finn mutters.

"Tastes like it, too," Gabe says brightly.

"And that lets you breathe underwater?" Remy says, scribbling notes.

"Makes it so you don't *have* to breathe," Striker corrects. "For a while, anyway. Five minutes. Maybe ten if you can stay calm and keep your pulse slow enough." She catches Cas's eye and nudges him in the ribs. "See? Another very sensible reason we should all practice meditation."

There's no antagonism to the nudge, so Cas must be forgiven. He really hadn't been trying to annoy Striker during their lesson earlier. It's only that meditation is terrible, and no one should do it, and Cas in particular *really* shouldn't do it, and besides, he's shit at it and not getting any better. If he's being honest with himself, he'd asked Striker all those questions because he was stalling. Putting off the moment when he would have to sit quietly with nothing to distract him from his own thoughts. His own thoughts have been feeling especially treacherous lately.

Gabe has shoved the little wax ball into his mouth. "Oh god," he says after he's swallowed, grimacing. "I forgot how chewy it was."

The minutes drag as they wait for the magic to take effect. At last, Striker says she can feel it working, and she and Gabe both draw in a few impossibly long breaths, testing themselves. They don't look any different from the outside. When they descend the ladder, one after the other, and dive down toward the wreck, Cas half expects them to pop back up a moment later, gasping for air.

They don't pop back up. The whale balls must have worked, then. Cas stands at the railing for much longer than he ought to, watching the blurry shapes of Gabe and Striker and trying to ignore the way his heart is skittering. This is fine, isn't it? He's fine. He can ride this feeling out. No reason to make a scene. Later, maybe, if the anxious pressure in his chest becomes too much, he'll find somewhere to hide away and have a good breakdown in private. He just has to keep his head on straight until then.

Still, of all the petty discomforts that come with a life at sea, this is the most inconvenient: Why does the *Mori* have to be surrounded by so much goddamn *water*?

Cas doesn't want to think about Eden. He doesn't want to think about the spring in the woods, or Smith's man forcing his head under the surface, trying to drown Cas's visions straight out of him. He doesn't want to think about ice-cold water creeping into his lungs.

He's been thinking about all of this constantly for the past week. The reminder is literally all around him. There's no escape. Even belowdecks, he can't block out the ship's rocking. When he closes his eyes to try to meditate, the rocking is all he feels, and he imagines himself set adrift on an endless sea, tossing on the waves of his mind.

"Don't scratch at that," Remy says, and Cas startles. He hadn't even realized he was picking at the scar on his face again. He clamps his scratching hand into a fist and raps it on the rail instead.

"It itches," he mutters, which is an understatement.

"Well, scratching it isn't going to make that stop, and it'll itch more if it gets infected."

"It's not going to get infected," Cas says, though he makes a mental note to ask Leo about this the next time he sees him.

Finn is squinting at him. "Are you all right? You seem . . . fuzzy."

Maybe she's worried Cas is going to have another vision. "I'm fine," he tells her. "Just impatient for them to find something, you know?"

"Let's get to work on our plan, then," Remy says, because of course she does. "I assume we'll still be heading on to Boston after we're finished here. I know the captain mentioned a contact, Díaz, who owns a bookshop there. I think we should make a list of other people or places we'd like to investigate in the city. There are probably more Order members based in Boston than anywhere else, and with how we left the seminary—"

"In flames, you mean?" Cas asks.

"Yes, in flames. The Order will have to move their operation somewhere, and Boston would make the most sense. Smith might very well be in the city already."

"Grand," Finn says. "Shall we track him down and shoot him in the head, then?"

"Don't be flippant," Remy snaps.

"I'm not. I genuinely think we should shoot him in the head. I'll do it, happily. You can't tell me he doesn't deserve it."

"Yes, fine, but . . ." Remy seems to be fumbling for an argument. "You'd get strung up for murder."

"So? I won't live long enough to see the noose anyway."

At that, Remy looks a little murderous herself. Finn has been making these sorts of comments for days, as if she's not at all bothered by her own impending death. But Cas is fairly sure her nonchalance is an act. He's spent enough years plastering humor over the unpleasant truths of his life to recognize the handiwork.

"Or is it my *immortal soul* you're worried about?" Finn adds. "Because that's already good and scuppered."

"*Stop it*," Remy says. "Just stop. If you're not going to let us help you, you can at least stop acting like you don't give a damn."

For a moment, they both stare at each other in a silent standoff—Finn, all sharp bones and fiery red hair, and Remy, with her deceptively soft exterior that can't quite hide her iron core. There's a strange energy running between the two of them, unexpectedly strong, like a rip current. Cas isn't about to wade into *that*. Maybe he ought to try to break the tension, but his mind has gone blank. He can't think of a single thing to say.

At last, Finn makes an angry snorting sound and storms off across the deck without a word.

Remy's nostrils flare. "I'm not going to apologize for trying to save her life."

Cas certainly isn't the one demanding that apology. "I'm with you," he says.

"We need Death's help."

"I know." Cas is painfully aware of the way Finn's fate rests in his hands—or in his mind's ability to focus for two goddamn seconds so he can make contact with Death. The guilt chafes him. He should be working harder during his lessons with Striker. He should be spending his every waking moment practicing meditation, even though the very idea of it makes him want to vomit. "I'm . . . trying," he says, though clearly he isn't trying hard enough.

"Right," Remy says. "And that's all well and good, but if you aren't able to . . ." She seems to catch herself. "If that isn't . . . producing . . . immediate . . . results," she says carefully, "we need to have other pieces in play."

She doesn't think Cas can do it, he realizes. She doesn't really believe he can figure out how to use his reaper's glass powers, or whatever they are, to communicate with Death in his mind.

Her lack of confidence in him shouldn't hurt so badly. Even *Cas* doesn't really think he can do it, does he? He's been telling everyone as much from the moment they came up with this plan.

The meditation lessons were Striker's idea. She offered to help him a day after the harrowing events at the Eden seminary, when they all sat down with the captain, and Cas explained, awkwardly, that he himself is the reaper's glass Captain Hobbes had been searching for. The captain thought this reaper's glass might let him contact his missing partner. Reverend Smith at the seminary believed Cas could do just that, and probably more. Supposedly, Cas's visions come from some sort of spiritual connection he shares with Death. But Cas has never been able to *control* the visions. It had never occurred to him to try.

Thus, meditation. Kit had described it like a river: Cas has been catching the runoff already, but if he wants to communicate with Death more deliberately, he needs to figure out how to reach the main current. Striker had described it as something like a prayer—quieting the mind, quieting the self, in order to connect with something larger.

Cas isn't sure *what* it's supposed to be like. He only knows he isn't doing it.

There's a splashing sound as Immortal Gabe surfaces a dozen yards from the *Mori*.

"We've found something!" Gabe calls.

Suddenly, most of the crew crowds around Cas and Remy at the rail in a flurry of excited voices. "What is it?" someone shouts back.

"No idea. Some sort of . . . panel? It's metal. And . . . I don't know . . . ominous. You'll see. Toss me a rope—we're going to rig up a harness for it."

The rope is tossed. The harness is tied. Mita adjusts the cables so the crew can use the windlass to hoist up the mysterious metal panel. *Ominous.* Cas hopes this is only Gabe being superstitious, though the fog has them all on edge.

While Gabe stays with their find to keep it secured in its sling, Striker climbs back aboard the *Mori* with a report.

"The wreck is a clipper," Striker says over the creaking of the windlass as it turns. "Or was. The hull is snapped clean in half, like . . ." She mimes breaking something over her knee, clicking her tongue against her teeth as she does it. The sound effect is a little too visceral. Cas shivers. "And she must've had a rough journey even *before* the storm that finally did her in. The mizzenmast had been broken and jury-rigged back together, and the fore and main took a beating as well."

Finn has returned to Remy's side, their earlier spat forgotten. "Bad luck," Finn mutters. She says it as if it's a tangible thing.

"Fortunately, the broken hull made it simple for us to get into the cargo hold," Striker says. "Less fortunately, someone else got here first. Everything in the hold was picked over."

"So the Order of Lazarus has already come and gone," Remy says. Cas wonders how hard she's biting her tongue to refrain from saying, *I knew it.*

Striker shrugs. "Could be scavengers, I suppose. But more likely the Order. The one panel we found was wedged behind the ladder, like it got stuck there while the ship was tossing around. Probably why they missed it when they came to take the rest."

"You think the ship down there was carrying more of . . . whatever it is that you've found?" Remy asks, and Striker nods.

"A lot more. We could see where they would've been stacked and strapped down."

Remy opens her mouth, probably to ask another question, and Striker laughs.

"Do you want to swim down and see the wreck for yourself?" she asks. "I think we've got one more whale ball."

Remy grimaces and pulls her coat a little tighter around her. "I'm not going swimming in the sea in March, thank you," she says primly.

"It'll be April tomorrow," Striker tells her, as if this makes all the difference. "Besides, you'd acclimate. What about you two? Any takers?"

She's turned to Cas and Finn now, and Cas works very hard to keep his voice normal. "I'll pass," he says.

Finn shrugs with one shoulder. "Can't swim."

"*That*, at least, is a decent excuse," Striker says, pointing a finger at Finn as if she's just won a round of cards. "Although if you're planning to stick around here, you're going to have to learn. Captain's orders."

The panel in its sling breaks the water's surface with a slight sucking sound. For a moment it hangs there, suspended over the sea: a flat slab of metal, tarnished by the salt water, but still shining vaguely gold. Striker goes to help Gabe back aboard while Captain Hobbes directs the other sailors hauling up the piece of metal.

Finn is watching the proceedings with her arms crossed. "Or I could just plan to keep my feet on the deck," she mutters.

"That plan works, until it doesn't," Remy says. "You'll learn easily enough. And I suppose it's not surprising the captain wants his sailors to know how to swim. I mean, he told us about the night he met his partner."

This sobers them all, because yes, Captain Hobbes did: He'd

been a common sailor aboard a merchant vessel that wrecked off Cape Cod, and he'd watched his crewmates drown around him one by one as they all struggled for shore. Death was supposed to take Hobbes that night, too. Though obviously the reaper made a different choice.

"Wait," Finn says, eyes narrowing. "Since when do *you* know how to swim?"

"Since—always!" Remy stammers, flushing. She looks absurdly defensive, though maybe it's fair, because Finn looks absurdly accusatory. "Since we were eight. Cas's nanny taught both of us one summer in Cedar Pond."

"We pestered her into it," Cas tells Finn.

"*You* pestered her," Remy says.

"Sure, but you wanted to learn as well!"

It feels fraught to reminisce about these years of childhood, before his and Remy's falling-out—and yet Cas would much rather talk about *this* than about shipwrecks and sailors drowning in the sea. Poor harangued Miss Eloise. She probably would have been fired if Cas's mother had ever found out about the swimming. And still she did it. Maybe Miss Eloise realized she could either teach Cas and Remy properly, under her own supervision, or live in terror that they'd go sneaking off to the pond anyway on their own.

Finn is still glowering at Remy, apparently put out that this piece of Remy's history hadn't been disclosed to her before now. But Remy is distracted.

"Did Striker say it's April tomorrow?" Remy asks. When Finn tips her head in confirmation, Remy says, "Cas, it's almost your birthday."

Cas blinks at her. Time aboard the *Mori* seems to move by its own rules; it's strange to imagine that the world back on shore has been carrying on without them. "Is it?" he says.

"Isn't your birthday the first of April?"

"Well," Cas says. "Yes."

Mita has finished tying off her line on the pin rail beside him, and her face breaks into a smile. "Happy birthday, lad," she says. "We ought to celebrate."

"We don't have to do that," Cas says quickly.

"We absolutely do," Gabe says as he joins them. He throws an arm over Cas's shoulders, which—fine, it's fine, except Gabe's sleeve is wet on the back of his neck and Cas really doesn't want to be touched right now. "Don't take away my excuse for a party. How old will you be turning, anyway—eleven? Twelve?"

"Oh, shut up." Cas is glad for the ribbing, though; it gives him an excuse to duck out of Gabe's grip.

"He's a very youthful seventy-two," Finn says.

The metal panel lands flat on the deck with a crash that makes Cas's teeth rattle, and they all gather around it. Captain Hobbes pulls away the ropes so they can get a good look at what they've found. There's an uncharacteristic quiet among the sailors. It is, indeed, ominous.

The surface of the metal panel is etched with an image of a man dressed in full armor, with only his face visible. His gauntleted hands are folded in prayer, and his eyes stare empty and lifeless at the sky.

"A . . . knight?" Cas guesses.

"He does look medieval, doesn't he?" Remy says.

Captain Hobbes paces slowly around the panel, examining it from different angles.

"I think it's a monumental brass," the captain says.

Cas waits four seconds for the captain to elaborate before impatience gets the better of him. "What's a monumental brass?"

"It would've been inlaid in a tomb. A life-size depiction of the deceased. They were popular in Europe. Perhaps the thirteenth or fourteenth century."

"Who was the deceased, then?" Striker asks. "Some self-righteous Christian celebrating his own self-righteous atrocities?"

The captain seems to consider this. "It's possible he was a Crusader."

Striker nods, satisfied. "Like I said."

The fog around them feels like a pall. Immortal Gabe's good humor has dropped away; he's watching the brass panel as if waiting for it to spring to life and attack them. And it's harder, now, for Cas to dismiss Gabe's earlier comment as superstition. There's something *wrong* about the object in front of them.

Remy has been sketching a rough outline of the figure onto a blank page of her research journal. "You said this is made from brass?" she asks the captain. When he nods, she continues, "Do you think the metal could be melted down? Forged into something new?"

Captain Hobbes turns his intense gaze onto Remy. "What do you have in mind?"

"Not me," Remy says, now flipping through her journal with a new kind of urgency. "But if we think there were more of these monumental brasses aboard that ship . . . and if we think they're what Smith and his men wanted so badly . . . Well, it's in all the grimoires. Brass is the metal used for sealing away evil spirits. Craft a vessel out of brass, and it's supposed to be capable of holding a spirit's power. Keeping the spirit contained."

Again, Cas feels a shiver like a cold finger tracing up his spine.

"I imagine that a piece of brass like *this*, with particular significance, would be even more powerful for that sort of thing," Remy says. She eyes the captain. "You told us the Order has tried to capture Death before, but they didn't have a way to hold him. What if—?"

But she's interrupted by a *shush*ing sound. Kit has been stationed on the quarterdeck, keeping up the watch while the captain and the others examine the brass. Now she darts to the captain's side, a finger pressed to her lips, signaling them all to quiet. She murmurs something to Captain Hobbes, too low for Cas to make out.

Then she nods in the direction of the starboard rail. The captain turns. When Cas turns, too, his stomach drops.

A patch of the white fog has become strangely solid. Because it isn't fog at all.

It's the sails of another ship, heading straight toward them.

III.

REMY

After Eden, when it became clear that Remy and her friends would be staying aboard the *Mori* a while longer, Kit assigned them all loosely to the larboard watch. This hasn't changed much about their day-to-day duties, but it does mean they have an official station where they're meant to report during a crisis. When all hands are called for an emergency, Remy, Finn, and Cas are supposed to join Mita at the foresail brace and wait for orders. Kit made them run drills of this three times in the last week.

Those drills prepared them for this moment. As the incoming ship emerges through the fog, most of the other sailors start moving quickly and quietly to their positions. But Remy stalls, lingering, keeping herself within earshot of Captain Hobbes and Kit. She wants to be *here*, where the decisions will be made—not stuck at the foresail.

And no one has technically called for all hands just yet. The bell on the mast is still silent. Remy will cling to this technicality for as long as she can.

"It's this damned fog," Kit tells the captain, voice low. "They shouldn't have been able to catch us by surprise in the open ocean."

"Have they spotted us?" Captain Hobbes asks.

"Can't say for certain."

"Better to assume they have, then. The Order?"

Kit doesn't reply, but her expression is grim. The captain nods.

"We'll assume that as well, until proven otherwise," he says.

Cas taps Remy's arm. "We're supposed to go with Mita."

"I know," Remy murmurs. "I'll be there in a moment."

On the distant ship, a line of signal flags has come into view. In the fog's blur, the flags look as if they're floating in midair, spots of blue, yellow, and white that inch ever higher above the deck.

"They're running up a message," Kit says. "Which means yes, they've definitely spotted us. I need the Marryat."

She and the captain start toward the quarterdeck, where their copy of Marryat's *Code of Signals* must be stored. Remy waits a casual five seconds before trailing after them as inconspicuously as she can.

"Where are you going?" Cas presses. But when Remy ignores him, he shakes his head and leaves her to it.

Remy pretends she's tidying rigging at the base of the quarterdeck stairs while Captain Hobbes and Kit consult the book. It takes an excruciating number of seconds for them to match the flags to their corresponding code. *Everything* about life aboard a ship feels slow to Remy these days. She hardly recognizes herself. When did she become so impatient? She used to be content to appreciate the process, to take the time needed to not only do each step but do it correctly. She spent so much of her life trapped in a state of eternal planning—imagining moves and countermoves in some chess match against herself, but never actually playing the match through to the end. Never playing it at all, except in her own mind. She could never quite turn those plans into action. Even their trip to Eden hadn't been her idea; she'd needed Finn and Cas to drag her into this by both hands.

Somehow, lately, *she's* become the person desperate to charge forward, while everyone around her seems to be dragging their feet.

Maybe, Remy thinks, she's just never had the proper motivation until now. Finn's confession about her demon deal set something in Remy alight, and Remy *has* to act, to find the answer, to keep Finn alive, because . . . well, because she has to. Full stop.

Kit pauses tracing her finger down the page as she finds the message at last. "It's a request to come alongside us and board," she reads, the slightest tremor in her voice.

Remy shouldn't feel this thrill of excitement—but it zings through her veins. After days of drifting through the fog, finally, something is about to happen.

Captain Hobbes focuses his spyglass with precision. "I've got the name," he says. "The *Clara Smith*."

"Smith?" Kit says sharply.

Remy knows she shouldn't, but the magnitude of this discovery overrides her common sense. "Clara is the name of Reverend John Smith's wife," Remy says.

Kit and the captain both turn to stare at her. Remy can't tell whether their surprise is over what she's actually said or only the fact that she's been eavesdropping.

Then Kit shakes her head with a kind of horrified wonder. "Goddamn. How did the Order find us out here?"

"They had the same coordinates," the captain reasons. "Maybe they've been lying in wait in case someone else came looking. Or maybe they doubled back for the piece of brass they left behind."

He closes his spyglass with a snap.

"All hands to stations," he says to Kit. So much for Remy's loophole. "Don't sound the bell, though. No signs of alarm. Signal that we consent to their boarding."

Kit calls the commands, and a sailor hurries to raise the *Mori*'s own signal flags as the crew takes their positions. Still, Remy doesn't move. She can hardly believe this is happening. Maybe the *Clara Smith* will have new information about Smith's plans. Maybe today they'll find some answer about how to stop him, or, better yet, how to release Finn from her deal.

Kit is eyeing the captain with similar disbelief. "We're going to meet with them?" she asks him.

"No. We're going to run."

"What?" The word bursts out of Remy before she can stop herself.

The captain whirls on her. "All hands to stations," he says again.

"Don't you want to know what the Order is doing out here?" Remy says.

"Get to your station. *Now*."

It's the sharpest Remy has ever heard him speak. Probably she deserves it. She resents him for it anyway as she gives up and retreats to her assigned post. The logical part of her knows the captain is making the wiser choice: It would be an absurd risk to invite the Order aboard, or even to let them bring their ship around. Does the *Clara Smith* have cannons? The *Mori* certainly doesn't. The only guns here are the captain's single pistol and Striker's extensive rifle collection belowdecks.

The less logical part of Remy doesn't care about any risk. She cares about saving Finn, which means she needs any and all information she can get, and the *Clara Smith* surely has *something*. In fairness to the captain, he doesn't know about Finn's demon deal. He can't understand why it's so crucial they find answers *now* rather than later.

The less logical part of Remy really might get her strung up for mutiny if she isn't careful. She feels like a chastened child as she joins Cas and Finn at the foresail brace.

Mita doesn't acknowledge Remy's delay; she only nods at her and passes her a handful of sail lines. But Cas and Finn are both watching Remy. Cas's expression is pointed; he definitely saw the captain snap at her.

"Don't," Remy tells him.

"I didn't say anything." He accepts a handful of ropes from Mita as well. "If I *was* going to say something, though—"

"Don't."

"Fine! I'm not saying anything!"

The lines tug in Remy's hand; the sail they're attached to is already straining, trying to open to the wind prematurely.

"Hold for my signal," Kit calls as she moves to the center of the deck. "We'll open sails all at once. Striker—the anchor."

Kit hands Striker a long, serrated knife, which Striker accepts with a grimace. "He's sure about this?" she asks.

Kit nods once. "We'll replace it in Boston. Wait for the signal to make the last cut. We want to get a running start before they realize what's happening."

Striker moves to the windlass and starts sawing at the largest cable there, a hemp rope several inches thick.

"Isn't that the anchor cable?" Remy asks.

"Yes," Striker says through gritted teeth. "Yes, it is."

"Don't we need that to haul the anchor back up?"

"Yes, we do." Striker keeps sawing.

"We're leaving the anchor behind," Mita says, her dark eyes wide with the realization. "Is the captain really doing a cut and run?"

"It's quicker," Striker says. "He's not taking any chances."

No, Remy thinks; no, he isn't. The frustration eats at her. She bites her tongue.

Cas has lost his hold on one of the sail lines; it flops out over the railing. He leans out to grab it, but he must lean too far, because for a moment he seems to wobble on the brink, caught off-balance. Mita snags his collar and hauls him back.

"Steady on," she says. "Are you all right?"

"Fine," Cas says, though he wears the stricken expression of one who's just brushed up against something alive and slithering in the dark. "I'm fine."

"Ready," Striker calls out, knife poised over the anchor cable's final fraying strand.

They all wait, watching Kit, who's watching the captain.

When the captain holds up a hand, Kit shouts, "Cast off! All sheets to the wind!"

Remy, Cas, Finn, and Mita release their sail lines all at once, and the largest sail at the foremast billows free with the sound of rumbling thunder. All around them, the other sheets unfurl as sailors pull them open. Striker hacks through the last fibers of the anchor cable, and the *Mori* lurches as it breaks away. The cut length of rope slips off the deck and falls to join the abandoned anchor in the deep.

The sheets snap tight as they catch the wind, and the ship sets sail away from the wreck and the *Clara Smith*. Away from any other answers Remy might have found here.

The *Memento Mori* sails into the fog.

The rest of the afternoon is eaten up with mindless labor—a long series of menial tasks to which Remy is assigned, all of them physically demanding but mentally dull. Her arms and back ache as she lays out rigging and helps Gabe set the studding sails, but her mind keeps racing, playing through the afternoon's events. Wondering about what they might have learned if only the captain hadn't ordered them to flee.

The *Clara Smith* has been out of sight for hours. But the heavy fog still hasn't lifted, and it's all too easy to imagine the other ship reappearing behind them at any moment. The captain has the *Mori* flying under full sail, harnessing every scrap of breeze, though the breeze isn't very obliging. Kit keeps cursing the wind. Apparently it's being unusually capricious, changing direction without warning and threatening to take the ship aback. Remy is sent aloft five different times to adjust the studding sails when the wind shifts. Not even two weeks ago, climbing up into the rigging had felt like a momentous accomplishment for her. Now it's a tedious routine.

She wouldn't mind the work so much if it weren't for the nagging suspicion that the work is her punishment for crossing the captain earlier. She can't help but feel she's being put in her place, reminded that she isn't in charge here.

At least they're on their way to Boston now. By this time tomorrow night, they'll be rounding Cape Cod, and they'll be in the city the day after.

Assuming the weather stops fighting them, anyway.

"I don't like the feeling of this wind," Kit says after Remy has adjusted the studding sail yet again and returned to the deck. "Or this fog. Something's brewing."

Remy's palms are sticky from climbing the tar-coated shrouds; she wipes them on her skirts. Captain Hobbes has retreated to his office belowdecks. The sun has set by now, and the main deck is unusually dark; they've avoided lighting the lanterns in case the *Clara Smith*, or another ship, is still out there in the fog and might spot the light.

The large brass panel from the shipwreck is still abovedeck. No one had wanted to try to maneuver it down into the cargo hold, so it's covered with a sheet and secured flat underneath where the jolly boat is stored.

Finn casts the sheet a wary glance as she comes to meet Remy.

"Have you seen Cas anywhere?" she asks.

The afternoon blurs together in Remy's mind. She remembers Cas helping Mita with the jib and flying jib at one point. But that could have been hours ago.

"Not for a while," Remy says. "Why?"

"We should go check on him."

"Why?" Remy says again. "Do you think he's off causing trouble somewhere?"

"That's not what I'm worried about."

The uneasiness in her voice is catching. Remy clenches and unclenches her hands. "It's not as if he can leave the ship," she points out.

"And yet he keeps disappearing, doesn't he? Remember the other day, he claimed he'd been belowdecks with Mita? Well, she told me later that she hadn't seen him all afternoon."

"He was probably working on meditation with Striker," Remy says.

That's what he *should* be doing now, she thinks. But it wouldn't make sense for him to lie about that. Besides, Striker is currently sitting with Kit on the quarterdeck, her head resting lightly against Kit's knee. And Cas is nowhere in sight.

"You know he's been . . . off . . . lately," Finn says in a low voice. "Don't pretend you haven't noticed."

Remy has noticed. She's just had too many other matters on her mind to want to deal with Cas's fickle moods right now. "He says he's fine!"

"And he'd never lie about that sort of thing, would he?" Finn asks in a tone that says she knows full well Cas would, and has before.

Unfortunately, she makes a good point. Remy sighs. "I'll help you look for him."

The lanterns belowdecks are burning, at least. Finn splits off to check the galley while Remy takes the crew's quarters. A few sailors are asleep in their bunks, and Remy is careful not to disturb them. She slips through the curtain into the fo'c'sle.

"*There* you are," she whispers. She can sense Cas on one of the bunks, although when the curtain falls closed behind her, it's too dark to really see him. She pulls the curtain back again to let in a little light.

There's no one on the bunk.

Remy's heart jolts. She could have sworn . . . but no. The fo'c'sle is empty. Why had she thought Cas was here? Did she actually *see* him? No, she thinks—only sensed him, the feeling of another person beside her in the dark. She'd imagined it, clearly. A trick of her weary mind.

She can't shake the feeling, though. There's a tingling sensation climbing along her scalp. For a second, she swears she hears someone *breathing*.

That's quite enough of that. Remy goes back to fetch one of the lanterns so she can light the fo'c'sle properly.

Empty. Just as she knew it was.

She inspects the bunk where she'd imagined she saw Cas. It isn't even Cas's bunk; it's Remy's. Her carpetbag is tangled among the blankets there, probably tossed around as the ship was floundering in the changing winds.

Remy opens her bag and checks that the contents are safe. Her research journal is a comforting weight in her hand; it helps settle her a little. At the bottom of the bag, wrapped inside a cloth sack, are two jars. One holds Remy's father's ashes. The other holds his eyes.

Remy takes a moment to make sure both jars are still tightly closed. She tucks one of her spare shirts around the jars as padding. She hasn't let herself think too much about what she's going to do with her father's remains, now that she's retrieved them from the seminary at Eden. Bring them home to her mother, she supposes. She feels strangely numb and businesslike about it. Not just the remains. All of it. The grief. She hasn't even cried since she learned her father was dead. Surely she should have cried by now.

Maybe the afternoon of tedious, endless work was a blessing. Maybe it's better for Remy to stay distracted, to keep moving, so the grief can't catch her.

Her scalp is tingling again—that odd sensation that she isn't alone.

A thought crosses her mind. A dangerous one. A foolish one.

Remy stares down at the cloth sack, which holds the jars, which hold what's left of her father.

No. She has no reason to believe in ghosts. Yes, fine, she can accept by now that reapers are real, and demons, and prophetic visions of deaths. But ghosts?

It doesn't matter, she decides. Even if ghosts *were* real, her father has been dead for eight years now without Remy even knowing it. And she's never before felt any sort of presence like *this*. Which means she's imagining the presence altogether. She closes the carpetbag quickly, but hooks it over her shoulder. Maybe it's better to keep the bag with her from now on.

"Any luck?"

Remy knocks her head into the upper bunk as she startles and scrambles upright. When she blinks away the stars, Finn is standing in the doorway, eyebrows raised.

"He isn't here," Remy says, rubbing at the sore spot on her head.

"Not in the galley, either," Finn tells her. "Or the dining area. Or any of the open cabins."

Remy tries to think. "Where else is there to go?"

Finn gnaws on her lower lip. It isn't a new habit, but Remy finds herself riveted for some reason, reluctant to look away.

"Cargo hold?" Finn guesses.

"Maybe."

Finn leads the way down the ladder into the cramped cargo hold at the bottom of the ship. The ceiling here is low; Remy has to bend over double to fit. They peer down the rows of crates and barrels, all secured under nets.

"Cas?" Remy calls.

The cargo hold is a familiar enough space; Remy, Finn, and Cas spent nearly a full day hiding here when they first stowed away on the *Mori*. But something about the flickering lamplight, with its dancing shadows, unsettles Remy. Or maybe she was already unsettled to begin with. She tugs her carpetbag a little higher up her arm.

"Cas," Finn hisses. "Are you down here?"

The ship around them seems to sway with a little more force. The wind must have changed direction yet again. Remy can almost feel the ballast shifting under the boards beneath her feet. The ballast had seemed counterintuitive when Striker explained it to them all—a layer of heavy stones laid out along the bottom of the ship's hold. Supposedly the stones help keep the ship balanced, though Remy still can't quite wrap her mind around the concept of deliberately weighing down a thing that's meant to float.

Remy's scalp has begun to prickle again. The sensation creeps slowly down to her neck, and then her back.

Finn's voice is a whisper as she asks Remy, "Do you feel . . . watched?"

"Maybe it's the cat," Remy whispers back. Although she could swear she saw the little black-and-white creature sleeping in the crew's quarters just a few minutes ago.

"Cas," Finn says in a warning tone, swinging the lantern to and fro. "If you're down here and not answering us—"

The ship gives a sudden lurch, and Finn gasps, and it's sheer instinct—Remy grabs onto her in the dark. Finn stumbles against her, the sharp bones of her shoulder jabbing into Remy's chest, her hair in Remy's face, salty and familiar. Finn has grabbed onto Remy's arm, too. They both cling to each other for longer than they really need to.

Remy wills herself to let go. But she doesn't actually move until Finn loosens her own grip and detaches herself.

"Cas will turn up," Finn says. Her cheeks are fiery red in the lantern's glow. "Like you said. It's not as if he left the ship. We should go."

With that, she darts back up the ladder. She takes the light with her. Remy stands in the dark for a moment, heart pounding, before she follows.

IV.

CAS

It's nearly impossible to find anywhere aboard the *Mori* to be alone, which is why Cas keeps ending up in the surgeon's cabin.

He'd tried the cargo hold first. A day after they sailed away from Eden—when the terror from that night caught up with him at last—Cas had fled down to the lowest level of the ship. He'd tucked himself behind a row of barrels near the stern, just outside the panel hiding the secret smugglers' compartment. The cargo hold *was* private. It was also, inconveniently, entirely below the waterline. The sea pressed in around him on all sides, crushing against the hull. The planks groaned under the weight of it. Water sweated through every hairline crack.

And suddenly Cas was back at Eden. Back under the water at the spring in the woods. He could feel the hand on his neck again, holding him under the surface, and he couldn't breathe, and he was going to drown—

He'd fled up the ladder, gasping. The lower deck was empty, though it wouldn't be for long. Cas couldn't let the others see him like this. He needed somewhere else to hide.

And the surgeon's cabin was right there, a few steps down the passageway. When Cas tested the door, it was unlocked. Over the past week, on the two or three other occasions when Cas has needed somewhere to break down in private—or eight other occasions, but who's counting—the cabin has always been empty.

He put off today's breakdown for as long as he could, though he'd felt the pieces building up. Their narrow escape from the *Clara Smith* had been officially too much. A slow climb to the top of the cliff—and then a swift push over the edge. As they were preparing to drop sails, when Cas had reached over the railing to grab that loose line, for a second, reality had forked. There was the scene that actually happened, where Mita pulled him back before his feet even left the deck. And then there was the scene that *could* have happened: Cas losing his balance, tumbling over the rail, plunging headfirst into the deep. The sensation of falling had felt so real that his stomach actually swooped, and he could swear he saw the water rising to meet him.

The image stays stuck in his mind as he makes a flimsy excuse and escapes belowdecks. That invented moment is a net, and he's tangled in it, and he can't quite convince his brain that the moment didn't happen and that everything's fine and he's safe. He doesn't *feel* safe. He feels like he's drowning anyway.

The door of the surgeon's cabin is ajar, as if the room is waiting for him. Cas darts inside. He leans against the back of the door and presses the heels of his hands to his eyes. He folds himself down, down, down, until he's small enough that he can let himself fall apart at last.

Christ, look at the state of him. Why can't he let this go? Cas didn't actually fall overboard, and even if he *did* fall overboard, he knows how to swim. He would've been fine. He and Remy used to race each other across Cedar Pond for hours, and Cas never used to be so terrified of drowning, because why would he be? But now he can't breathe, and his heart is fluttering like a torn sail in a squall, and his chest is squeezing in on itself—

"I'm sorry—do you want I should go?"

The voice comes from very, very close to him, and Cas leaps to his feet, eyes flying open. "Jesus Christ."

"No," Leo says, "it's only me."

He's sitting at the tiny desk built into the wall, a book spread open in front of him. His dark curls fall over his dark, serious eyes. His pencil is poised over a loose sheet of paper, as if he's been taking notes. Probably he *had* been taking notes before Cas came barging in without even looking. God, how had Cas missed him? He's three feet away, and there's an oil lamp burning on the desk. Cas would've noticed the cabin was occupied if he'd had a single one of his wits about him.

Instead, Cas stands gaping like a goldfish, utterly witless. And for some reason, *Leo* is the one apologizing.

"I'm sorry," Leo says again. "I thought at first that you knew I was here. But then I realized you *didn't* know, and I didn't know how to tell you. And I thought maybe I could just slip away without saying anything, but you're blocking the door, and then I decided that the longer I waited, the stranger it was going to be. But it's still strange, so I'm sorry. Are you all right?"

"Fine," Cas says in a voice that is very obviously not fine. It's a marvel his voice works at all. "I'm . . . fine. Just . . . felt a little faint, I guess, and . . ."

Leo's brows have pinched. "Is your binding vest too tight?" he asks.

It isn't, but Cas unfastens the buttons of the vest anyway with fumbling fingers. It doesn't help. He needs to pull himself together for long enough to escape this interaction and find somewhere more private. But his body has stopped taking orders. The floodgates have already opened, and the current now is too strong to force them shut again. Everything has gone sideways. The world feels very far away.

Leo says something, and then he's sitting down on the cabin floor beside Cas. Cas doesn't even remember sitting down himself. When did that happen? And then Leo is telling him to breathe, and showing him how: a long inhale through the nose, a longer exhale through the mouth. Cas tries to mirror him, but it's impossible. His lungs aren't working. His heart is beating too fast. It's probably going to give out at any second. Can a person die like this? Probably. Surely. A heart simply exhausting itself. Lungs refusing to pull air. And all the while, Leo just sits there, breathing in, breathing out, at a pace far too slow and deliberate for Cas to ever match.

Until eventually, painstakingly, Cas *can* match it. More or less. He inhales with Leo, and he exhales with Leo, and his breaths don't hitch quite so badly anymore. Slowly, the pressure in his chest begins to ease, and the world drifts back into focus around him.

"There've been a lot of recent breakthroughs about the physiology of the nervous system," Leo is saying in a low, even voice. "The brain impacts the body impacts the brain. I'm skeptical about the old 'melancholia' diagnosis, but if we trace back to the ideas of Galen—I'm sorry, I can stop talking."

"Please don't," Cas croaks. "Please keep talking." It helps. It gives Cas something else to focus on. Leo watches him for a moment with a doubtful expression, as if waiting for Cas to change his mind.

"All right," Leo says. "What do you know about the ancient Greeks' theories about the humors of the body?"

Cas knows absolutely nothing.

They sit side by side on the cabin floor while Leo explains it to him. Then Leo explains where the ancient Greeks' theories went wrong, and then he lays out the path from there to the more recent medical discoveries. Every so often, he asks Cas a question, or he makes Cas repeat something to confirm he understands. Cas can't just feign interest; he has to actually listen. Besides, it *is* sort of interesting. It's just complex enough that it requires all of his mental energy to follow. There's no space left to worry about anything else.

Eventually, Leo produces a handkerchief from his jacket pocket and hands it over. Cas had barely realized that he'd been crying earlier. Jesus Christ. He blows his nose.

"Better?" Leo asks him.

"I'm all right."

And he is, mostly. The worst of it has passed now; all that remains is that exhausted, fragile, hollowed-out sensation that always comes afterward. Cas feels like one of those delicate eggs his mother used to set out at Easter time—a decorated shell with all its insides dried and emptied out.

He wads the handkerchief into a ball and clears his throat. "I'm sorry about all that," he says, and he's relieved to hear that his voice sounds almost normal again. "I shouldn't have just barged in here. I didn't mean to interrupt."

"You didn't interrupt," Leo says quickly. "Or you did, I suppose, but nothing important. Besides, I'm the one who left the door open." He pauses for a moment, then adds, "And this is a good place to be alone, right? It's quiet. And the others know not to . . . That is, they won't bother you when you're in here."

He says it in a way that implies personal experience, and

the realization brings with it a fresh wave of guilt. This cabin is *Leo's* private space. Cas remembers the conversation he had with Leo some nights ago, during the crew's party on the beach. How had Leo described himself? *Too quiet, too . . . odd. Too easily overwhelmed.* This place is meant to be Leo's escape when the chaos of the ship becomes too much. He'd probably come down here looking for some peace and quiet, and then—

"Sorry," Cas says, starting to his feet. "I didn't mean to bother you. I should go."

Leo grabs him by the sleeve and tugs him back down. "That's not what I meant. I didn't mind the interruption, truly. I'd tell you if I did. I'm a terrible liar. Ask anyone."

Cas laughs at that, though it comes out a little wet. "Still. I shouldn't have . . . I don't know what happened."

"Has it happened before?" Leo asks.

Cas should lie and say that no, this has never happened before, and it certainly hasn't been happening fairly regularly over the past few days. And also nothing happened, and what is Leo talking about? And once again, Cas should probably be going now.

He doesn't say any of this. He doesn't say anything at all. Leo nods slowly.

"That makes sense," Leo says. "You went through something harrowing just a few days ago. I think this is a fair reaction."

Cas wrings the used handkerchief in his hands. "I'm better now, honestly. I just needed a minute to . . ." He waves at Leo's desk, trying to change the subject. "What were you working on?"

"Oh, that," Leo says. He stands and shows Cas the medical textbook on the desk. "I've been trying to copy down these diagrams, but I still can't get this one right."

The diagram shows a segment of bones and tendons—possibly a hand, though it's much more recognizable in the book's depiction. The version Leo has been drawing in his notebook is misshapen, as if the hand has been brutally chopped into several pieces and then strung together by the loosest lines.

"I borrowed the book from Gilly," Leo says as explanation. "The keeper at that lighthouse where we stopped in Maine. I've been trying to copy down the interesting bits before I have to return it to him. But most of the interesting bits are the pictures, and I can never get the pieces to fit together right." He sighs. "I should probably just wait till morning, and then trace it once the light's better."

Cas tilts the notebook in the lamplight, studying it. "I mean, you've got most of it. It's just this part on the side that's angled wrong. Can I—?"

He breaks off as his mind catches up with his mouth. Leo hadn't asked for help. But to his surprise, Leo thrusts a pencil and an erasing rubber into Cas's hand. He's watching Cas expectantly, and so there's nothing to do but erase the stray segment from the paper and start sketching it back in the proper place.

"I didn't know you could draw," Leo says after a few minutes.

Cas drops the pencil at once. "I can't."

"That drawing says differently," Leo says, nodding at his work. "What are you doing? Keep going."

Reluctantly, Cas returns to the page. He tries to focus on the lines, the scratch of pencil on paper, instead of Leo's eyes on him. Sure, Cas is decent at drawing. It's only because he took lessons as a child. Though he had plenty of lessons in piano, too, and in French, and he still can barely manage a minuet or a *je ne comprends pas.*

The drawing lessons were the only ones that stuck, probably

because Cas actually enjoyed them. He used to get lost in it—finding the core shapes within an object, sketching the pieces together, studying the textures and shadows to capture the ways those pieces interact. The whole world seemed to quiet as he focused on just this one thing.

Except his mother didn't appreciate him working patiently at a sketch of an interesting rock for an entire afternoon, especially when he wouldn't practice the piano for more than ten minutes. It was good for a young lady of society to be able to paint a nice landscape or two, yes, but that alone wouldn't land Cas a husband. His mother fired the drawing teacher. She told Cas to take the effort he'd put into drawing and use it for something that actually mattered.

Cas finishes fixing the diagram and hands it over for inspection. Leo compares it with the picture in the book and smiles.

"Can you help me with the rest of these?" Leo asks. "I've been struggling at this all evening, and you made it look absurdly easy." He hesitates. "You don't have to, of course. I know it's getting late. If you'd rather get to bed—"

"No," Cas says immediately. "I'd rather do this." He's exhausted, but he's not going to risk trying to sleep while his mind is still such a tangle. Although it's starting to feel a little less tangled than before. "Show me the others."

Cas spends the evening copying out diagrams from Gilly's book, and Leo hovers, then seems to realize he's hovering, then moves to sitting on the cabin's little bunk to take notes from some of his other textbooks. He reads passages from the books out loud sometimes, and he asks Cas what he thinks of them. It's as if he can sense when the silence is becoming too heavy, as if he can anticipate when Cas's mind is about to start spiraling again.

Leo's reading voice is soft and a little raspy. Cas feels quiet, for a while.

Eventually, when Cas's eyelids are starting to droop, Leo takes the pencil from him and invites Cas to sit on the little bunk, too. It ought to feel awkward and embarrassing, sitting shoulder to shoulder with Leo like this. This whole night ought to feel awkward and embarrassing. It probably will tomorrow. For tonight, Cas is too tired to care.

Maybe sleep won't be so terrible after all.

V.

FINN

That night, Finn dreams of flames.

She's always dreamed of flames. Her nightmares about hell started long before she sold her soul to a demon and sealed her fate. When she was a child, the priest at the old church in Knockadine preached about the unquenchable fires that would meet the unrepentant sinners in the hereafter—and Finn has never slept soundly since. For years, she's dreamed of a pit where she burned without end. She's watched her own skin sizzle and peel from her bones. She's watched it regrow so it can sizzle again.

Sometimes, in the dreams, she looks up to see her parents and her brother Kieran staring down at her. They stand safely atop a cliff, far removed from the hellfire. *They* are not the unrepentant sinners the priest had meant. Finn cries out to them to help her, but they won't answer. One by one, they look down at her, shake their heads, and walk away.

Which is the worse torment—the actual pain from the fire, or her family's disappointment as they see her for who she really is? In life, perhaps Finn has been able to hide from them the badness she's always sensed inside her. But the afterlife will reveal the truth.

She'd tried to hide her badness from the demon, too. When she asked Marbas to save Kieran's life, *she* knew that she was offering a shoddy deal, but it was all she had.

"I'm willing to pay," she'd told the demon. "Dearly."

"Your soul," Marbas said.

"Yes."

Finn felt her gaze pulled at last to look directly at him. Marbas's eyes had no irises or pupils—they were only flat black pools.

"Let's take a look, then," Marbas said.

In an instant, Finn wasn't standing in the Pendletons' barn anymore. She wasn't standing *anywhere*. She wasn't in her body; she was pure essence. She was guilt. She was shame. She was every sinful thing she'd ever done in her entire life. She was five years old, and a boy down the road had a shiny stone Finn wanted, and she pocketed it when he wasn't looking. She realized she could take trinkets—anything small—and no one ever noticed. She was never caught. She was seven, and she spilled tea all over one of Kieran's books, and instead of telling him, she shoved the ruined book back in its place as if nothing had happened. When he found it later, she denied any knowledge, and Kieran was so gullible that he believed her.

She was ten, and she broke a boy's nose on the packet ship from Ireland to America. It was self-defense, mostly, but she hadn't really needed to kick him in the face so many times or so fiercely to get her point across. She knew, secretly, that she'd enjoyed the violence of it.

She was eleven, and she started . . . noticing. She started watching other girls, and then having to stop herself from watching other girls. She stole glances at them like tiny bites of forbidden fruit. Their faces. Their lips. The soft, warm shapes of their bodies. The way those shapes made her feel. The girl who sold baskets at the artisan market in Lynn was lovely, and Finn's skin burned just thinking about her. She lingered in Finn's wayward mind long after the market was done. She haunted Finn's sleep. In dreams, the girl would cup one of her soft hands to Finn's cheek, and she'd press their mouths together, and she'd press their bodies together, and Finn would wake alone in her bed with an ache in a place that was forbidden.

All of this, the demon saw. And when Finn became a physical thing again, when the barn and the cold returned and she was standing again in the center of the summoning circle, she knew that the demon wasn't going to agree to this deal. He wouldn't take tarnished goods. He wouldn't trade for a soul that was so obviously already damned. Why bother? Marbas could cure Kieran's illness and drag Finn to hell now—or he could leave Kieran to die, and let Finn damn herself through her own sinful drives over a lifetime. To a demon, timeless and ageless, what difference was there between "now" and "later"?

She'd hoped she could conceal the depths of her own depravity from the demon—but of course the demon knew. He'd seen it all. More than that, he probably knew even *before* he pried into her memories.

Good, virtuous, heavenly girls didn't summon demons.

But the demon said, "All right. I accept your offer. Let's trade."

Finn stared at him, amazed. "I'm sorry?"

"I'm not sure that you are," the demon said. "It's probably better that way. You're an odd one, aren't you? You're so young, and yet you're powerful. You ask audacious things, and yet you feel no entitlement. Arrogant and lowly in equal measure. I confess, you intrigue me."

Finn had no idea what to make of this. She had never in her life felt powerful. She *had*, for most of her life, felt odd.

"Here are the terms," Marbas told her. "I will cure your

brother, Kieran Robinson, of his disease. At the moment you sign this contract, you'll sign to me your soul, and your brother's illness will leave him. His lungs will clear. He'll breathe deeply and fully. He'll wake, and he'll eat, and when he sleeps, his sleep will be restful."

As he spoke, a paper was in his hand with all of this written in tidy script. There was no moment of him writing, or even of the page appearing; it was simply there, as if it had been all along. The demon offered the paper to her—letting the page, but not his hand, cross the line of the triangle that still bound him.

Finn hesitated. This was too easy. "Is this a trick?" she asked.

The demon didn't blink. "I have no need for tricks."

Finn found that she believed him. Besides, if it was a trick, it hardly mattered. She had nothing else to lose except Kieran, and had no chance to save him, except this.

"If these terms suit you," the demon said, "you can sign. But the contract must be signed in fire."

Finn looked around her summoning circle, with its four lit candles positioned around the edges of it.

"No," Marbas said. "*Your* fire."

"I don't have fire," Finn said.

But she did.

The demon's instructions for her didn't come as words—only an awareness, a surge of knowledge. *This* was the forbidden fruit. Because there was, in fact, a fire in her. Perhaps it had always been there, and she'd simply never had access to it. She hadn't known to look for it. She hadn't known what it could do.

With the demon's guidance, she reached into that dark, yawning place inside her. She touched the fire. Then she touched the page. She wrote her name and sealed her fate.

Is this dream or memory that she's seeing now? Finn watches the scene as if from the outside; she sees the child who she once was summoning that fire. But the dream shifts, and the fire grows, far beyond anything that really happened the night Finn signed the contract. This fire keeps burning and consuming. It devours the paper and chars the dirt at her feet, breaking the lines of the summoning circle. The demon had called the fire *vitalis vis*, Finn's inner will, something inside her the demon unlocked. Soon, her fire will take the barn. The town. The whole world.

She feels arms around her, enveloping her, and Remy is there with her in the blazing barn. She pulls Finn against her chest and holds her tightly. Remy's dark eyes shine with the fire's light. There's a solidness to her. A heat. Finn can see the line of sweat glazing Remy's upper lip. She aches.

The flames will consume them both. Marbas's words echo through the inferno.

When Finn jolts awake, she's alone in the fo'c'sle.

For a long moment, she lies there in the dark, swaying with the rocking of the ship. She wills herself to forget the sensation of Remy's arms pulling her in. But Remy had held her just like that earlier this evening, when they'd both startled in the cargo hold. That had been real.

Marbas had said something, in the dream's final moment. Finn racks her mind, trying to disentangle the dream from the memory six years ago. Back then, just before Marbas vanished, he said, "We'll see you again soon."

But Finn doesn't think those are the words she just heard. Even now, the voice seems to echo in the empty cabin. As if Marbas had spoken not only in the dream but here, aloud, in the waking world.

A new message: "*We need to talk. Soon.*"

The darkness in the fo'c'sle presses in around her like a living thing. Is the demon somehow *here*? Now? Finn has tried to convince herself she imagined that feeling of being watched when she and Remy were in the cargo hold. She's tried to convince herself she imagined the shape watching her from the shadows outside the seminary.

She doesn't think she imagined it.

Finn is on her feet. Where are Remy and Cas? When Finn had announced she was going to bed that evening, Remy said she'd be along in a few minutes, though clearly she didn't follow through. They never did find Cas; he must be holed up somewhere, taking some time to himself. Finn would be a hypocrite to fault him for that. Most of the time, she's perfectly happy to be alone.

Finn can't be alone right now.

She's careful not to wake the sleeping sailors in the main crew's quarters as she passes through. She starts for the ladder. But a warm glow catches her eye, and she pauses on the lower deck. Lantern light spills out of one of the cabins down the passageway. The door of the surgeon's cabin is hanging wide open, and Finn is almost certain she recognizes the pair of boots discarded on the floor just inside it.

"Cas?" she whispers as she creeps toward the open door. "Are you—? Oh."

Inside the surgeon's cabin, Cas is curled on the small bunk, sleeping soundly with his head on Leo's leg. Leo holds a book open in one hand. His other hand gently smooths the hair over Cas's ear. He stops this when he spies Finn in the doorway, but otherwise he doesn't move.

"The latch on the door came loose," Leo says softly. "And I couldn't get up to fix it without waking him. You're looking for Cas?"

"I was, but—let him sleep," Finn says. "I'll talk to him later."

She closes the door behind her with a soft click before Leo can protest. It's the first time Finn has seen Cas asleep in days. He'd looked younger—relaxed for once. Not struggling to meditate so he can talk to Death. Not scheming with Remy about how to save Finn's life.

If it weren't for Finn—if it weren't for her demon deal—is this what Cas and Remy would be doing? Sailing with the crew of the *Mori*. Settling into themselves. Finn really is going to burn down her whole world by accident. Her contract with Marbas is of her own doing; it's *her* burden to bear, not Remy's or Cas's.

She never should have told them about the deal. She's certainly not going to tell the rest of the crew. Gabe has been muttering all day about that strange brass panel they'd recovered from the shipwreck; Finn overheard him earlier telling Striker he thinks it's cursed. Finn can't shake the feeling that Gabe is pointing his accusations in the wrong direction. *Finn* is the curse—the albatross from the Coleridge poem, a weight hanging around the necks of everyone aboard this ship. She's destined to doom the people she loves.

The cold fog lingers when Finn climbs the ladder to the main deck. Finn tugs down the sleeves of her knit jumper to warm her hands. The sailors on the night watch move quietly around her, going about their work. There truly is something unnatural about this fog. It's so thick that the tops of the *Mori*'s two masts seem to disappear into the night sky.

A lone figure sits on one of the mastheads, boots dangling high above the deck. It's such an improbable place to find Remy that Finn almost thinks she's imagined her there. She allows herself the brief pleasure of studying Remy. This is safe, for a moment.

From a distance. Anything more is dangerous; the more Finn eats of this forbidden fruit, the hungrier she feels for it. The fog and the moonlight cast Remy's pale face in silver. Even from here, Finn can see the familiar dimple that forms in her cheek when she's concentrating. She's bent over something in her lap—her journal, no doubt. Her soft skirts and the hem of her wool peacoat spill out around her and over the side of the platform. She's sitting precariously close to the edge.

Only as Finn starts up the web of rigging does she notice the line anchoring Remy to the mast. She's looped it firmly under both her arms, to hold her in place even if the ship pitches. Not precarious at all, then. Finn climbs toward Remy's perch slowly and carefully. The waves feel much rougher from up here; perhaps a storm really is on its way.

When Finn reaches the masthead, Remy closes her journal. She shifts her carpetbag to the side so that Finn can crawl up beside her.

"You couldn't sleep, either?" Remy says. She offers another rope for Finn to use to tether herself. Finn doesn't take it. She sits back from the edge, though, spine pressed against the mast. The wood is sturdy even as it sways, a tree trunk in the middle of the ocean.

"What are you working on?" Finn asks, nodding down at the closed journal.

Remy answers too quickly: "Nothing."

"You're always working on something."

"I'm just thinking."

"And you had to climb all the way up here to do it? They're making a real sailor of you."

Remy snorts. "Hardly. I just . . . needed a change in perspective."

Finn waits, though she doesn't look at Remy directly. In her periphery, the tips of Remy's fingers press against the cover of her journal one by one.

"I've decided to accept what I can't control," Remy says. "I can't *make* Cas talk to Death. He'll either figure it out, or he won't. In the meantime, I need to focus on what I *can* do."

Finn isn't about to accept this declaration at face value. For days, Remy has seemed wholly fixated on her plan to track down Death and persuade him to spare Finn. This sudden reversal feels fishy.

"You're . . . giving it up?" Finn asks.

"I'm not giving anything up," Remy says. "But I'm shifting my attention to a different objective. For the moment. If I just keep pestering Cas, I'm going to lose my mind."

Finn suspects the pestering isn't helping Cas's mind much, either. "What's the different objective?"

"Take down Smith. Take down the Order."

Remy says it so simply. Not a new goal, though Finn does feel a seed of relief. Perhaps Remy truly is ready to put that powerful brain of hers toward a better cause than trying to save Finn from her own foolish decision.

"Hmm," Finn says, still watching Remy in the corner of her eye. "Revenge?"

Remy's hand moves to her carpetbag, almost unwillingly, as if drawn toward the two jars Finn knows are still packed inside it. Remy tips her head, something between a shrug and a nod.

"I can get behind that," Finn says. She pokes at Remy's journal still in her lap. "Tell me what you've got."

Remy sighs. "Not much, unfortunately. I'm going to try to talk to the captain tomorrow. Offer to help with anything he's planning for Boston."

"An olive branch?" Finn asks.

Remy nods. "We really are working toward the same goal, in the end."

The fog hasn't dispersed, but it doesn't feel quite as worrisome at the moment. There's a sort of beauty to it. The ship below them is so quiet at this hour that it feels as if Finn and Remy are completely alone. Finn thinks of the nights they used to spend together at Dungeon Rock. The rock has always felt a little otherworldly. It isn't only the legends of pirates or the rumors that it's haunted; it's Finn's own personal lore, too. The nights she and Remy have spent there, watching the stars, talking about anything and everything, have made Dungeon Rock feel nearly sacred. When they met Cas there just a few weeks ago, they set into motion something bigger than any of them even knew.

Perhaps that feeling isn't about the place, though. Perhaps it's the people. There's a sacredness as she sits with Remy, and Finn is reluctant to break the silence. She wants to be here, in this moment, and let everything else fade away.

The night is cold, and Remy is warm as Finn edges forward and lets herself lean into Remy's shoulder. Finn shouldn't look at Remy from so close. Remy's lips are chapped and red from the sea wind. When Remy wraps an arm around her and pulls her in, the fire in Finn's stomach flickers, and this feels like a dare, even through layers of sweaters and coats.

Finn has had too many dreams like this, too. She's dreamed of cupping Remy's face in her hands and kissing her, fiercely and eagerly. She's dreamed of running her hands over Remy's bare skin, intertwining their bodies like ropes into knots.

But the flames will take everything in the end. They always do.

Finn can't. She shouldn't. Everything she touches, she burns.

VI.

REMY

"We need to lay out everything we know," Remy says as she and Finn stand at the large dining table the next morning. "And from there, everything we *don't* know."

She and Finn have the dining area to themselves now that breakfast has been put away. The last of the fog finally cleared at dawn, and most of the sailors have congregated on the main deck to soak up the sun after days without it. This portion of the lower deck opens to the stern, with its row of wide, glass-paned windows. Shreds of sunlight sneak inside, though the light is mostly blocked by one of the boats that's stored off the back of the quarterdeck.

All the better; Remy doesn't have time to bask. She's borrowed a pair of drawing slates and a piece of chalk from little seven-year-old Nessa, and now she arranges the slates side by side on the table. She labels them: *What we know*, and *What we don't know*.

"How can we lay out what we don't know?" Finn asks. "Isn't that contradictory?"

"Unresolved questions, then," Remy says, revising the heading on the second slate. "We need to know the questions so we can work out where to find answers."

Finn leans in to read her writing. For a moment, their hands brush on the edge of the table. It's absurd that this tiny, accidental touch sends a thrill shivering up Remy's arm. Remy thinks of Finn's wiry frame pressing into her last night as they sat together on the masthead. That physical contact between them had felt so natural and easy, almost casual. And yet not casual at all.

Remy can't think about it—not now. Finn finally seems willing to help her organize their next steps, and Remy wants to harness this momentum.

"Well, we know Smith's plan," Finn offers. "Capture Death; take control of his list."

"Right," Remy says. "Ashworth told Cas that Smith wants to 'trade out the names' of the people who are meant to die." The chalk makes a grating sound as Remy writes this down.

"Can he really do that?" Finn asks.

"And that's something we *don't* know, isn't it?" Remy says, and she notes the question on the second slate. "Whether it's possible, and if so, how. I wonder if that's why Smith wants a reaper's glass. Capturing Death is one matter; changing Death's list is another altogether. But if Cas's visions really are connected to that list, maybe Smith hopes to use the connection as his opening."

Cas is practicing meditation with Striker again this morning. Striker had seemed in good humor with her stomach full of bread and coffee; maybe that will improve her patience. Remy had tried to talk with the captain over breakfast, though the conversation was disappointingly brief. Captain Hobbes would only tell her that he intends to meet with his contact, Díaz, when they reach Boston. And Remy already knew that much.

She's certain the captain is working on other strategies; he's too much of a chess player to put all his focus on a single line of attack. He's treating Remy like a child, keeping her in the dark.

"It was Díaz who wrote the captain that note saying the Order had acquired a reaper's glass," Remy says now, thinking. "Or *thought* they had acquired one, anyway." The Order had mistakenly taken Henry Ashworth, then briefly acquired the *actual* reaper's glass before Cas got away from that place. "Do you think we can assume Díaz has a leak within the Order? Someone passing information?"

The cat has come to investigate whether there's any food left on the table. Finn has to catch her before she walks across the slates and scuffs the chalk.

"More than one someone," Finn says, cradling the squirming cat in her arms. "I think the note said two sources."

Remy tries to recall the exact wording of Díaz's note, though she'd been distracted when they found it their first week aboard the *Mori*. The memory makes her flush; Remy barely had time to read the note before she and Finn were caught in the act of rifling through Hobbes's office.

"Maybe Díaz's sources will know *how* Smith wants to use the reaper's glass," Remy says. "Or if there's some other way he intends to change Death's list." She wishes she had a third slate for *Where we might look for answers.* Her journal will have to do. She labels a blank page and writes down Díaz's name.

"Or why Smith wanted the brass," Finn prompts.

"Right. The brass." Remy returns to her first two lists. "Smith went to great lengths to track down that cargo ship after it wrecked. We don't know why he needs the rest of those brass panels, but clearly he wanted them badly."

Remy has missed this rhythm with Finn; she's relieved to have Finn engaging with her on this again. For years, Finn has been the one at Remy's side as they've investigated the Order of

Lazarus. There's a specific spark that lights up in Remy's brain when she tosses out some new idea and hears Finn catch it and toss it right back to her.

"Did you tell the captain your theory again?" Finn asks. "About Smith making a binding vessel for Death?"

"I did. He thought the theory might hold weight. Though he seemed reluctant to talk about it with me."

"Can't really blame him for that, can you?" Finn says, catching the cat once again and scratching her ears to distract her from the chalk. "The Order might be trying to build a magic box to lock up his partner. It's not a cheery conversation."

Remy hadn't thought about it that way; she's been too caught up in solving the puzzle of it. Maybe she shouldn't take Captain Hobbes's coldness so personally. She and the captain are both scrambling to protect someone they . . . well, someone they care very deeply about.

Remy's cheeks feel warm. She didn't exactly *lie* last night when she told Finn she was shifting her focus. It was probably a lie by omission, though, considering Remy didn't correct her when Finn assumed the wrong reason for this change. It's better this way; let Finn believe that Remy wants to take down the Order purely because she wants to avenge her father. Finn doesn't need to know this is only a more roundabout approach to the problem of finding Death.

This is the way Remy sees it: Death isn't *gone*; he's only in hiding, evading Smith's plan to capture him. The captain believes he's retreated "through the Veil," though he refused to elaborate on what exactly this means. Presumably, once the Order no longer poses a threat to him, Death will return. And if Remy, Cas, and Finn have helped *stop* that threat, it seems only fair that Death should agree, in a show of gratitude, to wipe the Mark of Death from Finn's soul.

Remy hopes Death will agree. She hopes they can find a way to stop Smith before Finn's demon comes to collect. It would be much easier for everyone if Cas could just work out how to talk to Death now.

A door opens in the passageway outside, and Cas storms out of the cabin where he and Striker have been working.

"Cas!" Remy calls through the open doorway. "In here."

Cas freezes. When he turns, he hasn't quite managed to clear the scowl from his face, though he's tempered it to a slight grimace.

"Any progress with the meditation?" Remy asks him.

The scowl returns in full force. "*No.*"

"Christ," Remy says. "It was only a question."

Cas groans as he joins them at the table, digging the heel of his hand into a spot between his furrowed eyebrows. "Sorry," he says. "Ignore me. Just . . . *god*. My head's killing me."

Remy straightens at once. "Are you going to have another vision?"

"What? No." Cas looks at her aghast. "Why would you ask that?"

"You said it always starts with a headache."

He'd told them all this the day after Eden, when Striker offered to help him with the meditation. She'd asked what Cas felt before a vision took him. They'd already witnessed the taking part, days before, when Cas had fainted into a vision in the middle of the main deck.

Finn has pulled out a chair for him. "Do you want to sit down?"

Cas doesn't take the chair. "Yes, the visions always start with a headache, but no, this isn't a vision. I don't *think* it's a vision. I think it's what happens when I spend the whole morning trying to *focus my thoughts*."

Remy opens her mouth to point out that Cas has been at it for less than an hour—but Finn shoots her a warning look. Right; new perspective. Remy isn't pestering. She closes her mouth.

Cas reaches for the closer of the two slates. "What's this? Are you making lists?"

"Remy's scheming," Finn tells him.

"I can see *that.*" He leans across the table to see Remy's open journal. "*Where we might look for answers,*" he reads. "Captain has a plan for that already, doesn't he? The friend who owns a bookshop."

"Yes, I know," Remy says, jabbing a finger at Díaz's name on the page. "That doesn't mean we can't have our own plans as well."

"What about that student?" Finn asks. "Daniel . . . Stewart?"

"Stevens," Remy corrects. "That's a good thought."

"Who's Daniel Stevens?" Cas asks as Remy adds Stevens's name to the list.

"A former student at the seminary. I exchanged letters with him for a while, trying to wheedle out information."

The cat has been sniffing at Cas's hand; she seems to realize he doesn't have food, either, and she jumps from the table and stalks out of the room. Cas shakes his head, rubbing at his forehead again.

"Right," he says. "I forgot. I still can't believe you had a secret correspondence with some boy in Eden."

"It wasn't like that. I wasn't *me.* Daniel Stevens thought I was a twenty-five-year-old private detective."

The open page of Remy's journal flutters a little; there must be a draft. Remy smooths it down.

"Why did he think that?" Cas asks.

"Because that's what I told him! He wouldn't have taken me seriously if he knew how young I was. Or how . . . *female*. Stevens helped me look into the disappearances."

Cas's golden-brown eyes have glazed over.

"The . . ." Remy sighs. "The ritual murders."

He blinks back to attention. "*Oh.* Those."

Remy's journal still won't stay open properly. The pages keep flapping back and forth. "I need another slate," Remy mutters.

"I'm surprised you haven't moved to writing straight on the tabletop," Cas says. To Finn, he adds, "Did she tell you about the time she wrote lists all over my bedroom floorboards? Swore the chalk would wipe clean with no trouble—"

"It *did* wipe clean," Remy cuts in. "Eventually."

"It didn't. You can still see it there if the light's just so. I had to put a rug over it."

"*Why* did you write lists all over Cas's floorboards?" Finn asks. She looks almost amused by this anecdote. Remy has the sour notion that she's the butt of this joke.

"We were trying to research the pirate treasure," Remy says. "Because we were eight, and Cas wouldn't stop talking about it."

Finn's eyebrows have shot up. "Pirate treasure?"

"Buried under Dungeon Rock. At least if you believe the stories. And I'd tracked down five different versions of the history, and I needed to write all the pieces in one place. And we didn't have a slate that was big enough."

"And after all that, we still didn't find the treasure," Cas says.

"Only because *you* have no follow-through!"

The journal on the table is still ruffling a little; Remy bends its spine backward before she lays it flat again. The pages finally stay put. Remy needs to focus.

"Daniel Stevens was planning to accept a post in Boston after he graduated from Eden," Remy says. "We could try to find him in the city. Though it's been a few years since I last wrote to him."

"Probably shouldn't just show up on his doorstep," Finn says. "He wouldn't even recognize you, would he? Seeing how you're *not* a twenty-five-year-old private detective."

Remy considers this. "I suppose we could find another way to reach out to him."

"*Or*," Cas says, "we could wait, and follow the captain's lead on all this."

"*You* want to wait," Remy says, incredulous.

Cas looks weary. "I want you to stop crossing him. You're going to get us thrown off the ship."

Would that really be the worst thing? Remy wonders. If the captain is so determined to set his own course without their input, they might as well split off in Boston and keep working at this on their own. Remy doesn't dare say this aloud. Cas has gotten too comfortable here with the crew; he's forgotten what's at stake.

Or maybe the stakes are different for him. Finn's eyes are darting between the two of them, wary. Remy feels something burning beneath her sternum. Cas has found a good future for himself here, aboard the *Mori*. Or at least he's on his way to finding one.

For Remy . . . She tries to imagine any future for herself that doesn't have Finn in it. The thought is unbearable.

"If you're so desperate for the captain to let us stay on," Remy tells Cas, "you really ought to get back to meditating."

"Rem," Finn cautions.

But Remy's patience has snapped. "Captain Hobbes wants to contact his partner—and there's exactly one person aboard his ship who can do that. So make yourself useful. Are you even *trying* to meditate?"

Cas doesn't answer; his jaw is clenched. He's moved to lean against the wall, arms folded tight.

Fine. Let him sulk. Remy whirls back to her lists, though she can feel Finn's reproachful gaze on her.

"He thinks everything's just going to magically work itself out," Remy tells Finn. "I suppose that's what happens when you've lived your entire life with a nice, comfortable cushion under you."

"That's low," Finn says, though they both know it's true.

"Well, the rest of us don't have that luxury. We have to work things out for ourselves." Remy snaps her journal shut. "Do you know who really would have answers? Death."

She gives Cas a pointed look. Cas doesn't respond. He's standing very still, fingers digging into his own arms as he hugs himself.

"I think you were right, actually," he says. His voice is strangely flat. "I think it's happening again."

The fight leaves Remy in one swift spill, a cup of water knocked on the floor. "Another vision?" she says.

Cas nods once. He's gazing at nothing, still leaning heavily against the wall as if it's all that's keeping him upright.

"Is it Finn?" Remy asks.

"Don't know yet. I won't know until . . ."

He doesn't finish the sentence. He's swaying a little. Finn reaches to steady him, but Cas suddenly snaps to focus and jerks away as if she might burn him.

"Don't touch me!" he bursts out. "When I . . ." He stares at Finn's outstretched hand. "I don't want to pull you in."

Of course, Remy thinks, as the understanding sinks in. This is what happened with Henry Ashworth. Weeks ago, when Cas had his first vision of Finn's death back on Long Beach, Ashworth had grabbed onto Cas's arm at the last moment. He'd been dragged into the vision right alongside Cas. Something about the physical connection, the skin-to-skin contact in that crucial moment. It's strange to think how everything that's come since—the three of them gathering at Dungeon Rock, their rescue mission, their time aboard the *Memento Mori*—unfurled from that single unwitting move on Ashworth's part.

Finn retreats, her hands raised in surrender. "All right," she says. "We won't touch you. But you need to lie down. You're going to fall."

Stiffly, Cas turns and starts toward the crew's quarters. Remy and Finn trail behind him without a word. Remy's mind feels sluggish. She feels useless. Should they call someone for help? Should she go fetch Leo, with his medical knowledge? But all the bunks are empty as they pass through the cabin, and she doesn't want to leave Cas alone right now.

Remy brings the lantern as they follow Cas into the fo'c'sle. The curtain drops back into place behind them like a veil, and they're shrouded and alone in this small, angled space reserved for the three of them.

Remy finally voices the idea that's been settling in her mind: "Maybe you *should* pull us in."

Cas's face is waxy in the lamplight. "What?"

"Or me, at least. You could show me, right? I could see what you see. If it *is* Finn—"

"No," Cas cuts in. "I'm not going to . . . You don't want to see that."

"Yes, I do! I could see what we're up against!"

"*No!*"

"Stop it." Finn's voice is a dagger, cold metal pressed against skin. "I already know what we're up against," she tells Remy. "Don't do this."

She's right, and Remy knows it, and it's still so tempting to keep pushing. Could Remy learn something here, anything, that might be the key to saving Finn? She has a morbid curiosity to witness the scene firsthand, the way Cas has twice already. The way her father witnessed these deaths for years before the Order found him.

Remy left her carpetbag back in the dining area. Her arm feels empty without it.

She takes a breath and steps back, trying to gather herself. She won't interfere. She can't.

This story isn't about her.

Cas lowers himself onto the nearest bunk with a shaky breath. He rolls onto his side, turning away from them.

"You don't have to stay," he says to the dark inner planks of the hull.

They stay, of course.

Remy knows the precise moment the vision takes him. She can't see his face, can't watch his eyelids flutter shut, but his tightened muscles go slack all at once, and she knows what must be happening. Is he witnessing Finn's death, again? What does it mean if Cas sees yet another way for her to die?

Remy tries to focus on counting the seconds. It feels like an eternity, though she knows it won't be. When Cas had his vision on the deck the other day, they didn't even have a chance to call for Leo before he came to.

Remy has reached a count of twelve when Cas speaks. It's only a syllable, the garbled word of a sleep-talker.

Remy and Finn both stare at each other. Finn's eyes are impossibly black.

"Did he just say . . . ?" Remy whispers.

The word was indistinct, and yet Remy feels certain.

Death, Cas had said.

He jolts then, and gasps, and sits up so quickly that Finn throws out a hand to stop him from slamming his head against the bunk above.

"Well?" Remy says.

Finn frowns at her. "Give him a moment."

Cas buries his face in his hands. He doesn't look at either of them.

"You . . . drowned," he says in a muffled voice. "In the sea. There was a storm, and you were struggling in the waves . . . and then the demon was there. Pulling you down."

Finn lets out a breath in a long, thin stream. In the silence, the air seems to whistle. She says, "I suppose I *should've* learned how to swim."

The attempt at levity doesn't land. "I don't think being able to swim will save you from a demon," Remy snaps.

"There was something else," Cas says. "Or . . . *someone* else. I couldn't see them, but . . . I heard a voice."

Remy waits for him to continue, but he doesn't. "What did it say?"

"I can't remember."

"You can't *remember*?"

Cas is shaking his head, face still covered. "There's usually no sound! I've never had to remember *words*, or . . ."

Remy grits her teeth and tries again. "What did the voice sound like?"

"It was . . . deep. Had an accent, I think. English, maybe? Or Irish?"

Finn looks as if she's holding herself together by a thread. "Well, which was it?" she asks. "English or Irish?"

Cas doesn't answer.

"There's a difference, you know, between English people and Irish ones."

"I know that! I'm just not good with accents!" Cas looks up at her at last to offer a helpless shrug. "Maybe it was German."

"Jesus Christ," Finn says.

"Think," Remy tells him. "What did the voice say?"

Cas presses his hands over his eyes again. "Strange."

Remy is going to grind her own teeth to dust. "Yes, we know it's strange."

"No, that's what he said. *Strange.* And then something about . . . *I thought they took this one already.*"

Cas isn't trying to avoid their gazes, Remy realizes. He's trying to *remember*—to cup the details of the vision in his hands, like water that wants to slip away.

"He'd seen Finn before, obviously. He seemed surprised she was still alive. He said . . . *Demons don't typically play with their food.*"

Cas sounds apologetic for even repeating this. The food, in this case, is Finn.

But Remy is scrambling to get her hands around something—a shred of hope. What does it mean, if the demon should have taken Finn already? What does it mean, that the demon *hasn't*?

"I thought the voice knew I was there, at first," Cas says. "I thought he was talking to *me.* And I tried to reply, but . . . You know when you're trying to speak, in a dream, and you can't get the words out? And so you push a little harder, and . . ."

"You said it aloud," Finn tells him, breathless and marveling.

When Cas finally looks at them, his face answers the question Remy knows is on all their minds.

"I think I just heard Death," Cas says.

Maybe he's been making progress with the meditation lessons after all.

VII.

CAS

Remy interrogates Cas about his vision for what feels like hours. He recounts it in painful, painstaking detail, over and over: the storm, and the churning waves, and the tiny dot of Finn as she vanished and resurfaced in the dark void of the sea. The shadow of the demon emerging from the deep. The tentacle of smoke dragging Finn beneath the surface. The bone-chilling cold. Cas's chest is squeezing, squeezing, as he remembers Finn gasping for air until her eyes went dim.

As Cas talks, Remy scribbles notes in her journal. She wonders aloud about what Death's words had meant. She makes Cas recount the whole vision yet again.

The more times Cas tells it, the more he doubts his own recollection. The actual memory starts to blur with his *telling* of the memory. It's like when he used to try to tell Miss Eloise about a nightmare that had woken him: Afterward, he was never quite sure how much was the real dream anymore, or how many pieces his mind had reshaped to make sense now that he was awake.

Had Death actually said that part about demons playing with food? Or did Cas imagine Death's surprise at seeing Finn once again? The whole vision feels like something Cas would imagine—of *course* he'd have to see a drowning, now. Maybe he manifested this particular death scenario himself, after days of flinching at the sight of the sea and getting pulled into the waves of his mind. Meditation is terrible. Cas stands by that.

Unfortunately, the meditation seems to be working. True, he hasn't fully *talked* with Death; the vision cut off just after Cas managed to say Death's name. But it feels like the start of something.

By the time Remy is satisfied, Cas's voice has turned hoarse from so much talking. It's possible the talking helped, though. Cas isn't going to tell Remy this. If she *hadn't* forced him to rehash the vision until he went numb to it, he'd probably have spent the rest of the day replaying it in his mind. Instead, he feels wrung out, every last drop squeezed from the sponge. His mind is refreshingly dry.

They join Finn abovedeck just in time for the midday meal. Finn left before Remy started asking Cas to describe her death a thousand times, thankfully. Cas can't eat. He feels achy and sick, which is probably from the vision, though Cas is also willing to blame it on the ship's bouncing. The eerie fog has been replaced by a wind that's aggressively strong. The *Mori* is positively galloping across the water today. It's good for speed. It's less good for Cas's stomach.

Leo comes to sit with him after he gets sick over the railing. He brings Cas water and a piece of dry bread, and Cas feels a little better for it. Leo has been very polite about Cas having fallen asleep on him last night. Cas is still waiting for his own embarrassment over that to catch up with him. Somehow, it hasn't yet. His stomach settles.

By evening, the low rise of Cape Cod has come into view on the horizon. The dusk sky is purple and clear, but Kit still claims it's going to storm soon. The violent wind hasn't let up, driving them with urgency toward shore.

Cas assumes the weather will put off Gabe's plans for Cas's birthday party that night. But the party happens anyway. As it turns out, Gabe has arranged for music, decorative bunting strung between the masts, and a special batch of biscuits put together by the cook, with raisins and a dash of molasses. This is a rare treat, according to Gabe. Cas appreciates the gesture more than the biscuits themselves, which taste almost the same as regular hardtack except with soggy, chewy bits mixed in. He nearly gags when he bites into one; the texture is offensive.

And still, all evening, people offer Cas biscuits and wish him well, and he smiles and thanks them and tries not to think about the elaborate dinner his mother had arranged for tonight. She'd been planning it for months, nominally for Cas's birthday, but really as an excuse to show off the new wallpaper she had shipped over from Paris for her dining room. There was a menu involving a lot of expensive veal and a guest list of nearly fifty people. Cas had no say in any of it.

He much prefers this party—even with the raisins. Even with the ocean wind chapping his face and the jaunty violins playing a little too loudly. Cas didn't have much say in this celebration, either, but at least it's actually for *him*. This is a crew of people whose company Cas genuinely enjoys, and who seem to enjoy his company in return.

He stuffs all the extra biscuits into the pockets of his coat. Maybe he can sneak them back into the basket when no one is looking.

"I have something for you," Leo says when he finds Cas in the festivities. Cas braces himself for another raisin biscuit. But Leo offers him a small, tidy book with a marbled cover.

"Thank you," Cas says automatically. There's no title on the book's spine. Cas racks his mind. "Did I . . . forget this in your cabin yesterday?"

"Oh, no! It's a gift. Or it's meant to be a gift, if you want it. For your birthday. Technically it's from the captain, but he has a whole shelf of them that he hasn't even touched, and he said I could take one. For you. As a gift."

Cas's stomach is doing something complicated and fluttery. He doesn't think it's seasickness now.

"Thank you," he says, more earnestly this time. He flips through the pages, but they're blank. "It's . . . empty?"

"Right," Leo says. "That's the idea. It's a ship's logbook—unused, obviously. I found one that doesn't have lines on the pages. I thought you might use it for drawing."

Cas feels very . . . *seen*. It isn't an unpleasant sensation, but it's a new one, and he's not sure what to do with it. He's been quiet for too long. Leo seems to falter.

"It just seemed like drawing . . . helped, maybe?" Leo says. "Yesterday, when you were—"

"Oh, sure!" Cas cuts in, because they really don't need to talk about how Cas was yesterday. "Sure, sure, sure. Yes, it helped a lot. I'm fine now. That was nothing. I'm loads better today. Completely fine."

Leo is looking at him oddly.

"Thanks for this," Cas says, waving the little book. "Really."

Leo turns to face the shoreline, so Cas can only see him in profile. There's a seam down the sleeve of Leo's wool jacket, a hole patched back together with tidy stitches.

"Can I say something?" Leo asks.

Nothing good will come from this, but Cas nods.

"Sometimes," Leo says, "you say that you're fine, but then you don't . . . seem . . . fine. It's a little confusing."

Cas still feels seen, but now it *is* an unpleasant sensation. He laughs once, awkward and too high. He laughs again. Which is ridiculous. He's only going to prove Leo's point.

"I'm sorry," Leo says, shoulders hunching. "I shouldn't have said anything. Let's get back to the party. Would you like more biscuits?"

Cas's pockets are filled with raisin biscuits already. He tucks the blank logbook into the waistband of his trousers as he trails after Leo anyway. The ship is pitching worse than ever, or maybe Cas is just feeling it more now. His headache from earlier is creeping back in. The choppy waves around the ship seem to leer at him.

The violins really are too loud. The wind rushes in his ears. Sound has gone slanted.

"Oh, there you are," Mita says as Cas passes her. "Have you got a minute? I could use your help with something."

Cas tells Leo to go on without him and follows Mita belowdecks. Once he's down the ladder, he manages to catch his balance. He looks around.

"What did you want help with?" he asks.

"Nothing," Mita says. "You just looked a little stricken. I thought you might need a moment to yourself."

Cas did, in fact, need a moment. He hadn't realized how badly until now, with the wind and the music dampened by the deck above.

Mita's smile is knowing. "Take all the time you need."

"It really is a nice party," Cas tells her. "I appreciate Gabe doing all this."

"He knows that," Mita says. "They all do. But it's meant to be a celebration—something you *get* to do, not *have* to. No one minds if you step away for a bit."

She makes it sound so simple. So obvious. Cas flops down against the ladder, letting the steps of it dig into his back. "I think I'm still getting used to that," he admits.

He isn't sure why he starts telling Mita about the birthday dinner his mother had planned for him. He thought he'd exhausted his voice earlier, with Remy. But this is different. Mita doesn't press him; she just lets him talk. Cas tips his head back to watch the night sky through the open hatch above. Clouds have started to gather there.

"The dress she ordered for me had all these ruffles, and these drooping sleeves—you should have seen it," Cas says. "Or, no, you shouldn't. No one should. It was hideous."

Mita laughs. "Not really to your tastes, I'm guessing."

"I don't think my tastes have ever come into it."

Cas wonders if his mother is still throwing the dinner without him. He wonders how his parents have been looking for him. Did they call the authorities when they realized he'd run away? Did they hire a team of private investigators? No one will find him out here, thank god, but the idea doesn't sit well with him.

He'll never know the answers to these questions anyway. He's never, ever going back there.

Eventually, when Cas has trailed off for a while, Mita says, "Well?"

"I think I could use a little more celebrating," Cas says, and starts to his feet.

The bell on the mainmast begins to clang, an urgent peal.

Mita's eyes are wide. "All hands," she says.

They both race back up the ladder.

On the main deck, Cas tries to make sense of the frenzy that's erupted where the party had just been. Nessa darts past him and through the hatch, the ship's cat bundled in her arms. Gabe is scrambling to gather the food and the decorative bunting. Cas helps him get it all into a crate. The clouds are thick overhead now, spitting rain.

By the time he and Gabe push the crate belowdecks and wrestle the hatch closed behind it, the rain has turned to an icy downpour.

This is fine, Cas tells himself as he heads for his station with Mita, just as Kit made them all practice. This is fine, I'm fine, everything's fine. Leo's words flit through his mind. Cas ignores them. He turns up the collar of his coat, though the rain is already seeping through it.

When he staggers to the foresail brace, Remy and Finn are nowhere in sight. Good. They must have gone to safety belowdecks, like Nessa and the cat. Finn, at the very least, shouldn't be out in this storm—not after the vision Cas had just hours ago.

Mita hands Cas the lines, and together they fight to take in the sail. The rain-slick deck tips beneath them as the ship is battered by the waves. More than once, Cas nearly slips. Gabe joins them and catches him by the arm.

"I don't like this," Gabe shouts over the wind as he takes the lines behind Cas. "It's been clear skies all day."

"Storms come on quickly," Mita shouts back.

A fork of lightning cuts the sky with a bone-rattling clap of thunder. It's so close to them that Cas swears he feels the electricity tingling on his skin.

"Not like this," Gabe says. "Not here. Not in April."

Cas doesn't have enough experience at sea to gauge what's normal and what isn't—but the rest of the crew has experience aplenty. Ever since Georges Bank, they've been in a constant refrain of *not normal*. Cas struggles not to shiver as they finish pulling up the sail. Something is happening here that isn't just weather.

The clouds overhead flash again. In the brief burst of lightning, Cas catches a glimpse of copper-bright hair.

Finn and Remy are standing on the deck twenty feet away from him. They seem to be locked in a fierce debate. Cas's mind is fuzzy with panic. Why the hell is Finn still here?

There's a whizzing, popping sound, almost like a patter of gunfire. The air feels strange and crackling. Someone is shouting. Cas can't think with the rain pelting his face.

A fiery light. An apocalyptic *boom*.

The fabric of the world blasts apart.

VIII.
FINN

Finn is sprawled across the deck. She can't quite work out how she got here. It's as if the force of whatever just happened has knocked loose the timeline in her mind. She blinks through the rain, trying to fit the events back into the right order. Her left shoulder hurts. She landed on it when she fell. No, when she was tackled. Striker tackled her. She tackled Remy, too, who's still halfway on top of Finn, pinning her to the deck. Striker had grabbed the two of them and hurled them out of the way when the lightning struck.

Because . . . Jesus, Mary, and Joseph. The *Mori* was just struck by lightning.

Remy is scrambling to her knees, though she stays hunched protectively over Finn. She's saying something. Finn's ears are ringing too badly for her to hear her. There are long splinters of wood stuck through Remy's coat sleeve. There are several more caught in her hair. Finn pulls one free of the wet curls. The splinter is at least six inches long. Remy's eyes are wide as she and Finn stare at each other, dazed, faces inches apart.

Over Remy's shoulder, Finn should be able to see the highest yards and sails of the foremast. But the yards and sails aren't there. The *mast* isn't there. She has an unobstructed view of the stormy, black sky, swirling clouds flashing with lightning.

Striker pulls Remy back and helps her to her feet. She hauls Finn up, too. The angle of the deck is wrong, everything set on a slope. Finn staggers, and Striker grabs her before she can start sliding toward the far rail.

"All right?" Striker asks her, then brushes a few of the splinters from Remy's sleeve. Striker's calmness now is probably a front, but Finn appreciates it. "We need to clear the debris. Get the weight rebalanced."

And at last, Finn sees it—the stump of the foremast. It ends maybe twenty feet above the deck, a charred stick split down the middle like a piece of firewood. The top half of the mast—sixty feet of massive pine spars—has shattered apart from the lightning strike, hurling the crossbeams down onto the *Mori*'s deck, everything snarled with torn sails and rigging.

This is the reason the ship is slanting so badly. One of the mangled yards is caught, hanging over the rail, loose sailcloth dragging into the sea. The lopsided weight of it has pulled the *Mori* nearly on her beam-ends.

Striker has already joined the crew working to push the broken yard overboard. Finn starts to follow her, but Remy seizes her hand.

"We need to get below!" Remy shouts. Her fingers are freezing. "*You* need to get below."

Another piece of the jumbled timeline in Finn's mind slots into place: They'd been arguing, just before the lightning. Remy wanted Finn to go weather the storm belowdecks. Finn refused. Finn knows it's foolhardy to stay here, but she can't bear the thought of hiding while Remy and the others battle this tempest.

"We need to help!" Finn says now, trying to tug Remy forward.

Fire is flickering amid the wreckage; one of the sails must have caught when the lightning hit. It's still burning now in spite of the pounding rain.

Remy has braced her boots on the pitching deck. "You can't be serious. Did you forget that Cas *just saw you die* in a storm?"

Finn didn't forget. But she can't shake the looming awareness that this storm is something unnatural. It's too sudden. Too targeted. Too close on the heels of Cas's latest vision.

Finn's eyes are pulled to the fallen spar with its sail trailing. The waterlogged fabric is threatening to drag the whole ship into the deep.

Albatross, Finn thinks.

She shakes her hand loose from Remy's grip. "We have to help," Finn says again.

The deck has been pulled to such a sharp angle that for a moment, everything goes quiet. The hull is shielding them from the oncoming wind. As Finn struggles not to slide down the slippery deck and into the sea, a memory surfaces in her mind: her brother Kieran reading her the story of Jonah when they were children. Kieran had been enthralled by Jonah's three-day ordeal in the belly of the whale. Finn was fascinated by the part that came just before that. Jonah had tried to evade the path God intended for him; he'd boarded a ship heading the opposite direction. The ship was plagued by terrible storms until the crew cast lots to determine who'd brought down this trouble upon them.

The trouble was Jonah. They threw Jonah overboard. The storms stopped.

But the crew of the *Mori* doesn't know that someone among them has a terrible secret. Finn stopped believing in coincidence long ago; it's clear to her, now, with some deep conviction that she can't quite put into words, that this storm is meant for her.

Jonah shouldn't have tried to outrun his own fate. If Finn were a nobler person, she'd fling herself off the ship now—before everyone else aboard it has to pay the price.

The deck suddenly heaves, and Remy stumbles against her, grabbing Finn's jumper and not letting go. Remy's carpetbag is still hooked over her arm, even now, and it presses into Finn's side. A cheer rings out—the sailors have managed to cut the dragging sail free. The world rocks as the *Mori* starts to level out.

"They don't need us here," Remy says, her mouth very close to Finn's ear.

But as the ship sways, the gusting winds return in full force, spreading the fire on the deck. Finn watches it with dazed horror. It's as if she's back in a nightmare, her own inner fire burning down the world.

This fire isn't hers, but a thought flickers in her mind: She can create fire. What if she can tame it, too?

Cas appears through the rain, clinging to a piece of rigging with both hands to keep his balance. "What are you doing? You can't be here!"

"I know!" Remy shouts. "That's what I've tried to tell her!"

"The fire," Finn says.

The flames have nearly blocked the hatch from view now. Striker and Mita are rushing to smother them.

Cas's face is grim as he tries to shove the rope into Finn's hands. "There's another hatch at the quarterdeck. Mita told me to take you below."

Remy accepts the lifeline from him. But Finn's mind is a blur. "What?"

"I don't like it, either, but she says they've got it handled. We'll only be in the way now."

Finn's fingers are numb as she takes the rope and holds fast. She's just in time, too. A massive wave hits the *Mori* from the side, crashing over the deck, shockingly cold. Finn is nearly knocked from her feet. She clings to the lifeline.

When the flood recedes, the fire on the deck is nearly extinguished. Remy coughs up salt water.

"Come on," Remy says, her voice fraying. "Please."

This "please" is what convinces Finn to move at last—or perhaps the freezing wave has jolted some sense into her. Finn feels like a coward for running away from this disaster of her own making. But at least if she goes to safety, Remy and Cas will go with her.

They stumble through the chaos, pulling themselves toward the quarterdeck using the rope Cas had found. The other end of their lifeline is fixed to a rail near the stern. Finn nearly trips on the brass panel that's still lashed in the middle of the deck. The boat that's usually stored above it has broken loose and swings wildly, tied on only one end. Finn can see the opening of the quarterdeck hatch ahead of them.

Then the second wave hits.

Finn swears she doesn't let go of the line. The rope is in her hands, fibers rough and real against her palms, and then it's stolen from her grip by the force of the water. She can't feel the deck underneath her anymore. She's choking on the sea. At any moment she's going to slam against the ship's rail, with a force that could break a person's spine.

But the collision never comes. She tries to grab for a rope, the rail, anything. There's nothing solid in the world. When she forces her eyes open and tries to see through the salt water, she isn't on the ship anymore. She's been thrown overboard. Thrown to the mercy of the sea, just as Cas's vision showed.

Everything is ocean.

Finn had been prepared to die six years ago when she signed the contract. If the demon had taken her then, she thinks she'd have gone without a fuss. Instead, she lived. She waited. The next year, as the anniversary of her demon deal approached, Finn braced herself again for death—but that day came and went without fanfare. She wondered if the demon might come to take her on her fifteenth birthday, or her sixteenth, or her eighteenth.

On the day Finn turned eighteen, Remy asked if she wanted to go celebrate in the woods at their usual spot at Dungeon Rock. Finn *wanted* to, yes; she always wanted to be with Remy. But she imagined the demon appearing in the woods that night; she imagined Remy's screams. Finn told Remy it was too cold outside, though it was only November. She spent the night of her eighteenth birthday in her little room at Mrs. Darner's, alone.

And still, the demon didn't come to collect.

For years, Finn has been trying not to stoke that fire within her. Better to let it burn out gently. Better to fade away. She's told herself not to make connections—though that never worked with Remy, and Finn can't bring herself to regret that.

It should be easy, now, letting go. The sea tosses her around till she's lost all sense of direction. It doesn't matter. Even if Finn *did* know how to swim, she doesn't think she'd make it to the surface. The others won't be able to see her out here, which means there's no rescue coming. The world underwater is almost peaceful after the wind and the rain above.

She's been too long without air. The fog of her mind is closing in. The roaring water in Finn's ears is so constant that it fades to nothing.

Perhaps here, at the end, Finn will find that quiet she's been waiting for—that elusive sense of peace as she accepts her fate at last.

Something grabs her in the dark.

Finn tries to scream. She's underwater. Opening her mouth only lets the water in. The thing touching her is startlingly solid. An arm. A tentacle.

It slithers around her middle, hooks her under both arms, and pulls.

And here, at the end, as the demon drags her through this directionless dark, there is no peace—only a primal ferocity. Had Finn failed so spectacularly all these years at not caring? Or has the fire been burning inside her all along, despite her best efforts?

Because she doesn't want to die. Not now. Not like this. She wants to live, and fight, and keep fighting. She wants to go back to Dungeon Rock with Remy, and with Cas, too. She wants to pass around the bottle while stars twinkle through the trees above them. She wants to let the ship's little black-and-white cat fall asleep in her lap, purring, while Finn scratches her ears. She wants to tell Kieran about the book she ruined when she spilled tea on it when she was seven. She wants to hug Kieran, fiercely. She wants to tell Kieran everything. She wants to tell *Remy* everything—that Finn is in love with her, that she's been in love with her for years. She wants to touch Remy's soft cheek and feel the skin under her fingers grow warm as Remy blushes. She wants to kiss Remy. On that dimple in her cheek. On her wind-chapped lips. Everywhere. She wants Remy to kiss her back. She wants to cut her hair short—not as short as Cas's, probably, but to her shoulders, and then let it grow, and then cut it short all over again. She wants to reinvent herself. She wants to grow old. She wants to breathe deeply without this crushing weight on her chest. She wants to sit with her friends on the beach and watch the sun rise over the sea.

So she fights. She tears at the tentacle snarled around her waist with all the strength left in her. She kicks at the demon. The water slows her movements, weakens the force, but she keeps kicking.

The grip around her only tightens. There's no escape. Finn fights anyway.

And by some miracle, her head breaks the surface and—

"Oh my god, stop kicking me!" a voice shouts in her ear. "I'm trying to get us to the buoy!"

Finn stops kicking. She coughs, and gasps, and coughs again, and she marvels at the fact that she's still alive.

There is no demon. It's Cas's voice shouting, Cas's arm wrapped around her. He's the one who dragged her to the surface, back into the world of the living and un-damned. He must have dived off the ship after her when she fell overboard. He's struggling to keep them both afloat now, swimming clumsily with one arm as he tries to tow Finn toward a shape tossing in the waves.

Finn clings to him. She lets herself be towed.

The buoy Cas hauls them to is a splintered plank of wood—part of a crate, Finn thinks, either knocked or thrown from the deck of the *Mori*. It seems too flimsy a thing to hold them in this angry sea, but Finn scrambles for it anyway, and she hears Cas breathe out, "*Oh*, thank god," as he lets her go. For a moment, they just bob there, both of them catching their breaths.

"You're all right?" Cas calls over the wind.

"Yes. You?"

"Grand," he says.

Between the dark and the downpour, it's impossible to see. Only when lightning cracks the sky can Finn make out the silhouette of the *Mori*, looking wrong and off-kilter with only one mast. The storm carried Finn so much farther away from the ship than she'd hoped. How did Cas manage to reach her out here? How did he even *find* her?

Finn is still waiting for the demon to grab her by the ankle and drag her down.

"What now?" Finn asks. Her voice sounds faint against the howling wind.

Cas shakes his head. "I don't know."

"Do we swim for the ship? Or swim to shore?"

"I don't know! This is as far as I . . ." It's too dark for Finn to make out his expression, but his voice is trembling. "The ship," he says after a moment. "I don't think we'll make it to shore. *Christ*, it's cold. Come on."

Together, they kick toward the *Mori*, clinging to their feeble raft as the waves rise and fall. But they're not making progress. Finn swears the ship is only growing more distant. The squall is still raging, a swirl of clouds that, from this angle, seems to be centered almost directly above the *Mori*. The ship is being batted like a toy in a child's washtub.

Finn's courage is faltering. She and Cas keep kicking. A swell knocks them back. Then another. Beside her, Cas spits water from his mouth and swears.

"Why aren't they stopping? Don't they know we're out here?"

Perhaps they don't—or perhaps they do, and they can't do anything to help regardless. In fair weather, the crew would deaden the ship's forward movement and bring the *Mori* back around to rescue them. But this isn't fair weather. And one of the masts is gone—and one of the anchors is gone, too, after their frantic escape from the *Clara Smith*. If the *Mori* stops moving forward, the wind and the waves will knock the ship into the perilous shoals around the Cape.

Finn thinks of the wrecked clipper at Georges Bank—the hull snapped in two.

What a precarious thing, Finn thinks, to sail aboard a wooden vessel on the open sea. The ship is their world, and it's a tiny speck; it's nothing to the storm that surrounds it. All the crew can do is keep running before the wind and hope that the other mast holds.

The *Mori* isn't coming back for them. Cas shouldn't have come back for her, either. At least if he'd stayed aboard the ship, Cas might have stood a chance. Now, he *and* Finn are going to die out here, by drowning, or freezing, or both.

"I'm sorry," Finn says. "I'm sorry."

Can Cas hear her? Does she even want him to? And this is what proves she's a terrible, selfish, damnable person: It's Finn's fault that Cas is going to die—and still, in this moment, she's glad she isn't alone.

Something emerges through the rain—a shape rising over the wave ahead of them. A boat. No—an angel. Her dark curls blow in a wild halo around her face, and she holds out the end of an oar for them.

"Grab on!" Remy shouts over the wind.

As Remy hauls first Finn, then Cas, into the jolly boat, Finn wonders if she's dreamed this. Perhaps the demon took her after all.

But this isn't hell. This is a rescue. The boat Remy somehow managed to bring out to meet them is leaking badly. Remy starts to bail the water with a bucket stowed under the seat, then seems to think better of it. She thrusts an oar at each of them.

"Come on," she says. "We need to row for shore."

But Cas doesn't take the oar from her. "The *Mori*," he says.

"They'll be all right," Remy tells him. "They can ride it out."

"We need to row for the ship!"

"Think this through! We'll never catch up with them, and even if we did, they can't haul the boat back up in this storm. It would be dangerous to try." Remy pushes her oar into the water, trying to steer the little boat alone. "We need to go ashore."

Cas grabs her arm to stop her rowing. "If we go to shore, we'll lose them!"

This is sheer panic; Finn doesn't think Remy's cool reasoning is going to sway Cas on this. Remy is quiet. She's still clutching the oar, fingers pressing one by one against the handle of it.

Then Remy says, "We're not going to lose them. Kit told me they're going to drop the anchors and wait for us. She said I should take you to shore until the storm has passed. There's a lighthouse, see? We'll aim for that. When there's daylight, we'll row out to meet the *Mori* again."

And it's a lie, Finn realizes. Remy is lying to them. It isn't only the factual error that gives her away, though Finn catches that, too—the *Mori* only has one anchor for now, which won't be enough to hold the ship in this weather. But it's the way Remy says it: not quite looking at either of them, her words a little too careful, too deliberate. Remy is a good liar. But Finn knows all her tells.

Cas doesn't, though. And the fear has him muddled; he doesn't notice the anchor-size hole in Remy's story. Perhaps Finn should call Remy to task for the lie. Instead, she lets Cas be convinced.

He nods. "All right." He takes the oar.

Together, they row for the lighthouse.

IX.
REMY

They battle toward shore for what feels like hours, taking turns at rowing and at frantically bailing out the water that's slowly flooding their jolly boat. Remy's arms are burning. She tries to keep her eyes fixed on the pinprick glow of the lighthouse through the rain. But she catches her gaze drifting to Finn—trying to soak up the fact of her, trying to reassure herself that Finn is alive. She's drenched and shivering and badly shaken, as they all are. But she's alive. If they manage to make it to land without their boat sinking, Remy is going to throw her arms around Finn and never let go.

Remy hadn't even seen Finn fall overboard. This is what haunts her. The massive wave had knocked Remy to her knees when it breached the deck, and by the time she regained her footing and looked around, Cas was already shucking off his coat and dashing toward the larboard rail. Finn was nowhere in sight. Remy's mind was too slow to work out what had happened. She only finally understood that Finn had been thrown into the sea when she saw Cas vault over the rail to go after her.

If Cas hadn't been there . . . If he hadn't been so quick to act . . .

Remy collects another bucket of water from their leaking boat. Finn nearly died tonight. It was too close. For days, Remy has been working tirelessly to find an escape from Finn's demon deal. She's accused Cas of not trying hard enough to save her.

But Cas had acted when it really mattered. If it had been left to Remy alone tonight, Finn probably would have drowned. Sure, she and Cas *both* might have drowned if Remy hadn't brought the jolly boat out to them—but that was more luck than anything. The boat had broken free of its ties on the deck and crashed through the railing; when Remy saw it there in the water, upright, it felt like a miracle. The most heroic thing *she* had to do was clamber down into it and start rowing.

Remy tosses another bucketful over the boat's side. They can't *all* just dive into the sea on pure impulse; someone needs to pause and work out a plan. This is what Remy tries to tell herself as she bails out more water. But the argument feels weak.

Cas hasn't said a word since they turned the boat toward land. They're all quiet, but his silence is the most noticeable. The rain has started to ease, at least. Remy has long since lost sight of the lighthouse, but the line of the shore slowly rises ahead of them.

When the boat finally scrapes in the sand, all three of them clamber out into the shallows to drag it up onto the beach. Remy tips it onto its side to pour out the last of the water. She ties it off to a scrubby tree in case the tide comes in. She probably shouldn't even bother; the hull is badly cracked and certainly not seaworthy. But it gives her something practical to do.

Finn has started toward the dunes that rise along this stretch of beach. Remy watches her hunched shoulders, the way she's hugging herself against the cold. They're going to need to find somewhere to warm up and dry off—and soon. Finn doesn't look back at her.

Cas is sitting folded over in the sand, forehead pressed against his knees. He's breathing hard, raggedly, though Remy doesn't think this is from physical exertion. *He* hadn't wrestled the boat onto its side.

"What's the matter?" Remy asks.

"Nothing." His voice is strange, though. He doesn't look up. "Just . . . give me a minute."

"We should keep moving," Remy tells him.

"I know."

"We need to find shelter."

"I *know*. I . . ."

His breath snags; the sentence goes unfinished. Without really thinking, Remy touches his shoulder. He flinches badly. When he glares up at her, his eyes are puffy and red. Maybe the salt water has irritated them.

"Give . . . me . . . a minute," he says again, his voice low and furious and not like him at all.

"I'm sorry," Remy says. "I'll just . . . I'm sorry."

She gives him a minute.

Finn is trying to climb one of the dunes, but her boots keep sinking in the sand.

"I think there's something just over the bluff," she says as Remy jogs to join her.

"The lighthouse?"

"No. But a structure, maybe."

They need to get a better view of where they've landed, anyway. The lighthouse could be miles up the beach. Remy finds a place where the dune isn't quite as steep, and they stagger up it, leaving a crumbling trail in the sand behind them.

Remy reaches the crest first. She turns back to help Finn, and Finn hangs on her arm as Remy pulls her to the more stable soil. The moment seems to stretch. They're both breathing hard. The front of Finn's sodden sweater is caked with sand, and it takes an embarrassing amount of restraint for Remy not to reach out and brush it off her chest.

When Finn moves away, she keeps her hand locked around Remy's. Which is perfectly normal, and something they've done a thousand times, and not something that should consume the majority of Remy's attention as Finn tugs her toward the weather-beaten building she'd seen from the beach.

Finn was right—it isn't a lighthouse. The tiny shack is built on wooden piles in the sand, and it leans slightly in the coastal wind. Several of the boards that make up the nearest wall have begun to rot away.

"Is it . . . occupied?" Finn asks as Remy peers through a gap in the siding.

"By a family of raccoons, maybe," Remy says. "Not by people."

Her voice sounds much steadier than she really feels. But with Finn's fingers still clutching hers, she can tell how Finn is trembling. Remy can be the steady one, can't she? She has to be.

Finn lets her go so Remy can pry open the latch on the rotting door. Together, they duck out of the wind and the misty rain.

Remy's eyes adjust slowly. There are no raccoons here, fortunately, though judging by the smell, there may have been at one time. The shack's wooden floor is scattered with straw, and a crumbling brick fireplace occupies one corner, sheltering a crate of supplies.

"It's a charity-house, I think," Remy says. "For survivors of shipwrecks, if they make it to shore. Mrs. Hinton with the Humane Society used to pester my mother to donate for things like this."

"Clearly they could use the donations," Finn mutters. She's picking at a stack of firewood by the door. The shack's walls have been leaking; the firewood looks damp.

Remy pulls out the supply crate and shakes out a few scratchy blankets. She, Finn, and Cas haven't come from a shipwreck, technically—but they came near enough. Remy has to trust that the *Mori* was able to ride out the storm. The alternative is too bleak to consider.

"This isn't exactly the Tremont, is it?" Cas's voice says from the doorway. "But I suppose it's better than nothing."

As he saunters inside to join them, he seems perfectly at ease again. It's too quick a turnaround from his red, puffy eyes on the beach just minutes ago. Remy feels as if she's gotten a peek backstage at the theater; she's suddenly noticing the stage effects.

In the scant moonlight through the open door, the scar on Cas's face looks ghastly.

Finn has propped a few logs in the fireplace and is digging through the rest of the meager supplies. "No matches," she says. "Or flint, either. Figures."

But *Finn* doesn't need matches. Remy catches her gaze and holds it like a challenge. They haven't talked about this—not really. Not since the night Finn first showed Remy this power, and they hardly talked about it then, either. When Finn confessed to Remy and Cas about her demon deal, she called the fire *vitalis vis*—a manifestation of her inner will. Something the demon taught her to harness so she could burn her name onto the contract.

Maybe Remy shouldn't encourage this; maybe it's dangerous for Finn to use some power a demon unlocked inside her. But Remy thinks of that night on a foggy beach with Finn, their hands cupped together, their faces close. She remembers the tiny flame dancing between them in Finn's palm.

She stares at Finn, and Finn stares back.

Finn closes her eyes. The logs in the fireplace flare to life. A bare moment later, a small but cheerful fire is burning there.

Cas is gaping at her. "How did you . . . ?"

Finn adds another log, turning away from them. "I told you already," she says. "Demon deal."

"When you said that thing about burning your name, I didn't think you meant you could *literally* . . ." He makes a wild gesture that involves a lot of wiggling his fingers at the crackling fire. "What the *hell*, Finn?"

"I think hell has something to do with it, yes."

Cas shakes his head, though he goes to join her at the hearth, warming his hands. Remy squeezes in beside them. She's almost afraid to check how her carpetbag has fared through the storm. But when she opens the clasp, her heart settles. Her journal is a little damp, but it will dry. The two jars bundled at the bottom of the bag are still safely intact.

Cas is peeling apart the pages of a small blue book, fanning the sodden paper in front of the fire to dry it.

"Where did you get that?" Remy asks.

"Birthday gift." He doesn't elaborate. "You didn't happen to grab my coat where I left it on the ship, did you?"

Maybe Remy should have, though the thought never crossed her mind in the confusion of the moment. "I didn't," she says. "I'm sorry. There wasn't time."

"Well, you had time to bring *your* whole carpetbag, so . . ."

There's an edge buried underneath his light tone that puts Remy on her back foot. "I already had my bag with me," she says.

"And my coat was right there on the deck."

"Are you really upset with me about this?"

"No." He snorts, as if the question is absurd. It *should* be absurd. Remy grits her teeth.

"I was distracted with trying to make sure you didn't drown, so no, I didn't pause to pick up your clothes."

"I'm not upset!"

He's definitely upset. He gives up on drying the waterlogged book and goes to crack open the shack's door again.

"The rain's nearly stopped," he says, peering over the dunes. "We can probably take the boat back out to meet them tonight, can't we? We don't need to wait till morning."

Finn catches Remy's gaze now—a challenge of a different sort. Finn knows, then, that Remy hadn't been entirely truthful with what she told Cas back in the boat. Finn raises her eyebrows. Remy doesn't respond.

"Well?" Cas says.

"The boat's in bad shape," Finn points out. A solid excuse, though it's only putting off the inevitable.

"Let's go look at it, then," Cas says. "We can figure out how to fix it, can't we?"

Finn's expectant eyebrows arch a little higher. Remy would much prefer to do this in the morning, when they're all warm and better rested.

"Why are you looking at each other like that?" Cas asks. "Do you think the boat's beyond fixing?"

Neither of them answers.

"The *Mori* has other boats, though," he reasons. "It's fine. It'll be fine. If we can't row out in the morning, they'll send someone over in the longboat to fetch us."

This is excruciating. Remy closes her eyes and braces for impact. "They're not going to come fetch us," she says.

"Oh." Cas is quiet. "Because we *can* fix the boat?"

"Because they're not there. They had to keep running before the wind, to make it through the storm. The *Mori* will be long gone by now."

"But you said they were dropping the anchors. You said that Kit . . ." An agonizing five seconds pass as he finally puts it together. "You lied."

The accusation in his voice is well earned—and still, Remy can't help but feel like this is mischaracterizing the situation as it happened. When she opens her eyes, Cas's face is unreadable.

"You weren't thinking clearly," she tells him.

"You *lied* to us," Cas says again. "What did Kit really say? Or did you even talk to her, before you took the boat? Does she know where we are?"

Remy looks to Finn, but Finn makes no move to help her. "I assume that at least one of them saw me—"

"You *assume*?"

His voice pitches high on the word. This reaction is the reason Remy lied to him in the first place, and still, the guilt starts to gnaw at her.

"There wasn't time!" Remy says. "I couldn't even see you and Finn at that point, and everything on the ship was madness. And the boat was just sitting on the water. So I took it."

"Then why did you say that you talked to Kit?"

"Because you wouldn't listen! You kept insisting we should go back to the ship—"

"We *should've* gone back to the ship!" Cas bursts out.

Remy can't reason with him when he's like this. He's started pacing, fingers snarled through the front of his hair, tugging on the wet tangles of it.

"Oh my god," Cas mutters. "Oh my *god.* They have no idea where we are. They don't even know if we're alive. And now we're stranded out here—"

"We're not stranded," Remy cuts in. "There's a lighthouse somewhere nearby. We can find it in the morning. We'll make our way to Boston, just as we planned."

"I should've *known* you'd do this!" Cas says.

"Do what? Save both of your lives?"

"Split from the captain at the first chance you got! You've *hated* having to let someone else call the signals—"

"That isn't what this is about," Remy snaps. But his words sink in like a splinter. Hadn't this very thought crossed her mind—that she could break off from Captain Hobbes and his crew once they reached Boston?

"Except you didn't just run off on your own, did you? You dragged both of us here with you! We might never see the *Mori* again—do you realize that?"

Remy's throat feels tight. "We'll meet them in Boston!"

"Oh, great. Foolproof. Because Boston's such a small place. What if we can't find them? Or they've left again by the time we arrive? What if they have to change course to make repairs? Do you even have a plan?"

He's circling the room, working himself up. Finn is still crouched beside the fireplace. Her eyes follow Cas's pacing like a cat watching a pendulum swing.

"Here's a plan for you," Remy says, though she knows she

shouldn't. "Death's symbol is carved in the *Mori's* figurehead. *He* can find the ship from anywhere. If you actually put your mind to contacting him—"

"*Jesus Christ*! If you're so convinced you could do it better, find a way to talk to Death yourself!"

"I'm trying to!" Remy shoots back.

"Oh, right." Cas's laugh is humorless. "Obsessing over the goddamn Order, because you think if you somehow manage to stop Smith, Death might pop out of hiding and grant you three wishes—"

Remy is startled that Cas has seen through her on this. She's even more startled by how flimsy he's made the whole idea sound. Temper flaring, she says, "It's better than just waiting for *you* to sort yourself out!"

Finn has shot to her feet. The shack around them feels very small. Remy is certain she had the high ground when they started this argument; she isn't sure how she lost it. Now, Cas has pulled up short in his pacing, stung, and Finn is watching Remy with a look of betrayal.

Remy needs to salvage this. She takes a long breath. She turns to Finn. "You knew I didn't really talk to Kit. But we *had* to come to shore—we never would have made it back to the ship. And you knew he wasn't going to agree to it otherwise."

Cas's eyes are flashing golden and dangerous in the firelight. "You knew?"

"I . . ." Finn starts. She doesn't go on. She looks wretched as she stands there, chin ducked, fingers worrying into the damp wool of her sweater.

The fight seems to leave Cas all at once. "Of course you'd take her side."

"Cas—"

"I need air." He lets the door slam behind him as he stomps into the night.

Remy considers going after him, but there's nothing to be gained, and she doesn't think he'll go far. Finn hasn't moved, either.

"Was he right?" Finn asks quietly. "Is that why you've redoubled your focus on Smith? You think if you take down the Order, you can petition Death to . . ."

She doesn't finish the sentence, and Remy doesn't deny it.

"You told me you'd given up on that," Finn says.

"No," Remy says, "I told you I was focusing on the things I can control."

Remy has plenty of regrets tonight, but this isn't one of them. If Finn is going to hate her for trying to save her life . . . well, let Finn hate her. The wind whistles through the shack's drafty walls.

Finn turns away from her. She retrieves the scratchy blankets. She pushes one at Remy. "We need to dry our clothes," Finn says.

She moves to the opposite corner after that, as if she needs to be as far away from Remy as this small room will allow. Remy tries not to let that sting. She keeps her eyes fixed determinedly in her own corner as she sheds her outer layers and spreads them on the floor. There was a time when she and Finn could have changed in front of each other without Remy thinking twice about it. Now, her skin seems to tingle the same way it had just before the lightning strike. It feels inexplicably scandalous for the two of them to stand in the same room in their underclothes, even facing away from each other, even with blankets wrapped around them.

When Remy finally gives up on fiddling with her drying coat, Finn is sitting by the hearth again. She's pulled her blanket up to her chin, so she's only a head atop a mountain of gray fabric. Remy watches the firelight dancing on her pale face.

There had been something so strange, earlier, about Finn's reluctance to go to safety belowdecks when the storm broke out.

"Are you . . . all right?" Remy says, though it isn't quite the question she wants to ask.

Finn doesn't look away from the fire. "Are any of us?"

Probably not. Remy sits beside her, though she keeps several inches between them, and Finn doesn't move any closer.

"Cas wasn't wrong, you know," Finn says. "It's very possible that everyone on the *Mori* thinks we're dead."

Remy has always thought of herself as a very deliberate person. But she hadn't thought *this* through. She should have told someone on the crew where she was going. Have they realized yet that Remy, Finn, and Cas never made it belowdecks? She tries to imagine their reactions—Striker. Kit. Mita. She feels ill. She has to try very hard *not* to imagine their reactions anymore.

"Someone probably saw me take the boat," Remy says.

Her stomach is still twisting into knots, though. If someone *did* see Remy leave, without telling anyone and without returning, it's hardly better. They probably assume she stole their jolly boat and ran away.

Remy *did* steal their jolly boat and run away.

The door of the shack opens again. Cas doesn't speak as he unlaces his boots and starts laying out his clothes beside Finn's.

"We have blankets," Remy tells him.

"I'm not speaking to you," Cas says, though he accepts the blanket she passes him.

The wooden floor is hard and uncomfortable when Remy lies down to try to sleep. She feels self-righteous, and she also feels rotten. If her body weren't so utterly spent from the night's events, she'd probably lie awake for hours, reviewing it in her mind, wondering what she might have done differently.

But they're all exhausted. Remy can hear Finn's breathing steadying out a few feet away from her, though the distance feels much farther. Sleep takes Remy quickly. The fire in the hearth smolders on.

X.

CAS

Cas wakes in a terrible mood.

His head feels like it's being squeezed between two bricks. His whole body is aching and sore after last night's frantic swim in a storm-tossed sea. Or maybe he's stiff from sleeping on the floor. Or from his vision yesterday. Or from the cold. The fire sputtered to nothing as they slept, and the shack's rotting walls let in an awful draft. None of their clothes have dried properly in the night. They have to put them on again damp. Cas has several long scratches on his arm from when Finn tried to fight him off in the water, and he has to keep his shirtsleeves carefully rolled down so Finn doesn't see and make a thing out of it.

All of it—the damp clothes, the scratches—would be bearable if only they were back aboard the *Memento Mori*. If Cas were on the *Mori* right now, Mita would be offering him a cup of coffee to warm him. Or Leo would give him a dubious-smelling salve for his scratched arm to prevent infection.

Everything would be fine if only Cas hadn't been goddamn *kidnapped.*

"You haven't been kidnapped," Remy scoffs when Cas says this aloud.

"I'm not speaking to you," he says again. "I'm speaking to Finn."

Finn glances up from the blanket she's folding. "Oh, I'm sorry, what did you say?"

"*I* don't see how it would meet the definition of a kidnapping anyway," Remy says, undeterred. "You climbed into the jolly boat willingly enough."

"Under false pretenses! You lied to us!"

Remy's long, infuriating sigh implies *Cas* is the one being unreasonable about this. "I'm sorry I didn't give you all the information," she says. "I don't see what difference it would have made, or what other option we had besides coming to shore, but you're right. I shouldn't have lied."

Cas thought an apology would make him feel better. It doesn't.

"I'm not speaking to you," he reminds her.

Slowly, as if she knows she's goading him but can't resist the technicality, Remy says, "You're literally speaking to me right now, though, in telling me that."

Cas has to go outside before he punches a hole through a wall. The rickety shack might not survive it.

The world feels bleak and washed out after the storm. The morning is colorless. Cas stands atop the dune and stares out at the water, willing the familiar sails of the *Mori* to appear on the horizon. He's clutching one of the scratchy blankets around him, because he doesn't have a coat, because Remy left it lying on the ship after he took it off to rescue Finn. It's hardly his biggest complaint at the moment, but it's somewhere on the list. The blanket makes him feel like a child stumbling out of bed after a bad dream.

The most frustrating part is that Cas knows, on some level, Remy has a point. They weren't going to be able to catch up with the *Mori* in their little boat. The raging storm had seen to that.

Cas doesn't regret diving in to save Finn, though he resents the fact that he had to. The whole storm had felt strangely targeted—the sort of bad luck that keeps building until luck seems to have nothing to do with it. Did the *Mori* make it through the squall? The crew has weathered countless storms before. Surely they weathered this one.

Even assuming they did—because Cas has to believe they did—he can't shake the terrible feeling that he's never going to see Mita or Leo or little Nessa or any of them again. The world aboard the *Mori* had felt like a dream. And this—standing alone and shivering on this windswept beach—feels like the inevitable waking, that awful, sinking realization that none of it was real. Or maybe it's worse to know that it *was* real, and *is* real, and is now out of his reach.

Is this what being eighteen feels like? Cas liked seventeen better.

They leave the shack behind and set off in search of the lighthouse, following the beach in the direction Remy claims is north. Cas trails behind her a minimum of thirty feet; when Remy tries to slow down for him, he pretends he has to retie his boot until she gives up and keeps walking.

He doesn't want to catch up with her. She's going to try to rehash their conversation from last night, to talk Cas around into begrudging agreement with her point of view. Cas would sooner eat raisins.

When Finn drops back to join him, though, Cas lets her, and they walk along the sand side by side for a while. He's less annoyed with Finn than he is with Remy. It's useless to blame Finn for going along with Remy's lie, anyway—like blaming a cat for hunting mice. She and Remy have been inseparable for years;

they're always going to choose each other over anyone else. Cas should know this by now.

At least Finn doesn't speak as she walks beside him; she doesn't try to justify her actions. She just falls into step at his side. She's breathing slowly and deliberately, the way Leo had in the surgeon's cabin. As they trek along the beach in silence, Cas feels his own breath slow a little to match.

It's midmorning when a tidy brick lighthouse emerges on the bluff ahead of them. A rumpled man is wrestling a heavy oil can across the yard. Cas lets Remy take the lead as she recounts the events of the previous night. The lighthouse keeper listens with mounting horror.

"We saw the lightning strike your ship," the keeper says. "We were watching in case she wrecked and the crew needed rescue—but she righted herself and sailed away. We didn't realize anyone had washed ashore, or else we'd have . . . good lord. *Ambrose!*"

He shouts this last bit, and a second man pokes his head out of the doorway of the gray-shingled keepers' quarters.

"Darling, I've *told* you, you don't have to—oh." The man is wearing very few clothes, and he quickly shuts the door again, so his voice is muffled from inside. "I'm so sorry. I didn't know we had company."

"I was going to ask you to put on the kettle," the lighthouse keeper calls through the door. His face is flushed as he turns back to Remy. "Would you all like tea?"

They squeeze in around the table of the cramped kitchen inside. The lighthouse keeper introduces himself as Mr. Spencer; the other man, Mr. Ambrose, is his assistant keeper, who joins them a few minutes later after going to put on trousers.

"We don't get a lot of guests out here," Mr. Spencer tells them as they wait for the water to boil. "And most of them are of the marooned variety, like you three. It's not a bad trek to Provincetown, though. We can take you in the wagon."

"Do you think there's a ship there heading to Boston?" Remy asks.

"Oh, certainly. There's a packet that makes the trip most days. The captain won't mind taking on a few passengers."

The heat in the kitchen ought to have loosened Cas's muscles by now, but he can't relax. He'd been bracing himself for Spencer to say, *won't mind taking on a few women.* He's *still* bracing himself, even though Spencer hadn't said it.

And what if he had? Cas wonders what these lighthouse keepers see when they look at him, Finn, and Remy. It shouldn't matter. He should be worrying about more important things than whatever sex these strangers might have assumed for him at a glance.

And still it needles him, like a splinter digging under his fingernail. He's glad Remy is doing most of the talking. He feels like he's been knocked off-balance. Cas spent years teaching himself how to be Miss Cassandra Sterling—how to smile politely, how to fold his hands, practicing all of it until he'd nearly perfected the act. And then he ran away and found himself aboard the *Mori*, where he slowly realized he didn't *have* to act anymore. Where he could just be Cas, and from the beginning, the sailors simply took him at his word on that.

Now that they're back on shore, Cas feels like he's stumbled into hostile territory. He's overthinking everything. He doesn't know where to put his arms.

But Spencer and Ambrose seem friendly enough, and the tea is fortifying. It does warm Cas a little. He thinks about Ambrose's "darling," his state of undress when he thought he and his housemate were alone. A few weeks ago, Cas might have written this off as nothing. And maybe it *is* nothing.

Or maybe, he thinks, as he, Remy, and Finn ride in awkward silence in the back of Spencer's wagon, Spencer and Ambrose have been wondering at the same time what these three shipwreck survivors make of *them*.

The wagon's wheels get stuck in the sand just beyond the edge of town. Remy thanks Spencer profusely for all his help, and the three of them make their way into Provincetown on foot.

They find the town's wharf easily, a cluster of docks lined with fishing boats and schooners. Cas and Finn lurk nearby while Remy negotiates with the captain of the next packet boat bound for Boston. The packet won't leave until the afternoon, though, and once Remy has secured their passage, they go to find lunch at a tavern across the street. The tavern has wide, airy windows that look out over the wharf.

Cas hasn't eaten anything since the bite of raisin biscuit last night, and his appetite is catching up with him. The money he stole from his father is still stowed in Remy's carpetbag, so Cas orders soup for them all, and bread, and a decent-looking port wine from behind the bar.

The glass of port wine earns him a raised eyebrow from Remy. "Don't you think it's a little early in the day for that?" she asks as he returns to their table.

"No," Cas says. "No, I do not."

Finn makes a thin humming noise as she picks at her soup.

"What?" Remy asks.

"Nothing," Finn mutters. "Only I've seen *you* drink earlier in the day than this."

"Not in public. It's different." Remy is frowning at Cas's glass like a disapproving mother.

"I'm not speaking to you," Cas reminds her.

The alcohol dulls his headache, though, or at least it makes him a little less aware of the headache. He's a little less painfully aware of his own body. When he finishes the first glass, he orders a second, just to get a rise out of Remy.

And rise she does. "Really?"

"I'm not the one who keeps a secret liquor stash at Dungeon Rock," Cas tells her.

"Like I said—*not in public.*"

"Mmm." Cas takes a deliberately noisy slurp of his port wine. "Dungeon Rock is public."

"How? It's in the middle of the woods."

"It's haunted, though. You're getting drunk in front of the ghosts."

Cas had only said it to rile her, but she's more visibly riled by this comment than he could have hoped for. "There's no such thing," Remy says, knuckles white around her soup spoon. "And even if there were, Dungeon Rock is not *haunted.*"

"Mr. Anderson says it is. He says he met a ghost of a pirate out there who bet him twenty dollars on a round of cards—"

"Well, Mr. Anderson drinks even more than you do! And I thought you weren't speaking to me!"

Cas considers this. "I'm not," he says. "I'm speaking *near* you."

Remy drops her spoon back into the bowl with a clatter and stands. "You're a child."

She leaves their sack of money, at least, before she takes her carpetbag and stalks outside. Through the window, Cas and Finn watch her cross the street onto the little beach beside the wharf.

"Do you have to antagonize her like that?" Finn asks.

"You did it, too."

"Right, and I shouldn't have."

Remy has disappeared from view behind the dock's pilings. Finn chews on her bottom lip. She's twitching to follow; Cas can see it. He drains the rest of his glass in one go. He knows he's being petulant, and he can't bring himself to stop. He feels like a stringed instrument tuned too tightly, ready to snap at any moment.

Finn is still staring out the window after Remy.

"Go on, then," Cas tells her, more bitterly than he means to. "Doesn't one of you turn into a pumpkin if you spend too much time apart?"

Finn's expression turns cool. She pushes out her chair.

"Don't forget to pay for our meal," she says, nudging their bag of coins at Cas, and then she trails Remy outside.

Cas sulks at the table for only a minute. The second glass of port wine was a mistake. The first glass was likely a mistake, too, though Cas will never admit it. His headache has returned with a vengeance. When he stands, the room spins for a moment. It doesn't help that he probably *would* have forgotten to pay if Finn hadn't reminded him. Because Cas has never had to pay for his own meals before, because there's always been someone else to pay for him, because Remy was right, and he *has* lived his whole life with a comfortable cushion under him. He doesn't know how to exist in the world. What is he even meant to do with the money?

The tavern is nearly empty; a lone employee is washing glasses behind the bar. Cas counts out a pile of coins from his bag and leaves them by his empty soup bowl.

"I've . . . left the money on the table?" he tells the barkeep, like a question.

The man doesn't even look up from the glass he's scrubbing. "That's fine. Have a nice day, miss."

It's like being knocked across the face with a pillow—not painful, exactly, but startling all the same. *Miss*. The barkeep still isn't looking at him; he'd made the assumption on voice alone. Maybe that should be a comfort, but it isn't.

Cas hurries out of the tavern and starts up the wharf toward the packet boat. He just needs to keep his head down. Keep quiet. Don't talk any more than he needs to until he's back aboard the *Mori*.

He ducks his chin into his shirt collar. He feels exposed. Playing the part of Miss Cassandra Sterling was never comfortable, but at least then, he knew where he stood. He knew what people saw when they looked at him—what they expected. Now, every interaction with a stranger feels like wading out into the unknown.

And he really *does* intend to keep his head down, except that a group of sailors from the packet boat's crew spots him before he can reach the gangplank. A hand claps Cas on the shoulder.

"Hey, we were just talking about your friend," the sailor who's touching him says. He's a ruddy-faced tower of a man, and Cas has to physically crane his neck to take him in. "The girl who was with you earlier. Is she spoken for?"

Cas is too fuzzy-headed for this. "What?"

"Not the scrawny one," the sailor says. "The pretty one."

"The *bossy* one," one of his mates chimes in with an unpleasant grin.

Cas feels as if he's watching this interaction through a very thick pane of glass. Remy? Are they talking about Remy?

The man with his hand on Cas's shoulder laughs unabashedly. "What can I say? I like a domineering woman."

It's slowly dawning on Cas that he's never in his life heard a man speak to him like this. He's rarely heard men speak like this at all—only snippets of conversation overheard after supper, when the gentlemen have moved to the next room to smoke cigars away from their wives and daughters.

"So?" the sailor asks. "Does she have a mister? Or is she free for the taking?"

He wouldn't be speaking like this if he thought Cas was a woman. Maybe that should be a relief after the barkeep's casual *miss*, but it feels like whiplash. The chummy hand on Cas's shoulder feels dirty. Why is this man talking about Remy like she's a piece of overripe fruit left at the market stand?

Through his daze, Cas hears himself say, "She isn't *free for the taking*."

The man's eyes widen for a moment, and he pulls his hand away. "Oh, Christ," he says. "Is she yours?"

But Remy doesn't *belong to* Cas. She doesn't belong to anyone. Is this what men are like when they're only among themselves? Cas was furious the first time Henry was invited to join that post-supper rite of masculinity. He'd pestered Henry for every detail afterward, and Henry told him it was very dull, and that he'd much rather be allowed to stay back with Cas and the women in the parlor. But still, after that, he went with the men every time.

"Apologies, mate," the sailor is saying. "I didn't realize. If she's ever too much for you to handle, though . . ." He waggles his eyebrows in an implying sort of way and makes a crude cupping gesture with both of his hands.

And Cas has had enough. "What's that supposed to mean?"

The man tries to give him an affable knock on the shoulder. Cas ducks away. "Lighten up, mate. No offense meant."

"I'd say that gesture was pretty offensive, though. Evocative, too. Do you want to show us again?"

Half a dozen other sailors have circled around them. There's an eager thrum in the air. The man doesn't make the cupping motion again.

"I'm just curious about what exactly you were hoping to handle," Cas says, voice rising. "Did you mean you wanted to touch her *breasts*?"

Someone gives a low whistle, as if Cas has just said something unfathomably crass. Maybe he has. The sailor laughs nervously. "It was just a joke."

"I don't think it was, though. I think you're trying to pull it back into a joke now, before your friends realize what a massive lout you'd be if it wasn't."

The rumble of laughter from the group has a daring edge to it. One of the other men shakes his head at Cas. "Christ, kid. Let it go."

The sailor definitely wouldn't *hit* Cas if he thought Cas was a woman, either. Cas has the brash impulse to stick his hand in the fire and see what happens.

"I have an idea," Cas says loudly. "Why don't you explain your joke to all of us, from the beginning. And then *we* can decide whether it was funny—or whether you're just a scummy, spineless piss-pot of a man who shouldn't be allowed to show his face in public."

As it turns out, the sailor does not think Cas is a woman.

XI.
REMY

Remy sits on the beach with her back pressed against one of the old wooden pilings of the wharf. She relishes the silence. She knew Cas would be angry when he found out Remy had lied to him. Somehow, she hadn't expected him to *stay* angry. When they were children, his temper would always come on like a summer storm—immediate and all-consuming, but the downpour could never last. He'd rage and rant, caught in some unreachable place in his own mind where Remy couldn't touch him, and then the squall would blow itself out. A few minutes later, he'd be back to smiling and joking as if nothing had happened.

His simmering resentment this morning feels different—a storm system that's still brewing and might yet whip up into a hurricane. Cas had been nearly out of his mind with panic last night when he realized the *Mori* was not, in fact, waiting for them. Remy is exhausted. How can he even care about that right now, when Finn's days are numbered? It's a selfish thought. Maybe Remy had underestimated just how much the ship means to him. Still, she saved both their lives last night and hasn't gotten so much as a thank-you for it.

Even Finn resents her, because Remy lied to her as well, or at least was less than forthcoming about her intentions. Remy watches the waves eating away at the shoreline. She's appreciated having clear tasks ahead of her up until now: find the lighthouse, find a ship, make their way to Boston. She wants to keep charging ahead; otherwise, she might have to actually confront whether this feeling in which she's wallowing is self-pity or self-hatred.

She opens her carpetbag and rummages around for her research journal. A hand touches the back of her shoulder. Finn must have crept up on her, silent as always.

Remy turns.

No one is there.

Remy brushes at the spot on her shoulder quickly. She brushes it again. An insect must have landed there. Or it was just the wind rustling her coat.

She opens her journal, irritated. Cas's throwaway comment about ghosts has gotten in her head, which irritates her even more. She can't look at the jars of her father's remains in her carpetbag. Better not to dwell. This is yet another motivation to keep moving, but at least this one is well practiced. Remy has been running from *this* grief for years—long before she even knew that "grief" was the word for it.

She finds the page where she'd started listing the people they should talk to: Díaz, and Daniel Stevens. She's tempted to add Death to the list, but she doesn't. She's kept all the letters from Daniel Stevens fastened in her journal; did he ever give Remy a specific forwarding address for after he graduated from the seminary? Remy doesn't think he did, but she finds his old letters and skims through them anyway.

She has that same prickling sensation that someone is watching her. She can't give in to this. When she hears footsteps behind her, she forces herself not to turn to look in case she's imagining them.

But a shadow passes over her, and Finn is there. She sits down beside Remy in the sand. Remy closes her journal. The two of them watch a seagull pecking at something in the surf.

"I know you're angry with me, too," Remy says.

Finn doesn't speak. A wave rolls in, then retreats.

"I could pretend I'm sorry that I misled you about what I was really planning, but I'm not," Remy says. "So I won't."

Finn releases a long breath in time with the next ebbing wave. She leans against Remy's shoulder.

"I'm not angry with you," Finn says very quietly.

When Remy looks down at her, Finn meets her gaze. Finn's eyes are so dark that under the gray sky, her irises and pupils are almost the same color.

Remy doesn't want to imagine existing in a world where these eyes have gone lifeless.

"I want to be angry with you," Finn says. "I *should* be. Because I've told you to leave this be, to stop trying to save me from a circumstance that we both know is of my own making. And you haven't."

The place where Finn's shoulder presses into Remy's feels like a lifeline. For years, she and Finn have been able to touch each other so easily. Sitting just like this. Walking down the street arm in arm. Hands brushing across an open book. Legs draped over each other as they watched the stars at Dungeon Rock. Remy isn't sure when she started to feel this sharp awareness of her own body. Awareness of *Finn's* body.

It feels dangerous. And still, she doesn't want to pull away.

There's a freckle above Finn's left eye, just inside the arch of her eyebrow. Remy can't stop staring at it.

"Last night, in the storm . . ." Finn's voice catches, and Remy realizes very suddenly that her eyes have gone shiny. "I really thought it was the end."

In all the time they've known each other, Remy has never seen Finn cry. She feels something crushing inside her chest, squeezing her heart. "I did, too," Remy says.

"And . . . I didn't want it to be the end."

Finn whispers it like a confession. Like there's something shameful in admitting this, even though Remy has been waiting for these words. Hearing them now, Remy doesn't know what to say.

"I . . . *don't* . . . want it to be the end," Finn amends. Her voice is so thin. "And I don't know if there truly is some way to change it now, or any way you can actually fix it, but . . . if you're still willing to try . . ."

The first tear spills over and darts down Finn's cheek, and Remy wraps her in her arms. She draws Finn in like water flooding an open field.

"Of course," Remy says into the tangle of Finn's hair. "Of course. We're going to figure something out."

"There are things I haven't done, or . . . said . . ."

Finn's shaky breath is tickling against Remy's neck, under her collar.

"Perhaps I don't need to say them," Finn murmurs. "Or shouldn't. I don't know. Perhaps you've known all along, for years, just . . . watching me make a fool of myself."

Remy feels as if she's floating, even as she's shockingly present in this moment. "When have you ever made a fool of yourself?" Remy asks.

"With you? Constantly."

Finn stiffens, as if she's said too much. It's so subtle a change that Remy might not have noticed if she didn't have Finn so firmly locked in her arms. Finn shifts slightly, and though Remy thinks the effort might physically kill her, she loosens her grip and lets Finn break apart from her.

"We don't need to talk about it," Finn says, face in shadow.

"Talk about what?" Remy asks.

Finn dries her eyes with the heel of her hand. "Probably better that we don't. Spare us both the embarrassment, right?"

She's about to stand and walk away from this moment, and Remy catches her fingers. "Finn."

It's the feeling of sudden clarity when the end of a chess match comes into view. When you understand all at once how the moves will inevitably play out. *There are things I haven't done, or . . . said . . . Perhaps you've known all along.* Remy *hasn't* known all along. But maybe she's sensed Finn's feelings for her, for a time, anyway, without letting herself admit it.

Without letting herself *want* it.

Remy knows now. With thrilling confidence. And considering how this not-quite-admission from Finn has set Remy's heart soaring, Remy knows her own feelings, too. She's been too terrified to allow herself the question, but if the question is allowed, so is the answer.

Remy wants to kiss Finn.

Finn is still sitting beside her, watching her. Their hands are clamped together in the sand.

Somewhere in the back of Remy's mind, there's a list of reasons she *shouldn't* kiss Finn. Which is revealing in itself. How long has Remy been thinking about this? The most obvious reason is this: Finn is a girl, and Remy is a girl, and that simply isn't done. But *why* isn't it done? Because of some arbitrary rules of a religion that Remy stopped believing in long ago? She goes to church most Sundays, but she hasn't listened to Pastor Dekker's sermons since she learned about his ties to the Order. Surely any worthwhile God would condemn the Order's abductions and murders with far more vehemence than he'd condemn Remy for kissing someone who happens to be a girl.

And women *can* desire other women; Remy knew it even before she met Striker and Kit aboard the *Mori*. She knew about Finn's escapades with other girls in town, and she wondered why *learning* about Finn's escapades had made her so ... *indignant* isn't quite the right word ... jealous, though she couldn't have said before what she was jealous about. When she'd walked in on Finn and Mary Lassiter months ago, Remy felt like all her organs had been carved from the hollow cavity of her chest. And still, she didn't let herself really consider *why*.

Another reason Remy has told herself she shouldn't kiss Finn: People in town would talk. But people *have* been talking about her and her family for years, even when Remy stayed perfectly in line and followed their every rule. Why had she cared so much? Now that she's seen more of the world, Windover seems terribly small. And away from her family, it's easier for Remy to let herself be selfish. *Finn* is the place Remy has been letting herself be selfish.

She wants to kiss Finn.

It might be dangerous, kissing in public. This pocket of beach is blocked from view by the dock, but someone could see them from the road. Finn is wearing her trousers, though. From a distance, she could pass for a boy. If she and Remy were spotted kissing, it might be a scandal, but they wouldn't be arrested for it. Does Remy want to kiss Finn because she's dressed as a boy? Of course not. She wants to kiss Finn because she's *Finn*.

The most terrifying reason Remy shouldn't is this: If she kisses Finn now, there's no undoing it. They're both tumbling off a cliff that they can't climb back up. But Remy is falling already, whether or not their lips have actually touched, and she doesn't *want* to go back, because she wants to kiss Finn.

Remy works through this list in her mind, and she dismantles the points on it one by one. When the list is gone, it leaves only resolve.

Remy is *going to* kiss Finn.

She cups Finn's soft cheek in her hand. Finn's breath catches, but she doesn't pull away.

There are voices from the dock above them. A *raised* voice. Familiar. The world around them crashes back into focus; Remy has waited too long. Finn blinks, startled, dark eyes flitting toward the commotion on the dock.

"Is that Cas?" she says.

She scrambles to her feet and starts back toward the road. Remy follows, though she feels groggy, like she's just been jolted from a dream. The warmth of Finn's skin is still burning on her fingertips.

As they run down the dock, though, Remy is suddenly wide awake.

Cas is facing off with a man twice his size, surrounded by at least half a dozen onlookers. The man throws a right hook. Cas doubles over. He's crumpled like a wet sheet of newspaper. When Remy reaches him, Cas is clutching his jaw, and he lets Remy drag him away from the circle of sailors.

Finn has stepped into the group's center, feet planted between Cas and his assailant. She glowers up at the man who punched him. There's a glint of metal in her hand—the blade of Finn's tidy little knife. The one Kit gave her at Eden.

"Well?" Finn says.

The man scowls down at her knife. "Your friend doesn't know what's good for him," he grunts.

"Probably not," Finn says. "The real question is, do you?"

Two of the other sailors hook the man by both arms and haul him back toward the packet. Finn stands her ground as the group disperses. Remy's entire body is buzzing. Finn is standing right here, quiet and fierce and magnificent, and Remy had been a second away from kissing her, only she spent so long running through the moves in her own mind that she missed her moment. And then Cas ruined everything. Remy rounds on him.

"What the hell were you thinking?"

Cas is rubbing at his jaw. "*He* hit *me*."

"Clearly you did something to provoke him!"

"You didn't hear how he was talking about you," Cas mutters.

"And so you thought you'd, what, defend my honor? I didn't ask you to do that!"

"And I didn't ask you to get involved! I had it handled."

"You obviously didn't!"

The captain of the packet is coming up the dock toward them, expression sour. He can't be pleased that Cas got into an altercation with one of his crew. Remy will need to smooth this over. She'll need to be pleasant and obliging and politely apologetic. She knows by now how to do all of this with ease, and she's angrier than ever that she has to.

Finn has tucked her knife away. Remy pushes down every ugly emotion and prepares her most respectable smile.

XII.
FINN

The packet's captain is still willing to take them to Boston once Remy is through with him—and once she's doubled their passenger fees and promised that Cas will stay safely out of the crew's way for the duration of the journey. The schooner is quite a bit smaller than the *Mori*, and the lower deck is cramped as the three of them settle in. They're wedged between bags of mail and crates of goods being shipped from the Cape. Everything smells of fish.

Remy stays for a while to continue lecturing Cas for his foolishness, but once the packet is out to sea, she retreats abovedeck. Cas is sitting on the floor with his knees drawn up to his chest. Finn moves a mailbag so she can take a seat beside him.

Cas has pried a loose nail from one of the crates, and he drags the point of it back and forth across the boards between his feet.

"You're not going to go check on her?" he says, nodding after Remy.

Finn thinks of Remy's arms tight around her on the beach—so comforting, so comfortable, that Finn almost slipped and said the thing she's been thinking for too many years. She could swear she'd watched some new resolve forming in Remy before her very eyes, when Remy snagged Finn's hand and held her there. Finn had almost—*almost*—believed Remy was going to kiss her.

This day has all of them too high-strung. Finn needs time to get her head on straight.

"I'm not going anywhere," she tells Cas.

Remy will be all right, Finn thinks; she's less certain about Cas. He's still dragging the nail across the planks, hard enough to make an awful scraping sound, but not quite hard enough to scratch the wood.

"How's your jaw?" Finn asks.

He brushes it against his shoulder, as if trying to wipe a stray bit of food off it. "Didn't even really hurt," he says. "Just surprised me."

His jaw hasn't bruised yet; perhaps it won't. The wound from Smith's knife is far more visible than the place where the sailor had hit him.

"Next time someone comes at you like that," Finn says, "give him a quick knee to the groin. That's the easiest way."

Cas scrapes the nail for a while. "Noted," he says.

"What *were* you thinking?" Finn asks him. It's a question Remy already posed, but Finn keeps her tone curious rather than accusatory.

"I wasn't."

Finn snorts. "Fair enough."

"I know I should've walked away. He just . . . got under my skin." Cas pokes the nail against his own knee, as if testing whether he can feel it through his trousers. "Is that really how men talk to each other?"

Finn considers this. "Some of them, clearly."

"I don't want to be like that."

"Good. I wouldn't be friends with you if you were."

Finn watches him press the sharp end of the nail against the palm of his hand, then return to scratching it against the floorboards. She wants to tell him that he can be a man without being *that* sort of man. She wants to tell him he doesn't have anything to prove. She hadn't known Cas well before they all set out on this journey—but even she can recognize how he's settled over the last two weeks, despite everything else that's happened. It's as if being *him* has given Cas a fixed point to hold on to amid the chaos.

Perhaps this is something he has to prove only to himself, then. They both know plenty of men by now who treat other people with respect, regardless of their sex: Leo, Immortal Gabe, Captain Hobbes himself. Finn thinks of her brother, who's always led with gentleness.

"Kieran and I took a packet like this when we came over from Ireland," Finn says. "Well, bigger than this one. There was this older boy who tried to steal from us."

Cas throws a sideways look at her. "Did you give him a knee to the groin?"

"No. I pushed him down and kicked him in the face."

That startles a laugh out of him. "Did you?"

"Broke his nose," Finn admits.

"Jesus."

"Well, it wasn't as if *Kieran* was going to fight him. Christ, can you imagine?"

Cas turns to fully stare at her now. "Yes," he says. "What do you mean, *can I imagine*? I've seen your brother's shoulders! They're massive!"

"Kieran isn't like that, though," Finn says. "He's . . . soft." She can sense Cas about to make a face, and she adds, "It isn't a bad thing."

Kieran is probably back out to sea again by now; he's kept his little apartment in Windover all this time, but he never stays there for long. A few months after his miraculous recovery, Kieran decided he wanted to see the world. He talked of signing on with a whaling ship first. Then he spoke with a few actual whalers and seemed to realize what a whaling ship *does.* The boys in town tried to tease him for getting green around the gills over a bit of blood, but Kieran took a position on a merchant ship instead, and he learned the ropes, and he's grown from a sixteen-year-old greenhand into a promising twenty-two-year-old second mate.

Finn didn't want Kieran to take to sea. She'd only just pulled him back from the brink of death, at a cost he could never know. And a sailor's life is a dangerous one.

Still, Finn is glad he didn't become a whaler, at least. She remembers his distress on the evening after he talked with the whalers, when she sat with him on the little stone bridge over Cedar Brook. Kieran couldn't fathom the idea of slaughtering a living creature for a bit of oil. And Finn couldn't fathom her brother's kind heart surviving in such a world.

She never actually *told* him she didn't want him to take to sea, back then. She bit her tongue. Finn was going to die anyway, and she convinced herself it would be better for Kieran to be away from Windover when it happened.

It's possible she's been deluding herself. It's possible her death would be equally terrible for him either way. Finn's heart feels squeezed in a vise's grip.

Cas has lost the nail somewhere. He's started drumming his fingers on the toes of his boots instead, a rhythm like quiet rainfall. If it weren't for Finn, he'd still be happily aboard the *Mori* right now.

"I never thanked you," Finn says.

"For what?"

Finn blinks at him, incredulous, and waits.

"Oh," Cas says. "Last night?"

"You saved my life," Finn says. "I was a goner. How did you even manage to find me out there?"

"I don't know. I just did."

He looks almost embarrassed to be discussing this. When he rubs a hand over the back of his neck, he reminds Finn so much of Kieran, even though the two of them are completely different.

"Well," Finn tells him, "I appreciate it."

Cas goes back to drumming his fingers. "It still wouldn't have mattered if the demon actually showed up. I keep thinking about what Death said, in the vision. Do you know *why* the demon's been toying with you?"

Last night, as she slept on the shack's floor, Finn had dreamed of Marbas again. She's certain this time about the demon's words: *We need to talk.* But what on earth is Finn meant to do with that? She knows of only one way to talk to a demon. And even she isn't foolish enough to resummon the entity who's supposed to kill her any day now.

"I have no idea," Finn says.

"I wonder if there's something special about you," Cas says. "Maybe the demon's chosen you for some . . . purpose."

"Why would a demon choose me?"

"I don't know. Why did I become the reaper's glass? Maybe there's roles we're both meant to play in all this."

But this sort of story makes sense in Cas's world, Finn thinks. It doesn't make sense in hers. Someone like Cas *would* have some magical power bestowed on him. Meanwhile, the only reason Finn has any power at all is because she had the audacity to steal a spell book. She strong-armed her way into a world of magic that was never meant for her.

Audacity. The word stirs a memory. What had Marbas said, that night when she summoned him? *You ask audacious things. Arrogant and lowly in equal measure.* She can't let herself go down this road of speculation.

"There are other people who've sold their souls to demons," Finn says. "Perhaps the demons are toying with all of us."

"Death didn't seem to think so. And the demon gave you your . . ." Cas waves his fingers to imitate flames springing to life in his hands. "Right? I can't imagine that everyone who's tied up in a demon deal is able to do *that*."

"I think they can, though," Finn says. "They have to. It's how you sign the contract. And the demon didn't give me the fire, he just . . . unlocked it."

Finn tries to remember that moment when she became aware of her own *vitalis vis*. Marbas's words echo in her mind: *You have fire aplenty, don't you?*

"I think the fire is something everyone's got, to some degree," she tells Cas. "They just can't bring it to the surface like that."

Cas gives a skeptical *hmm*. "I don't buy it."

She can't tell him that Marbas apparently wants to speak with her. Cas will do something rash, or he'll tell Remy, and then *Remy* will do something rash.

Remy already has plans for when they reach Boston. Whether or not they can actually find Death, whether or not Death can save her, Finn suspects that's a far safer strategy than going face-to-face with the demon himself.

"Perhaps Díaz will know something more about it," Finn says. "Or the Order. We'll figure it out. And for what it's worth, I do think we have a good shot at reuniting with the *Mori* in Boston. I think it's too early to worry."

Cas makes an airy gesture with his hand. "You know me. I never worry about anything."

"I *do* know you," Finn says. "Well enough to know that you often worry, deeply, about all sorts of things. Including the possibility that the rest of us might catch on to just how deeply worried you actually are."

Cas looks as if she's just caught him with his hand in the church money-box. "Oh," he says.

"Did you think we didn't notice?"

"No." He reconsiders. "Maybe."

Perhaps they've all been feigning steadiness, Finn thinks. Trying to spare each other the worry. It hasn't worked. Remy is careening toward a crash, too; Finn can sense how perilously close she is to dashing apart on the shoals. What can any of them hold on to in this choppy sea?

Perhaps Finn should go find Remy on the deck. But after that daring look in Remy's eye on the beach, the idea of standing beside her right now and *not* touching her makes Finn want to set herself on fire.

And Cas seems to have calmed a little. There's a strange sort of balance, with the three of them. None of them is the steady rock in this storm, but they've stayed afloat this long all the same.

Finn thinks about the remedy she's heard Leo recommend for seasickness: focusing your eyes on a spot on the horizon. One fixed point, so that the body can see and understand the fluctuation it's been feeling. Finn thinks she can see something taking shape on that horizon, if she looks closely enough.

She isn't sure the sailor's life is for her. But it's been a long time since she's let herself imagine much of a life at all. And that's something, at least.

XIII.
CAS

The packet boat makes its landing in Boston in the late afternoon. Cas doesn't make eye contact with any of the sailors on deck as he, Remy, and Finn debark. Then they're down the gangplank and set loose in the city.

"All right," Cas says. "Which way to the dock where we found the *Mori* last time?"

Remy seems happy to push past their earlier quarrel and focus on business. "I think we're south of Union Wharf right now," she says. "But I'm not sure if they use the same berth on every visit."

That isn't very encouraging. Cas forces himself to breathe. "Well, let's start at Union Wharf, anyway. We can search the other wharves after if we need to."

"We can't just wander up and down every wharf in Boston," Remy says. "Besides, we don't even know if the *Mori* has arrived yet. If they had to stop to repair the mast—"

She must realize she's about to wade right back into the quarrel, though, because she breaks off and turns to Finn in a plea for help.

"Customhouse?" Finn says.

Remy's face clears. "Yes! Yes, that's exactly where we should go. The city's customhouse will have records on every ship in the harbor. If the *Mori* has arrived, the captain will have to register there, to declare his cargo and pay any fees."

Cas can't tell if this is a genuine plan or if Remy is lying again to placate him. "Does Captain Hobbes really do any of that, though?" he asks. "Considering the *Mori*'s a"—he drops his voice at the last moment when he remembers they're discussing this on a public dock—"smuggling ship."

"He'll still have to declare something," Finn says.

"That's right," Remy says. "When we were here last time, the dockmaster's ledger *did* have a record of some of the *Mori*'s cargo. Just not the dozen casks of whiskey hidden in the secret compartment."

"Or the magical artifacts," Finn says.

"Or the magical artifacts," Remy agrees.

The fact that it was Finn's idea first, not Remy's, makes Cas feel a little better about it. Finn waits with him while Remy goes to ask someone for directions to the customhouse. Cas's haze of port wine has mostly worn off, but he still feels off-balance. Maybe he's just adjusting to being back on land again after finally getting his sea legs.

He's not sure he ever really *got* his sea legs, though. His precarious footing now feels like something different. He thinks of the *Mori*'s ballast—the layer of stones at the bottom of the ship that's meant to keep everything balanced. Striker had warned that if the ship were knocked sideways with enough force, the ballast might shift; the rocks and cargo could slide around and settle in the wrong positions, throwing off the whole center of gravity. Cas wonders if there's any way to fix that, once it's happened. Maybe something inside him has been permanently knocked askew.

Remy's directions guide them to a moldering brick exterior on a side street just off the waterfront. The vestibule of the customhouse is dimly lit and crowded, everyone trying to pack in their business before the offices close for the day. Cas had worried that he, Remy, and Finn, in their bedraggled state, would be conspicuously underdressed here—but the crowd ranges from gentlemanly ships' owners to ruddy-faced officers to threadbare common sailors like the three of them. If anything, Remy's skirts seem the most out of place. Still, no one stops them as they join a line to speak with one of the clerks at the desk.

"I'll claim I'm looking for the ship my husband was sailing on," Remy says.

Finn makes a face. "Husband?"

"Or brother, maybe. I just want to have our story straight. I'm not sure what the clerk will ask."

The hairs on the back of Cas's neck have prickled to attention. When he turns around, he meets the gaze of a gentleman standing in the next line. The man's eyes are an eerie, pale blue, and for a second, Cas could swear the man is staring straight at him. Sizing him up. Cas looks away quickly.

"I can say that I was told this particular brigantine would be arriving soon but I'm not sure where they'll berth," Remy goes on. "Or will the clerk wonder why I wasn't told that part as well? What do you think?"

"I think you're overthinking this," Finn tells her.

Cas's skin is still prickling. It takes everything in him not to turn around again.

"Is that man in the next line staring at us?" he asks quietly. Remy starts to crane her neck to see, and Cas grabs her arm. "No, don't *look*."

Remy frowns. "How can I know if someone's staring at us if I'm not allowed to look?"

"Fine, you can look, just . . . be subtle about it. He's near the counter. In the top hat."

Remy adjusts the carpetbag on her shoulder as a pretense for turning. After a moment, she makes a humming sound.

"I see him," she says. "And he isn't staring. He did look this way for a moment, but he's talking with the clerk now. See?"

Cas risks a glance over his shoulder. Sure enough, the gentleman has reached the front of his line. He's presenting a stack of papers to one of the clerks at the desk.

"Do you know him?" Remy asks.

"No. He just . . . never mind."

Cas doesn't even know what he'd been afraid of. It's not as if anyone here is going to recognize him, right? Not so far from Windover. And not with Cas dressed as he is—even if the person was specifically sent by Cas's parents to look for him.

Have his parents sent anyone? Contacted the police, or hired someone to track Cas down after he ran away? It isn't the first time this thought has occurred to him, but it feels more pressing now that he's back on shore.

They've reached the front of their own line. Remy presents her story to the clerk, who doesn't seem to care at all about Remy's reasons for asking after the *Mori*. The clerk makes her write down the ship's name and class on a scrap of paper. Then he sighs, then sighs again, to make sure Remy understands just how put out he is over having to do his job.

"I suppose I'll go check the logbooks," the clerk says, and he trundles off.

Remy mutters something rude under her breath. Finn is

standing with her arms crossed tightly. Cas glances down the length of the desk, where the other clerks are conducting their business.

The man in the top hat is staring at him. *Again.*

This time, Cas doesn't look away. He forces himself to hold the man's gaze for several seconds—a test. If the man really *isn't* staring at him, or if he doesn't *mean* to be staring, surely he'll turn away first.

The man doesn't turn away. He's still talking with the clerk, and yet his eyes don't leave Cas.

Cas's heart is jumping in his chest like a spooked rabbit. He feels . . . *scrutinized.*

"So that man is definitely staring now," he says.

Remy's head twitches to see, even as the man returns to his papers at last.

"Are you certain you don't know him?" Remy asks. "Could he be one of your parents' friends?"

"Christ, I hope not," Cas says.

"He seems the sort, though, doesn't he? Or maybe he's just one of those proper, pompous types. Maybe he's judging you for being out and about in public in only your shirtsleeves."

Cas is only out and about in his shirtsleeves because Remy didn't bother to retrieve his coat from the *Mori*'s deck. He grits his teeth and fiddles with his cuffs, though it's not as if he can manifest a jacket at the moment.

"Maybe," he says, dubious. "Or do you think he's . . . you know . . . guessed?"

"Guessed what?" Finn asks.

"That you and I aren't boys. Not proper ones, anyway."

Finn's eyebrow arches as she surveys Cas up and down. "You're proper enough."

"You know what I mean."

"I don't see how he could know," Remy says. "Or what business it is of his either way. It's not as if you're breaking any laws by wearing trousers." She frowns, considering. "I don't *think* you're breaking any laws."

"Is this your idea of being helpful?" Finn asks her.

The clerk returns at that moment, though he hasn't brought the logbook with him, which doesn't bode well. The *Mori* hasn't arrived yet. Cas knew better than to hope. The clerk starts explaining in a bored monotone the timetable under which a ship's captain would make his report.

But Cas stops listening. He can't shake the ridiculous feeling that every person in this room is watching him. He can't gauge which of his fears are rational or irrational anymore. He feels unreasonably twitchy.

"I'm going to get some air," he mutters to Finn. "Meet me outside when you're finished."

Finn seems wary, but she nods. "Don't go far."

The shadows have grown long as the sun dropped lower in the sky, taking the afternoon warmth with it. Cas wanders partway down the sidewalk, though he heeds Finn's words and doesn't round the corner. A few carriages and drivers wait along the curb, their horses shifting from foot to foot on the cobblestones. A seagull squawks from a nearby rooftop.

Cas leans against the brick wall of the building next door and drags a fingernail back and forth through the grout. He tries to breathe the way Leo showed him—in through the nose, out through the mouth. There's a terrible smell from the nearby waterfront. Not the fresh, salty breeze of the open sea, but something dank and fishy. The end of the street offers a narrow view of the harbor, with its wharves and warehouses and countless ships. And none of those ships are the *Mori*.

In through the nose, out through the mouth. It's too early to worry. No one out here on the street is paying him any mind, at least. The man in the top hat probably hadn't meant to stare. Cas is imagining things. He's just anxious to be back at sea, back among the crew, where he doesn't have to look over his shoulder all the time. Everything is fine.

"Excuse me," a voice says.

Cas whirls around. The man in the top hat is standing right behind him. His hands are tucked into the pockets of his wool greatcoat, and he smiles down at Cas, easy and genial, though the smile doesn't quite touch his pale eyes.

"Sorry," Cas says. His heart is skittering again. There's plenty of space on the sidewalk, and still, automatically, he presses himself farther into the wall. "Am I . . . blocking the way?"

"Not at all," the man says. He pauses, surveying Cas. "I believe you and I have an acquaintance in common."

The possibilities are knocking around in Cas's mind: Maybe this man has mistaken him for someone else. Maybe he's a swindler, and he's taken Cas for an easy mark. Maybe he's a private investigator hired by Mr. and Mrs. Sterling.

Maybe he's a member of the Order.

"Do we?" Cas manages. His voice is much too high.

"Oh, yes," the man says. "Reverend John Smith. He's going to be very pleased to see you."

There's a rushing sound in Cas's ears. He can't quite believe this is happening.

"Come," the man says. "I have a carriage just around the corner."

By his tone, he fully expects Cas to give in to politeness and accept this invitation. Cas doesn't move. And yet maybe the man had good reason to lean on manners, because Cas ought to be screaming and running for his life, and instead he hears himself stammer out, "I'd rather not."

The man's smile doesn't falter. All this time, his hands have stayed in his coat pockets, as if he's trying to prove he's not a threat. But now he pulls one hand out—just far enough to show Cas the handle of the small, dark pistol hooked around his finger.

There's something absurd about the tiny gun. It's so small, like a toy. Like a gentleman playing at violence. It's also very real. The sight of it cuts a rope loose inside Cas's chest, and he feels like he's falling, falling, falling.

The man dangles the gun, confirming that Cas has seen the glint of its metal shaft. Then he reaches for Cas's arm.

"Right this way," the man says.

The hand coming for him finally jolts Cas from his stupor. He swats the man's arm away. The man scowls down at him. He's tall, though not as tall as the sailor Cas scuffled with back on the Provincetown docks. Finn and Remy aren't here to save him this time.

Cas slams his knee into the man's groin as hard as he can. He takes off running.

XIV.
REMY

For the second time today, Remy and Finn arrive too late to stop Cas from coming to blows with a stranger. This time, though, it's Cas who lands the blow, and his opponent who's left doubled over on the sidewalk. The man's top hat has fallen off; he's swearing. Remy bursts outside just in time to see the man shove the tiny gun back into his pocket before he starts sprinting down the street, trailing Cas by a dozen yards.

Remy and Finn chase after both of them.

Remy hates running. She especially hates running in skirts. She has to hike them up so she doesn't trip and break her face on the sidewalk. A stabbing pain has already started in her side. She should have taken Cas's concerns in the customhouse more seriously. *He'd* sensed this man was dangerous, and Remy had barely given it a second thought until Finn saw the man follow Cas outside. And now they're on this madcap dash through the city, trying not to lose Cas in the tangled streets, because Remy has no idea how they'll track him down again if they do. How does anyone find anyone around here? They should have agreed on a meeting point in case the three of them were separated.

Cas has started toward the broad stone wharves that jut out into the harbor, which keeps him in view. Unfortunately, it also keeps him in his pursuer's view. He keeps glancing over his shoulder, checking the man's progress behind him.

"Where the hell is he going?" Finn gasps out.

"No idea." It's possible Cas has no idea, either. It's possible his only directional thought is to get *away*.

But he's nearing the end of the wharf, and he seems to realize now it's a dead end. He looks backward again, and it's a mistake—he trips over something that Remy can't see, and then he's on the ground. The man stands over him. His pistol is out, glinting in the evening sun. Is he really going to shoot Cas right here in the open?

Remy and Finn both put on a burst of speed, but Finn gets there first. She tackles the man from behind. He staggers, thrown off-balance, but only briefly—he slithers out of Finn's grip like the snake that he is. Finn is left holding his coat while he rounds on all three of them, gun still in hand.

"Even better," the man says. A single lock of his sleek blond hair has fallen out of place. "You've brought company."

Cas is scrambling to his feet. But Remy doesn't take her eyes from the gun. For once, there isn't a single thought in her mind as she lunges forward and knocks it from the man's grip. It's pure instinct. The gun hits the stones with a satisfying clatter. The man reaches to retrieve it, and Remy runs at him, throwing the whole of her weight against him, pushing him toward the wharf's edge.

He staggers back a step. Then another. His foot hits one of the stone pilings behind him, and he topples backward into the harbor.

Remy nearly overbalances and falls in after him, but Finn and Cas haul her back. For a second, the three of them stand there, clinging to each other, watching the gentleman splashing and sputtering in the water below.

"Who the hell is he?" Remy gasps out.

"Order." Cas sounds badly winded, too. "Said he knew Smith."

People are running toward them, drawn by the commotion. At any moment, someone is going to arrive to help fish their attacker out of the water. And Remy doesn't want to stick around for that.

"Come on," she says. "We need to get out of here."

They shoulder through the growing crowd of onlookers and start running again before someone can try to stop them. More running. Remy will grumble about it later. For now, she's too busy trying to keep herself oriented in these winding streets—and basking in the relief that none of them were shot.

The relief is overpowering; Remy gives up on her sense of direction. Striker told her once about Manhattan, with its tidy grid of streets and avenues. This pocket of Boston is the opposite. The roads are a jumble, the meandering paths of herd animals paved over and immortalized into the modern age.

By the time Finn pulls them both back and slows to a walk, they're terribly lost. But Remy is confident, at least, that they've lost anyone who might have tried to follow them.

"I think we're out of immediate danger now," Finn says, her voice a thin wheeze. "Running will only make us more conspicuous."

Remy isn't about to argue. She feels like there's a knife in her side every time she breathes. They walk for several more minutes, stone-faced and deliberate, until they find a secluded alley they can slip into.

"Thank god," Remy says.

She collapses against one of the alley walls. Cas is trying to brush the grit from the knees of his trousers. Finn has something clutched to her chest—a bundle of dark fabric.

"You still have his coat," Remy realizes, marveling.

Finn shakes out the man's woolen greatcoat. "I figured he might have something useful in the pockets."

"Gun," Cas says. "He had a gun. *That* was in his pocket."

"I know. I picked that up, as well. You said he was with the Order?"

Cas nods grimly. "He wanted to take me to Smith. Said Smith would be pleased to see me. That's when I hit him with my knee."

"I told you it was effective," Finn says.

"How did you find me?"

"We saw him following you outside," Remy tells him. "Or . . . Finn saw." The guilt is writhing in Remy's stomach. "I'm sorry. I should've listened when you pointed that man out."

"Not your fault." Cas gives up on brushing off his clothes. "I didn't anticipate him pulling a gun on me, either."

Maybe he understands, though, that Remy is apologizing for more than just today. It's the same old conflict, echoing through the years. It's as if they're still ten years old, and Cas is trying to tell Remy the truth about her father, and Remy doesn't want to hear him. Her first instinct is still to doubt him, even almost a decade later.

Finn has drawn out a leather pocketbook from the man's coat, and now she unfolds a piece of paper from it. As her eyes flick back and forth, her usual glower turns into a scowl.

"I think I know how he recognized you," Finn says. Cas moves to see what she's found, and Finn seems to backtrack. "You don't need to read—"

Cas snatches the page from her hands. Remy cranes to read over his shoulder.

The note isn't handwritten like Remy expected—it's printed

in a small, tidy typeface. This is the sort of thing someone has produced in bulk, meant for wide distribution. The text lays out a sort of wanted notice, with a description of a person who *must be apprehended and brought into our Order's custody with all haste*.

The person described is very obviously Cas. But it doesn't describe *him* at all. The person is approximately Cas's height, with Cas's cropped brown hair, and Cas's fair skin, and a scar, recent, running from brow to cheekbone on the left side of the face. The note concludes with a remark that this young lady—because according to the notice, it *is* a young lady—*is likely to be disguised in the dressings of a young man*.

The signature is only initials: *J.S.*

"Looks like Smith still wants a reaper's glass," Cas says. He's rubbing at the wound on his face again. This must have been what caught the man's attention, Remy realizes. There are probably hundreds of people in Boston who match Cas's general height, hair, and complexion. But the scar is noticeable. It's distinctive. Back at Eden, when Smith attacked him and left him bleeding, Cas was marked.

Remy studies the page again. How quickly did Smith have to work to get these notices printed? Has he only distributed them among the Order members in Boston—or does Smith's entire organization now have a description of Cas in hand? Cas might be hunted across the whole of New England.

Finn is examining another sheaf of papers. When she sees Remy looking, though, she shoves them back into the coat pocket. Her eyes flick to Cas, and she shakes her head: *not now*. Whatever she's found needs to wait until they can speak privately.

Cas is too preoccupied with the wanted notice to catch any of this.

"Are you all right?" Finn asks him.

"Aside from running for my life across half the city? Yeah, I'm great."

He looks worn thin, though. He's still reading and rereading Smith's description: *likely to be disguised in the dressings of a young man.* Maybe this line shouldn't have taken Remy by surprise, but she feels like she's swallowed a glass of spoiled milk. Cas isn't *disguised*. He's just . . . Cas. When they were sailing with the *Mori*, it all seemed so uncomplicated.

As perturbing as Remy finds all of this, Cas must be feeling it tenfold. It's no wonder he's been so out of sorts since they came ashore. Remy resolves to be a little more patient with him.

Finn snatches the paper from Cas's hands. She frowns at the words there.

She tears the paper in half, then in half again. With a flare of heat and light, Finn burns the pieces right there in her hand. Smith's wanted notice turns to ash in seconds.

Cas is gaping at her. "Don't we need that?"

"Why would we need that?" Finn asks flatly.

"I guess we don't."

"Take this," Finn says, and she presses the little pistol into Remy's hand. Remy isn't sure what it says about her that she accepts it.

"What am *I* supposed to do with this?"

"I don't know. But you know how to use it better than I do."

Remy empties the bullets and tucks the gun into her carpetbag. "We need to get off the street," she says. She eyes Cas, who's scratching at the scar on his face again. "We need to get *you* off the street."

"Where is there to go?" Cas says. "The *Mori* isn't here yet."

"How much money do we have left? Enough for a hotel?"

Cas shrugs a little helplessly as he draws out their bag of coins. "I don't know how much that costs."

"Depends," Finn tells him. "Do you need to stay at the Tremont? Or could you make do with humbler accommodations?"

With how snappish Cas has been today, Remy expects him to take offense at that. To her surprise, he huffs a laugh and offers Finn the money bag.

"As long as no one's shooting at me, I'll take whatever accommodations we can get," Cas says. Finn counts the bag's contents and gives a low whistle.

"Jesus. We probably *could* stay at the Tremont with this."

"They do have a very good breakfast there," Cas tells her.

It's as if Finn burned away something else, too, when she incinerated Smith's wanted notice. Remy is struck by the ease between the two of them. Is it new, or had she just not noticed it until now? Her life used to be neatly divided into two eras: the years before her father disappeared, when she and Cas were inseparable friends. And the years after, when she met Finn. Now, those years are folding into some new age they're all entering together.

Finn turns Cas around by both shoulders and pushes him toward the mouth of the alley. "Come on," she says. "We're going to make a common man of you yet."

Remy trails after them into the warmth of the setting sunlight.

XV.

FINN

They rent a room at the first hotel they can find. It's hardly the luxurious Tremont, but it's still the most expensive place Finn has ever stayed. She's certain someone in the lobby is going to take one look at her and toss her back on the street. Even Cas looks out of place here in his present state.

But the man at the front desk seems perfectly happy to accept their money. It's better, anyway, to draw a few judgmental looks from the other guests than to risk another Order member recognizing Cas while they wander the city in search of cheaper lodging. Once they've locked themselves inside their room on the third floor, Finn can breathe a little more easily. The room is at least triple the size of Finn's maid's quarters at Mrs. Darner's, though somehow it's crammed with five times the furniture. Besides an enormous bed, there's a writing desk, several stools, an ornate gilded mirror, a bureau, two side tables, and a pair of chairs nestled beneath the room's gabled window.

Cas seems unimpressed with it all. He's kneeling on one of the chairs to get a view of the street outside, which is barely visible over the sloping eave of the roof.

Finn still has the Order member's coat bundled in her arms. She pushes it to the back of one of the bureau's drawers while Cas isn't watching. She isn't sure why she'd kept the additional papers in the man's pocket a secret from him. She barely had time to look through them in the alley—just enough to confirm they were registration documents for a ship. Probably this was what the man had been discussing with the clerk back at the customhouse.

It could be nothing. But now that they know the papers' bearer is part of the Order, it could be something, as well.

Finn wants to get Remy's opinion before they decide whether the ship named in the papers is worth investigating. And with the entire Order on the hunt, Cas is going to have to stay locked inside this room for the foreseeable future. That's going to be a bitter enough pill for him to swallow even without the added temptation of a vendetta to chase.

Remy's mind seems to have followed a similar track.

"Finn and I will go back out tomorrow to track down Díaz's bookshop," Remy says. "When the *Mori* does arrive, Díaz might know how to get in touch with the captain."

It's possible she thinks this reminder about the *Mori* will cheer him, but Cas doesn't seem cheered. "You're really going to make me wait here while you go off and have adventures?"

"We're not *having adventures*. We're gathering information. And there are far worse places to wait than this," she adds, gesturing around at the room's fine furnishings.

"I know. I know. It's fine." Cas sighs and flings himself onto the bed, sinking into the soft mattress with his arms outstretched. "This is much nicer than the shack."

For all its furniture, the room has only one bed. Finn hadn't even considered it when they told the man in the lobby they'd take whichever room was least expensive. It shouldn't be an issue. Before the beach in Provincetown—before that moment when, to be clear, nothing even happened, and perhaps Finn is a fool for imagining something nearly did—it *wouldn't* have been an issue.

Remy is eyeing the bed, her cheeks flushed.

Is it possible something really *did* nearly happen in Provincetown?

"I can sleep on the rug," Finn murmurs, to spare them both.

Cas sits up to stare at her as if she's just suggested she might leap out a window. "Are you joking? This bed is massive. We can all fit."

He isn't wrong. And the mattress does seem far more tempting than sleeping on the floor. Finn can't look at Remy as she carefully sits on one edge of the bed. The blankets shift as Remy claims the opposite side. Surprisingly, Cas doesn't seem to mind being sandwiched between them. Finn suspects the events of the day have left him far more rattled than he's letting on.

When Finn falls asleep later that night, she dreams of flames, as usual.

Afterward, she remembers the dream in pieces: The fiery pit in hell, with her parents on the distant clifftop. The foggy beach beneath the lighthouse, and the dancing flame cupped in Finn's hands that sets Remy's face aglow. Fire spreading over Finn's skin. Over Remy's skin. Flames that aren't painful, but warm and thrilling. The candles Finn placed around her summoning circle in the barn six years ago. Firelight reflecting in the flat black pools of Marbas's eyes.

Marbas spreads his arms toward the trappings of the ritual that surround him: the stubby candles, the spell book, the summoning circle drawn in the dirt. The gesture feels like an invitation.

We need to talk.

As Finn lies on the edge of the bed, waiting for the first rays of morning sun to filter through the curtains, she turns over Marbas's words. The demon wants her to summon him again. It's undeniable now, and it doesn't make any sense. In the visions Cas has described, the demon seems to appear at will; surely Finn doesn't need to *summon* Marbas for him to collect. And she's growing more and more certain that Marbas *has* appeared for her—at least once back at Eden, and possibly aboard the *Mori* in the days since. She can't shake the memory of that presence both she and Remy felt in the cargo hold.

The room around her is dark enough that Finn can almost imagine those shadowy tentacles creeping toward her now. But the demon isn't here; she feels no real danger. Cas keeps moving around in his sleep, nudging Finn lightly with his foot. Remy breathes deeply and evenly from the other side of the bed.

If the demon wants to talk with her so badly, why is he poking at Finn's dreams instead of appearing in the flesh—or in the shadowy substance of . . . whatever he is?

Perhaps that's it: The creature Finn saw outside the seminary—the creature Cas has described from his visions—is a different form of Marbas than the man she negotiated with six years ago. The ritual from the grimoire had summoned the column of smoke and then forced that smoke to take a human form.

Or perhaps it *allowed* the demon to take a human form. To speak with her, in a way he otherwise couldn't.

If Marbas is going to such lengths to persuade Finn to summon him . . . it's possible the demon really *does* want to talk, and talk only.

In the darkness, Finn lets the hope blossom in her. By the time dawn finally comes, it feels like a fool's hope. Remy and

Cas are both still sleeping when Finn lets herself slip from the bed. Cas has sprawled out across the mattress in a way that *does* make it feel too small for them all. Remy is on her side, curled in on herself. There's a troubled line between her brows. Finn has a fleeting thought that Remy is dreaming of *her*—that she's working through the puzzle of how to save Finn, even in her sleep.

If she manages to wake with the answer, she can spare them all a lot of trouble. Then Finn won't even have to decide whether or not to tell the others about Marbas's message.

Finn tears her eyes away from Remy's dark curls splayed across the pillow. She quietly retrieves the Order member's stolen coat from the bureau. Remy *would* dream of puzzles, Finn thinks, her cheeks hot. Finn's dreams about Remy tend to be of a very different sort.

Finn brings the coat to the window so she can read the registration papers in the early morning light. The ship they reference is called the *White Swallow*, and its manifest shows that it was originally scheduled to depart from Boston for Eden three days ago. But plans must have changed; the manifest was amended. The departure has been postponed indefinitely.

Finn commits as many of the details as she can to memory. When she hears the others begin to stir, she returns the coat and papers to their hiding spot.

"How long will you be gone?" Cas asks later that morning as Remy and Finn prepare to set out.

"I don't know," Remy tells him. "We're not even sure where the bookshop is yet."

"How long do you *think* you'll be gone, though?"

"I don't know! A few hours, maybe?"

Finn would wager this guess is overly optimistic. But Cas looks like he's in physical pain. "A few *hours*?"

"We'll be back as soon as we can," Remy says.

"What am I supposed to do in the meantime?"

"Stay inside! We'll ask one of the maids to bring up food for you."

"So I'm supposed to just sit here?"

"That's the idea, yes," Remy says. She bites her lip for a moment, then adds, "It might be a good time to practice meditation."

This suggestion was clearly a mistake. Cas scowls. Finn thought he and Remy reached a truce yesterday, but the truce seems a tenuous thing. Finn opens the door and pushes Remy out into the hall before either of them can draw swords again.

"We'll be back soon," Finn tells Cas, like an apology. Then she closes the door in his face.

Finn and Remy plan to start their search at City Hall, where Remy thinks they can ask after property records to find the bookshop in Díaz's name. They've barely stepped out onto the street before Remy says, "What else was in that man's pocket yesterday?"

"You don't waste any time, do you?" Finn says.

"It's been eating at me all night. I've been dying for a moment to ask you about it, but we really haven't had any privacy, have we?"

Pink patches bloom on both of Remy's cheeks. Finn wonders if she's thinking about the *last* semi-private moment the two of them had back on the beach. The unspoken memory hangs between them like an electric current—the popping sound before a lightning strike.

Or perhaps this is wishful thinking on Finn's part.

But the buzzing energy doesn't fade as they set off into the city. The two of them aren't alone here, and yet the bustling crowd makes them anonymous. At one point, Remy takes Finn's hand to pull her across the street, and she doesn't let go even once they're safely on the next sidewalk. Finn doesn't know what to make of it. She's distracted as she relays everything she remembers from the *White Swallow*'s paperwork.

"It sounds promising," Remy says. "We'll add the *White Swallow* to our list of places to investigate. It's good you didn't tell Cas, though. He'd probably go running straight to the docks. And after yesterday, it does seem more and more likely that Smith is in the city now."

The thought of Cas stewing back at the hotel, alone, doesn't sit well with Finn. She knows it's for the best, but even so. Remy keeps her fingers intertwined with Finn's until they've reached City Hall.

But when Remy asks at the records desk about the bookstore, the clerk tells them they're in the wrong place; property records are kept at a storage building a twenty-minute walk up the road. The man at the storage building says he'll need a few days to find them anything, but he claims the head librarian at the Boston Athenaeum knows every street and shop in the city, and if they need an answer more quickly, perhaps they should ask him instead. By the time the librarian points them to a little shop on the edge of Beacon Hill, nearly two hours have passed. The sun has come out in full force, and sweat soaks through Finn's shirt.

There's comfort in this familiar back-and-forth journey of hunting down information, though. Finn barely even minds her aching feet. She likes watching Remy in her element. They keep bumping into each other as they squeeze past people on the narrow sidewalks, and every accidental touch sets Finn's heart fluttering. She's so far gone, it's almost comical. How on earth has she survived existing in Remy's presence for this long?

The bookshop in Beacon Hill is nondescript and underwhelming after the circles they've walked in search of it. It's a garden-level flat, with curtains drawn across the knee-high windows along the sidewalk. They might have missed it altogether if it weren't for the peeling sign on the door that reads simply: *BOOKS*. When Finn trails Remy down the stairs and inside, it seems they're the shop's only customers.

They're the only people in the shop whatsoever, Finn realizes.

"Hello?" Remy calls as the door swings shut behind them.

A voice calls from a back room: "I'll be out in a moment."

Remy clasps her hands awkwardly in front of her as they wait. With the windows covered, the only light comes from a lamp dangling from the low ceiling. The shop is tiny. Most of the walls are crammed with books, and plenty of the floor, as well. On a table in the middle of the room, the tomes are stacked several inches higher than the top of Finn's head. Everything smells of dust.

A person emerges from a doorway in the corner.

"Oh, hello," Remy says, slipping at once into the practiced, polished version of herself that's best for convincing people to help them. "I hope it's all right that we just came in. The door was unlocked."

The person is peering at Remy in the lamplight. "Have we met?"

"No," Remy says. "I don't believe so, at least. We're looking for a Mr. or . . . Miss Díaz." She seems to have realized too late that they were never told a proper introduction for the captain's contact. If said contact is the person standing before them, who's wearing both a skirt and a waistcoat with cravat, Finn isn't immediately sure which title to use, either.

"I'm Díaz," the person says. Which isn't an answer. Or perhaps it is. They're still studying Remy very closely. "Are you certain we haven't met? I don't forget a face, and I could swear I've seen yours before."

Finn expects Remy to lie; Remy has often given a false name when she's digging for information about the Order. But Díaz's intense scrutiny seems to have rattled her, and when Remy falls back on her most polite reflexes, she answers with the truth.

"Remy DeWindt," she says, extending a hand to shake.

Díaz doesn't take the hand. Their eyes have widened. "DeWindt," they say. "That's it. You must be his daughter."

XVI.

CAS

Cas can cross the hotel room with seven short strides in one direction. Ten strides in the other. He paces back and forth on the longer side. He *would* take the diagonal, corner to corner, to maximize the space, but the bed is in the way. Ten paces back and forth is all he gets.

A maid brings up a plate of breakfast for him, just as Remy promised. Cas can only pick at it. That restless pressure in his chest is building. The distant chime of a church bell tells him it hasn't even been an hour since Remy and Finn left. Cas is going to lose his mind in here. He's spent too much of his life locked in his bedroom at his parents' house; isolation has long been his mother's preferred method for managing Cas. As if keeping him shut away might make his excessive energy just fizzle out. Usually, it only bottled up the energy until Cas exploded.

But locking him in his room for days at a time did keep the explosions contained—and, more importantly, it prevented Cas from embarrassing his mother when she had guests over. Cas doesn't think his parents ever really wanted a child. His father wanted an heir to carry on the Sterling name, and his mother wanted a fancy, well-trained pet she could trot out in front of company and then shut back in the kennel. Cas was a miserable failure on both counts.

He used to chart out the escape routes, on those long afternoons trapped in his bedroom. He'd imagine crawling out the window and somehow making his way down the ivy on the corner of the house, or maybe trying to jump into a shrub. He never actually attempted this. He probably would have broken both his legs and been stuck inside even longer.

The window of their hotel room opens onto the roof, at least, which seems more practical than the sheer two-story drop from the window at home. Cas finds himself eyeing the convenient brick chimney outside, wondering if he could climb down it. The street is barely visible from this angle, but he can see the shadows shifting on the surrounding rooftops as the morning creeps by.

The bell chimes again. Another hour.

Remy and Finn still aren't back.

He paces until someone in the room below him hammers on the ceiling and shouts at him to stop clomping around like a horse. He throws himself down on the enormous bed. He groans into the pillow. He pulls out his blank logbook from Leo, which has finally mostly dried out, and he tries to smooth the wrinkled pages. It's useless. The logbook is ruined. He feels absurdly close to crying over this.

He really does try to meditate, for a while. He sits cross-legged on the bed and closes his eyes. He tries to remember how Striker had described it. She said that some forms of meditation use awareness of your own body, focusing on breathing and posture to help you ground yourself in the moment. And some meditation is about detaching from the body altogether, letting your consciousness wander freely.

Cas is terrible at both kinds. His body is too twitchy to sit still the way Striker kept telling him to. And his mind is plenty good at wandering, sure, but never where he wants it to go. He's thinking about the *Memento Mori*, and fuming at Remy for lying to him, and sulking over Remy and Finn running off to explore the city without him. When he tries to actively *stop* thinking, his mind is a storm, and he's drowning in the spring at Eden, or drowning in the ocean as he desperately searches for Finn. He resumes his pacing. The person downstairs resumes pounding on the ceiling.

Cas finds a pencil in the drawer of the writing desk, though. And even though the pages of the logbook are crinkly and badly discolored, he can still draw on them. It's better than trying to meditate, anyway.

He tries to draw the *Memento Mori*. But without the ship in front of him for reference, it's unrecognizable. He turns the drawing into a violent scribble. He tries again. It's a disaster. He tears out both pages, crumples them into a ball, and hurls it at the wall as hard as he can.

The throw isn't very satisfying. But the scribbling and the tearing paper felt good, for a moment. It feels good to destroy something, bit by bit, even if that something is already beyond saving.

So Cas gives up on drawing anything in particular. He just scribbles. Shapes and smudges and abstract pencil marks. He's still thinking about Remy, and Finn, and the night they all got drunk on brandy together at Dungeon Rock, and the other nights that Remy and Finn have apparently spent at Dungeon Rock without him, because Cas and Remy didn't speak for eight years and that still bothers Cas more than he wants to admit.

But he's also not really thinking about anything at all. This is better than pacing. Cas is grounded in his body *and* detached from it at the same time, and time seems to stop existing altogether, and he stops counting the church bells.

He scribbles, and he tears, and he throws, and he scribbles again, until his mind goes blessedly quiet.

XVII.

REMY

Díaz knew Remy's father.

As Díaz locks up the shop for the morning and uncovers chairs for them from beneath the piles of books, Remy wonders at the odds of this. The coincidence feels too bizarre to believe. But maybe it isn't such a stretch. Remy knew her father had acquired his occult books *somewhere*, and clearly he hadn't purchased them at a store in Windover or Lynn. It had never occurred to her to seek out this cramped bookshop in Boston, a short train ride away.

The world is so much larger than she'd imagined. But as Remy has moved from only researching the supernatural to facing it head-on, this world feels smaller, too. These threads—reapers, demons, visions of deaths, the Order of Lazarus, Captain Hobbes's ties to the occult market—are all more interconnected than Remy realized. And her father had been tugging at the same threads, when he was alive. Maybe it's inevitable that Remy's research would bring her stumbling onto a path he trod long ago.

Díaz knew Remy's father.

Everyone has always told Remy she takes after her father. There was a time she resented this—her square jaw, her overlarge nose. Now, it's a stab to the chest to have a stranger recognize these familiar features at a glance.

Already, Díaz hardly feels like a stranger. Because again: Díaz *knew Remy's father.*

"I remember when he first turned up here," Díaz says as they bring out a plate of dry sandwiches from the back apartment. They have to rearrange the books on the table to make space. "It must've been . . . lord, ten years ago now? Twelve? He said he'd heard I could source books on topics that were unusual, and he was looking for information about prophetic visions."

"Did you sell him something?" Remy asks.

"Of course. I *do* source books on topics that are unusual. He kept coming back for years, a new question every few months. And then he stopped."

Díaz hasn't asked outright, but Remy makes herself say it.

"He died," Remy says. It occurs to her that this is the first time she's said it aloud, or at least so bluntly. Her throat feels very tight. "He . . . was killed. Eight years ago."

Díaz has finally set down the sandwiches. For a moment, they go very still.

"I'm sorry," Díaz says.

Then they turn abruptly and walk away. Finn catches Remy's eye, a question. Remy shrugs. In a way, she appreciates this strangely matter-of-fact reaction more than if Díaz fell over themselves offering condolences.

Díaz has retreated behind the counter in the corner. Remy is a little embarrassed to admit that she still can't work out whether Díaz is a man or a woman. At a glance, she'd taken Díaz's clothing for a dress—but the bust seems much closer to a gentleman's suit than a gown, and when Díaz climbs up on a stool to retrieve something from an upper shelf, the skirts hike up to reveal trousers and riding boots underneath. Their sleek black hair is pulled back in a way that seems more about practicality than fashion.

Does it really matter, Remy wonders absently, one way or the other? Probably not. Of all the questions she has right now, this seems like one that can wait.

Díaz returns to the table and presents Remy with an enormous stack of books.

"I used to set books aside for him," Díaz says. "When I came across one I thought he'd want to read."

Whatever Remy had been expecting, it wasn't this. She's reeling as she takes in the titles on the spines before her. The books themselves are unfamiliar, but the subjects aren't; any of these would fit perfectly among the other titles her father locked inside the window-seat bench in his study.

"You've been keeping these for eight years?" Remy hears herself ask.

Díaz shrugs. "Just in case."

This simple kindness is too much. Remy wants to weep. And Díaz isn't the only one of them who held on to hope that Charles DeWindt was still alive, even after nearly a decade without a word. Remy's carpetbag feels heavy on her lap. There's a stinging sensation behind her eyes.

Finn shifts in her chair so that her knee presses against Remy's, a warm and grounding force.

Remy blinks away any tears before they can fall and tries to concentrate on business. "We've been sailing with Captain Edward Hobbes and his crew, on the *Memento Mori*," she says to Díaz. "You know him."

It isn't really a question, but Díaz nods. "I do."

"Have you heard from him recently? In the last day or two?"

Díaz considers this. "No, not for a few weeks. Did he find that reaper's glass he was looking for at Eden?"

Remy isn't sure how much she should disclose. "He did, actually."

"Good," Díaz says, and they don't push for details.

"We were hoping the reaper's glass could contact Death," Remy says carefully. "But we haven't had much luck yet. The captain thinks Death has gone into hiding somewhere—maybe beyond the Veil. Do you know any more about what that means?"

Díaz's expression is soft. "You really are your father's daughter, aren't you?" they say, and they maneuver a book out of the stack they just brought over. "The Veil is a sort of barrier. Between our world and . . . well, I don't know much about what's *beyond* the Veil, but I know it isn't a place, exactly. At least it isn't something tethered to space and time the way we are. Do you know how dreams seem to exist in their own reality? It's like that."

This is a much more abstract answer than Remy was hoping for. But Finn, who hasn't spoken a single word since they stepped into the bookshop, now says quietly, "A dream space." As if this makes perfect sense.

Díaz nods again. They're flipping through the book's pages. "Spirits can reach through the Veil sometimes. I suppose it would make sense that Death could move back and forth through that barrier when he wants to."

Remy has finally gotten a look at the title of the book Díaz is searching: *Remarkable Apparitions of Spectres, Spirits, and Ghosts*. She can't quite tamp down her own annoyance.

"Ghost stories?" Remy says. She stops herself just short of adding, *Really?*

Finn kicks her gently on the ankle. "Are you truly still a skeptic, after everything?"

The possible implications attached to this question feel too fraught to really consider right now. "No," Remy says, "I suppose not."

"You said that spirits can reach through the Veil?" Finn asks Díaz.

"Sometimes," Díaz says. "For a moment or two."

"And if Death is on the other side of the Veil now, can we—or the reaper's glass—reach back? To talk to Death, while he's in that dream space?"

"Possibly." Díaz holds open *Remarkable Apparitions*, and Remy skims enough to realize the passage they've presented her with is describing a séance. "Most of the time, when a spirit manages to reach through the Veil, the connection is unsteady. Just a momentary touch. Or a figure you glimpse out of the corner of your eye. To have a *conversation*, you'd need to find a stronger tether for the spirit to grasp. Or, better yet, multiple tethers. Something the spirit touched in life, or the place where the spirit died."

Remy is trying very hard not to think about that feeling of another presence she felt in the fo'c'sle days ago. It's all she can think about. "That won't work for Death, though, will it?" she says, trying to focus. "He was never alive."

Díaz blinks at her. "Of course he was."

This snaps Remy to attention. "What?"

"He was a mortal man before he became a reaper," Díaz says.

The captain certainly never mentioned *this.* Remy feels piqued. No one tells her anything. "What could we use as a tether, then? Do you know where Death . . . died?" Remy asks, then has to take a moment to marvel at that question and look at this absurd, incredible world in which she's found herself.

"I'm sorry," Díaz says. "I don't. I've never met him myself, and there isn't much about reapers in the written record. Mr. Hobbes would probably know, though."

Yes, Remy thinks, annoyed and eager all at once. Yes, he would.

"And you said he found the reaper's glass," Díaz says. "I'd wager the glass can act as one tether to contact Death through the Veil. For a more stable bridge, you'd want to find more points of connection. But wait." Díaz frowns, as if something has just occurred to them. "If Mr. Hobbes has the reaper's glass, that means Smith doesn't. And that doesn't make any sense."

Remy feels a tickle of unease. "Why doesn't that make sense?"

Díaz is quiet. They seem to be debating something.

"Have you ever heard of the Order of Lazarus?" Díaz asks.

Remy knows too much about the Order by now to summarize with any efficiency. Before she can overthink it, she fishes her journal out of her carpetbag and offers it to Díaz. Díaz's mouth falls slightly open as they scan the pages.

"Fair enough," Díaz says. "All right. It doesn't make sense because Smith is still acting like he *has* the reaper's glass. He's called a huge gathering of his followers for this evening; supposedly, he has everything arranged to move into his endgame. He's calling it the Order's *final checkmate*."

"That's redundant," Remy says, though it's hardly what's important here. Smith probably doesn't even play chess.

"How do you know about this?" Finn asks Díaz.

Díaz is still looking through the journal. "I have sources."

"Servants?" Finn guesses.

Díaz shrugs. "If the men in Smith's Order want the undivided loyalty of their house staffs, they ought to pay them better." They offer the journal back to Remy. "Smith hasn't been particularly quiet about this event tonight, though. Which is worrisome. He's getting bolder."

"Where is the meeting?" Remy asks. "And when?"

Finn is watching Remy closely. A few days ago, Finn probably would have been urging caution; she would have tried to talk Remy out of going anywhere near this gathering of Order members tonight. A few weeks ago, it probably would have been *Remy* urging caution.

The storm off Cape Cod—Finn's narrow escape from the jaws of death—has shifted something for both of them. Finn seems ready to fight now. And Remy would rather take the risk, whatever happens, than live with the regret of *not* taking it. If Finn dies without Remy having done absolutely anything and everything she can to stop the Order and talk to Death . . . Remy will never forgive herself.

"Six o'clock," Díaz says. "At High Street Chapel. It isn't far from here. I have a map in the back."

Finn stays in the main shop, looking through the stack of books, while Remy trails Díaz into a little apartment through the door behind the counter. Díaz could have brought the map out to them, she knows. But a question has been burning in her, and while she's reflecting on things she'd regret . . . the thought of leaving Díaz's shop without asking it is altogether too much.

"The spirits who can reach through the Veil," Remy says as Díaz hunts around for a map of the city. "Those are people who've died?"

Díaz nods. They've pulled out a roll of paper, but they don't unfurl it yet.

"If I thought I . . . sensed . . . something," Remy says. "Or someone. How would I . . . know?"

The question seems almost childish, now that she's brought it into the light. But Díaz is looking at her thoughtfully.

"Are you asking how you'd know if you sensed someone?" Díaz says. "Or are you asking how you'd know who it was?"

Remy's bag feels very warm under her arm. "Either?" she says. "Both?"

Díaz spreads the map over a little table and gestures to Remy to hold the corners flat.

"Both are very good questions," Díaz says, even as they point out the corner where High Street Chapel is. "I'm not sure I can answer. I will say that the space just beyond the Veil, where a spirit might be able to reach through . . . I don't think spirits stay there forever. I don't think they're meant to. That's part of the reaper's role—to help them move on and find peace."

Díaz is still speaking theoretically, but Remy suspects they know exactly who she's thinking of.

"Right," Remy says. "That's what I expected. I'm just imagining things."

"I didn't say that."

Díaz waits, though, as Remy leans in to chart the route she and Finn will take from here. The church really isn't far.

"He used to get that same look on his face," Díaz says quietly. "The one you've got right now. Like he was always putting together some puzzle in his mind."

The gentle observation knocks Remy straight out of her

thoughts; whatever composure she's managed to regather goes scattering in the wind.

Díaz turns away. "Sometimes a ghost is a literal spirit," they say. "Sometimes it's memory. Grief is a funny thing."

Remy wonders if Díaz, too, experienced a remarkable apparition today. She's glad she and Finn found this bookshop and intersected with this person, if only briefly.

Remy is growing more and more certain she's sensed a presence these past few days. She's less certain that presence is her father. She can find a sort of peace with that, she thinks.

But she's never been good at accepting mysteries.

XVIII.
FINN

Díaz promises to tell Captain Hobbes that Finn and Remy are in the city if or when the *Mori* arrives and makes contact. Finn and Remy leave the bookshop in the early afternoon. Remy is quiet; Finn suspects she's digesting far more than the sandwiches. Their visit with Díaz did yield a few answers, but it also opened far more questions.

"Should we go back to the hotel?" Finn asks. They have hours before the Order's gathering is scheduled to begin.

"We'd pass High Street Chapel on our way back to the hotel anyway," Remy says. "We should scout it out now, before Smith or his men arrive to set up for tonight. We might be able to find somewhere inside we can hide and wait until this evening."

She's pressing the fingers of her right hand against her thumb one by one, the way she does when she's thinking.

"And if we go back to the hotel, you know that Cas is going to want to come with us tonight," she adds.

He will; Finn can't deny it. It's possible Smith has found some way to move forward with his plans even without the reaper's glass—but Finn doesn't think he's truly given up on finding Cas. A man tried to kidnap Cas off the street just yesterday. A gathering of Order members is the last place Cas should be.

They spot the bell tower of High Street Chapel first—then

the rest of the church comes into view, with soaring columns and walls of golden-brown stone. A small cemetery with a wrought-iron fence abuts the building. Inside, a midday service is underway, which makes it easy for Finn and Remy to slip in and join the congregation.

The ground floor is all private boxes for the wealthy families who can afford them. But a spiral staircase leads up to the balcony that wraps around the church on three sides. Finn and Remy slide into a pew.

If this were a Catholic mass, Finn might be able to place how much longer the service will last. She has no idea here, though. On the rare occasions she's attended Protestant services, she's always felt like she was watching the proceedings distorted through a bottle—familiar pieces, but the shapes all different. It's been years since she last went to a Catholic mass; probably she'd feel like she was watching *that* through a bottle these days, too. She's an interloper as she and Remy fold their hands and pretend to pray.

The hymn the congregants are singing is one she recognizes, though. If she closed her eyes, she could be back in the old stone church in Knockadine, squeezed into the pew between her mother and Kieran. Her childhood in Ireland grows hazier by the year, but those church services are vividly clear. Finn remembers in visceral detail the priest's descriptions of hell. She remembers when he listed sodomites among the sinners—and when she first understood what he meant by that. These men who would lie with other men were equivalent with murderers or thieves, at least according to the priest. In the same breath that Finn learned such desires were possible, she also learned they were a terrible sin.

There's a knot inside Finn's heart. A swirl of confusion that she thought she'd given up picking at when she bargained with a demon and resigned herself to hell. She's picking at that knot again. She can't stop herself. She's been picking at it for days—ever since they boarded the *Mori*. When Finn was with other girls back in Windover—kissing, and sometimes more than kissing—the pleasure she felt was always tinged with shame. She took that as proof that the thing she'd done was shameful.

But she can see now how she was fed that sense of shame deliberately. And what if the priest in Knockadine was wrong? Finn has seen women kiss aboard the *Memento Mori*. She's seen how Kit and Striker care for each other, and how deeply the captain is devoted to his partner. It isn't murder. It isn't thievery. It's love, pure and simple. The priest's condemnation doesn't make any sense.

Finn's mother once told her that when a person dies—when they meet Saint Peter at the gates of heaven—every question they've ever wondered about the world will be answered. Finn isn't bound for heaven, though. If paradise is learning answers to all your questions, perhaps this tangle of doubt inside Finn is just a precursor to hell.

The church's organ is playing loudly enough to cover Remy's words from eavesdroppers as she leans close to Finn. Finn's skin is on fire.

"This balcony could be a good vantage point," Remy murmurs. "And the railing is high enough that we could stay out of sight from anyone down below. I imagine the members of Smith's secret Order are the sort who'd expect a private box—not seats in the balcony pews."

When the service finishes, Remy rises to leave with the others. She doesn't make her way to the staircase they came up at the back of the church, though. Instead, she ducks her head and moves toward a different stairwell at the front, near the altar. Finn follows. This staircase continues up another story. The trapdoor at the top is latched, but there's no lock on it. Remy and Finn ascend into the church's attic.

The attic is only a small, sloping storage space beneath the peaked roof. It's warm but not stuffy; slatted windows on either end of the building allow a slight breeze. Through one of them, Finn can see the churchgoers spilling out onto the street below.

"I don't think this space is used much," Remy says, running a hand over a box of old hymnals. "There's a lot of dust. It's probably safe for us to wait here until this evening."

Again, Finn feels a pang of guilt over Cas; they're abandoning him for much longer than they intended. But she isn't sure how early the Order might arrive to make any preparations for their meeting tonight. If she and Remy leave the church now, they might not be able to get back in without attracting attention.

It's better to wait here. She turns away from the window.

She realizes, with a sudden, very palpable tension in her body, that this is the first time she and Remy have been truly alone since the beach in Provincetown.

Remy seems to have realized it as well. She's standing halfway across the attic, but even from here, Finn can see how red her face is.

"I shouldn't have said anything, on the beach," Finn blurts out.

But she and Remy have both tried to speak at the same time. She has no idea what Remy said; it's possible Finn's words were equally indecipherable. Finn's cheeks are hot. She's probably blushing an even brighter shade than Remy.

"You go first," Remy says.

"We don't have to talk about it," Finn tells her.

"We do, though. We do have to talk about it. Or . . . we don't *have* to, but I *want* to talk about it, because . . . well, because I want to. What were you going to say yesterday? On the beach?"

Finn doesn't answer that. She can wait this out. The silence between them stretches. Finn's heart feels like it's being pushed through the rusty meat grinder in Mrs. Darner's kitchen.

Remy groans and points her gaze at the sloped ceiling. "If I'm wrong about what you were going to say, this is going to be mortifying. But . . ." She seems to notice how intently Finn is watching her, because she falters. "Stop looking at me."

"Where am I meant to look?" Finn asks.

"I don't know. Just . . . fine, I won't look at you." Remy actually turns around then, so Finn can only see the back of her. "All right. You and I have been friends for a long time. *Are* . . . friends. And I want to *continue* being friends. But I also want to . . ."

She stops abruptly. She takes a breath. She seems to reset. Finn has a terrifying, breathtaking suspicion of where this conversation is heading. She can't let herself hope for it. She's probably wrong. At any moment, cold reality is going to smack her in the face and set her straight.

"Here's the thing," Remy says. "It's always been very clear what I'm supposed to do with my life, right? Find a husband—hopefully someone I can halfway tolerate, but we both know the reality is just any man who's willing to marry me. And then I'll spend the rest of my life keeping his house and making supper for him, and maybe, if I'm lucky, we'll get along well enough to enjoy each other's company, or . . . I don't know . . . sit and talk by the fire sometimes."

She's speaking very fast, as if she's afraid that at any moment she's going to lose her nerve, and she wants to get out as many words as possible before then.

"And it's always seemed so silly to me," Remy says, "because why would I find some random man to do all these things with, when I'd much rather do them with *you*?"

There's a part of Finn that doesn't believe this is really happening. This *can't* be happening. Because when you imagine something a thousand times, a thousand different ways, that something can never actually come to pass.

But Remy is still talking, hurtling toward the cliff. "And I know that isn't how it works, and I know there are other things that are supposed to ... *happen* ... when you're married, and things I'd be meant to *do* with a husband, and, and, and ..."

It isn't like her to stammer, but Remy seems to be running out of words at last. She manages one final burst.

"And so what does it mean, if I'd rather do *those* things with you, as well?"

Finn is dead. It's the only explanation. She drowned in the sea two days ago, and everything since, including this conversation, is a marvelous dream.

"What things?" Finn says. It isn't a question, but it is. She needs Remy to say it.

Remy turns back to look at her at last. "You know what I mean."

"What things," Finn says again.

A challenge. She and Remy stare at each other across the church attic.

"Oh, lord," Remy says.

She strides forward to close the distance between them. Her fingers brush Finn's arm. Her shoulder. The spot just beneath Finn's jaw. Finn's breath is ragged as the wind at sea. Remy is going to finish what she started on the beach in Provincetown. It's all been real. Finn will never doubt again.

Remy leans in and kisses her.

It's gentle. A light touch of lips. Even this sets a fire stirring in Finn's gut. Remy wants this. *Has* wanted this. Finn is allowed to want it, too.

When Remy pulls back, just a little, the fire inside Finn is still gasping for air.

Finn waits for the shame to hit her, the way it always has before.

It doesn't hit her now.

Remy's eyes are dark pools as she gazes down at Finn. Finn has imagined kissing Remy for so long. Now that it's finally happening, Finn feels like she's somehow unraveling the secrets of the universe. The knot in her heart uncoils. The priest back in Knockadine was just a man; the shame he fed her was poison. Finn can let it seep away. Her pleasure in this moment is pure and undiluted.

Remy is waiting, her lips still an inch from Finn's. A question of her own.

Finn lets her fingers snag in the curls of Remy's hair as she kisses her back, deeply. Remy's body arches into hers to close the space between them. As Finn grazes Remy's bottom lip with her teeth and hears Remy gasp, the fire inside her shifts—not a wild burst anymore, a flare that burns itself out, but a steadier heat. Something warm and nourishing. It's like walking outside on the first sunny spring morning after a long winter. The feeling of golden sunlight warming your face, when you'd almost convinced yourself the sun would never shine again.

They tangle together beneath the attic's window in a patch of afternoon light. Remy's lips on hers feels like the most natural thing in the world. Finn will never meet Saint Peter at the gates of heaven. Perhaps she'll never have that blessed moment of clarity.

She doesn't care. This is better.

XIX.
CAS

When the distant church bell rings the hour, Cas returns to himself and realizes he can't feel several of his fingers. He drops the pencil. His hand *hurts*. He hadn't noticed it until now. He's ravenously hungry, and his mouth is parched. The hotel room around him is strewn with scribbled, crumpled paper.

He counts the bell's chimes: five. Somehow, it's five o'clock.

And Remy and Finn still haven't returned.

This is just like them, Cas fumes as he tries to shake the numbness from his hand. They've left Cas here, alone, for the entire day, while they run around the city doing god knows what.

But on the heels of his annoyance comes a twinge of worry. What *have* they been doing all day? Surely it didn't take them this long to find the bookshop. Is it possible they ran into trouble? Or ran into the Order again? The man who chased Cas last night probably got a good look at Remy and Finn, too. He might have gone straight to Smith after he crawled back out of the harbor. Smith could have circulated descriptions of Remy and Finn to every Order member in Boston by now.

What if they've been caught?

The sky outside has an orange tinge to it. The sun will be setting soon. Smith might have Remy and Finn in his grasp even now. And Cas has spent the whole afternoon sitting uselessly in this hotel room, doodling.

He needs to go look for them. He has only the vaguest idea where to start, but maybe he can track down the bookshop. Retrace Remy and Finn's steps. He'll need a disguise, though—something to make the gash on his face a little less obvious.

Remy left her tarpaulin hat here. Cas tests out a few ways to angle the brim as he studies his reflection in the gilded mirror.

It's something, at least. Where did Finn put the coat she stole from the Order member? Cas could swear she still had it when they came to the hotel last night, and he could swear she didn't take it with her this morning. He checks all the corners of the room, and all the drawers of the bureau, and under the bed. It's only when he's checking the bureau *again* that he finds the coat pushed all the way to the back of the drawer.

Which is odd. It's an odd place for Finn to put something—unless she was actively trying to hide it. Maybe she suspected Cas would use the coat to try to sneak out. He can argue with her about it once he's sure she and Remy are safe. The sleeves of the coat are several inches too long for him, and he's swimming in the shoulders. If he flips up the collar, though, it does help cover his scar.

As he checks himself in the mirror again, the coat makes a papery rustling sound. Cas feels around in the pockets of it. He pulls out a sheaf of papers. This can't be the wanted notice from Smith; Finn burned that yesterday. He clears a spot on the floor amid his torn scribbles and spreads out these new pages to read.

As he slowly puts together the meaning of these registration papers for the *White Swallow*, his worry over Remy and Finn shifts back to annoyance. Then it grows into something bigger.

Angrier. It's their deception in the jolly boat all over again. The coat's hiding spot makes a terrible sort of sense now. Finn and Remy are still keeping secrets from him. Finn sat beside Cas on the packet boat yesterday and told him she wasn't going anywhere, and it was a lie. It was another goddamn lie.

There aren't enough pages left in his logbook to tear and crumple and throw this growing rage out of his body. There isn't enough paper in the world. Cas has never felt so abandoned. No, that isn't true—he felt this abandoned once before, when he told Remy about his first vision and Remy cut Cas out of her life. Cas should take his things and not leave a note and set off to find the *Mori* without them.

But Remy and Finn might be in trouble.

Cas stares at his own fuming face in the mirror. Hat brim tipped down, coat collar turned up. The disguise isn't bad.

If Remy and Finn have gotten themselves caught, Cas can't just leave them to Smith. And if they *haven't* gotten caught, he's going to hunt them down and throw both of *them* into the harbor. They probably haven't come back yet because they've gone to investigate the *White Swallow* by themselves.

To hell with it.

The man in the hotel lobby gives Cas directions to the wharf listed on the ship's papers. It takes Cas a few tries to find the wharf; he's gotten used to just following Remy around the city. But he doesn't need her. He can do this himself. He keeps his face tucked as much out of sight as he can, and he paces the docks, studying each ship anchored here, checking the name on the stern.

The smell of the ocean breeze is familiar and reassuring. With each ship he passes, Cas half imagines he'll spot a skeletal figurehead. The *Mori* isn't here, though. Finn and Remy aren't here, either. On the dock nearest him, a sailor with a thick gray beard is trying to lower a huge bundle of lumber onto a barge in the water.

"Boy!" the sailor calls out to someone. "You! Boy! Lend me a hand!"

It takes Cas several seconds too long to realize the sailor is talking to *him*. He doubles back quickly and catches the stack of boards before it overbalances. Another sailor with a wiry frame runs to help Cas and the man settle the load into the barge.

The bearded man climbs back up onto the dock with surprising agility. He has to be at least sixty. "Thanks for that."

He's eyeing Cas curiously as he dusts off his hands. Cas ducks his chin a little farther into his coat collar.

"You haven't been to sea before, have you?" the sailor guesses.

Cas forces himself to breathe. The man wasn't sizing him up to see if he fit Smith's wanted notice; he was sizing Cas up to see if he was a hopeless greenhand.

"I have," Cas says, though his voice comes out a little tight. "Once."

The man grins at him. "You'll get that sailor's swagger soon enough, then. What ship?"

Cas isn't sure how to answer this.

"What's the name of the ship you're sailing with?" the younger man who's joined them clarifies. "Or are you looking for work? Foster here knows most of these crews. We can point you to a captain who's reputable."

An idea strikes Cas, and he speaks before he can think too hard about it: "I'm . . . sailing with the *White Swallow*," he says.

The man with the beard, Foster, winces. "Oh, lord."

"Is that the one with the cursed casket?" the younger sailor asks.

"Cursed casket?" Cas echoes.

Foster frowns at his crewmate. "Don't frighten the lad!"

"He should be frightened! He'd be safer putting in his resignation before the *Swallow* goes out to sea. That's what Brock and Hernandez did."

"What's wrong with the *White Swallow*?" Cas asks.

The two sailors seem to debate something between themselves. Then the younger of them turns to Cas with the wise air of an older brother offering advice.

"Look," the sailor tells Cas. "Hernandez isn't even superstitious. If *he* says something aboard that ship goes against God and nature . . . Well, he and Brock can tell you better than I can. Do you like faro?"

Cas has played faro exactly once, with Immortal Gabe, who did a terrible job of explaining the rules. It's also possible that the game Gabe explained wasn't faro at all, because it looked nothing like the table to which these two sailors lead Cas, in a tavern a few streets away. Remy would probably be furious if she knew Cas had followed a pair of strangers into a makeshift gambling hall. At the moment, that only raises the gambling hall's appeal.

At the faro table, Cas is introduced to Brock and Hernandez. He also meets Schneider, and Kelly, and half a dozen other sea dogs who've heard a wide range of rumors about the *White Swallow* and her mysterious cargo.

As the sailors call cards and swap coins with the dealer, this is what Cas gathers: A week ago, or maybe two, a group of gentlemen brought a large box about the size of a coffin aboard the *White Swallow*. The box was covered with a sheet when they loaded it, but several of the men caught a glimpse of the metal underneath. One claims the box was made of gold. Another thinks it was bronze. When Cas asks if it could have been brass, they both concede the point. The specific metal isn't important, anyway; what's important is that it's cursed. Hernandez swears it is, and Hernandez isn't even superstitious.

"It's simple fact," Hernandez says. "Even the *Swallow*'s captain knows it's cursed. He had to bring in some holy man to put a spell on it—to ward off evil."

The tavern is loud and impossibly stuffy. Cas feels like he might pass out in his oversize coat. "What sort of holy man?" he asks.

"A minister. Or reverend. Something like that."

Cas has a very bad feeling about this. "Do you remember what he looked like?"

Hernandez and Brock both think for a moment. "In his fifties, maybe?" Brock says. "He had gray hair. And he wore these little spectacles."

Cas is sitting at the dining table back at Eden, watching Reverend John Smith push his spectacles up his nose. He's sprawled in the woods behind the seminary, and Smith is crouching over him with his knife raised. The tavern feels very far away.

"I don't know what exactly the *Swallow*'s wrapped up with," Hernandez is saying, "but it's nothing good. They've even rigged her with cannons. That was the final straw for me. If I wanted to sail on a gunship, I'd have joined the navy. You should put in your notice, too. Or just don't show up when she sails tonight."

This jolts Cas back to himself. "Tonight?"

"Isn't that when she's scheduled to haul out? I thought the

Swallow was finally casting off as soon as your captain gets back from his big meeting."

"Careful," Brock says.

Hernandez waves him off. "If those rich bastards didn't want us to know, they shouldn't have been whispering about it all over Boston. Might as well have printed a notice in the newspaper."

"What meeting?" Cas asks, but Hernandez ignores him.

"It's not enough for these posh men to just *be* in a secret society. They have to make sure the rest of us *know* they're in a secret society. That's half the thrill for them."

"What secret society?" Cas presses. "What meeting?"

As Brock tells him about the rumored gathering at High Street Chapel, Cas has the same strange sensation he felt during that awful tea at the Eden seminary—the moment he realized that Smith had known all along about Cas's visions. The suspicion takes him slowly, like chilly rain seeping through his coat. Smith had bristled, once, at Cas describing the Order of Lazarus as a "secret society"—but spreading the word so openly about an Order meeting seems brazen, even for him.

"When did you all hear about this?" Cas says. "When did they start spreading the word?"

"Hmm. This morning? Maybe late last night."

Probably mere hours after the *White Swallow*'s captain told Smith that Cas, Remy, and Finn were in the city. Cas has walked into too many traps by now—he's finally learning to recognize the smell. Surely Remy and Finn wouldn't be so foolish as to show up at the Chapel tonight.

But they never came back to the hotel.

And it's nearly six o'clock now. The meeting will be starting any minute.

Cas grits his teeth and gets one of the sailors to point him to High Street Chapel. He thanks them for their help and takes off into the city. When he finds Remy and Finn, he's going to murder them both.

Assuming Smith doesn't do it first.

XX.

REMY

Beneath the sweat and salty sea grime, Finn smells a little like smoke. Not the choking, acidic soot of the city, but the sweet scent of a campfire. Burning cedar or hickory. Remy must have known this, even if not consciously, because the scent is so familiar, now that she's noticed it. Now that she can lie on the floor of the attic with Finn nestled against her.

Their lazy afternoon here feels like a dream. A part of Remy is bracing for everything to collapse around her; she doesn't know how to let herself be happy. The rest of Remy doesn't care. She *is* happy.

"Did you really mean it?" Remy asks. "What you said on the beach."

She half expects Finn to groan and brush this off. To her surprise, Finn rolls over to look at her. "Which part?" she asks.

"When you said . . . *for years.*"

Finn's face is guileless. "Yes," she says.

Remy can't believe it's taken them so long to have this conversation. "When were you going to tell me?"

"I wasn't."

Their faces are so close that Remy would be able to see if there were even a shred of embarrassment in Finn's expression. There isn't.

"I wasn't going to push anything," Finn murmurs. "If you didn't want this."

"I want this," Remy says. She doesn't let herself overthink it. She says it because it's true. "I don't think I realized I wanted this, or . . . was allowed to want it. But I do."

Finn kisses her again. Remy drinks in that campfire smell.

When the sun has dropped low through the attic's window, the spell breaks. The Order's gathering will begin soon. Remy and Finn peer through the slats and take in the view of the street.

There's a surprisingly large crowd gathered just outside the church's main doors—and not the sorts of people Remy has come to expect as members of the Order of Lazarus. Smith recruits men who have money and power. The people assembled here come from a lowlier social class than Remy thought Smith would bother with.

Maybe that's why this crowd is locked outside, Remy thinks. An expensive-looking carriage has just rolled to a stop on the street in front of the church's doors. Two hulking men in dark coats begin to shove back the throng of onlookers on the steps to clear a path. A man, woman, and three children, all finely dressed, climb down from the carriage and disappear into the church.

"Díaz did say that Smith was hardly bothering to keep this a secret," Finn says. "I suppose word got out."

Clearly it did. Nothing about this sits well with Remy. She can't blame these people for their curiosity, though; she and Finn are hardly different. Remy is glad they came to the church early so they were able to get inside.

The orange sunlight through the slats is falling across Finn's face in stripes.

Remy is glad they came to the church early for several other reasons, too.

"We need to talk about our plan," Finn says, still watching the crowd through the window. "We're not trying to *stop* Smith tonight, are we? We're only here for information."

Remy plays through it in her mind. She has the little gun Finn stole from the man on the wharf yesterday. From the balcony, she could probably get Smith in her sights. But every line of moves she imagines after that leads to her and Finn swarmed by Order members, badly outnumbered, both of them captured or killed. And Remy can't risk that—now more than ever.

"Agreed," she says. "We'll listen from our corner in the balcony. We won't engage. We'll wait to leave until everyone's dispersed. I think we'll have a much clearer idea of what Smith is planning before the night is over, though."

Finn nods slowly. "What then?"

"Then we can regroup with the *Mori*," Remy says. "We'll tell the captain what we've learned and work with him to decide what's next."

Finn blinks at her, surprised. Remy is surprised herself. But she thinks she's beginning to understand Captain Hobbes a little better. She's chafed at his insistence on taking the slower, safer path instead of charging ahead, risks be damned. But the captain has been trying to protect someone he loves, too.

Remy has been ready to burn down the world to save Finn's life. She still might, if she has to. But if there's another way . . . when it comes down to it, she needs there to still *be* a world at the end of this.

She wants to get to love Finn for years and years.

Remy retrieves her carpetbag from the corner where she left

it and checks the little gun. This pistol is very different from the rifles Striker taught Remy to use—but Remy can work out how to load the bullets. Finn watches her keenly.

"Only as a last resort," Remy says.

Finn gnaws on her lip. "If it comes to that, I can set the church on fire, too."

Remy doesn't know whether to laugh or groan. "Is that your solution to everything now?"

"It's gotten us out of scrapes before, hasn't it?"

Remy tucks the gun back into her bag. "Last resort," she says. A promise.

"Last resort," Finn agrees.

They wait until the bell in the tower above begins to chime the hour, then use its clamor to cover their footsteps as they creep back down from the attic. The church's balcony is empty, just as they predicted. When the ringing is finished, Remy can hear the murmurs of a different sort of congregation assembling.

Remy risks a quick glimpse over the railing to get a view of the altar and the boxes below. Even with the family they saw get out of the carriage, Remy underestimated how many women and children would be here. Some of the Order members must have come alone, but many have brought their wives. A few boxes hold whole broods of children, sniffling and drowsy at this evening hour. A woman near the front cradles a baby, while the man at her side frowns in disapproval every time the baby fusses.

Remy had been imagining this night to be some dark ritual with men in robes and masks—not something like a normal church service. At the altar, a slight, pale, gray-haired man stands with his hands folded behind his back, preparing to climb up to the pulpit to speak. Remy's throat tightens. This is Reverend John Smith.

Pastor Dekker is beside him. The last time Remy and Finn saw Dekker, he was cowering in the burning seminary. Now, his wheat-blond hair is perfectly sleek, his jacket clean and pressed. Remy spies another familiar figure, and revulsion rises in her as she watches Henry Ashworth take a seat in one of the boxes. How can Ashworth still be loyal to Smith, after Smith nearly killed Cas at Eden? Cas risked everything trying to help Ashworth escape the Order—and here Ashworth remains, of his own free will.

Remy settles back behind the railing, pushing down her fury. She hates all of these men, with their wealth and power and entitlement. But she hates some of them more personally than others.

A hush falls over the church. Reverend Smith must have ascended to his pulpit.

"Thank you," Smith says, "for joining us here this evening. It isn't often that we invite our women and children into this assembly, but they are part of our flock. Welcome."

Finn is pressed against Remy's side, her body clenched in anticipation. In the glimpses Remy has caught of Reverend John Smith, she's thought him unimpressive and unassuming. But there's a command to his quiet voice, carried through the cavernous space by the Chapel's acoustics.

"You are here this evening because you are men of God," Smith says. "You protect your dependents from the corruption of the world. For our world *has* been corrupted; the rabble outside shows us that."

He pauses, letting the voices from the crowd on the steps drift through the locked doors. What separates this "rabble" from the congregation Smith has allowed inside tonight? He can claim some sort of moral difference—but it's transparently clear to Remy that the real difference is money.

"There are monstrous forces on this earth that twist the will of God. But the Lord has granted me the tools to turn the power of these monsters—these *reapers*—toward a righteous purpose. At last, we have the means to capture one of these reapers. We can put to rights this reaper's list, so that our wives, sons, and daughters—who you've raised to be righteous and holy—will not be stolen before their time. They will be saved. And those who are *not* righteous, *not* holy, will be purged. Using this creature's power, we will reshape our world in God's image."

For years, as Remy sat through Pastor Dekker's Sunday services, she practiced disconnecting herself, listening through a veil of numbness. It was the only way to stop herself from going mad at the hypocrisy. Someone has carved graffiti into the balcony's railing, and Remy focuses on the initials gouged into the wood so she doesn't scream.

"We have crafted a vessel to bind this reaper," Smith continues. "A holy casket forged from a metal so potent that the sea itself tried to bury it. Even the ship that was carrying this brass across the ocean was wrecked and pulled to the depths. But the Lord granted me knowledge of the wreck's location—and a holy rite that could protect this metal for the remainder of its journey."

Finn has gone very pale. Remy wonders if she, too, is thinking of Smith's office at Eden—the evidence of a demon-summoning ritual Smith performed. It certainly wasn't *the Lord* who gave Smith those coordinates.

But Finn whispers, inexplicably, "It wasn't me. It was the brass. The storm, the fog . . ."

She's right, Remy realizes. And Gabe's terrible instinct about that brass panel had been right, too. The unnatural fog over Georges Bank had centered on the wrecked ship; when the crew hauled the remaining piece of brass aboard the *Mori*, the fog followed. Then the harsh, capricious winds. Then the aberrant storm that had whipped into a frenzy directly over the ship. The worst of the weather had passed by the time Remy, Finn, and Cas reached shore—but what if they only believed it passed *because* they went to shore? If the tempest was centered on that panel of brass stowed on the *Mori*'s deck . . .

The crew might be battling the sea's curse even now. Or worse. Remy feels ill.

Smith is still speaking. "The casket is ready. But in this final hour, the Lord has presented us with one final test of faith: The reaper, aware of our efforts to constrain him, has fled."

Remy is jolted all over again. How does Smith know that Death has gone into hiding?

"This cowardice cannot deter our holy mission. For I have prayed, and God showed me the way. We no longer need to capture this creature of Death. I will take up his vacated post."

Finn's fingers are locked around Remy's.

"I will become a new Death," Smith says calmly. "A holy Death. I will use this power to bring about God's kingdom on earth."

Remy stares at the graffiti on the balcony's railing. She feels numb. Her emotions are mud, and she can't wade through them. When she peers down into the body of the church, Smith is descending the pulpit's steps.

"I've gathered you all here in preparation for this final ritual," Smith says. "Some of you are here because you've lost someone; you know firsthand the pain this creature has inflicted. Some of you are here because you are protectors. I invite you to bring forward your dependents, that I may lay hands on them and grant them asylum from the coming floods."

Finn is still clutching one of Remy's hands. With her other, Remy touches the grip of the pistol in her coat pocket. She doesn't draw it out; she can't risk it, even though it feels like the only rational solution. Remy's mind is a haze of anger. Death's role is to shepherd the souls of people who've already died—not to *kill* them. The reaper Smith wants to supersede hasn't "inflicted pain."

But Smith has. Smith murdered Remy's father. He's murdered others, too.

Finn's grip tightens, as if she can tell Remy is on the verge of doing something reckless. Remy forces herself to breathe. Murmurs echo from the church below as the Order members and their families approach Smith at the altar one by one.

At the end of the procession, a blond-haired woman stands alone. She holds a bundle of something in her arms—a blanket. The woman is silently weeping.

Finn tracks Remy's gaze and whispers, "Smith's wife."

So this is Clara Smith. Remy hasn't seen her before, though Cas and Finn must have met her at the seminary. She has a sinking suspicion who the blanket in her arms once belonged to: Cas told them, after Eden, about the daughter Smith lost years ago in a shipwreck.

Remy doesn't doubt that Clara Smith's tears are real. She can't fathom this sort of loss.

But Smith isn't the only person here who's lost someone—and he's been the direct cause of that loss for others. For Remy. He's decided that his own family's grief outweighs that of anyone else. Death is one thing all the money and power in the world hasn't allowed him to control—until now. Others deserve to suffer loss; he should be exempt.

Clara Smith has reached the front of the church. She stands before her husband with the empty blanket cradled in her arms.

"My daughter," Smith says quietly, though his voice still resonates. "Viola. Another victim of this reaper. When the Lord raised Lazarus from the dead, his miracle strengthened the faith of his believers. When I step into this holy power, Viola will be a symbol of God's greatness and mercy. She will be our new Lazarus."

It's never been just about controlling who lives and who dies, Remy realizes through her tangle of emotions. For Smith, this is personal.

He thinks he can bring his own daughter back to life.

"Tonight, we begin our pilgrimage to the place where Viola was stolen from us," Smith says. "For her soul to be returned, for her to walk the earth with us again, there must be a sacrifice."

Remy knows in her gut who he intends to sacrifice. If Smith has truly moved on from his plan to capture and control Death, he shouldn't need the reaper's glass anymore—and yet he circulated those wanted notices. An Order member tried to kidnap Cas just yesterday.

In the silence, Remy can hear the raised voices from the crowd locked outside. The congregants in their boxes rustle with unease.

"Ignore the masses at our gates," Smith tells them. "I knew that spreading word of our gathering tonight would draw the rabble. But I needed to ensure our evening's special guests received our invitation."

With horror, Remy hears the footsteps on the stairs on either side of them.

"I believe they're waiting in the balcony," Smith says.

XXI.
FINN

Finn was wrong before, when she thought that learning all the answers at once would be paradise. This is too much. Her head feels like it's been cracked open and stuffed with too many revelations in a row. The storm aboard the *Mori* wasn't her fault after all; it was the brass panel, not Finn, that brought a curse down upon them. She can't catch her breath. Every new piece of information has her reeling all over again: Smith knows that Death has gone into hiding. Smith intends to become a reaper himself. Smith plans to raise his own daughter from the dead. Smith needs a sacrifice.

Smith knows Finn and Remy are here.

Remy's eyes are wide as she and Finn crouch there, both of them frozen with shock. But as footsteps thunder up the stairs on either side of them, it's Remy who acts first. She's on her feet, pulling Finn up, too. The little gun is in her hand. She stands at the balcony's railing and aims it down at Smith.

She fires.

The gunshot is earsplitting and wrong inside this church. Several voices scream. The people in the boxes below begin to run for cover.

But Smith is still standing at the head of his congregation, staring straight up at Remy and Finn. Unscathed. Remy's shot has missed. Men spill into the balcony around them, at least six of them, all with guns of their own.

"Drop it," one of the men barks at Remy. "The gun. Drop it."

Finn doesn't think she's going to. Remy hasn't taken her eyes from Smith in the church below.

But there's no time to reload—and even if there were, they can't fight the whole Order. Finn doesn't think Remy has it in her to try to shoot anyone here besides Smith.

She lets the little gun fall from her grip.

"Is the reaper's glass with them?" Smith calls up to his men. His eyes narrow as he takes in Remy and Finn—only two of them, not three. The man who shouted at Remy shakes his head.

As Smith's men fan out to search the rest of the balcony for Cas, Finn looks for exits. The Order members are blocking both stairwells. She and Remy might be able to shove their way through if they can catch them off guard, but it's just as likely they'll be grabbed and dragged down to Smith. They'd be fools to jump from the balcony; they won't be able to run with a broken leg, or a broken skull. Is there any chance they could break one of the windows and climb down from the ledge outside?

When Finn catches Remy's eye, she suspects Remy is doing a similar calculation.

Smith's men have finished their search; one of them calls down to Smith that Cas isn't here. But Dekker has gone to meet Smith, and he murmurs something in his ear.

"I see," Smith says. Even now, with his congregation in turmoil, his voice manages to rise above the din. "It had been revealed to me, before, that the reaper's glass should be our sacrifice. But the Lord works in mysterious ways."

Smith's eyes fix on Remy.

"Perhaps God has delivered us a sacrifice all the same," he says.

At the word "sacrifice," everything in Finn's mind goes white.

She and Remy aren't going to jump from a balcony or climb out a window. Finn has one weapon left, and the time has come to use it. With a sense of utter calm, Finn watches the men approach them. She watches one of them reach for Remy. He's young, probably Kieran's age, and a patchy mustache dusts his upper lip.

Finn touches the man's sleeve. The fire spills out of her effortlessly. In a second, she sets the man's jacket ablaze.

The man screams, lurching away from them both, trying to smother the flames on his arm. Finn grabs for the man behind him and lights his coat on fire, too. Remy runs at the third man and does something like a kick between his legs. He stumbles, though she didn't land the blow as effectively as Cas managed on his would-be assassin yesterday. They'll have to work on that, Finn thinks. But first, they have to get out of here.

Finn places her hand on the wooden railing of the balcony. This isn't like conjuring a tiny flame in her palm, and it isn't like when she burned the seminary by stoking a fire that was already in the hearth. This is pure will—conjuring an inferno from nothing in an instant.

She closes her eyes and pushes with everything in her. The railing ignites beneath her palm. Flames explode out around her, as if the balcony's floor had been doused with alcohol. The pews, the carpet, the entire balcony is burning.

This is the fire Finn has dreamed about, terrifying and wonderful at once. The flames cascade out of her. She can burn the world. The Order members are running from them. Their mouths open to scream, but Finn can't hear anything over the rushing conflagration.

Remy has grabbed Finn's hand. The fire has dodged around them both, just as it did at Eden. Even in Finn's dreams, the flames never hurt Remy. Remy is shouting something. With utter trust that Finn's fire won't burn either one of them, she drags Finn straight through it and down the nearest staircase.

The main body of the church is in chaos. Several more men rush at them as they reach the ground floor. Finn throws a wall of flame at them, holding them back, but cutting off the route she and Remy could've taken to the front doors. Smoke clouds the air. Remy is coughing. Finn can't see Smith or Dekker through the haze.

There's a side door, Finn thinks. If she and Remy can just get outside . . .

But Finn's head is starting to feel very strange. There's a pressure building there. She's further and further outside her own body. She tells her feet to move toward the door. Her feet don't respond. Remy is holding her upright, but Finn only knows this by sight; she can't feel the touch of Remy's arms around her.

Remy is shouting something again. How long has Remy been shouting at her? The words don't make any sense.

Finn has drawn more fire from that pit inside her than she's ever drawn before. If this fire really is her *vitalis vis*, her inner will . . . Finn is pointing all her energy toward sustaining the flames outside her; there's not enough left to sustain *herself.* Her body is abandoning its other functions. She's dimly aware of Remy dragging her toward the side door, of Smith and Dekker and an army of other men running to intercept them. She and Remy aren't going to make it.

The world turns very dark.

Finn thinks, distantly, that this is the natural next step. Her vision has given out, too. But the darkness is moving. Finn can still see it. A shape unfurls in the space between Smith's group and the door—a creature of smoke and shadow, tentacles and too many limbs.

Finn recognizes this figure: the same column of smoke that she once watched turn into a man inside the triangle of the summoning ritual.

The demon has come to collect at last.

Chips of ice have formed in Finn's veins and are working their way toward her heart. This is how Finn dies. How she was always going to die. She fought, during the storm, when she thought the demon grabbed her in the sea. She doesn't have enough energy left in her to fight now. She's a guttering candle that's run out of wax. She can't do anything except cling to Remy, who's clinging to her, just waiting for the end.

The demon stands in a single unburned circle, emanating cold. Watching them.

Then the demon turns away, toward Smith. Looming over the Order members. Holding them back.

It's one too many revelations for Finn to wrap her spent mind around: The demon isn't just letting them escape.

The demon is *helping* them escape.

Remy drags Finn through the side door and into the clear air.

Finn's consciousness keeps flickering through the pieces that come next. It's still light out. Dusk, but not dark. They're in the gated cemetery outside the church. Remy is coughing from the smoke. Perhaps Finn is coughing, too. Then they're on the ground. The soil and grass beneath Finn's hand are damp. She leans her cheek against the cool granite of the headstone that Remy has propped her against.

"Oh god," Remy is whispering as sound drifts back into Finn's awareness. "Oh god. Oh god. What can I do? What do you need?"

She's wiping at Finn's face with the sleeve of her coat. The fabric comes away dark and wet. Finn's nose is bleeding.

"We can't stay here," Finn manages to say.

"I know. But you can't walk. I can try to carry you, maybe, but—"

She breaks off with a swear. A young man in a dark coat is running through the cemetery toward them. Remy starts to her feet, preparing to fight him off.

But when the man hisses out, "*There* you are," it's Cas's voice.

Remy drags Cas out of view behind the headstone with them. "What are you doing here?"

"What am *I*—?" Cas is wheezing from the run. "I've been looking for you! Don't go inside the church. Smith's laid a trap."

"We know that now," Remy snaps.

But they hadn't known until it was too late. Remy and Finn fell for Smith's ruse without a second thought.

"What's wrong with her?" Cas asks. He must have noticed Finn still slumped against the headstone. She's so tired.

"I'm fine," she murmurs.

"She isn't," Remy says.

"And—Jesus Christ, is the church on *fire*? Is that your solution to everything?"

Remy had said the same thing, but mercifully, neither of them stops to rub it in just now. "We need to move," Remy says. "Can you help me carry her?"

Finn feels herself lifted between them, an arm draped

helplessly over each of their shoulders. She thinks she's coming back to herself, except she blinks and finds that they've somehow left the cemetery. She blinks again, and they're on a completely different street. It's humiliating to have to let them tote her around like this, but when she tries to walk, she's clumsy and disoriented. She's going to send all three of them sprawling.

Remy and Cas are arguing about where to go next. Then they seem to have agreed to return to the hotel but are arguing about the directions. And then they're just arguing, even as they stagger down yet another street.

"You were supposed to be waiting at the hotel," Remy says.

"And *you* were supposed to be back in a few hours!"

"I said we'd try to be back. Something came up."

Cas snorts. "Clearly."

"Díaz gave us a lead, so we followed it. I'm sorry we didn't double back to tell you, but—"

"No, you're not," Cas cuts in.

"Fine, I'm not!"

"Probably not sorry for hiding the *White Swallow*'s papers, either. I found those, by the way. You just decided to keep that piece of information to yourself?"

Finn manages to find her voice at last. "That was my fault," she tells Cas. "Don't blame Remy for that."

"Don't worry. I'm plenty angry with both of you. When you didn't come back, I went to poke around the docks—"

"You *what*?" Remy says.

"—and it turns out Smith *did* build some cursed box out of those brass panels—"

"You could have been recognized!" Remy cuts in. "And we already know about the casket! Smith's plan has changed, anyway—he's not trying to capture Death anymore. He figured out somehow that Death has gone into hiding."

"He—oh, damn it all!"

They're being too loud, drawing too many eyes as they hobble down the street, an awkward six-legged creature.

"Cas." Remy's voice is wary. "What did you do?"

"I . . . told Henry something about that. At Eden."

"You *told Ashworth*?"

"I didn't know he was going to tell Smith!"

"I can't believe this," Remy says. "I can't believe you'd be so foolish as to—"

"I'm not the one who went running straight into Smith's trap!"

Cas is shaking, Finn realizes—fury, or fear, or a combination of both. Remy falls silent; she doesn't have a rebuttal. Finn maneuvers herself out of their grip and regains her footing.

"I'm all right," she says. "I can walk."

Remy lets her go, though she seems reluctant about it. "Your nose is still bleeding."

Finn wipes at the blood as they cross another road. The streets are becoming more familiar; she thinks they're near the hotel now. Has anyone followed them from the church? Finn has been too bleary to pay attention, but they haven't been nabbed by the Order yet, which is promising.

"You're right," Finn tells Cas as they make the final turn onto the street where their hotel awaits. "We should have come back and told you, when we knew we were going to be gone so long."

"Yes," Cas says. "You should have."

"I'm sorry."

His face is mostly hidden by his hat brim and the turned-up

collar of his coat. But Finn thinks something in his expression softens. He nods at her once.

They attract far more attention in the hotel lobby than Finn would like. She and Remy probably reek of smoke, and based on how the clerk blanches when he catches sight of Finn's face, it's possible she hasn't done as much to wipe the blood from it as she'd hoped. No one stops them, though, as they stumble upstairs to their room.

When Cas gets the door unlocked, Finn barely makes it inside before her knees give out. She feels right on the edge of fainting. She lets herself sink to the floor while her head clears again.

But Remy has frozen on the threshold. "What happened here?"

The room looks as if it's been ransacked. Papers are strewn across the floor around Finn, some crumpled, some torn into pieces. Finn catches scraps of pencil drawings on them. It's as if a sketchbook exploded.

Cas sweeps a few of the crumpled drawings into a pile with his foot.

"Nothing happened," he says, still cross. "I was bored."

"Christ, Cas. I thought someone had broken in!"

"Oh, so *now* you're worried about what might have happened while you were gone the *entire day*."

Remy has locked the door of their room behind them. "Do you even want to hear about what we learned at the church? And from Díaz?"

Cas's desire to fight this out is clearly warring with his curiosity. The curiosity must win, because he tosses the Order member's oversize coat onto the bed and says curtly, "What did you learn?"

As Remy recounts the discoveries of the day, Finn stays on the floor, head between her knees. She's recovering, slowly but steadily. Whatever happened back there, when she pushed her fire too far, it doesn't seem to be permanent. The horror is finally catching up with her, though. If Finn had kept pushing, would her body have simply collapsed? Would she have died?

And why did the demon stop her? Marbas could have watched her burn out, or he could have killed Finn himself. Either way, Finn's side of her contract would have been fulfilled. But Marbas intervened, and Finn is still alive.

We need to talk.

"So Smith thinks he can . . . become . . . Death?" Cas says. "And raise his daughter from the dead?"

Remy's face is grim. "So it seems. He wanted to sacrifice you to bring her back."

"Well, I don't like *that*," Cas says, which might be his greatest understatement yet.

"We need to get out of the city. I don't know if Smith still plans to set sail tonight, or if he'll keep trying to hunt you—and us—down. But it isn't safe for us to stay here."

"I could've told you the meeting was a trap," Cas mutters.

"Yes, well done. You guessed right for once."

It's cruel of her, Finn thinks, but Cas is pressing on a fresh wound. Remy is surely berating herself for this already. She'll probably keep berating herself for the next thousand years.

Cas is glaring at her. "Don't be an ass. I was going out of my mind this afternoon thinking you two had been caught, or killed, or—"

"Well, we weren't," Remy cuts in.

"That's the best defense you've got? Really?"

Remy hasn't told him, obviously, the details of how she and Finn spent their afternoon in the church attic. Finn still doesn't feel shame over it—but she does feel guilt, now, as she considers it from Cas's point of view. She hadn't meant to frighten him.

"Like I said," Remy tells him. "Díaz gave us a lead. If we'd come back here first, we would've had a much more difficult time sneaking into the church without—"

"Without what? Without being spotted? How did that work out for you?"

Remy is holding herself tightly. "You're really enjoying this, aren't you?"

"Trust me—I'm not."

"At least I didn't tell *Henry Ashworth* about Death being missing."

Cas laughs, bitter and humorless. "I can't believe you're being self-righteous even now."

"I'm not *self-righteous*!"

"You're so convinced you're smarter than everyone else! And clearly you know better than we do what's best for us, and that means you're perfectly justified when you lie, and keep secrets—"

"Remy didn't know about the *White Swallow*'s papers," Finn says again. She's trying to rein in this conflict, but Cas rounds on her.

"And you're just as bad as she is!" he snarls. "You think you're protecting us by not telling us anything, but we're in this, too! We have been the whole time."

They've all reached the point in this relationship where they can see each other a little too clearly. Every shot fired now hits its mark with deadly aim. Because isn't this exactly what Finn has told herself for the last six years—that she's protecting Kieran by keeping the deal she made a secret from him?

She can't meet Cas's gaze. She picks up one of the crumpled drawings just to have something else to look at.

"We need to make a plan," Remy tells Cas. "We can fight about this later."

"No!" Cas says. "No, we're doing this now, because otherwise we're never going to!"

Cas's sketch takes up most of the page, all jagged lines and shading. Finn turns it a little. Something about the shape strikes her as familiar.

"This is *why* we don't tell you things, you know," Remy is saying. "You're a powder keg, Cas! Ever since we came to shore—"

"Since you *forced* us to come to shore," Cas snaps.

Remy sighs, exasperated. "I already apologized for lying to you in the jolly boat. What else do you want?"

"I want you to stop running off without me and leaving me in the dark!"

"Why did you draw all these?" Finn asks.

This seems to startle Cas from his rage. He glares down at her. "What?"

Finn smooths out another of the crumpled pages, then a third. The smudgy pencil images are nearly identical. And she's finally recognized the shape Cas has been sketching.

"Why did you draw all these pictures of Dungeon Rock?"

XXII.

REMY

Cas snatches the drawing from Finn's hands, frowning. Remy takes another paper from the floor and studies it. The sketch looks abstract at first—just random lines and cross-hatching.

Then Remy rotates it. The image is half finished, but its likeness to Dungeon Rock is uncanny. The silhouette alone fills Remy with an unexpected nostalgia, like catching a whiff of the specific strain of tea her mother used to brew when she was ill.

"I wasn't drawing Dungeon Rock," Cas snaps. It's clear he thinks Finn is trying to distract him from their argument, and he doesn't like it. But he studies the page more closely. "I didn't *mean* to draw Dungeon Rock."

"What did you think you were drawing?" Remy asks.

"Nothing! I was just scribbling."

"Well, you kept scribbling the same shape," Finn tells him. "Over and over."

She's unfolding page after page, handing them to Remy, who hands them to Cas. Cas drops the whole stack on the floor again, as if at a loss for what else to do. Every sketch matches.

"I was trying to meditate, at first," he says. "Only I felt like I was losing my mind. And I had my book from Leo, and he'd said something about— It doesn't matter."

"I think it might matter, actually," Remy says. An idea has

occurred to her. It's impossible, and yet . . . "What if you *were* meditating? Or something like it, anyway."

Remy's mind is spinning so quickly that she wonders if it might overheat. The idea isn't impossible. It's *very* possible. As she considers it further, it seems almost obvious.

It's been a decade since Remy and Cas dug for treasure at Dungeon Rock. Remy hasn't thought much about the details of the pirate legend for years. But the details are still tucked away in her mind—etched into her memory as stubbornly as the chalk that apparently still lingers on the floor of Cas's childhood bedroom.

At eight years old, Remy had gathered accounts from as many sources as she could. Annoyingly, the accounts never quite lined up. Her father told Remy the story *he'd* been told, or at least what he remembered of it. Old Mrs. Darner let Remy look through the journal of her several-times-great-grandfather. Mr. Pendleton and his cousin Mr. Hirsch had their own conflicting versions of events. Mr. Hirsch—to prove he was the authority on the matter—lent Remy his copy of *The History of Lynn* by Alonzo Lewis. Even this historian seemed dubious about the legend, but if it did really happen, he dated it to 1658.

All versions of the story involved at least one pirate on the lam, who evaded the British navy by rowing up the Saugus River. Mrs. Darner claimed the rowboat held a dozen pirates. Alonzo Lewis thought it was four. Mr. Pendleton believed the wanted man was alone. All agreed that the pirates—whatever the number—took shelter somewhere in the Lynn Woods, though the shelter might have been the cave under the rock, or it might have been a tent nearby. Or it might have been a small house they built in a glen beside a bluff, with a garden and a view of the sea.

According to Remy's father, the residents of Lynn held little fondness for the British authorities of the time; they kept their mouths shut about the fugitives' camp and traded with them when they could. Old Mrs. Darner said one of the pirates even whittled toys for the children in town. She showed Remy a wooden carving inherited from her several-times-great-grandfather, a tiny bear that could fit in Remy's palm.

The British navy found the pirates eventually, though. Of that, every account was certain. At least one of the pirates—a man named Thomas Veal, if *The History of Lynn* could be believed—escaped the noose by hiding in the cave where the group had stashed their gold. But within the year, an earthquake trapped him inside. Thomas Veal, presumably, died under that rock. Any stolen gold that may have existed was buried forever. And Dungeon Rock got its name.

Remy is working her way through a theory now. With each new scrap of evidence, she thinks the theory will finally fall apart. Instead, it only grows sturdier.

"I need to make a list," Remy says.

Cas and Finn are both staring at her dubiously. But Remy needs to lay out all the pieces in one place. She doesn't have Nessa's slates now; she scrambles through her carpetbag for her journal. Cas offers a pencil from the writing desk without a word.

"Tell me everything we know about Death," Remy says, pencil poised over the page.

"You mean . . . as a concept?" Cas asks.

"No—the captain's Death. We know he was alive, once. Díaz told us that."

"Was he?" Cas's surprise seems overshadowed by his bafflement at Remy's list making. He shakes his head. "Well, we know he fancies men."

Remy isn't sure how relevant this is, but she writes it down anyway. "What else?"

"He's good at chess," Finn offers.

"Right," Remy says. "And at carving. He carved the *Mori*'s figurehead, didn't he?"

"And that little skeleton toy of Nessa's," Cas adds.

Remy had forgotten about that. Her brain sparks with an image of the tiny carved bear in Mrs. Darner's hand.

"We know he's at least a hundred years old," Finn says. "Probably older. Possibly much older."

"Old enough that he could've died—or become Death—around 1658, maybe?" Remy says.

Finn's eyebrows are doing something complicated. "I suppose."

"That's . . . very specific," Cas says.

"Just the other day," Remy prompts him, "I asked the captain how we could know whether you were the reaper's glass for *his* reaper. And he asked where your visions take place, and then where Windover was. Do you remember what we told him?"

Cas hesitates. "The North Shore?"

"Near the Lynn Woods," Remy says. "I mentioned the woods specifically. And Captain Hobbes seemed absolutely certain after that. Because he knows his partner has a tie to that place."

She snatches up another drawing of Dungeon Rock and waves it in Cas's face.

"You said you were trying to meditate, right? You were trying to connect with Death. And then you drew—"

Cas swats the paper from her hand and turns to Finn, as if looking for a second opinion. Finn is still sitting on the floor, but she's staring up at him with widened eyes.

"That person you mentioned, who said he met a pirate ghost in the woods," Finn says.

"Mr. Anderson? He was drunk, though. You don't really think a ghost challenged him to a game of cards—"

"It wasn't a game of cards," Remy cuts in. "I've heard Mr. Anderson tell that story a dozen times. He always said it was *chess*."

Remy watches Cas's face go through several stages: surprise, doubt, and finally acceptance. Slowly, he sinks to the floor beside Finn. He looks like a man who just briefly met God.

"Jesus, Mary, and Joseph," Finn breathes. "Not a ghost. It was probably Death himself."

Cas is fully lying on the floor now, staring at the ceiling. "What do we do with all this?"

"Díaz thinks you can talk to Death through the Veil," Remy tells him. "Because you're the reaper's glass. But the connection will be steadier if you have another tether. Something else for Death to hold on to."

"Like anchor cables," Cas says, sitting up. "For mooring. That's how Mita described it. Two points of connection are steadier than one."

Remy blinks at him. He seems to have come to terms with this concept much more quickly than she did. "Exactly like that," Remy says. "Anyway, Díaz told us that the place where a spirit died would be a tether, too."

"Oh," Cas says. He takes this in. "Oh, no. We have to go back to Dungeon Rock, don't we?"

The words have barely escaped his mouth before someone knocks on the door.

XXIII.

CAS

As the knock echoes in their hotel room, Cas, Remy, and Finn stare at each other in open-mouthed silence.

The person outside knocks again, a little harder. Cas's manners get the better of him.

"Yes?" he says. Remy shoots him an agitated look.

"Sorry to bother you," a young voice calls through the door. Cas thinks it's the maid who brought him breakfast this morning. "Your visitors have arrived a bit early. Shall I have them wait in the sitting room, or would you like me to escort them upstairs?"

Visitors? Remy mouths at Cas. She still looks agitated, as if she thinks Cas might have actually invited company.

"Visitors?" Cas asks the maid.

"The two gentlemen. I apologize; I didn't catch their names."

At the word "gentlemen," Finn has already started to her feet. She seems steadier now, though she's still worryingly pale. Remy shuts her journal and reaches for her carpetbag. Cas tries to gather the crumpled papers still littering the floor.

"We'll . . . we'll be down in a few minutes," he says, even as Remy waves at him to stop talking. If they were followed from the church . . . or if the Order asked the clerk in the lobby if he'd seen three people fitting Cas's, Remy's, and Finn's descriptions . . .

Through the door, the maid lets out a surprised sound. "Pardon me, sirs. They'll be down shortly. I didn't realize you'd—"

Cas gives up on clearing the papers. The men looking for them are not waiting in the sitting room downstairs. Cas never really intended to use the escape route he'd charted earlier—but there isn't time to think about it now. He makes for the window. When he slides it open and scrambles out onto the roof, Remy and Finn follow without a word.

The slope of the roof is much steeper than it had looked from inside. Cas's boots slide on the shingles as he crawls to the brick chimney at the edge.

Remy's voice is a hiss. "We can't climb down this!"

"Would you rather stay put and have a chat with the Order?" Cas shoots back. "Or maybe we should just set the hotel on fire."

Finn makes a huffing sound and slips past him. She wiggles her foot into a gap between the bricks.

As it turns out, they *can* climb down it.

Their days at sea have served them well; Cas doesn't think he'd have had the nerve to scale two stories of sheer brickwork if he hadn't already practiced scaling the *Mori*'s rigging. Or maybe he would have found the nerve when it came down to it. Once they've all reached the sidewalk, scraped but still standing, they run for the next corner. All Cas can do is hope they've escaped from sight before the Order members in their room realize they made a break for it.

Night has fallen, at least. A boy on the next street is lighting the lamps one by one. Cas's stolen coat and hat are back in their abandoned room. But if they encounter the Order out here, his half-hearted disguise would hardly save him.

“Where are we going?” he gasps. If he never has to run for his life through this city again, he’ll be happy.

“Rail depot, I think,” Remy says. “The last train won’t have left yet. That’s the quickest way back to Windover.”

Right. Because they’re going back to Windover.

Cas is half waiting for the Order to catch them as Remy leads them through the darkened streets to the station. He’s half waiting for the Order as they purchase their tickets and lurk on the platform. A sick part of him almost *hopes* they’ll be caught. If they’re caught, at least they don’t have to go home.

When the train arrives, he digs his fingernails into his palms and follows Remy and Finn aboard.

If Smith really does plan to become a new Death, it’s more urgent than ever that the *actual* Death come back into play. This is bigger than just saving Finn from her demon—though that’s weighing on Cas’s mind, too. He can’t quite believe that she and Remy faced the demon this very evening at the church. He can’t quite believe they got away.

But they need Death to stop the Order of Lazarus, too, before Smith breaks some balance in the world that can’t be unbroken. What Smith intends—enacting his own sort of arbitrary justice by culling those he deems unworthy . . . Cas is going to be sick if he thinks too hard about it. He’s sick over it already.

So yes—they need to talk to Death. And after days of useless attempts at meditation, Cas finally has a real plan on how to do that.

He wishes that plan were taking them anywhere else.

As the train screeches away from the station, Remy brings out her journal again. She opens it to the list she started back at the hotel and now starts recording everything she remembers about

Dungeon Rock and the pirate Thomas Veal. Cas peers over her shoulder to watch her write; it's a welcome distraction. He wonders if Remy is trying to distract herself, too.

"It's a strange coincidence, isn't it?" Remy says. "Our whole lives, we were a mile away from this place—long before we knew about Death, or the Veil . . ."

"It probably *isn't* a coincidence," Cas says.

Remy stops writing. "How so?"

"I mean, our houses are on the same street," he says, putting the theory together even as he speaks. "Right on the edge of the woods. First your father becomes a reaper's glass, and then me?"

The odds of that have always struck Cas as curious. Though even Smith hadn't seemed to understand much about how a reaper's glass was chosen.

"It actually makes sense now, though, doesn't it?" Cas says. "If Death is tied to the rock. We were just nearby."

Remy makes a humming sound. "It can't *only* be about proximity, though. There must be other factors, too. When my father . . . died . . . when the visions passed to you . . . you weren't the only person living on that street."

The weight in her voice isn't sadness, exactly. Cas isn't sure what to call it. He isn't sure he's heard Remy say aloud, until this moment, that her father is dead, even though she's known it since Eden.

Cas is so tired. He's tired of fighting with her. He leans his forehead against the cool window, so that the train's shaking makes his teeth jostle around in his skull.

"It should've been you," he says quietly. "*You* should've become the reaper's glass. You would've figured out this meditation stuff in a day."

Remy had been noting something else in her journal, but now her pencil goes still. "I don't think I would have, actually," she says. "Maybe I thought that, once, but . . ."

She trails off. Outside the train window, the lights of the city are dropping away. The darkened landscape flashes by in a tableau of forests and fields.

"I haven't been very fair to you," Remy says after a long time. "Or very kind."

Cas's throat feels thick in a way that's embarrassing to acknowledge. "It's fine," he says. "We've all . . . said things."

Finn is lying on the bench opposite them, eyes closed, though Cas suspects she's still awake.

"Well, Finn hasn't," he amends.

Finn cracks open an eye. "I've *thought* things," she says.

It's easy, Cas thinks, for him and Remy to fall back into their old patterns, as if they're still ten years old. It's comforting and infuriating at once. Cas wishes sometimes they could just push onward, as if their childhood feud never happened.

Remy closes her journal and holds it there on her lap.

"I don't really believe I'm smarter than everyone else," she says. "I *wish* I was smarter. And then I'm constantly reminded that I'm not."

Cas can't pretend their childhood feud never happened. They're not the same people they were back then. Maybe that isn't a bad thing.

"You are fairly smart, though," Cas tells her begrudgingly.

Remy pokes him in the shoulder. "You are, too."

Cas snorts. She's only saying it because she feels guilty for their argument earlier, and probably for their several arguments before it.

“I mean that!” Remy insists. “You think of things I don’t. Make connections that never would have occurred to me. There are different ways to be clever.”

Cas has spent most of his life being reminded of his own inadequacies: He’s too impatient, too impulsive. He asks too many questions. He forgets things he’s been taught. His mother dubbed him “willful” and “disobedient,” and sometimes Cas *was* willful and disobedient—but other times, he really did try to do what was asked of him, only he couldn’t quite figure out how. His mother berated him the same, whether he tried or didn’t.

“I don’t blame you for telling Ashworth that Death is missing,” Remy says suddenly. “I don’t think it really mattered. Smith was going to get here one way or another. It isn’t your fault. You know that, right?”

Everything has always been Cas’s fault—or at least his parents told him it was. He feels suddenly wobbly. He hadn’t realized how badly he’d needed to hear that.

Remy is watching him too closely. He is not going to cry.

“Do you think Henry went back home, after we left him at Eden?” Cas asks. “After everything that happened.”

Finn is sitting up now; she’s given up the pretense of sleep. She and Remy seem to be having a private conversation with their eyebrows.

Remy chews on the inside of her cheek. “You said you don’t want us to keep secrets from you, right?” she asks Cas.

Cas did say that. But the fact that she’s asking, now, tells him already.

“We saw Ashworth at the church tonight,” Remy admits. “With Smith. With the Order.”

“Oh.”

Cas turns back to the window so he doesn't have to meet their eyes. He doesn't want to see the pity. Henry's involvement with the Order shouldn't matter to him anymore. Even if Henry had realized the error of his ways, Cas isn't sure their relationship could be salvaged.

It still stings that Henry *hasn't* realized the error of his ways.

Cas's eyes are burning—the press of tears despite his best efforts. He keeps his forehead crushed against the window so the others can't see.

Why do they have to go back to Windover? There's nothing for Cas there. Remy and Finn have family in town, people they're probably eager to see, but Cas can't bear the thought of facing his own parents right now. When all of this is over—even if they survive this—where is Cas going to *go*? He, Remy, and Finn were waiting for the *Mori* in Boston, and now they're not waiting anymore, and Cas can't shake the feeling that this train is carrying them all away from the only bearable future that exists for him.

Maybe it would have been better if he never knew that future was an option. If he'd never gotten to live like this. There was a time when Cas had resigned himself to the life presented to him. He could play the part of Miss Cassandra Sterling well enough to satisfy most people, even if his mother never quite believed the act. It would have been exhausting and depressing. It wouldn't have been a *good* life, exactly.

But it might have been good enough—if he hadn't known there was anything else.

It's so much harder, now that he knows what it feels like to recognize himself in the mirror. To take a breath and feel it truly fill his lungs. To let that comfortable, quiet warmth settle somewhere in his heart. He never realized before how badly he was struggling, until he cut his hair and boarded the *Mori* and *didn't* have to struggle in that way.

For a while, anyway. Not forever. Cas almost wishes he could erase this knowledge from his mind. He could let his hair grow long again, could put on a puffy-sleeved gown and a forced smile. But he can't go back.

He doesn't truly want to erase the knowledge. He doesn't *want* to go back.

But without the *Mori*, he has no idea how to go forward, either.

In the window's reflection, he can see Remy watching him. Reading him. Even after their feud, with years of distance between them, she knows him too well; she's guessed what he's thinking.

"We're still going to find the *Mori*," Remy says. "Death will know where the ship is. When you talk to him—"

"*If*," Cas corrects. He can't help it.

Remy doesn't falter. "*When* you talk to him," she says deliberately, "you can ask him to take a message to the captain. You can set up a rendezvous."

It might be nothing—the fact that she said *you*, not *we*. Cas tries to clear the lump from his throat. "What are you two going to do?" he asks.

Remy turns to study Finn. "I suppose that depends on . . . well, a lot of things. If Death can wipe Finn's name from his list . . . I suppose she'll be free, won't she? And if he knows how to stop Smith from becoming a reaper himself . . . we'll all be free. To do anything we'd like."

"Right," Cas says. He feels hollowed out. He isn't sure what answer he'd wanted from her. But it wasn't that.

At the rail depot in Lynn, they hire a hack instead of taking the public coach line to Windover, where someone might recognize them. Remy has the driver drop them on the edge of town, where they can hike straight into the woods. Cas is grateful for it. He feels more settled walking this familiar path through the trees. His feet still recall this route instinctively, even if he's only returned to the rock once since his falling-out with Remy. It feels right, Cas thinks, to be back here now. All three of them back in the place where they first came together.

Finn has somehow acquired a lantern; Cas wonders if she stole it from someone's porch as he and Remy were climbing out of the carriage. She holds it up to illuminate Dungeon Rock as the silhouette looms into view ahead of them—the same shape Cas spent the whole afternoon mindlessly sketching.

"What do we do now?" Remy asks. What she really means, though, is, *What do* you *do now?*

Cas had hoped he'd somehow know, when faced with this moment. He doesn't know. He approaches the rock carefully. He rests his palm on the cool surface of one of the boulders. Back when the three of them met here the first time, Remy said something about physical touch—that it can be a means of spiritual connection. It was how Cas dragged Henry into his vision on the beach; Henry had been touching his arm when the vision took him.

If this is the place where Death died . . . if Cas is trying to access his own spiritual connection with Death . . .

He's touching the rock, though, and he doesn't feel any different. Cas closes his eyes. He tries to focus. The night has turned chilly again. Remy and Finn are both breathing too loudly. He can *feel* them staring at him, waiting for something momentous to happen.

His closed eyes feel twitchy. He opens them again.

"Anything?" Remy asks.

Cas shakes his head.

He starts pacing. He tries to remember what he felt back in the hotel room, when he was drawing. But that's the problem, isn't it? It hardly felt like anything; the whole afternoon is a blur. He needs to make his brain go quiet, but it's like trying to force himself to fall asleep: The harder he tries, the more his mind resists it. He can't just *will* this into working.

The pacing helps, though. And here, there's no one to pound on the ceiling and shout at him for clomping around.

"Which way is the river?" he asks Remy. Her expression is questioning, and he adds, "That's the direction the pirates came from, right?"

Remy takes a moment to orient herself. "West," she says, gesturing. She and Finn both follow as Cas weaves his way through the trees where she's pointed.

It's difficult to navigate with just one lamp among the three of them. But the moon is out, and Cas's eyes adjust to the darkness. They walk slowly and without talking. Even here, away from Dungeon Rock itself, this path is familiar. Cas and Remy spent years of their childhoods playing among these trees. The Lynn Woods were one of the rare places where Cas used to feel like himself back then, even if he couldn't have described what that meant in so many words.

Here's the little creek where he and Remy used to toss rocks. Somewhere farther through the trees is the pond where Miss Eloise taught them to swim. This is the stretch of trail where they used to race each other. Cas usually won those races, though not always—and yes, here's the tree that always marked their finish line. And this was the strawberry patch. They planted the seeds in the spring, probably too early, and they worried the last frost had killed them off. But the plants sprouted anyway. Later that summer, when they lifted the leaves, they found tiny red berries the size of a thumbnail—

No. Cas stops walking. That isn't right. He's never planted strawberries. He's never planted anything in his entire life.

Yet he can't shake the memory of it. It's like the moment of waking up from a dream, trying to remember how much is real.

"Was there a summer when we grew strawberries here?" he asks Remy.

"Strawberries?" She sounds perplexed by the question. "No. I don't remember ever finding strawberries in these woods."

"Not finding them. *Growing* them. From seeds. Did we ever . . . ?"

Remy's face seems guarded. "No," she says. "We never grew strawberries. Why are you asking that?"

Cas swallows. "Because I have a memory of growing strawberries here."

He feels half awake, his drifting mind conjuring these pieces like truth. They *can't* be true. The rational part of him knows that. But the details are all there when he reaches for them. Dirt under his fingernails. The sweet, slightly tart taste of the berries as they ripened.

"We didn't think they were going to come up," he says. "And then one morning . . ."

He can picture that little burst of red under the leaves so clearly. The moment of discovery. It feels so real.

Maybe it's not that the memory isn't real. Maybe the memory isn't *his.* He's remembering through someone else, from a time long before Cas was born. The world feels blurry. He feels drunk even though he doesn't have a drop of alcohol in him.

Remy is chewing on the inside of her cheek, clearly unsure what to make of this. But Finn says, "What else do you remember?"

Cas starts walking again. *He* isn't sure what to make of this. But the path ahead of him seems straight enough for him to close his eyes for a moment. He lets reality tangle again.

"There were flowers, too," he says. "These little orange-yellow blossoms. Those weren't edible—they weren't useful in the same way as growing food, but they were . . . nice. Homey." He can picture the tiny flowers perfectly, and the name springs to his mind: "*Caltha palustris*."

Remy draws in a sharp breath, and Cas opens his eyes. Ten feet ahead of him, just within the glow of the lantern, is a patch of golden flowers.

It's impossible, and yet Cas knew they'd be there. "You're seeing those," he says. "Right?"

Remy crouches to examine one of the flowers. "How do you know the Latin name for these?"

"I don't know. I just do." Cas has to remind himself to breathe. "I know it sounds mad."

"It does," Finn says. "Keep going."

Cas tries to rack his mind. It's not so different from trying to remember a vision. The details have a sort of shimmer to them, as if some part of Cas knows he's seeing through eyes that aren't his own.

"We—they—were growing their own food," Cas says as the memories snarl together. "It wasn't always safe to go into town, so . . . better to have a garden. And it was peaceful. It felt like purpose. That's what the carvings were, too. I—he—would set them out for the children. He never had children of his own. He wasn't sure he wanted them. But . . . he did want a family."

He *had* a family. The memories are flooding Cas now, but they're all getting mixed up with Cas's own. Standing aboard the *Mori*'s deck, helping Mita and Gabe with the sails. Sipping coffee in the galley with Leo while Nessa regales them both with a story she made up. And then images that don't belong to Cas at all. He's walking through these woods, one arm slung over his friend's shoulder. His brother? His lover? His home. The touch is so comfortable, so right. He would die for this man. Around them, the garden blooms. They've all made this, together. A place to survive, but also do more than survive. A place to be happy.

The memories blur because Cas *knows* these feelings—the warmth of this garden, and the warmth of the crew who welcomed him with a generosity he can barely understand. The warmth of his friends, still walking on either side of him.

It all fits into the legend Remy told them—Cas can see that—and yet the legend was so small. It left out so many things. It left out all the *feeling*. It left out the love.

A high bluff has started to rise just off the side of their path. The trees clear, opening up into a little grotto, painted silver in the moonlight.

"The camp was here," Cas says. "They built a house. And there was a well, too, right around—"

His boot catches something on the ground. He nearly goes sprawling, except that Remy grabs him by the back of his shirt.

"Good lord," she breathes. The old well is filled in now, thankfully, but the ring of weathered stones is still there, half buried in the grass.

Remy stares down at the remnants of the well as Cas regains his balance.

"Good lord," she says again. "I mean, I *knew* that something was happening, but . . . this is real, isn't it? It's all . . . *real*."

"It ended like you said," Cas tells her. Now that they've entered the clearing, a new emotion has descended on him from somewhere outside himself. A heaviness. A sorrow. He doesn't know a word big enough. "They were found out, at the end of the summer. Arrested and killed. He wasn't here when they were taken. He'd gone out for supplies, and when he came back . . . he was alone."

Cas hasn't lived long enough to have known anything like the weight of this despair, compounding over the years. The regret is going to crush him. He wasn't there with them, at the end. He didn't get to say goodbye. He didn't get to comfort them, in their final moments.

His cheek is wet. He wipes his eyes.

Remy is watching Cas intently. "When you say *he* . . ."

"You've pieced that together already, haven't you?" the man says.

It takes Cas's mind a moment to catch up. It takes him a moment to wonder, *What man*? The figure is standing with them in the clearing, tall and pale, with curling brown hair that falls past his shoulders and the slightest stubble of a beard. Was he here just a moment ago? He can't have been. But Cas's mind keeps trying to convince him the man was standing here all along.

"It doesn't seem to matter how many years pass," the man tells Cas, with that deep sadness in his gaze. "I think a part of me's always going to stay trapped in that moment. When I knew I failed them."

Remy and Finn are both staring at the man, too. Which

means this isn't part of the memory. The man crouches to examine something on the ground: more of the tiny golden flowers. *Caltha palustris.* When he runs his fingers over the blooms, they ruffle at his touch. Which means he isn't a ghost, either.

"We didn't plant these," the man says. "Not here, anyway. They must've spread. Nigh on two centuries left unattended, and look, they're thriving all on their own."

His voice is deep, and he speaks with an accent—English, maybe, or Irish. Probably not German. It's a voice that's familiar.

"Are you real?" Cas asks.

The man smiles. His sadness has fallen away. "As real as any of you."

"And you're really . . . here?"

The man plucks one of the golden blossoms from the ground. He stands and holds it out to Cas, evidence that yes, he's really here.

"You're the one who's been poking at me through the Veil," the man says. "You're the glass."

Cas accepts the flower from his hand. "And you're Death."

XXIV.
FINN

Death is definitely Irish, not English.

There's something shockingly casual about him as he stands in the clearing and surveys Cas, Remy, and Finn. Perhaps after two hundred years of existence, it takes more than this moment to stagger him. Finn is feeling plenty staggered. This man is the reaper about whom they've heard so much—there's no other explanation—but she can't quite believe they're truly seeing him, at last, in the flesh.

He isn't studying all three of them now. He's studying Finn.

"I know you," Death tells her. "That demon still hasn't taken you, then? But you're Marked. I can see it on you."

Finn can't speak. She carried the secret of her demon deal for six years without telling another soul. She intended to carry it to her grave. But Death has taken one look at her and seen the truth laid bare.

Remy has stepped forward to stand at Finn's side. Finn could kiss her all over again.

"We need your help," Remy tells Death. Surely she's just as much in awe as the rest of them, but her voice is perfectly even. "You can see for yourself why. Captain Hobbes told us that you wiped the Mark of Death from his soul twenty years ago. We're asking you to do the same for Finn." She reaches for Finn's hand. "Please."

Death eyes their clasped fingers. "He told you that?"

"Yes," Cas joins in. "We've been sailing with him. On the *Memento Mori.*"

"Is that so?" Death's pale, pointed face is cool. "I know everyone in his crew. I don't know you three."

"We . . . haven't been with him very long," Cas admits.

"Clearly." Death's gaze is intense; Finn is glad he's moved it to Cas now instead of her. "I've felt you trying to nudge me."

"Why didn't you answer?" Remy asks.

"I did," Death says. "I'm here, aren't I?"

Remy's grip on Finn's hand has tightened a little. "Why didn't you answer *sooner*?"

"I've been busy. And trying to lie low. I know what the Order of Lazarus is planning. I know they've built a binding vessel for me. I don't know if it could really hold me—but the demons seem to think there's a chance. It's why they've been collecting on all their bargains."

"*All* their bargains?" Finn asks. It's possible this shouldn't be a surprise. She knew she couldn't be the only person whose soul is tied up in a contract with a demon. And Cas suspected Smith had done something to prompt all the demons to collect—not only Marbas. The implications of this hadn't hit her properly until now.

Death has already pushed onward, though. "Never a good sign. You know when everyone goes to the shop at once to buy lamp oil and food before a storm hits? It's like that. Except it takes a pretty massive storm to frighten *demons.*"

"Have the demons collected all the others?" Finn presses. She isn't sure she wants the answer. While she's been waiting to die by a demon's hand, how many others already have?

"Most of them," Death says coolly. "Are you having regrets?

Nearly all of them did in the end, too. Was it worth it—whatever you sold your soul for?"

The question is blunt, but somehow, the way Death says it, it isn't cruel. "Yes," Finn says. "It was worth it."

Remy still hasn't let go of her hand. Her tone is protective as she tells Death, "She saved her brother."

Death's dark eyebrows rise. "All right," he says. "I'll admit that's a new one."

"Will you help us, then?" Remy asks. "We know you can do it. Will you wipe the Mark from her soul?"

Death is quiet for so long that even Finn feels herself fraying under the silence. She's starting to realize this might simply be the leisurely way of someone who isn't mortal—someone whose time isn't limited.

"Let's walk," Death says. "I need to stretch my legs. It's always strange, being back in the material world. And if you know so much, you can tell me what you know about Smith and his plans."

He's shifted back into that casual, almost careless manner. Finn wonders if it's an act—if he's adopted this cavalier tone to hide a more troubling, or troubled, emotion underneath. He strikes her as far more curious about Smith's plans than he's letting on.

There's nothing to do but follow Death as he starts along the trail, then veers off it, picking his way through the brush to start climbing one of the bluffs that shelters the little glen. Finn holds the lantern as high as she can to help the others. Death doesn't seem to need the light.

He doesn't interrupt as Remy recounts, piece by piece, everything they learned earlier this evening about Smith's plan to replace Death and raise his own daughter from the dead.

"Ah," Death says when she's finished. "He's been working for years to find a way to bring her back. All sorts of mad attempts—but this does seem the closest he's gotten."

"Can he do it, then?" Remy asks. "Can a reaper truly bring back someone who's died?"

"I don't know." Death is still striding forward with ease; the three of them have to scramble to keep up. The ground is damp, and Finn keeps slipping on the leaves as the slope grows steeper. "It *shouldn't* be possible. And Smith might do it anyway."

Finn doesn't like the sound of that.

"This is part of what I've been busy with," Death says. "Beyond the Veil. I haven't just been hiding. I've been learning, or trying to, anyway. There are spirits trapped there who know things, if you're willing to take the time to hear them out."

"Spirits, like . . . ghosts?" Cas asks. "Is Smith's daughter there?"

"No," Death says. "I wondered that, too. But she's moved on."

"Moved on to where?"

"I don't know."

Remy stops walking. "What do you mean, you don't know? Isn't that your job? Aren't you meant to shepherd souls through the Veil, or—"

"I don't shepherd them *through the Veil*," Death scoffs, as if this is an absurd conclusion to have drawn, though Finn isn't sure it is. "The souls are already through the Veil. They're dead."

Death sidles between two thorny bushes, then holds back the branches to help the others pass through. He sighs.

"How can I put this simply?" he says. "Beyond the Veil, it's a sort of transition. An in-between."

"Díaz called it a dream space," Finn offers.

Death nods at her. But Remy hums; she clearly finds this explanation inadequate.

"Think of it like a rail depot," Death says. "With trains coming and going. I help the souls of people who've died find their way aboard the right train. I see them off. But I don't go with them."

"So Viola Smith has already gotten on a train?" Cas says.

"It isn't *actually* a train, but . . . fine, yes. You understand the idea."

"But you said there are still spirits trapped there," Remy prompts.

"Right," Death says. "Smith has been tampering with all sorts of things that aren't meant to be tampered with, trying to reverse death. He's killed people. Sacrificed them. Scraped their souls raw in the process."

Cas's eyes are wide. "The ritual murders."

"Now those spirits can't move on," Death says. "That's who I was talking to, beyond the Veil. Understandably, they want Smith stopped, too."

"Because he stole their train tickets!" Cas says. "And now they're stuck at the station!"

Death scrubs a hand over his face, as if he regrets ever offering this metaphor. "It isn't actually a train!"

"If Viola Smith has already gotten on a—if she's already moved on," Remy says, "is it even possible for Smith to bring her back to life? Would *you* be able to do it?"

"I would never try," Death says. "That isn't how it's meant to work."

"Yes, but *could* you? Because Smith certainly thinks you can—or he thinks *he* can if he becomes Death in your place." They've nearly reached the crest of the bluff now, and Remy pauses to catch her breath. "*Can* he become Death, now that you're back?"

"Again," Death says, "no. And he might do it anyway."

His frustration, Finn realizes, isn't with any of them. His *real* frustration is with Smith and the Order. Finn thinks Death is more disturbed by Smith so flagrantly defying the laws of nature than he wants to let on. He's trying not to frighten them. Finn has spent plenty of time on the other side of this sort of deception. The fact that Death himself is working so hard to keep his fears in check makes Finn more frightened than anything.

Death has come to the top of the bluff, and as Finn joins him there with the others, for a breath, she forgets everything else. They've climbed much higher than she realized. The hill drops away down a sudden cliff, and they can see for miles: a perfect view of the bay, the strip of beach near Nahant, and the ocean beyond.

"There it is," Death says quietly, as if greeting an old friend. "The sea."

His unhurried manner is catching; they've spent so much of this evening racing from one spot to the next, but for a moment, they all stand and take in the view.

"This is why you chose this place," Remy says quietly. "Isn't it? Why you made camp in that specific glen. I remember reading about this bluff. You thought you'd be able to see if the navy was coming."

Death doesn't turn his gaze from the distant water. "We *should've* seen," he says. "Perhaps they did, and they just didn't have enough time."

He says it ruefully—the tone of someone who's now had more time than he's known what to do with.

"I don't know how Smith intends to become Death," he says. "It isn't meant to be something you choose. It's . . . a mantle, I think. Passed from one reaper to the next. I can only guess at what the reaper before saw in me. I was out of my mind with grief, after everyone was gone. I was just . . . biding my time."

Finn has spent the last six years biding her time, waiting to die.

"And then the earthquake," Death says. "And then I died. And then I . . . *was* . . . Death. I could see the souls, beyond the Veil, and talk to them. I could comfort them. The way I never got to for my . . ." He pauses, as if trying to decide on a word that's big enough. "Family," he finishes.

"Maybe Smith does still need to capture you," Remy says. "Maybe he thinks he can force you to pass your mantle on to him."

"Well, he's out of luck, then. I couldn't pass this role on to him even if I wanted. I don't know how."

"How did the reaper before you do it?" Remy asks.

Death shakes his head. "I didn't get to ask. Not about that—not about any of this. You know what you need to know when you need it. If I knew how to pass along this mantle and die properly, I would've done it decades ago."

There's something so stark about the admission. Death is looking at Finn now, though she hasn't spoken. Another truth laid bare.

"I thought I could bring comfort to people, at first," Death says. "Perhaps I did. But we're not meant to live forever. It all started to feel meaningless."

It's the opposite of Finn's conundrum—too *much* time instead of too little—and yet she understands the feeling he's describing perfectly.

"And then I met *him.*" Finn knows he's talking about the

captain. "I didn't even know him, really. But . . . listening to him . . . it was the first time I'd felt anything in so long. I saved him on a whim, if I'm being honest. And then I slowly fell in love with him."

He's still staring out at the sea.

"What we're asking of you isn't a whim," Remy says. "We need you to save Finn, the way you saved your partner."

"I can't," Death says.

"You can, though." Remy's impatience is getting the better of her. If Finn's inner will is made of fire, Remy's is made of steel. "You've done it before. You just told us."

"I saved him, yes, from drowning. I brought him to shore." He turns to Finn. "But you're not going to die a natural death. Your soul is bound to a demon. I can't save you from that. I'm sorry."

Cas's face has turned skeptical, though. "That isn't all you did for the captain," Cas says. "You didn't just save him from drowning. You did something else."

Death turns to frown at him, but Cas doesn't falter.

"Because I tried that," Cas goes on. "When I saw people in my visions—I used to try to stop the visions from coming true. I *did* stop them, sometimes. But all of them still died, just in different ways from what I'd seen."

Death looks caught out.

"The list only shows one version of their death, yes," he admits. "Even if you prevent that single moment, they're still Marked."

"But you wiped the Mark from the captain's soul," Remy presses. "You did it once. You can do it again for Finn."

"You can't wipe the Mark from a soul," Death says. He closes his eyes. Bracing himself. "You can transfer it, though."

Finn has a sudden realization. Cas must be realizing it, too.

"So . . . you traded the names on the list," Cas says quietly. "You did exactly what Smith is planning to do."

"I know. I'm not proud of it," Death says. "There's a reason I never told Edward the real cost of what I did. How he was saved."

Cas looks troubled. "Who died in his place?"

"Would it make you feel better if I said it was a terrible man? Someone who hurt people. Someone bad."

Yes, Finn thinks. Obviously, yes. She can tell just by Remy's face that Remy agrees.

But Cas's expression hasn't cleared. "I don't know," he says. "I don't know that it would. Because Smith would say exactly the same thing about us, wouldn't he? And obviously *he* shouldn't get to decide who lives or dies, but . . ."

He lets that hang. Finn thinks, perhaps, that Remy had been right: When Cas became the reaper's glass, it wasn't only because of proximity.

Death rests a hand on Cas's shoulder. "It doesn't make me feel better, either," Death admits.

"I'm not saying you shouldn't have saved the captain," Cas says. "I'm grateful you did. Objectively, the world's a better place because of him."

"And it still wasn't for me to decide." Death takes a long breath. "I'd do it again, though."

Cas nods. "I figured."

Finn wonders if Death wishes he'd told his partner the truth back then—the real cost. She wonders how he's carried the weight of this secret for nearly twenty years. That has a cost, too.

"I'm not going to ask you to transfer my Mark onto someone else," Finn says.

Death studies her. Remy takes Finn's hand. Ever since she

learned about Finn's demon deal—ever since Finn admitted to her that she was going to die—Remy has been working toward this moment. And now this moment has come to nothing. Death can't help them. He can't save Finn from the choice she made six years ago. Finn can't look at Remy; she can't bear to see the weight of the disappointment on her face.

But Death says, "There might be another way."

Finn has a sudden suspicion that Death knows about Marbas and her dreams. That he knows there's something Finn isn't telling him or the others.

Perhaps he just recognizes a fellow secret-keeper.

"How?" Remy says. "What can we do?" The hope in her voice is going to break Finn's heart. But Finn can let this hope nourish her, too. Remy's determination has carried them all this far.

"You're only Marked because a demon holds your soul in a contract," Death tells Finn. "You don't need to transfer the Mark. You just need to get out of your deal."

"What can we *do*, though?" Remy presses.

Remy isn't going to like it. *Finn* doesn't like it. But there's no way around this now.

"I need to summon Marbas," Finn says.

XXV.
REMY

Remy thought her capacity for shock had already been reached this evening. It hasn't. As Finn describes her dreams and the demon's requests to speak with her, Remy wonders if this new revelation will be the one that breaks her. Finn's tone is too flat, too practical for the gravity of this conversation. Remy feels sick with nerves.

It's easier to analyze this discomfort than to let herself feel it, though. Remy isn't sure her stress now is really about Marbas or whatever he might want with Finn. *That* part makes a terrible sort of sense after his appearance at the church: If he'd really wanted to collect on Finn's bargain, he would have. Instead, he helped them both escape from the Order. Clearly he has something else in mind for Finn.

No, the part that's bothering Remy now is the fact that Finn hadn't told her any of this before. Marbas has been urging Finn to summon him for days—and Finn never breathed a word about it. Remy thought the two of them got everything out in the open during their glorious afternoon in the church attic. *She* aired her deepest thoughts and secrets. But apparently Finn had kept some secrets still.

Remy forces herself to focus on the practicalities, not this sudden surge of insecurity that she doesn't know what to do with.

"Is it true," Remy asks Death, "that Marbas can't adopt a human form unless he's been summoned?"

"I suppose," Death says. "These sorts of demons can't offer their bargains unsolicited. If they could, I imagine the demographic of people tied up in their deals would be very different." He's eyeing Finn curiously. "You're not much like Marbas's usual dupes."

Finn bristles. "I wasn't *duped* into anything."

Death doesn't argue with her over that, though Remy senses the age in his eyes as he looks at Finn. Finn was a child when she made her deal. In Death's eyes, she's probably a child still.

"Do you believe he might be willing to negotiate, then?" Remy asks.

Death makes a vague gesture of assent. "You can't trust a demon's intentions. But you can trust their word. They'll use every loophole and technicality in the book, but they won't lie outright." He turns to Finn. "It seems your demon wants something from you. Which means you just might have leverage to get him to amend your contract in a way that's airtight. If a new deal is signed, he'll be bound to it."

Remy is good at technicalities, though. She's still holding Finn's hand, and when Finn meets her gaze, Remy's doubts melt away. They can do this, together.

Remy has one more question for Death, and she isn't sure she'll find a better time to ask it. "When you were beyond the Veil," she says, "with the souls Smith trapped there. Was the previous reaper's glass one of them?"

Finn and Cas both turn to look at her sharply. Remy can't meet their gazes. This evening has brought a whirlwind of emotions, but with this new hope to hold on to, she thinks she can weather the answer.

She sees the answer in Death's eyes even before he says it.

"No," Death says. "He wasn't. He's moved on, as well."

Something inside Remy settles. She isn't relieved. She isn't disappointed. She just . . . is.

Cas has been uncharacteristically quiet through this exchange. Remy thinks his eyes snag as he notices her fingers intertwined with Finn's. Cas shoves his hands in his pockets as Death turns to address him.

"I need to go to the *Mori*. I can't bring you with me," Death says, and Remy doesn't miss how Cas's face falls at that, though he tries to hide it. "But I can take a message." Death's expression is troubled as he adds, "I've been gone much longer than I meant to be. He must be worried."

Remy doesn't have to ask who he means. "He is," she says.

Death's gaze turns distant for a moment, and then he says, "They're approaching Boston Harbor. If I catch him now, he can bring the *Mori* to rendezvous with you on one of the beaches near the mouth of the river. Probably before dawn."

Cas's eyes have lit up, and Death heads off his question before he can even ask it.

"They're all right," Death tells him. "And I'm sure they'll be glad to know *you're* all right. It sounds like the three of you have some business to handle here first. Once you're finished, meet us in the harbor." He offers Cas a smile. "I promise you'll see them again."

A promise from Death is no casual thing. Cas seems as if a weight has been lifted off him.

Then Finn, Remy, and Cas stand alone atop the bluff. Remy didn't see Death vanish; it's as if he was never here. Except he was, and everything is different now.

Finn's hand is still tucked in Remy's. She doesn't let go as they start hiking back through the woods toward town. It's all too much; it's almost a relief for Remy to let her mind be occupied by logistics instead of everything that's happened, and everything that might happen yet.

"So how do we summon a demon?" Cas asks. He runs a hand through his hair. "Not a question I ever thought I'd be asking, but here we are."

"I'll need the spell book," Finn says. "Probably best to use the same one I did before, if we can get it."

She eyes Remy, apologetic, and Remy appreciates that this, at least, isn't a secret anymore. "One of my father's?" Remy asks.

Finn nods. "The *Lemegeton.*"

"I can get it."

If Remy is being honest, she's glad for the excuse. They're walking back toward Windover even at this moment, and Remy knows, on some level, that she needs to speak with her mother. She's holding the carpetbag that contains her father's remains.

Both she and her mother need some sort of closure.

"And we'll need a place to draw the circle," Finn says. "Somewhere indoors. We can't risk the lines being broken by a bit of wind."

"Would there be enough space in my father's study?" Remy asks.

Finn shoots her a sideways look. "Do you really want to summon a demon with your mother and sisters in the house?"

No; Remy does not. They're nearing the edge of the woods now, and Finn lets her hand go at last.

"I think Kieran is back out to sea again," Finn says. "I'll scout

out his apartment, make sure he isn't there. Assuming it's empty, that should be big enough."

"I'll . . . wait here, I guess?" Cas says, like it's a question.

He doesn't look happy about it. Finn considers him, then gives his shoulder a short, reassuring squeeze. "I'll be quick."

Remy feels like a ghost herself as she approaches her family's home.

For eight years, Remy imagined the scene of her father's homecoming. A cool, clear night not unlike this one. A tap on the front door. Her father standing on the porch, scooping Remy into a hug and never letting go.

This is a homecoming, but not the one she wanted. This is Remy fishing the spare key from its hiding place beneath the elderberry bush. When she slips inside, no one runs to greet her. It's late. It's very late.

And she carries what's left of her father in two jars inside her bag.

There are footsteps on the stair landing. Her mother is in her nightclothes, blinking sleep from her eyes as she takes in the intruder.

"Oh," she breathes as she recognizes Remy. "I didn't know you were coming home tonight. I'd have waited up. Did you write?"

The sight of her mother has made something inside Remy seize up. "I didn't write," Remy says. Her mother must hear the weight in her voice, or she sees something in Remy's face. Her brow furrows as she starts down the stairs.

"Is everything all right? What's happened?"

Everything isn't all right. It hasn't been for a long time. Before they set out on this journey, Remy told her mother she was going to spend a few weeks in Boston working as a short-term nanny.

The truth is so much more far-fetched that she doesn't even know where to begin.

Her mother has reached the bottom of the stairs now. She sets down her candle, takes Remy by both her shoulders, and studies her in the flickering light.

"Darling," she says, so gently that Remy wants to cry. "What's the matter?"

"I haven't been honest with you," Remy whispers.

Remy hasn't been honest with her mother for a very long time. In those early days after her father left—after he was killed—it had seemed like the only option. Her mother could barely get out of bed most days. She certainly couldn't care for herself or her daughters. Remy took care of all of them. She handled the household and the finances for years, and she handled the harder truths, as well. She never told her mother about the letter her father sent, or the journal, or the conspiracy he'd gotten tied up in that had prevented him from coming home. How could she tell her frail, broken mother these things? She had no choice.

This is what she believed in the beginning, anyway. But there's always a choice. Remy's mother has changed since then. *Remy* has changed. Eight years into these lies of omission, she's starting to think the lies were easier, but not kinder.

"Come with me upstairs," her mother says. "We'll talk."

The fire in her mother's room is still lit, and Remy lets herself be guided there, onto the bed, where she can lean into her mother's warm embrace in a way she hasn't done for years. When she was a child, she used to fit into these arms very differently. She's missed this, though.

She shows her mother the letter her father sent, just before he died. *My love*, he wrote. *I didn't choose to leave you; this is the first thing you should know. Please tell Remy, Prue, and little Gracie that I didn't choose to leave them, either.*

Remy shows her mother the journal, too. She watches her mother turn the pages and realize just how little she's known of her daughter's life, and her husband's before.

Remy doesn't show her the jars still bundled in her bag. She can spare her mother the sight. But she tells her. She says the words.

They hold each other. They weep.

Remy has been trying to outrun this feeling for so long, and at last she plants her feet in the sand and lets the wave crash over her. Her mother hugs her tightly as Remy shakes and sobs against her. It's possible, Remy thinks, that her mother has known the truth on some level all along. This is only the closing note on a song she's already played.

Remy has been in denial about it for years. She thought she could be the steady one through this conversation. She isn't. But as she breaks apart now, her mother holds the pieces and cradles her until she can breathe again.

Remy breathes. She keeps breathing. She doesn't know how much time has passed.

"I can't stay long," Remy whispers. "Not tonight. But . . . I had to bring him back here. And I'll come back. I swear." Her carpetbag is tucked against her mother's other side. Remy is going to start crying all over again. "I suppose we should bury him, shouldn't we?"

Remy's mother is still holding her. She smooths the curls of Remy's hair, absently working out the tangles the way she did when Remy was young.

"We should," her mother says. "But I don't know if I can bring myself to do it just yet. And . . . I don't know if I can bring myself to leave him *here*."

This isn't something Remy had expected her to say. Remy turns so she can see her mother's face. "What do you mean?"

"I've been wondering, more and more, whether it's worth it for us to stay. And I think the answer is clear now."

Remy stares at her. "You want to leave Windover?"

"Don't you?"

Of course Remy has thought about it. In glimpses. In hopes she'd quickly squash. Windover is a familiar place, but it's never been a particularly comfortable one for her—even before her father was gone. And after he was gone, it became hostile. She's spent every day since trying to prove herself to the people here. Why has she done it? Holding on to the past, probably. She couldn't imagine leaving this town when it was the last place she'd seen her father—her last tie to the life she and her family used to live.

Is this closure? Remy isn't sure that anything has closed. She isn't sure it ever will. But a new door may be opening in front of her anyway—new possibilities for the future.

"I think," her mother says, "that we need a fresh start."

"But the house," Remy says.

"Damn the house."

Has Remy ever heard her mother swear before? Even her mother seems surprised by the words coming out of her mouth. But she doesn't falter.

"We can sell it," she says. "Probably not for much, but for enough to get us started somewhere else. We don't need this sort of space. We never have. Even your father knew it. He used to talk about running off, to somewhere no one knew us, and living in a tiny cottage, and raising you girls. A simple life. That's all he really wanted."

Remy's head is resting on her shoulder still.

"We've all spent too long trying to claw our way back into the good graces of these people who were all too eager to cast us off," her mother says. "I think it's time to move on."

"I think you're right," Remy admits—surprised at herself, and yet not surprised at all.

"You've carried us all for a long time," her mother says into her hair. "And you shouldn't have had to. I'm sorry for that."

"Don't be sorry," Remy says. "I wanted to—"

"I know. I'm sorry and I'm grateful. Both at once."

Remy thinks about how much of her life she's devoted to her family, and her mother, and to trying to convince the world that the DeWindts were good and respectable and deserved to be here. Who was she trying to convince? It was always going to be useless, and it was never going to be enough, and her mother and sisters had never asked her to do any of it. It was a role she took on for herself, pretending it was what they needed.

Maybe it *was* what they needed, once. Maybe it isn't what they need anymore.

XXVI.
CAS

Cas should have stayed on the bluff in the woods, with the view of the harbor where he could watch for the *Mori*. Instead, he paces just within the fringe of the trees, waiting for Finn and Remy to come back. He's too close to Windover—too close to his parents' house. Even from here, he can see his mother's back garden, with its perfectly pruned shrubs and gravel paths. The tidy geometry of the garden feels at odds with the untamed woodland just beyond it.

Cas lurks in the woodland. He watches the lights flickering from a few of the windows at the back of the Sterlings' enormous house. His father is still awake, probably reading in his study. His mother must be in the bedroom upstairs. And the kitchen window is aglow; apparently at least one of the house staff is working even at this late hour.

The door of the kitchen opens. A young woman lugs a bucket of scraps outside. Cas recognizes Penelope, his maid. She has a shawl tugged around her against the night chill.

Cas thinks he's well hidden in the shadows of the trees, but suddenly Penelope drops her bucket with a clatter.

"Excuse me!" she calls as she strides across the garden toward him.

"I'm sorry," Cas says, fumbling backward. "I'm so sorry."

"Excuse me, sir, you cannot—"

But she breaks off as she recognizes Cas, and her eyes go wide. She's about to start apologizing for calling Cas "sir," and he can't possibly tell her that her "sir" made something pleasant flutter in his chest, so he cuts her off.

"Hi, Pen."

"Oh," Penelope says. "Hello."

Her face is impossible to read in the moonlight. She takes in Cas, with his vest and trousers and newly cut hair, and she doesn't apologize after all. Cas is more grateful for this than he can say.

"How are you?" he asks.

Penelope lets out an incredulous laugh. "How am *I*? I'm the same as always. How are *you*? Has your term finished already?"

Cas blinks at her. "Term?"

"At the school. At Miss Hill's School in . . ." But the realization is dawning on her face, just as it's settling like a rock in Cas's stomach. Slowly, Penelope says, "I see. You haven't really been at finishing school, have you?"

"No," Cas says. "Is that what she's been telling everyone?"

Penelope doesn't answer. This silent confirmation hangs in the air.

Cas isn't sure how he hadn't predicted this. It shouldn't even be a surprise. He's been imagining his mother sending out search parties and investigators, doing everything she could to track him down—but why would she? Sending people out looking for him would mean admitting that Cas had run away. And Cas having run away would mean admitting she didn't have control over Cas, and never had. It would mean scandal, and gossip, and a damaged reputation that could jeopardize any future marriage prospects, even with the family's money.

Of course Mrs. Sterling would make up some story to keep Cas's absence under wraps. Of course she'd lie and say she'd sent Cas away to finishing school. She's been threatening him with finishing school for years, though she never followed through; Cas always figured she was too worried about what trouble he might get up to if allowed outside her own careful supervision.

Based on how Cas has spent the last two weeks, she was probably right to worry.

But it's depressing to realize his mother has wallpapered over his absence so neatly. Did she and his father even try to look for him?

"She was a bit strange about it, when she told us," Penelope is saying. "And I did wonder why she wouldn't let me pack any of your things for you. Or see you off on the day you were meant to leave. But you haven't been at Miss Hill's at all, then. I can't say I'm not relieved."

Cas isn't sure what to make of this. "Relieved?"

Penelope leans in, almost conspiratorially. "Lord knows that place has a reputation. Apparently Miss Hill prides herself on breaking the spirits of even the most spirited young . . . people."

Cas is almost certain she'd been about to say "young ladies," and the subtle change of direction nearly sends him to tears.

"Oh," he says.

"And if I'm being honest, I've always rather liked your spirit."

Cas feels incredibly touched by this. For the hundredth time in the past few days, he feels a tightness in his throat suspiciously similar to the feeling of being about to cry. He swallows it down.

"Where have you been, then?" Penelope asks. "If you haven't been at Miss Hill's. Did you run away?"

"It's . . . a long story."

"You're safe, though?" She eyes the half-healed scar on his face.

"Yes," Cas says. "Mostly."

"Are you coming inside? Would you like me to let them know you're—"

"*No.*" Cas is almost startled by his own vehemence. "No, I—that's all right. I don't need to—" He knows he's babbling and he can't stop it. "I mean, they probably don't even want to see me. Do they? Not like . . ."

He doesn't elaborate, but Penelope's gaze flicks to his cut hair, and he suspects she's gotten the gist. She considers.

"Do you want the answer that will make you feel better?" Penelope asks. "Or do you want the truth?"

And that's the answer right there. In the silence, she seems to realize it.

"I'm sorry," Penelope says. "I shouldn't—I mean, I know it's not my place. And I know family can be . . . complicated."

Cas's stomach is twisting uncomfortably. "I don't want to face them," he admits quietly. "I don't think I'm ready to—but it feels cowardly, to just walk away forever."

Penelope raises an eyebrow at him. "You don't have to decide 'forever.' You can just decide for now. *Forever* is a very long time."

It feels obvious when she says it that way. More approachable. Cas doesn't have to know yet whether he's *ever* going to speak to his parents again—whether there's a relationship there worth trying to rebuild. He only has to decide what he wants to do in this moment.

And in this moment, he knows he isn't ready.

Penelope is still eyeing him. "Aren't you cold?" she asks. "Are you really out here without even a jacket?"

“I’m not cold. I’m fine,” Cas says, although he’s started to shiver.

“Wait here. I’ll be right back,” Penelope says. She must realize he’s about to bolt, because she adds, “I won’t tell your mother you’re outside. I’m only going to grab . . . Just *wait here.*”

Cas waits.

A few minutes later, Penelope slips back out through the kitchen door. She’s carrying a bundle of brown fabric. It’s only when she shoves the bundle into his arms that Cas places it: his father’s old hunting jacket. The fabric is worn but still sturdy, made of some sort of heavy, weatherproof cotton, the collar lined with flannel.

“It’s not perfect, but it’s better than nothing,” Penelope says as Cas tugs the jacket on. “The almanac says we’re heading for another cold spell. I’ll not have you dying of exposure out here.”

“You won’t get in trouble for stealing this, will you?” Cas asks her.

“Is it really stealing,” Penelope asks, “if it’s from *your* family, and I’m bringing it to *you*? Besides, they won’t miss it. It’s been stuffed in a storage trunk for longer than I’ve been employed here. When was the last time you saw your father go out shooting?”

Cas huffs a laugh. “I’m not sure I ever have.”

Honestly, it was probably Cas who wore this jacket most recently. He used to borrow it to romp around in the woods with Remy—though he was so small back then that its hem nearly reached his ankles.

Now, the jacket hangs to his knees, just as it’s meant to.

“Thank you,” he says.

“If you need anything else while you’re in town,” Penelope says, “don’t hesitate to come find me. I’m happy to help steal back any of your other belongings. You know which window is mine, right?"

Cas confirms he does. He feels numb at this easy kindness from her. "I can't thank you enough."

"I'm glad you're well," Penelope says, and maybe Cas is imagining it, but he thinks what she's really saying is, *I'm glad you're happy.*

And he is.

A slight figure is hurrying toward them, skirting the edge of the garden from the road.

"You were meant to wait by the path," Finn says in a low voice as she approaches. "The apartment's empty. We can use it for—"

She breaks off abruptly as she realizes Cas is standing not with Remy but with Penelope. Finn's whole body has gone rigid. Her face seems very, very red, though it's difficult to be certain in the moonlight.

"Oh, hello," Penelope says, good-natured as always.

"Right," Cas says. "Pen, this is Finn. Finn—"

"We've met," Finn says flatly.

"We certainly have."

Penelope is giving Finn a strangely expectant look—as if waiting for permission for something. Finn heaves a sigh. Her chin has jutted out, and her breath makes her bangs ruffle up.

"Fine," she tells Penelope. "It's fine. He's . . ." Finn eyes Cas up and down with an evaluating sort of gaze. "Familiar."

Cas is seized all at once with an overwhelming suspicion that the two of them have slept together. "Oh!" he says. "You've . . . *met.*"

"Jesus, Mary, and Joseph. Don't make a thing of it."

"It was years ago now, and we broke it off quickly," Penelope says. "*I* broke it off. I could tell Finn's affections lay with . . . someone else."

She seems more amused than embarrassed by this whole affair, though Finn is definitely blushing now.

"Don't make a thing of it," Finn snaps again, and Cas holds up his hands in a ceasefire gesture.

"I'm not making anything!"

He feels absurdly light, though, as he and Finn wait for Remy on the edge of the woods. True, they're about to try to summon a demon and hope that the demon doesn't murder Finn on sight. But they also have a real plan again. And the *Mori* is probably sailing toward them even now.

Remy takes a long time to meet them, and when she does, her face is puffy and red. She's obviously been crying. Cas thinks that's probably a good sign. She's brought the grimoire as promised, along with chalk and candles.

Kieran Robinson lives in the attic apartment of a boardinghouse on the south side of Windover. The ceilings are low and slanted, but once they've pushed the sparse furniture out of the way, there's plenty of space on the floor. They're all quiet and focused as Remy sets up the candles and Finn shows Cas the summoning circle from the grimoire.

"You know this chalk is going to be hell to clean up," Cas says as he copies the diagrams onto the floorboards.

"We can worry about scrubbing Kieran's floors once we've all made it through this," Finn says.

Cas appreciates she hasn't said, *if we make it through this*, or, worse, You *can worry about scrubbing Kieran's floors.* Her gallows humor is gone. They really might be able to pull this off.

He draws the snake as well as he can to match the book's

image, then marks the triangle off on one side, where the demon will appear. Remy keeps standing back and appraising the candles she's placed, then frowning and moving them a few inches.

"I don't think the details of the ritual really matter," Finn says. "I'm not sure how much they ever did. But now . . . Marbas *wants* to be summoned."

Remy adjusts the final candle and takes a long breath.

"Can we stay with you?" she asks quietly.

Cas really thinks Finn is going to say no. If Remy had asked it differently—if she'd said, *Do you want us to stay with you?*—he thinks Finn *would* have said no.

But she looks between them, and she says, "Please. Please stay."

They stand on either side of her within the summoning circle. The apartment is eerily quiet as Finn reads the Latin recitation from the book.

When the column of smoke appears, it brings with it the same icy cold Cas has felt in every vision of Finn's death. But the shifting creature of smoke doesn't chase her the way Cas has seen; it doesn't plunge a dark tentacle through Finn's chest and snuff out her life. The shadow moves within the triangle's bounds until it forms into the figure of a man.

"*Finally*," Marbas says. "You want to make a new deal, don't you? Let's talk."

XXVII.

REMY

This is a trap. Remy knows it's a trap. They've fought through too many obstacles to reach this point; they've faced too many disappointments. To have the demon himself propose a change to Finn's deal, after everything, feels far too convenient a solution for Remy to trust.

The man who stands before them inside the triangle of chalk looks nothing like the shadowy monster that had appeared back in the Chapel. If Remy hadn't witnessed the transformation herself, she almost wouldn't believe this was Marbas. But the man's eyes have no whites around them, no pupils or irises; they're black, swirling pools—evidence that the creature of smoke is still lurking beneath the facade.

She remembers this *feeling* from the church, too. Kieran's attic apartment was surprisingly cozy, warmed by the rising heat from the stoves of his neighbors below. With the demon's appearance, the room has gone frigidly cold.

Finn hasn't flinched. As Marbas studies her with those pit-like eyes, Remy fights the urge to step forward and put herself between Finn and the demon.

But Finn's voice is shockingly steady as she says, "Why? *Why* are you willing to renegotiate, after all this time?"

"All this time?" the demon echoes. "I forget how impatient

you mortals are. It hasn't really been so long. Do you wish I'd collected on our bargain sooner?"

Now Finn does flinch, as if the demon's casual barb has hit skin. The chill of the room is sinking deep into Remy's bones. *Has* Finn wished this, before? Remy thinks of Finn's words on the beach, the way she'd whispered them like a confession: *I don't want it to be the end.* An admission not only to Remy, but to Finn herself, because it hadn't always been true.

Remy is still learning Finn, piece by piece. She wants to cry. She wants to destroy the demon. She wants to wrap Finn in her arms.

She wants to do whatever's required to make it to the other side of this.

"Let's get to the heart of it," the demon tells Finn. "I'm willing to renegotiate because I believe you might be useful to me. You *have* been useful to me. You broke into the Eden seminary and sent those men scurrying like rats. This very evening, you set fire to a church with John Smith and all his followers inside. I can't pretend I haven't enjoyed it."

"I didn't do any of that for *your* benefit," Finn says sharply.

"Even better. Our aims have naturally aligned. You want to bring an end to the Order of Lazarus? So do I."

For the first time since Marbas appeared, Finn turns away from him. She casts her eyes toward Remy. Finn is keeping her expression deliberately blank, but this isn't her usual neutral glower; it's tinged with something new. Hope, maybe. Remy's heart is in her throat.

"You want to stop Smith and the Order?" Finn says.

"Yes," the demon says simply.

"Why?"

"Does it matter?"

"Yes," Finn says. "Of course it matters. If you're going to use me as your pawn, I want to know what your game is."

"I don't think you understand the role of a pawn," Marbas says coolly.

He tilts his head slightly as he considers her, though. The gesture strikes Remy as deeply inhuman.

"Smith seeks to break the world," the demon says. "I would prefer he didn't. I like the world as it is. Is that enough of a reason for you?"

"That's why you've been watching me?" Finn asks. "Watching *us*. At Eden—on the ship—"

"At Eden, yes. On your ship . . . no. I do have other interests that require my attention."

This takes Remy aback; it cuts straight through the strings of Remy's newest theory. If the demon is telling the truth—and according to Death, the demon must be telling the truth—Marbas *wasn't* the presence Remy felt watching her aboard the *Mori*. She can't dwell on it right now. Maybe Díaz was right after all; maybe Remy's haunting isn't such a literal one.

Remy is well aware that she isn't the driver of this conversation—but Finn has glanced sideways at her again, and it feels like an invitation. Remy clears her throat.

"If you don't want Smith to succeed in his plans," she says, "why did you make a deal with him?"

"I didn't," Marbas says.

"A demon did. Finn saw the summoning circle in Smith's office. We know how he got the location of that ship after it wrecked."

Marbas's sharp face has pinched with disdain. "Demons don't all act in accord. Do humans?"

It feels like a weak defense, but Remy doesn't have a rebuttal. Marbas sniffs.

"Some of my kin believe they'll fare better in this storm if they form the right allegiances," he says. "I'd rather the storm never come to pass."

Cas has been standing stiffly on Finn's other side. Now that Remy has spoken, though, he asks, "Why can't you just kill Smith yourself?"

The demon regards him with indifference. "I have no claim on *his* soul. Without a contract, I cannot intervene so directly."

"Can't?" Cas demands. "Or won't?"

Marbas doesn't answer.

"That's what I thought." Cas's voice betrays his frustration. "You say you want him stopped, but you're too afraid to cross him yourself—in case he comes out on top after all. You want to hedge your bets."

"And what of it?" Marbas says.

"You pretend you're better than the demons who helped Smith," Cas tells him. "But you're too much of a coward to actually stand up to him. You want Finn to do your dirty work, to take all the risk—"

"Her soul is bound to me," Marbas hisses. "If you'd prefer, I can leave the current bargain in place and collect just as—"

"No."

All three of them say it at once. Cas takes a physical step backward, chagrined, though he stays within the confines of the circle on the floor. He clamps his mouth shut. Finn's hands are clenched very tightly into fists at her sides.

Remy reaches out and touches the back of Finn's hand—the same way Finn has taken Remy's arm countless times over the years, to ground her, to pull Remy back when she's about to drift away. Finn's hand is warm, or maybe Remy's fingers are so cold in this icy room that it only feels that way.

Finn straightens her posture a little. She draws a bracing breath.

"What terms are you proposing?" Finn asks the demon.

Marbas is holding a small sheet of paper, crisp and new. Remy didn't see the paper appear. He extends it carefully toward Finn so that she can take it without having to reach over the chalk lines of the triangle drawn on the floor.

As if by reflex, Finn angles the page so that Remy can read it with her. There are far fewer words here than Remy expected—not a new contract, but an amendment to the contract Finn made and signed six years ago.

"I will release my claim on your soul," the demon says, "if you fulfill two simple provisions. First, keep the reaper Thomas Veal at his post. And second, kill the Reverend Smith."

Remy reads the lines over and over again, trying to find the trick. *Kill John Smith, the would-be usurper of Death. Maintain the present Death in his post. When these terms have been met, the previous bargain will be declared void.*

"What does this mean for Kieran?" Remy asks.

The demon's head tilts again. The movement is almost reptilian.

"Right," Finn says. "In the previous bargain, you saved Kieran's life. I obviously don't want that undone."

"Your brother's illness is already cured," Marbas says. "I won't reverse that. Kieran Robinson will be free to continue living his life. As will you."

"We'd prefer to get that in writing," Remy says.

The demon sighs. When Remy looks down at the paper in Finn's hand again, the words have changed: *When these terms have been met, Fionnuala Robinson's soul will be released from all claims upon it.*

"And what exactly do you mean by *kill*?" Remy asks. "You say, *kill John Smith.* Does that mean you expect Finn to murder him directly? What if someone else murders him? Or Smith dies in some other way?"

"That would satisfy me," Marbas says, and he waves a hand. The page now reads, *Finish John Smith, the would-be usurper of Death.* "Consider it a trade: You offered your soul to save your brother. When the Reverend Smith meets his end, I will take his soul in your stead. I'm not typically in the business of accepting souls indirectly—but the scales must balance, and John Smith has traded plenty of souls that aren't his own. He traded someone else's soul for those coordinates you mentioned."

It's new information, but it isn't a shock. Remy thinks of her father and all the others Smith has murdered at Eden. Smith has always been too willing to sacrifice other people for his own ends.

Finn's mouth has pulled into a thin line. She pushes the page into Remy's hands, and Remy reads and rereads it, scrambling to come up with any other technicalities Marbas might exploit. Cas is reading it, too, silently mouthing the words.

Remy doesn't push or plead, much as she wants to. Finn has to make this decision herself. Her gaze flicks from Remy to Cas and back again. The two of them haven't agreed on much for the past few days; now, they're a united front.

When Finn faces Marbas once again, her jaw has set. Remy touches Finn's sleeve again; she lets her hand rest on the wrinkled wool of Finn's sweater. On Finn's other side, Cas does the same.

A burst of warmth cuts through the room's chill. Finn has conjured a flame in the palm of her hand. She touches the paper, and she signs her full name at the bottom of the amended contract.

She doesn't have to pass the page back to the demon. He's already holding it, studying it. He nods once. He folds the paper and tucks it inside his dark jacket.

"It is done," the demon says. "If you fulfill these provisions, you'll never see me again."

"Wait," Finn says suddenly.

There's a ragged edge to her voice. Remy can hear it, though she can also see how Finn is straining to maintain her composure.

"What would have happened, at the church, earlier, if you hadn't stopped me?" Finn asks.

"You would have died," Marbas says.

Without the fire in Finn's hand, the air has turned cold again. An icy dread is forming around Remy's heart.

"*Why* did you stop me?" Finn says. "I could've kept pushing. I might've taken Smith down with me."

"No," Marbas says. "You wouldn't have. It wasn't your moment. If you're going to burn out in a glorious blaze, you must make it count."

Remy doesn't like the way Marbas is scrutinizing Finn. She tightens her grip on Finn's arm.

"I said before that you intrigue me," the demon tells her. "You've been powerless for much of your life. And still, until recently, you've barely even touched the power I unlocked within you. If you were willing to embrace it . . . what might you do?"

With that, the demon is gone.

Finn makes a choking sound and slumps, as if her knees can't hold the weight of her. Remy's heart seizes. She catches Finn and lowers both of them to the floor. For one terrifying moment, she thinks something has gone wrong: Marbas lied to them. Marbas snuffed Finn's life straight out of her as he vanished.

But Finn is crying. Sobs of pure relief. It's a sound Remy has never heard from her before, and for the second time tonight, she lets her own tears spill out. They both kneel there on the floor, shaking, while Remy holds Finn in her arms and Cas leans against them and murmurs, "You did it. You really did it. You found a way out."

Finn has been carrying this burden for longer than Remy even knew. She isn't out of the woods yet—but the path has emerged ahead of her. The clearing is in view, sunlight gleaming through the open trees.

Remy feels like she's drifting in a delirious dream as she clutches Finn more tightly than she ever has before. They curl together, silent and spent, and Finn breathes. She breathes.

A key rattles in the lock of the apartment door.

It happens too quickly for Remy's dazed mind to react. When the door of the little apartment opens, Finn, Remy, and Cas are still huddled on the floor, surrounded by the trappings of a demon-summoning ritual: candles and chalk markings and the snake drawn on the floorboards.

The young man in the doorway freezes with his key still in the lock. As he takes in the scene, his muscular shoulders hunch, and his eyebrows rise so high they nearly disappear under his shock of copper-red hair.

"Jesus, Mary, and Joseph," Kieran Robinson says. "What the hell is this?"

XXVIII.
FINN

Last summer, Finn met with Mary Lassiter at the Lynn Cattle Show, and Remy stumbled upon them while Finn's hands were busy under Mary's blouse. Finn had thought she'd never in her life experience that level of mortification again.

But it's a different sort of horror to have her brother walk in on the tail end of a demon-summoning ritual Finn has performed in his own home. At least her tumble with Mary Lassiter had been self-explanatory. How on earth is Finn meant to explain *this*?

Kieran is still fixed in the doorway, mouth hanging open.

"What are you doing here?" Finn asks, scrambling to her feet.

Kieran's mouth closes. He frowns. "It's my apartment. What are *you* doing here?"

"I thought you'd gone to sea," Finn says.

It doesn't really answer his question, or at least it doesn't answer the question well. Kieran glances down the narrow staircase behind him, probably fretting that their voices might wake his neighbors. Because Kieran is the sort of conscientious person who's always fretting about such things. He shuts the apartment door behind him.

"I signed on with a different ship," Kieran tells her. "I don't sail out for another week."

"But you weren't home. I came to check—"

"I was out!"

"Out *where*? It's nearly two in the morning."

"I don't think I'm the one who has to answer questions right now!" Kieran says, but he's rubbing a hand on the back of his neck—the way he always does when he's embarrassed. A flush is creeping up from under the collar of his jacket. "When I gave you a spare key, I didn't really expect you to just turn up any time you liked. Besides, I thought *you* were in Maine."

"We were," Finn says. "We're back now."

"And in my apartment. And doing . . . whatever *this* is." He gestures at the chalk snake and the demon's triangle on the floor. Two smudgy black spots mar the boards in the triangle's center—shadowy footprints. "Finn, what *is* this?"

Finn doesn't even know where to begin. Just moments ago, she was sobbing on the floor in Remy's arms. Her nose hasn't stopped running from it. She wipes it on her sleeve. Remy is still crouched just behind her, silent, clearly at a loss for how to salvage this situation.

It's Cas who pushes to his feet first. He dusts the chalk from his palms and extends one hand to Kieran, confident and polite, as if this is a perfectly normal occurrence all around.

"I'm not sure we've officially met," Cas says, as Kieran shakes his hand with a dazed expression. "Cas Sterling. I assume you know Remy already. You have a lovely home. I apologize for breaking into it—and for the mess. Remy and I can clean this up if the two of you would like to . . . talk?"

His breezy confidence holds until the last word—but even Cas can't quite pass this off as normal. He's waggling his eyebrows at Finn in a sort of question. Finn does not want to talk.

She has absolutely no idea what she's meant to say to her brother right now.

But Kieran is already starting for the door of his little bedroom, and he tugs Finn by the arm, snot-covered sleeve and all.

"Yes," Kieran says. "Yes, I think we need to do that."

Finn considers shaking herself loose, seizing Remy and Cas, and bolting out of the apartment. She doesn't do it—but she considers it.

Kieran hauls her into the other room. It's a cramped, low-ceilinged space, tucked under the eave of the roof; the slope of it reminds Finn of the *Mori*'s fo'c'sle. A trunk stands open beside the little bed, halfway packed, clothes tossed into it haphazardly. If Finn had bothered to peek in *this* room when she was checking the apartment earlier, she might have realized Kieran hadn't left town yet. Instead, she was a fool, and her inspection was half-hearted, and now she's suffering the consequences.

Kieran shuts the door and turns to face her. Waiting.

"It wasn't what it looked like," Finn tells him.

"I don't even *know* what that looked like," Kieran says. "What's going on?"

Finn can still lie to him. If Kieran had walked in before Marbas vanished, she probably would've been sunk—but she has options now. She can tell Kieran the ritual was a game, or a failed experiment. Some sort of childish nonsense. She racks her mind.

"Why did you really go to Maine?" Kieran asks. "And with . . . ? I mean, I figured you were traveling with Remy, sure. I never in a thousand years would've figured *Cas Sterling*. You failed to mention *that* when you asked if I could get you those sets of men's clothes."

Finn tries to make her voice work. It hardly even matters

what she tells him; she just needs to choose a story and stick to it with enough persistence. Kieran will take some convincing, but Finn has convinced him of plenty of other lies.

Her brother's weakness is that at his heart, he fundamentally doesn't understand that someone can look him dead in the eye and tell a bold-faced falsehood.

"Finn," Kieran says. "Talk to me. Now."

Finn has exploited Kieran's trusting nature too many times before. She doesn't want to lie to him anymore.

She has no idea how to tell him the truth.

Kieran closes his half-packed trunk and sits on top of it. He bows forward, elbows propped on his knees, hands folded as if he's about to pray.

"We don't really talk anymore," Kieran says. "Do we?"

He sounds so suddenly weary that Finn finds her voice at last. "We talk," she says.

"Not *really*, though. You don't, anyway. I ask you a question, and you brush right past it, or you turn it back around on me and think I don't notice. And I tried not to pry, because god knows you're allowed your secrets. And I was so afraid you'd push me away."

Finn realizes, to her horror, that Kieran's eyes have gone glassy and wet.

"But that's happened anyway, hasn't it?" Kieran says.

Finn hasn't meant to push him away. Or perhaps she has—only she hoped he wouldn't notice she was doing it. She's tried so hard not to hurt him.

Kieran asks, "Have I done something wrong?"

"No," Finn says. "No, of course not."

Her own tears are too close to the surface. She sits on the edge of Kieran's mattress. She wrings the corner of his frayed blanket in her hands. She never wanted Kieran to know about the deal she made to save him. For years, she's planned to take that secret to her grave. But she thinks of everything Death told them tonight—about the secret he's kept from his partner for twenty years. She could see how it weighed on him. He's been trudging around for nearly two decades with his pockets loaded up with stones.

"You haven't done anything wrong," she tells her brother. "But I have."

It's time for a confession.

Finn had learned to keep secrets from her brother well before she made the demon deal. But that choice opened up a gulf between them that Finn has never been able to bridge. She's never even tried to. It's strange, she thinks, to grow up as siblings, to be inseparable, and then to find yourselves on such separate paths.

The deal Finn made six years ago is, on its surface, nearly the same as what Smith is trying to do now. Finn knows this. The only real difference is that Finn traded *her own* life to keep Kieran safe; Smith wants to trade other people's.

Perhaps that's a world of difference.

Kieran listens as Finn tells him everything, piece by piece. He takes it in, only interrupting her with a few questions, and Finn is grateful for it. She isn't sure he'll believe her, at first, about the demon, and Death, and Cas's visions of the future. He seems to take it all in stride, though. After all, he was raised on stories of Catholic miracles and Irish fairy folk, too.

The part he seems to struggle to believe is the fact that Finn was going to die in his place.

By the time Finn has finished talking, her own eyes are dry. But Kieran is crying in earnest.

"Why?" he says. "Why would you make that deal?"

Finn isn't sure she can explain something so obvious. "I couldn't let you die."

"But *you* would've instead! How is that any better? How was I meant to live with that?"

"You weren't meant to know."

Kieran is shaking his head, over and over. He drops his face in his hands. His shoulders are shuddering with quiet sobs. Finn wants to pat him on the back, to hug him while he processes this, and she can't bring herself to do it. She's the one who brought this hurt on him.

"It's going to be all right," Finn promises. Perhaps she shouldn't promise it—not when the contract is still outstanding, not when she and Remy and Cas still might fail to meet Marbas's demands—but she can't just sit here and watch him cry. "I can fix it. We've found a way out. That's what we were doing, tonight, with the summoning circle."

Kieran looks up at her sharply. "What do you mean, '*fix it*'?"

"There's something I have to do," Finn says. "And once it's done . . . the demon's going to let me go after all."

Finn can't blame him for looking doubtful. She still hardly believes it herself, even as she clings to it.

"He'll let you live?" Kieran asks.

Finn nods.

"And you won't go to hell?"

This question is more complicated, and Finn isn't sure what to say. Kieran doesn't rush her. He just watches and waits.

Finn can't look at him as she says, "I think I was always going to hell. The demon just would've gotten me there faster."

"Why would you go to hell?" Kieran asks. "Why would you think that?"

They really don't need to have this conversation. Finn is well aware of the rumors that circulate about her in town—about her dalliances with other girls. The rumors aren't wrong, and it's her own fault that they've spread. She hasn't been as careful as she ought to have been, when she's brought girls home, or gone to their homes, or met up with them in tents at the cattle show. She hasn't cared enough about her own life to bother being careful.

So she knows what people in Windover say about her. She doesn't know if *Kieran* has heard what they say.

"Finn," Kieran says. There's an unexpected steel in his voice. "I'm glad you've found a way out of . . . whatever this is. I'm glad the demon will let you go. But . . . this doesn't *fix* everything. You see that, don't you? Cards on the table. Why did you believe you were always going to hell?"

Finn cannot possibly tell him the reason.

"Because you've gone to bed with girls?" Kieran asks.

Apparently Kieran *has* heard. Once again, Finn was happier leaving this question unanswered. Now it's her turn to bury her face in her hands. "Jesus Christ," she says.

"Is that why?" Kieran presses. "I'm not trying to embarrass you, I swear. I'm just trying to understand."

"Yes," Finn says. "No. I don't know."

She's been dreaming about hell since she was a child—since the priest in Knockadine first described it. For nearly as long as she can remember, she's suspected, on some level, it's where she'll end up. It felt simpler, for a while, to blame her demon deal. It's felt simpler to blame what the priest would've called her "unnatural desires."

But she's sensed a badness in her bones far longer than any of that. A shame at the core of her. She can't place where it came from. It's simply always been.

Kieran heard all the same sermons that Finn did, growing up. She isn't quite sure what the difference between them is. Something is different, though, clearly, because Kieran can't understand why Finn would believe this, in the same way he can't understand how a person can blatantly lie. Because Kieran's core isn't shame. Because Kieran is *good*.

"It isn't only that," Finn admits. "Or . . . wasn't. I think it's longer than that. For as long as I can remember . . . I think I knew there was something wrong with me."

"Finn Robinson," Kieran says sharply.

It's the same tone their mother used to use when they were children, when Finn and Kieran were getting into nonsense. Finn still has been too afraid to touch him—but now Kieran pulls her in and hugs her fiercely, squeezing her so tightly she can hardly breathe.

"There is absolutely nothing wrong with you," Kieran says.

Finn doesn't believe him—but a part of her *wants* to believe him, and that's a start. She's never been good at being gentle with herself. She's never been good at accepting love, even as, more and more, she finds herself surrounded by it. She's tried to turn down the invitations, and the invitations keep coming.

She has to fulfill Marbas's terms; she has to fight, to live through this, because she wants more time to bask in this warmth.

Kieran is still hugging her. Finn wriggles away just enough that she can see his face.

"Do you remember that book of yours?" Finn asks him. "The one that got tea all over it. That was me. I was reading it, and I spilled."

Kieran's expression is baffled. "What book? When?"

"When we were children. When you were, I don't know, eleven?"

"Why would I remember that?" Kieran asks, then laughs wetly at the look on Finn's face. "If it'll make you feel better, you can buy me a new one."

Kieran clears his throat and lets her go.

"Cards on the table," he says. "You wanted to know why I was coming home late tonight, right? Well, here it is: I was with Ben Mulligan."

He's scrubbing the back of his neck again.

"Where'd you go with Ben Mulligan at this hour?" Finn asks.

"We were at his house," Kieran tells her. When she doesn't respond, he adds, "In his room."

He's tipping his head in a funny way as if trying to signal something, though Finn can't work out what the message is.

"Doing what?" she asks.

Kieran stares at her. "Screwing!" he says. "Finn, we were screwing."

He says this as if it was absolutely obvious, and perhaps it should've been. Finn's mind has gone perfectly blank. Absurdly, all she can think to say is, "Ben Mulligan is a man!"

"I'm aware!" Kieran says. To her relief, he laughs; Finn's reaction is too irrational to even really sting him. He shakes his head as he adds, "I didn't think you of all people would fuss at me for that."

"I'm not fussing! I'm . . . just trying to wrap my head around it." Finn shakes her head, too. Of all the revelations this night has brought, this is the one that's going to do her in. "How did I not know about this?" she asks.

"I figured you wouldn't want to talk about it!" Kieran says.

"I didn't know there was anything to talk *about*."

How long has it been since the Robinson siblings last talked openly? Have they *ever* talked openly? Or has Finn been so determined to keep her brother away from her own pollution that she's kept him out of her life?

They could have both saved themselves so much loneliness and heartache.

Finn knows she, Remy, and Cas still have a massive undertaking ahead of them. It's a frail thread they're clinging to, trying to save Finn from her fate. But for this moment, she sits with Kieran, and Finn gives voice to all the words that have gone unspoken between them. She tells him everything.

"You're leaving again," Kieran says after Finn has told him about the *Mori* meeting them at the beach.

"I'll come back," Finn says, and she wills it to be true. "I'll try my absolute damnedest to come back."

Kieran stands abruptly. "I'm coming with you. Just let me put together a bag."

Finn stares at him. "You can't."

"'Course I can. I'm not letting you disappear again, am I? And I'm certainly not going to let you do this alone!"

"I'm not alone," Finn says. "Remy and Cas are coming with me. And the crew of the *Memento Mori*."

"And me," Kieran says.

He isn't asking for permission. He's stating it as fact.

Finn wants to keep arguing—but part of her doesn't want

to argue at all. She's missed this. She's missed her brother. She's missed this ease between them. She can't believe she's agreeing to this. Perhaps she *isn't* agreeing to it. But they aren't children anymore. Kieran has been making his own decisions in the world for a long time now, and he's decided this.

"This ship we're meeting," Kieran says as he opens his trunk and starts shuffling through his clothes. "The crew will let me join up, won't they?"

Finn can't help it; she laughs. "Oh, you'll fit right in," she tells him.

XXIX.

CAS

Cas *knew* the chalk wasn't going to clean easily. While he puts away the extra candles and gathers their supplies, Remy sets to work scrubbing at the outline of the snake on Kieran's floorboards. The snake remains stubbornly in place. Remy scrubs harder. The lines scuff a little under her cleaning brush, but they don't fade much.

Cas watches this for a few minutes before he takes pity on her and brings up a bowl of water from the pump outside. He joins Remy on the floor with a washrag. The *Mori* probably hasn't arrived yet, and even if it has, Finn needs time to talk with her brother. They can't leave yet. Together, Cas and Remy swab the wooden boards and the chalk lines start to dissolve.

"You were right about the chalk," Remy says, sweating a little from the effort. "You're welcome to remind me of this moment the next time I doubt you."

"I will," Cas says.

He's too tired for animosity, though. Or too relieved at the turns this night has taken. He isn't sure he truly believed, before now, that there was a way for Finn to survive this.

"This has been one of our wilder nights, hasn't it?" Cas says.

Remy snorts at the understatement. "One of them? You brought Death himself out of hiding to talk to us."

"And you negotiated with a demon." Cas dips his rag into the bowl again and goes back to scouring the snake's tail. "Do you really trust that the demon will let Finn go?"

Remy has surely been asking herself the same question. "Death said the language of the deal is binding," she says. "I don't think we have any other choice *but* to trust him."

"And you really think we can do it? Stop Smith, take down the Order . . ."

"We have to."

So they will. It's as simple as that. Remy wipes the sweat from her brow; her hand leaves a white streak of chalk dust there instead.

"I'm sorry," she says suddenly. "For how I've been acting toward you. I don't think I actually said that earlier, and I should have. I think I've been so focused on finding a way to save her, I couldn't really see anything else."

It isn't the first apology she's given him since they washed ashore, but it's the most sincere. "Can't really blame you," Cas admits. "I think we both lost our heads a bit. I'm sorry I've been a powder keg."

"Honestly, there are times when a powder keg is exactly what's needed," Remy tells him.

They clean in silence for a few minutes. Remy glances toward the closed door, where Finn and Kieran are still talking in the next room. The actual words are too muffled to make out, but Cas can hear the quiet lilt of Finn's voice.

"Can I tell you something?" Remy asks.

Cas nods at her.

"Even if it's . . . well, it isn't *embarrassing*, exactly," she says. "Or maybe it is. And I'm not sure how you're going to take it, and it might change how you think of me—"

Cas's alarm is mounting. "Now you absolutely have to tell me," he says.

Remy sits back on her heels. She's very deliberately avoiding his gaze. "This afternoon, while we were waiting at the church, we . . . that is, Finn and I . . . the two of us . . . kissed."

Cas thinks she's going to continue. He waits, dubious. Remy doesn't say anything. She's running her thumb back and forth across the bristles of her chalk-covered brush.

"And?" Cas says.

"And what?"

"Is that what you wanted to tell me?"

Remy drops the brush into her lap. "Yes," she says. "Yes, that's it."

Cas lets out a breath. Remy's nervousness in the prelude had him bracing for the worst.

"Is that . . . all right?" Remy says.

"Why are you asking *me*?"

She's watching him too closely, trying to parse his reaction. Still trying to guess how he's taking this news. Cas doesn't even know how he's taking it. Mostly, he finds himself unsurprised.

"I mean, I'm still not happy that you went to the church without telling me," he says. "But we already fought about that. And no, this doesn't change how I think of you. This was hardly the first time you and Finn kissed, was it?"

He says it without much thought, but Remy startles, her eyes wide and blinking in the candlelight.

"Was it?" Cas asks.

"Yes!" she says. "Yes, it was the first time we— You thought we'd kissed before?"

"I don't know," Cas says. "I just assumed!" Remy's eyes somehow grow wider. Her face is so red she looks like she might explode. "The two of you are literally always together! It really wasn't a stretch!"

Remy starts back in with her brush, though it's only for show; she's working on a section of floor that doesn't have any chalk on it.

"Well, we hadn't," she says, clearly trying to make this conversation calm and businesslike despite her blushing. "Not until today. And I thought we were . . . I thought everything was . . . I don't know. I'm not sure what to make of it. Finn is difficult to read."

"Have you talked to her?" Cas asks. "About what it meant, or . . . where things stand between you?"

Remy pauses her brushing to give him a deeply disbelieving look.

"You're making a face like that's a ridiculous suggestion, and I don't think it's a ridiculous suggestion," Cas says. "You should just ask her. That's what Henry and I did."

Remy jostles the bowl and sends water slopping all over the floor.

"Wait," she says. "Did you kiss Henry Ashworth?"

Cas shouldn't have to feel defensive about this, but he feels defensive anyway. "Not recently!" he says.

"When?" Remy demands. "Why?"

"Because we were practically engaged! It was . . . two years ago, maybe? We tried it out a few times—kissing, and—and then Henry asked if I enjoyed it, and I said it was fine, but a little boring. So we stopped."

"You told him it was *boring*?" Remy looks as if she's trying very hard not to laugh. "I suppose with Henry Ashworth, it probably would be."

"I don't think it was Henry's fault," Cas says. "I just don't think kissing is for me."

Remy turns to help wipe up the water she spilled. The bit of snake under the puddle scrubs away much more easily than it had with just a damp rag. Maybe this is what they should've been doing all along.

"I mean, it *is* sort of boring, isn't it?" Cas says. "There's the initial novelty, sure, but then that wears off, and then I was thinking about a dozen other things I could be doing instead."

Remy pauses to tuck a stray curl behind her ear, though the hair bounces free again almost immediately. "I suppose it's different for everyone," she says.

Based on her continued flush, Cas suspects *she* didn't find it boring when she was with Finn.

"Do you think you'd enjoy it more if it was with someone you really liked?" Remy asks.

"Maybe." Cas is too tired to put up a front, though. "Probably not," he says. "I've never really understood the appeal, to be honest."

He can't quite believe he's telling her this. It's only Remy, though, and compared with everything else the two of them have been through, this admission feels hardly consequential. Cas is still untangling the pieces: Who he thought he was supposed to be, before. What he thought he was supposed to want. All the rules of the life he thought he had to live. He and Remy have both broken most of those rules by now. What's one more?

He's missed Remy, he realizes. He's missed having someone to talk to like this. Even when he and Henry were close, Cas always finished their conversations with a lingering worry that he'd said too much.

By this point, he's said too much in front of Remy so many times that it can't possibly matter anymore.

"You and Leo seem to get along well," Remy says.

"What's that got to do with anything?"

Remy gives him a pursed-lips, raised-eyebrows look and waits. Cas pretends he doesn't know what the look means. Remy purses her lips more dramatically and raises her eyebrows even higher.

Cas has changed his mind; talking with Remy is terrible. He throws his chalky rag at her.

"Yes, fine, I like Leo a lot, and yes, we get along well, and he let me fall asleep on his leg the other day," he says. "And no, I still don't feel particularly driven to kiss him."

Remy is making a different face now, though it's just as embarrassing as her previous one. "He let you fall asleep on his leg?"

"Yes," Cas says, still defensive for no good reason.

Remy offers the cloth back to him, and Cas snatches it away.

"That's . . . really nice, actually," Remy says.

"Yes," Cas grumbles. "It was nice. Leo's nice. Aren't we supposed to be talking about *you*? You're the one who started this."

"I did," Remy says, sounding a little dazed. Maybe she can't quite believe they're talking about this, either.

Cas pours a bit more water on the floor. The chalk lines haven't completely disappeared, but they've turned ghostlike; Cas can only really see them if he's actively looking for them. Marbas's shoes have left black, smudgy footprints on the floorboards. Cas suspects their bowl of water won't be enough to clean *those* up.

“Thank you for telling me,” Cas says. “And I’m happy for you. Really.”

Something else is eating at Cas, even as he tries to ignore it. Remy has set down her brush again. She must hear in his tone that he’s winding up to a *but.*

Cas can’t look at her. He weighs each word carefully as he says, “I don’t want to feel like I’m the third wheel on a two-wheeled cart.”

It’s humiliating to admit. It also has to be said. This is why they shouldn’t have conversations at two in the morning.

Or maybe it’s exactly why they *should* have conversations at two in the morning.

“That’s a three-wheeled cart, though,” Remy says.

Cas blinks at her. “What?”

“What you’re describing. If the cart has three wheels, then by definition, it’s a three-wheeled cart.”

Cas doesn’t know whether to laugh or roll his eyes. He drops his washrag in the bowl instead. “You know what I mean.”

“I do,” Remy tells him. “I do know what you mean. And I’m sorry that we’ve made you feel that way. I don’t *want* you to feel that way.” Her face is utterly sincere as she says, “I’m really glad you’re here.”

This shouldn’t be enough to set Cas crying, but the tears are burning behind his eyes again. For the first time in days, though, he feels something inside him—that off-balance weight, the shifted ballast—settle back into place. A new center of gravity.

“A three-wheeled cart is a much better design, if you think about it,” Remy says. “It’s more stable. And it’s better for maneuvering around corners—”

The door of the little side room opens before Cas can throw

his cloth at her again. Finn emerges, her face splotchy and red. From behind her, there's a clamor of objects being tossed around quickly.

"Kieran's coming with us," Finn says without prelude. "Is that all right?"

Remy is staring at her wide-eyed. "Are *you* all right with it?"

"No," Finn says. "But I warned him about the risks, and he insists on coming anyway, and I'm not sure I have a leg to stand on to tell him no."

"And does he . . . know about . . . ?" Cas isn't even sure which part to ask about. Kieran is shuffling around in the room behind her, but he can probably still hear their conversation.

"He knows everything," Finn says.

That's a relief, at least. Cas isn't sure he could manage being cagey about Death or the demon or anything they're planning to do once they meet back up with the *Mori*. He wonders if Finn's brother is a bit of a madman, to have his sister dump everything about this world of magic onto him at once and then insist on coming along.

It's so wild that Cas almost laughs. Maybe he's delirious.

Kieran appears at Finn's side with a bag tossed over his shoulder. He's obviously been crying, too. His face is splotchy in precisely the same places Finn's is; they really do look a lot alike.

"What've you two been talking about?" Finn asks, clearly trying to change the topic.

"Kissing," Cas tells her.

Remy lets out a strangled squawk.

"I didn't say *who* you've been kissing!" Cas points out, while Remy dives at him and Finn becomes interested in anything but her brother's reaction. Remy gets a hand clapped over Cas's mouth.

"Well, Cas kissed Henry Ashworth," Remy announces. Cas tries, and fails, to bite her.

"Oh, Ashworth?" Kieran says. "I just bumped into him on the Common tonight."

For at least a second, Cas could swear his heart has stopped pumping. The very air in the room seems to freeze. Cas and Remy have upended the bowl again in their tussle, and the last of the water seeps slowly across the floorboards. All three of them are staring at Kieran.

"What did you just say?" Finn asks.

Kieran's offhand demeanor is faltering under their shocked gazes. "Henry Ashworth," he says. "I saw him when I was walking home."

"Tonight?"

"Yes! Why, what's the matter?"

Cas sits beside the empty water bowl. He feels like he's listening to this conversation from the bottom of a well. Distantly, he's aware of Remy and Finn both pressing Kieran to confirm that yes, it was Henry Ashworth, and yes, he was in Windover, and yes, this happened approximately thirty minutes ago, and yes, Kieran is absolutely certain it was Henry Ashworth.

"What's the matter?" Kieran asks again. "Have you been looking for him?"

They were, once. Cas went to the Eden seminary looking for Henry, and then Henry stayed with Smith, even after he saw everything Smith was capable of and everything he intended. Remy and Finn are still talking, speculating about how Henry can be *here*, in Windover, tonight, after he was just at the Order gathering in Boston this evening.

"Was he with anyone?" Remy asks Kieran. "Or was he alone?"

"I think he was with a few other men?" Kieran says. "I didn't know them, though."

"Gentlemen?" Remy presses, and Kieran nods.

"Did the Order follow us *again*?" Finn says.

"They must have. How else could they know we were coming to Windover?"

But a thought has occurred to Cas. "The drawings," he says. "At the hotel."

Remy's face falls as she realizes. "You think Ashworth recognized Dungeon Rock?"

"Or Dekker did. Or both of them."

Cas can't think. He can't process any of this. Remy puts a hand on his shoulder as if trying to keep his mind from drifting away.

"It doesn't matter," Remy says. "What matters is that we need to get out of town. We need to meet the *Mori* on the beach. We can only hope that if Smith or his men are in Windover, they came by train, too. Or coach. If they came by sea . . ."

She doesn't have to finish the sentence. If the Order came by ship, the *Mori* might be cut off before ever reaching the beach where they're supposed to rendezvous.

"How do we get out of town without being seen?" Finn asks.

Remy is clearly struggling to come up with an answer. "I don't suppose you have an enclosed wagon sitting around?" she asks Kieran.

It's a sarcastic question borne of desperation. But Cas's mind is racing. The Sterling family has an enclosed carriage. They have *several* enclosed carriages—more than Cas's parents even really use. Cas thinks of the offer Penelope made when they talked in his parents' back garden.

"I think I know someone who can help," he says.

Cas sends Kieran with a note, and with detailed instructions about which window to tap on so he can talk to Penelope without waking the rest of the Sterling household. Finn seems reluctant for Kieran to go on this errand alone, but they don't have any other choice; of the four of them, only Kieran can avoid notice if he encounters Henry again, or anyone else connected with the Order who might be prowling around Windover. Cas would much rather do anything besides wait, *again*, stuck and hiding from the Order just like he did at the hotel. At least he isn't alone this time.

Cas, Remy, and Finn clean what chalk they can from the floorboards while they wait. When Kieran returns, they meet him down on the street and duck inside the Sterlings' humblest single-horse carriage.

Cas feels like time has snagged, past and present all caught in a tangle. He's back in Windover, riding in one of the Sterlings' vehicles, toward the very beach where he first witnessed Finn's death and accidentally dragged Henry into his vision. And Henry is back here, too, somewhere in this darkened town. Cas keeps the curtains drawn over the carriage's windows, blocking out the view of the too-familiar streets.

As Kieran nudges the horse into motion outside, Finn leans against Remy and lets her head droop onto her shoulder. Her eyes are closed. Cas catches Remy's gaze and gives a small smile as Remy wraps an arm around Finn's slumped shoulders.

Cas leans back on his own bench and props his boots on the seat.

"I'll be happy if I never have to come back here again," he says.

Remy makes a humming sound. "It's been a few hours since Death left us on the bluff," she says. "The *Mori* might be waiting for us in the harbor by now."

"Thank god. Can't say I'm looking forward to the seasickness, but I'm looking forward to everything else."

Remy is watching him closely. "Where do you think you'll go, when we're through with all this?"

"I'll stay with the *Mori*," Cas says. "Obviously."

"Why is that obvious? You were just complaining about being seasick."

"Well, sure, but . . . where else is there?"

Finn sits up now, eyes opening. Remy is still staring at him.

"What do you mean, *where else is there*?" Remy says. "Anywhere."

"Not for *me*, though."

Maybe it's different for Remy and Finn; Cas isn't sure. Maybe his friends can manage coming back to Windover and living as they wish in secret. Cas is exhausted by the very idea. He can't go back to the life he would've had here. And he can't spend the rest of his life on alert, bracing before every interaction. Worrying over how every stranger on the street might perceive him. Moderating his movements and the pitch of his voice. It isn't an *act* in the same way—but it still feels like a performance of a different sort.

"Cas," Remy says. "Do you actually *want* to live aboard a ship year-round?"

"No." Cas is surprised by how easily this answer comes out of him. "But I want to be with Mita, and Leo, and Gabe, and . . . *everyone*. And *they* all live aboard a ship."

"And they're not setting off on three-year whaling voyages to the Pacific," Remy says. "They're sailing up and down the coast. They come to shore all the time. You could still *see* them even if you didn't stay aboard the *Mori*."

"Where would I go, though?" Cas tugs on his waistcoat—the binding vest Mita and Leo sewed for him. "Who else is going to . . . you know . . . understand?"

Remy purses her lips. "Do you really believe they're the only ones?" she asks. "We stumbled onto the *Mori* practically by accident. Even by simple probability, I find it unlikely that crew has the only people on earth who would *understand*."

Cas starts to argue with her—but his mind flits to Penelope, who took in his new haircut and clothes this very evening and didn't even question him. He thinks of the two lighthouse keepers on Cape Cod, Spencer and Ambrose.

"They're definitely not the only ones," Finn says.

The wheels of the carriage rattle on the road, dipping in and out of the well-worn ruts in the dirt. Cas's head feels scrambled.

"I'm not coming back to Windover," he says.

"Of course not," Remy says. "We'll find another place to live. Or we'll make a place, if it comes to that."

Remy must see the absolute shock on his face at that "we."

"I'm not coming back to Windover, either," she says. "Not permanently. I don't think I realized it until I talked with my mother—or maybe I just didn't want to admit it to myself. I'll come back to help her pack up and sell the house. But now that we've seen so much else . . . this town just seems so *small*, doesn't it?"

She isn't talking about the square mileage. The world is so much vaster, and the people in it more varied, than Cas understood even a month ago.

As Finn squeezes Remy's hand, her mouth tips into the slightest smile.

"I'm not coming back here, either," Finn says.

"Right," Remy says. "So where should we all go?"

Cas has been thinking of it as a choice between two options: go back home, or go with the *Mori*. He can't quite wrap his mind around this.

"The *Memento Mori* didn't spring up out of nowhere," Remy says. "Captain Hobbes built that ship into the home it is—and Mita, and Striker, and all of them. We can make a place, too. It doesn't have to be a ship."

"We could grow a garden," Finn says, and Cas wonders if she, too, is thinking of Death's grotto in the woods. "Or a farm."

Remy is nodding. "Somewhere along the shore. Along the *Mori*'s sailing route. A cottage by the sea."

Cas thinks of Spencer and Ambrose, bustling around their little kitchen on Cape Cod. "Or a lighthouse?" he says.

Remy smiles. "Exactly. We'll build the lives we want to have. Starting with the three of us. Cas . . ."

She switches benches to clamber over beside him, and Finn crushes in on his other side, even though the seat isn't really wide enough.

"We're not going to leave you behind," Remy says, and she squeezes him tight.

Cas lets himself cry until the carriage rolls to a stop on the beach. Then he wipes his eyes and tries to pull himself together. But when he throws open the door, the sight of Mita, Leo, Striker, and Gabe standing by the longboat sets him off again. And then Leo is running toward him, waving and grinning, and Mita pulls

Cas in and kisses him on the top of the head, and it's fine that he's crying. He doesn't even care. Everything is a tearful, joyful blur.

"Kit *thought* she saw Remy take off in the jolly boat," Leo says as Finn introduces Kieran to the others. "That night, during the storm. So we *hoped* you were alive. But we didn't really know anything until Death showed up on the deck tonight and said he'd spoken with you—"

"Leo's been out of his mind with worry over you all," Gabe says, giving Cas's hair an affectionate tousle.

"Of course I was! I'm glad they're all right!" Leo offers Cas a clean handkerchief. "I'm glad you're all right."

"We all are," Mita says.

Out in the deeper water of the harbor the *Mori* stands at anchor, furled sails stark against the night sky. A man is grinning at them from the prow—Death himself, standing above the skeletal figurehead he carved.

Remy explains as quickly as she can about Henry and the Order in Windover. A few other small boats are tied off along this stretch of beach, but no ships are in sight besides the *Mori*. Between the rocks and low cliffs that flank the harbor, Cas has a wide view out to the open sea. Hopefully the other boats here are from locals; hopefully Henry and his companions arrived in Windover by train or coach.

They all climb into the longboat and start rowing toward the *Mori*. If they can just make it back to the ship, and if the *Mori* can make it to open water, they'll regroup and decide how to track Smith and stop his plans, now that Death has returned. As the *Mori* comes into clearer view, Cas can see that the lightning-struck mast has been repaired.

"I'm glad *you're* all right, after that storm," he tells Mita.

"It was close," she admits. "Fortunately, Gabe made the brilliant call to toss that piece of monumental brass overboard. After that, we were able to ride out the storm. It took me time to jury-rig the mast, though."

"And you got the ship balanced again," Cas says. It isn't really a question; he can see that the *Mori* is. "So the ballast settled back into place?"

"Of course," Mita says. "We just had to rake it a bit, once the winds were calmer."

Remy is sitting on Cas's other side, and she reaches over to squeeze his hand. Cas's heart feels full. He thinks they might just make it through this.

When they clamber aboard the *Mori* again, it's a flurry of movement as they all rush to set sails. Kieran falls in effortlessly with the crew; his experience at sea shows. Cas takes up his post with Mita at the foresail brace. Death joins Captain Hobbes and Kit on the quarterdeck. The reunion is abridged; there isn't time to stop and exchange the proper hellos just yet.

Cas isn't sure where they'll head next. It's possible even Captain Hobbes isn't certain. But they'll have more options once they're out of the harbor and sailing into open waters.

They don't make it out of the harbor.

Cas and Mita have only just set the foresail when Mita swears. Cas scans the horizon, and he understands why.

Another ship has rounded the low cliffs at the end of the peninsula—cutting off the *Mori*'s route to the sea. The ship is larger than the *Mori*; even Cas can tell that much. He never actually laid eyes on the *White Swallow* when he searched the docks in Boston—but he'd wager nearly anything he's laying eyes on her now.

The Order has found them.

Cas feels oddly resigned as he watches the ship approach. The sailors around him have fallen silent. Kit's and Captain Hobbes's voices carry from the quarterdeck.

"They've run up signal flags," Kit says. The guidebook is already open in her hand. "They're requesting to send over a boarding party to negotiate."

Just as the *Clara Smith* signaled at Georges Bank. It isn't really a request, though—just as the Order member's polite invitation to Cas outside the Boston customhouse wasn't really a request. At Cas's side, Finn has tensed. Remy steps up beside her and threads their fingers together, jaw set as she waits for orders.

"We can outrun them," Captain Hobbes says. "Drop every sail, and tack to larboard. Make for the opening. They're going to try to cut us off, but we've got the wind. They can't touch us."

As Mita passes him the lines, a terrible thought surfaces in Cas's mind. Something Hernandez said back at the faro table. *If I'd wanted to sail on a gunship, I'd have joined the navy.*

Captain Hobbes thinks the *White Swallow* is a typical merchant vessel.

"Wait," Cas shouts. "They've got cannons—"

He's too late; the *White Swallow*'s crew has realized the *Mori* intends to flee. There's a *boom* from across the harbor. A puff of smoke. A whizzing sound, and then the crack of wood.

The first cannonball hits the jury-rigged mast.

XXX.

REMY

The mast splinters like a stick snapped over a knee. Remy watches the upper sails teeter and fall with the dazed sensation of time looping back on itself: They've been here before. But this is so much worse than the storm off Cape Cod—not a random act of nature, not the crossfire of some curse. This is a direct attack, premeditated and deliberate. And the *White Swallow* has cut them right over the recent scar. All of Mita's engineering, all of the crew's hard work, undone in a second by a single cannon shot.

The top half of the mainmast lands with a crash. The deck pitches. But Remy is braced for it this time, and she's still on her feet. She, Finn, and Cas all rush into the fray with the other sailors. At Mita's direction, they cut through the tangled lines and bundle the slack sailcloth out of the way. Remy's nerves are scraped raw, but the knife is steady in her hand.

"Was that a warning shot?" Remy asks.

"I don't think you call it a warning shot when it takes out the mast," Gabe says. "That was an attack."

"They're running up another message," someone calls.

A second line of flags is rising above the *White Swallow*'s deck. Again, Remy is rocked by the repetition of this moment, so similar to the *Clara Smith* hailing them on approach. But the captain had a plan back then. An escape route. Now, they're trapped in the harbor, with a foremast that's twice shattered, and the *White Swallow* angling to intercept them. The captain's plan to outrun them might have worked if the *Swallow* was unarmed.

They won't make it far if they try to run now.

Captain Hobbes stands on the quarterdeck, steady as always, but his shoulders are tense. Remy edges closer to his post, Finn trailing behind her. Kit relays the meaning of the signal flags word by word as she flips through the Marryat:

"Give . . . him . . . up," Kit says.

Remy feels very cold. "Give *who* up?" she asks, looking to her friends. "Cas? The reaper's glass?"

Cas has followed her toward the quarterdeck, too, his face pale. But he shakes his head. Across the expanse of water, the men aboard the *White Swallow* have hoisted something onto the main deck. Remy catches a glint of metal. Gold-tinted, but not gold.

Smith's creation—the casket made of cursed brass—is being loaded onto a boat.

"If it was me they wanted, they wouldn't say *him*," Cas says quietly. He's spied the casket, too. "They know we have Death."

Remy is still braced for another cannonball, but the *White Swallow* doesn't fire again. Not yet, anyway. Kieran, Gabe, and the other sailors finish pushing the bulk of the splintered mast over the rail, and the ship rocks, rebalancing. Remy knows she ought to report back to her post near the bow, but she stays where she is, waiting while the captain and his partner debate.

"No," Captain Hobbes says, in a tone that leaves no room to argue. "You're not giving yourself up."

"It's not my preferred option, I'll admit," Death says.

"It's not an option at all."

The *White Swallow* has apparently lost patience with their delay; another *boom* echoes across the harbor.

"*Hit the deck!*" Striker shouts, and Remy drops to her knees, Finn at her side. The *Mori* lurches as the cannonball hits with the ruinous cracking of wood.

But when Remy dares to raise her head and look around the deck, she can't find the damage. She catches a brief glimpse of Cas huddled by the rail with Leo. They both appear unharmed.

Kit sprints toward the hatch belowdecks. "Goddammit. God*dammit*. We need to patch the hull! Starboard watch, get below, *now*!"

A horrible realization settles in: Remy can't see the damage on the main deck because the shot was lower, through the *Mori*'s hull. The ship must be taking on water.

The Order is going to sink them. Or at least Smith is proving that he *can* sink them, if they don't give him what he wants. Not a warning, but a show of power.

The sailors on Kit's watch are running belowdecks after her. Kieran goes with them, but Finn, Remy, and Cas all stay put. Finn's grip is tight on Remy's arm, her eyes wide and frightened. Her hair has come loose from where she'd tied it back; it swirls around her like a veil of fire. A few strands are stuck to her lip. Remy resists brushing them off, and then realizes there's no reason not to. She reaches out and tucks Finn's stray hair behind her ear.

"We haven't gotten to talk," Remy says suddenly.

Finn stares at her. "What?"

"After the church, after—everything—we haven't talked. About where we stand."

"You want to do this *now*?" Finn says.

Remy doesn't want to do this now, but she wants to do it

sometime, and she's terrified they won't have another moment. They don't even really have *this* moment. Captain Hobbes and Death are locked in a heated discussion on the quarterdeck.

"I'm not going to stand by while he blows your ship to pieces," Death says. "Signal that we'll negotiate. I'll agree to go with him."

"No," Captain Hobbes says.

"What's the worst he can do to me? Kill me?"

The captain's face is grim. "Don't joke about that."

"I'm not joking. He can lock me in a box, but he can't do anything more. Meanwhile, he *could* kill every other person aboard this ship."

Remy's heart is pounding as she holds Finn's gaze.

"We'll talk," Finn promises. "When we make it through this, we'll talk as much as you'd like."

Remy was determined already, but this solidifies her resolve. They're all going to make it through this. They have to.

"If you give yourself up, what then?" the captain asks his partner, his tone sharp. "Smith isn't going to *negotiate*. Not in good faith."

"Perhaps not, but it'll buy you time."

Striker is at the rail, a spyglass pressed to her eye. "They're reloading the cannons," she calls back to the captain.

Captain Hobbes's jaw is clenched tight. His fingers are twitching ever so slightly, as if he's running calculations in his mind, playing through chess moves and countermoves.

For once, Remy is glad she isn't the person who has to make this decision.

"Run up a white flag," Captain Hobbes says, and Striker and Gabe both rush to follow the order. The captain turns to his partner. "You're not giving yourself up," he says firmly. "But you're right. We need time."

Gabe and Striker get the flag raised before the *White Swallow* fires again. The crew of the distant ship is working to lower a boat, the brass casket propped in the center of it. Remy thinks she recognizes Reverend John Smith climbing aboard to sit at the stern.

There's a shout from the rail on the other side, and Finn tugs Remy with her to see. A second boat is approaching from the beach. Remy watches one of the boats that had been tied off in the sand as it slowly rows across the harbor toward the *Mori*. She knows who's going to be aboard it even before she spies him.

"Henry," Cas says. He's joined Remy and Finn at the rail; Remy didn't hear him approach. Leo has gone belowdecks to help Kit, Mita, and the crew working to patch the hole in the *Mori*'s side.

"You need to hide," Finn tells Cas.

He doesn't move. He's staring at the approaching boat as if transfixed. But Finn is right—and if the boat is close enough for them to recognize Henry Ashworth, that means it's close enough for its passengers to recognize Cas, too.

Remy drops into a crouch and yanks on Cas's hand, dragging him behind the gunwale and out of sight.

"*Cas*," she hisses. "They can't know you're here. If Smith is still trying to capture Death, he'll need the reaper's glass to control the list. And if he's trying to *become* Death, he wants you as his sacrifice."

Cas blinks at her, dazed. "You were right," he says. "Henry's still with them."

"We knew he would be." Remy's words come out more harshly than she means them to. They don't have time for this. But it's different, Remy realizes, for Cas to hear secondhand that Henry Ashworth is still working with the Order; now he's seeing it with his own eyes.

"I don't understand," Cas is saying, shaking his head. "Why is he still working with Smith?"

It's Finn who answers. "I don't know," Finn tells him. "I don't know how he's justified it to himself. Or *if* he's justified it. It could be he's just . . . drifting with the current now."

Maybe Ashworth thinks he can ride this out and avoid making a choice. But that's a choice in itself.

Finn shakes Cas by the arm, rousing him from his daze at last. "Go down to the cargo hold," Finn says. "The hidden compartment. Shut yourself in."

Cas's face is still ashen, but he nods. He crawls to the hatch and disappears belowdecks.

"Should we hide, as well?" Remy murmurs to Finn. They probably should. Smith has already indicated he's perfectly willing to use one of *them* as a sacrifice instead.

But anyone else aboard this ship is at risk, too. And Remy and Finn have a job to do.

Finish John Smith, the would-be usurper of Death.

Striker has brought up several spare rifles from belowdecks. Remy watches the two boats approaching the *Mori*: on one side, Ashworth and the gentlemen who must have accompanied him into town; on the other, Smith and his men with the cursed brass casket.

Finn's mouth is set in a thin line as she says, "I'm not hiding anymore."

When Striker offers Remy one of her rifles, Remy accepts it.

The boat with the brass casket reaches the *Mori* first. The Reverend John Smith climbs aboard the *Mori*—alone.

It's a bold, baffling move. It unnerves Remy more than she'd like to admit. As far as she can tell, he isn't even armed. What is his strategy here? Remy can't work out what he's thinking.

Finn takes Remy's hand. With her other hand, Remy grips the strap of the rifle Striker gave her. They could kill Smith so easily. End all of this right now.

But Remy has played straight into Smith's hand too many times. A move like this has to be a trap.

Smith takes in their small group, then the pieces of the broken mast and torn sail still splayed across the deck. Smith looks physically unintimidating as he surveys the *Mori*, but his calmness puts Remy even more on edge.

"I'll have to ask that you set aside your weapons before I bring my men aboard," Smith says. "A precaution. I'm sure you understand."

"I'm sure *you* understand why my crew and I have taken up arms," Captain Hobbes says evenly. "Considering you fired on my ship unprovoked."

"Hmm," Smith says. "Are *you* the captain?"

He says this with contempt; he wants them to know he doesn't believe a man like Captain Hobbes deserves this title. Remy could just shoot Smith here. She really could. At the captain's side, Death hisses through his teeth.

"Yes," Captain Hobbes says without flinching. "I'm the captain."

"I'd hardly say our attack on your vessel was unprovoked," Smith says. "You were going to flee. I'd prefer to finish this tonight."

His eyes land on Death.

"This is what will happen," Smith says. "Your crew will set

aside their weapons. My men will board. We'll send your people safely belowdecks. This . . . *reaper*,"—he says this word with contempt, too—"will allow himself to be locked in a casket we've prepared especially for him. And my men will throw that casket to the bottom of the sea."

"That isn't going to happen," Captain Hobbes says.

"Or I can signal my crew to fire on your ship again."

It's eerie to watch the standoff between these two men, both of them unflappable.

"With you aboard?" Captain Hobbes says.

"That's a risk I'm willing to take."

"And if we decide to just kill you now?"

Smith is entirely unfazed. "Then the good crew of the *White Swallow* destroys your ship with a few more rounds of cannon fire, and my men in the longboat shoot anyone in the water who tries to flee this vessel as it wrecks." Smith watches this sink in. "I thought that might dissuade you. Tell your crew to disarm."

Captain Hobbes glances back at Death, Striker, Remy, Finn, and the handful of other sailors on the main deck. They'll be badly outnumbered if Smith brings his men aboard. But they're outgunned already, and at the moment, the only insurance they have against Smith ordering the *Swallow* to fire on the *Mori* once again is Smith's own presence here. Smith seems worryingly unconcerned about the risk to his own life.

There's another calculation to be made: Surely Smith won't order his men to sink the *Mori* while a dozen of his followers are aboard as well. Remy suspects Captain Hobbes is thinking the same thing. In this long-distance battle between the two ships, when only the *Swallow* has cannons, the *Mori* has no way to fight back.

If they can change the terms of the fight to hand-to-hand combat, the crew might at least have a chance.

Captain Hobbes turns to his crew.

"Stand down," he says.

Striker looks like she might argue, but she doesn't. Remy feels numb as she sets her rifle in a pile on the deck with Striker's and the others.

The boat with Henry Ashworth and the men from town has reached the *Mori* as well. At Smith's command, the Order members from both boats climb up onto the main deck. Even if the *Mori*'s full crew were abovedeck, they'd be outnumbered two to one.

"Now to business," Smith says. He turns to Remy. "Where is the reaper's glass?"

Remy suspected this would be coming.

"Do you mean Cas?" she asks Smith. "He isn't here. He stayed behind in Windover."

Smith's eyes narrow a little as he studies her. "Why?"

Remy forces herself to imagine this alternate story—one where she and Cas couldn't make amends. No crying and hugging in the carriage, no reconciliations. A split that they couldn't resolve, and so they went their separate ways. It's easier to imagine than she'd like. She's been carrying this ache since their first falling-out when they were ten years old.

Quietly, she says, "We fought."

It's more difficult to convince someone of a lie they don't *want* to believe. But Smith is wavering. Remy can tell.

Pastor Dekker and Henry Ashworth have boarded the *Mori* by now. Smith looks between them, gauging their reactions to this.

"I . . . don't know," Ashworth says. "I'd be surprised, if . . . Cas . . . remained in Windover willingly."

Smith turns back to the captain. "You won't mind if my men search your ship."

It's clear the captain *does* mind, but he doesn't answer.

"Bring the reaper's glass to me," Smith tells his men. "Lock anyone else you find away in the cabins. Tell them that if any of them try to put up a fight, I'll shoot their captain in the head."

Smith delivers the threat with absolutely no emotion. This is all business to him. But Death has stepped forward, more serious than Remy has seen him yet. "You don't want to play this game."

"Do you believe I'm playing?" Smith says.

Captain Hobbes rests a hand on Death's shoulder, and Death is quiet. Remy's chest aches. How many times has Finn touched Remy's arm, or put a hand on her shoulder, to ground her in just the same way?

Smith's men are hurrying belowdecks. Remy tries to catch Ashworth's eye, but he avoids her.

Remy's pulse is rushing in her ears as the Order members search belowdecks.

"I meant what I said," Smith tells the captain. "You and your crew will be safe, so long as the reaper, and the reaper's glass, come with us without a fuss. You have my word on that."

"Your word isn't worth much," Captain Hobbes tells him.

Captain Hobbes and his partner are looking at each other now, trying to communicate without words. Probably continuing their debate over whether Death should actually give himself up. Remy doesn't like how keenly Smith is watching them—as if he can sense the depth of feelings that run between them.

Remy's own mind is racing. If Smith *is* telling the truth, if he truly will allow the crew of the *Mori* to go free if Death cooperates . . . Death said himself that Smith can't kill him. Even if he's trapped in a cursed box at the bottom of the sea, they could find him and rescue him when this is all over. They still have another of the whale balls that Striker and Gabe used to dive the wreck over Georges Bank.

They need Smith to believe he's won—to believe that Death is out of the game.

Before Remy can overthink it, she says, "The Sarratt Position."

Both Death and the captain turn to stare at her. Smith is scrutinizing her, too, and Remy is careful not to give too much away on her face. Smith will surely put together that she's speaking in code; all she can hope is that he won't understand what the code actually means. She recalls Díaz's report that Smith said the Order was approaching the *final checkmate.*

Smith is a strategist—but he isn't a chess player.

"The Sarratt Position," Remy says again. "His preferred endgame. You know it?"

Understanding has flickered in Death's gaze. "I'm familiar." He raises an eyebrow at the captain and says, "The Sarratt Position."

"No," Captain Hobbes says.

"We don't have another option," Death says. Smith's eyes are keen, and Remy worries for a moment that he'll piece together their true meaning. Death seems to have the same fear. He adds, "Sometimes you have to make the sacrifice move."

The Sarratt Position isn't a sacrifice move, though. Not really. The chess strategist Jacob Sarratt sometimes sacrificed his queen, temporarily, while simultaneously setting up a pawn to reach the far side of the board. The pawn would be promoted, and the queen would come back into play. It's a loss, but only a provisional one. A temporary setback.

And Death and Captain Hobbes, chess masters that they are, both know it.

"No," the captain tells his partner. "I won't let you do this."

"It isn't up to you," Death says. There's a sadness in his voice. "I know you're the captain of this vessel. But this part isn't your choice."

Finn's fingers have tightened around Remy's. There's a stabbing feeling in Remy's chest.

"You know I have to make this right," Death says.

Remy sees the look on the captain's face and knows all at once that Death told him the truth, tonight, when he went to the *Memento Mori* and asked the captain to reroute. The secret Death kept from his partner for nearly twenty years is a secret no more.

Smith's men have returned to the main deck, and they haven't found Cas. Remy's knees nearly go weak with relief when she hears the news. A muscle in Smith's jaw twitches.

"I see," Smith says. "The reaper's glass is a loose end I'll have to tie up later. Or perhaps this will be inconsequential once the reaper has been dealt with." He turns to Death. "I thought I would need the power of the reaper's glass to control your list of souls who've been Marked. But I'll have a list of my own soon."

His gaze is still darting back and forth between Death and the captain.

"And there are other ways to control a person," Smith says.

He picks up one of the rifles lying on the deck. He points it at Captain Hobbes.

"*Don't!*" Death bursts out, stepping in between them, even as Smith's men pull the captain away from him. "Don't you dare touch him. I'll cooperate. See? I'm cooperating."

Remy blinks, and Death is gone. He vanishes before her eyes. No—he's in the Order's boat, still floating beside the *Mori*, with the brass casket nestled in the bottom of it. Remy eyes the pile of rifles still on the deck, wondering if she could grab one quickly enough to make any difference.

She doesn't try for it. She needs to survive this. It takes three of Smith's men to hold back Captain Hobbes as Death climbs into the terrible casket of his own free will. Two of the Order members clamber down to the boat after him. Death lets himself be locked inside. The casket's metal hinges creak shut with a sound like screaming.

When Smith's men tip the casket over the boat's edge, Remy draws in a sharp breath.

But the casket doesn't sink right away. Smith said he'd throw it to the bottom of the sea, but the metal floats on the surface. The vessel might not be completely watertight, but it's close, and at the moment it's full of air despite the metal's weight.

The men push the casket away from the boat, and it drifts out across the placid water of the harbor like a strange, golden raft.

"What's he doing?" Finn whispers, voice loud enough for only Remy to hear.

Remy tracks her gaze. Smith has drawn out a small book, not so different from the dozens of books Remy has studied over the years. The sorts of books hidden in her father's window-seat bench. The sorts of books he got from Díaz.

"The metal of this casket carries with it a curse," Smith says. "It seems the ocean itself doesn't want this brass to be found. I was able to leverage a protection spell, a sort of ward, in order to transport it this far. But I don't need that protection anymore, do I?"

He smiles.

"Let the ocean bury it after all," he says.

A chill washes over Remy as Smith starts reading a recitation in a language that might be Latin. For a moment, the brass of the casket seems to glow, a thousand lines of light surrounding it like a cocoon. The lines are moving, though. Retracting.

Smith finishes reading, and whatever had been protecting the casket is gone. The bare metal is exposed once again—and unhidden.

The dark sky covers over with storm clouds, just as it had that night the *Mori* rounded Cape Cod. The calm waters in the harbor churn, as if stirred by angry creatures just below the surface. The ocean froths. The water swirls, moving into a whirlpool—like a portal directly to hell.

Remy knows the casket isn't going to drop gently to the bottom of the harbor. This is why Smith didn't bother bringing Death in his casket out to the open sea, where he could sink the casket somewhere it would be harder to find. It doesn't matter where Smith abandons the casket. He's letting the curse and the ocean do the hiding *for* him.

The sea rises up and swallows Death.

"*No!*" Captain Hobbes's voice is tangled, wrenched from his gut. Remy has never seen him like this. In the short time she's known him, he's been eternally composed, calm. But this blows him past his limit. At a flick of Smith's hand, the men holding the captain drag him toward the hatch, to lock him away with the other sailors belowdecks. Striker tries to fight, too, and is restrained. Finn is all tension at Remy's side.

Everything Smith does hurts the people Remy cares about—and she's had enough.

Remy dives for the pile of weapons still left on the deck.

There's enough chaos around her that no one notices her movement except Finn. Remy lifts her rifle, the one Striker taught her with.

Remy shot Smith once before, back at the seminary, when he was attacking Cas. She put a bullet through Smith's shoulder, but she'd been aiming for his chest. She'd tried to shoot him again at the church. What a terrified, frantic girl she'd been back then.

She's still terrified, but a calm settles over her. The focus of years of research. Of a clear path laid out ahead of her. The moment of finding an answer that makes everything else make sense.

She fires the rifle.

This time, she doesn't miss. She shoots Smith directly through the head, and he crumples.

XXXI.

FINN

The Reverend John Smith is dead.

Pastor Dekker and the Order members seem at a loss for what to do. Murmurs break out, then bickering. Ashworth has turned very pale. He's staring down at Smith's broken form, at the splatter of blood and gore in his thinning gray hair, at the pool of blood spilling out around him on the deck. The red sinks into the crevices between the deck's planks and seeps out in tiny branching rivers.

For all his scheming and threatening and pontificating, Smith is—was—just a man. A creature of flesh and blood. And now he's dead.

Finn's mind races. Remy is still standing with the gun in her hand. Could it really be so simple? Finn's shock slowly molds itself into relief. This will surely satisfy the terms of her new deal with Marbas: *Finish John Smith, the would-be usurper of Death. Maintain the present Death in his post.* They'll need to find Death and free him from his casket somehow, but that task feels almost achievable with Smith dead and the Order out of the way.

The night sky fades to gray as a heavy fog descends, cold and thick, like the fog at Georges Bank. The ocean is still roiling around the spot where the casket was sucked into it. They've faced this much—they can face an angry ocean. Perhaps Marbas can even be persuaded to give them the coordinates to find Death. Finn might actually be able to free herself from her deal.

Finn can see a future that hadn't been fully real to her until now. She can see—

Something strange is happening.

The tiny rivers of blood on the deck have reversed their course. Water flowing upstream.

The crumpled body begins to move.

Slowly, Smith stands. He straightens his coat. The blood is gone, and he brushes a bit of grime from his sleeve. The red mark on his forehead where Remy's bullet had entered is quickly fading.

"Ah," Smith says. "It's satisfying when a plan comes together, is it not?"

Remy is still gripping the rifle, the first to recover her senses while the rest of them stand agape. She levels the barrel at Smith once again.

"Don't pretend that this was your plan," she says.

"Perhaps not the exact path I would have taken. And yet here we are, at the intended destination."

Smith removes a handkerchief from his pocket and begins to polish his spectacles.

"I knew it would come to this eventually," he says, eerily calm. "It had to. I've made the preparations. I said the spells. I performed the final rites. All so that I'd be ready to seize the moment and take up this mantle when the time was right." He returns the spectacles to his nose. "A man cannot become Death while he still lives."

He's a ghost, Finn thinks. She's staring at a ghost. Even Dekker is watching Smith open-mouthed. But when Smith steps forward, the boards beneath his shoes creak under the weight. He takes the spell book from Dekker. He holds it in his real, material hands.

This is no ghost. He's solid—solid as Death had been when he'd appeared to them in the grotto.

If Smith isn't alive, and he isn't a ghost . . .

"What . . . ?" Dekker breathes, still taking in Smith's form with something like wonder. "What is this?"

Smith's mouth twitches into a smile, as if he's amused by the question.

"Death," he says.

Remy aims the rifle at him and fires again. The bullet doesn't hit him. It doesn't miss, either. It simply . . . *isn't*. Something in Finn's perception rearranges, and the world ripples, and there was never a bullet at all.

One of Smith's men wrests the gun from Remy's hands. She's shocked enough to let it happen. Finn knows they need to fight, but the captain has already been taken belowdecks, and they're badly outnumbered, and she has no idea what to *do*. It should have been impossible for Smith to become Death, and he's done it anyway. How do you fight a force of nature?

He turns to where Ashworth stands with two other men barely older than he is. These aren't prominent members of the Order of Lazarus; these are the flunkies, the acolytes.

"I need to sail out to open water, in order to complete our ritual tonight," Smith says. "I need you to stay here, aboard this ship, and make sure the crew is contained. I won't have them interfere as I do what must be done."

Ashworth still looks ill, his face bone-white. But he nods.

Smith turns to Remy.

"There would have been a nice symmetry in using the reaper's glass as the sacrifice," he muses. "But perhaps I'll need to craft a new reaper's glass as I begin my work. And there will be symmetry all the same in using the daughter of Charles DeWindt." He nods at Remy and tells his men, "Put her in the boat. Send the rest of them belowdecks."

Finn's fear and rage are tangled together in a storm of white, as if the fog that now surrounds the ship is clouding her mind, too. She can't think as she steps forward, putting herself between Remy and Smith's men.

Remy takes Finn by the arm, though, and spins her around, so Finn is facing her instead of the approaching Order members. Remy's eyes are wide and dark in the misty lamplight. Finn doesn't have a plan. *Remy* is the planner, and they're out of options, and they're out of time.

"We haven't gotten to talk," Finn breathes, delirious. She promised Remy they'd talk when they make it through this.

"We will," Remy says.

And because Finn has already confessed her deepest truths tonight, and because she suspects Remy already knows, she says one more truth: "I love you."

Remy pulls her in and kisses her. It doesn't matter that they're surrounded by Smith and the Order of Lazarus. It doesn't matter what anyone else will think of them. For all her throwing caution to the wind, Finn has never kissed a girl in public before. The fire inside Finn is blazing hot. There's a fire in Remy, too, even if it's less literal. Finn wants to stay huddled in this warmth.

A hand is on her elbow, jerking her away. She and Remy are broken apart. Pastor Dekker sneers.

"You probably *should* sink this ship of degenerates," he tells Smith.

Smith's expression is stony. "They have a role to play, as well, as we reshape this world. For the righteous to be saved, someone must be struck down. The blood of these sinners will give us balance."

Finn hears herself laugh. "*You* don't decide that balance. You're just a man."

Remy steps between her and Smith before he can strike her.

"Go with the others," Remy tells Finn. "I'm going to figure something out."

There's a fire still burning in her eyes. The animal instinct in Finn fights for dominance, begging her not to leave Remy. She has to squash that instinct for now. She loves Remy enough to trust that Remy knows what she's doing. Finn lets herself be shuffled toward the hatch.

On the lower deck, the rest of the crew has already been shoved into cabins. The doors are braced shut from the outside with heavy crates, or with rope knotted expertly around the handles. There are far more sailors in the crew of the *Mori* than individual cabins aboard the ship, so Finn has to assume they've been locked away in twos or threes—good. Perhaps they can do some conspiring of their own. The door of the surgeon's cabin keeps pounding and shaking, as if someone is kicking it from the inside. Striker, Finn guesses. The muffled shouting in Yiddish confirms this.

Finn thinks Ashworth will shut her away with the others—but he pauses in the passageway. He waves at the other Order members to go back up on deck. They don't fully retreat, but they step back toward the ladder, out of earshot.

Ashworth won't quite look at Finn as he says carefully, "You traveled with . . . Cas. To Eden."

It isn't a question, so Finn doesn't reply. She does note the deliberateness with which he says this. Not Cas's full name, not *Miss Sterling.* She isn't sure what to make of it.

"And I assume you've been traveling together since," Ashworth says.

"If you're going to ask where he is, don't bother," Finn says. "We already told you. He stayed behind in Windover."

Ashworth massages his temple with one hand. "I know that isn't true. I might not know Cas as well as I thought. But I know he wouldn't do *that.*"

Finn hadn't expected Ashworth to follow Remy's and Finn's leads in referring to Cas as *him.* She isn't sure what to make of that, either. They stare at each other, like they're locked in a game of cards and bluffs, waiting to see which of them will break first. She studies Ashworth's face in the lamplight. She knows he and Cas talked back at the seminary. She has no idea of the extent of that conversation. Understandably, Cas hasn't been much inclined to revisit it in the days since.

Finn is very aware that for every second she sizes up Henry Ashworth, she's being sized up, too.

"He told me you were a friend," Ashworth says quietly.

It's not some grand statement. It's incredibly obvious, and still, Finn feels unexpectedly touched by this knowledge. *Friend.*

"You don't need to tell me where he is," Ashworth says. "Just tell me if he's safe."

"He's safe," Finn says.

Ashworth slumps back against one of the walls, rubbing his face in relief. It's very undignified. His gaze has turned glassy. A bead of sweat drips down his forehead.

"But he won't be, if Smith has his way," Finn continues.

"You've heard what Smith intends now, from his own mouth. He wanted to use Cas as a sacrifice."

"No," Ashworth says quickly. "No, he wants Cas's power. The reaper's glass connection, the visions. That's all."

"Is that what he told you?" Finn asks.

Ashworth might be even more gullible than Kieran if he truly believes Smith was going to let Cas live. Finn doesn't have time for this. Even now, her heart is pounding as she thinks about Remy being hauled into a boat with Smith.

"Cas *is* the reaper's glass," Finn says. "Smith planned to murder him. He probably still will, if he can get his hands on him. And he's going to murder Remy. *That's* the man you've allied yourself with."

Ashworth looks as if he's struggling even to stay upright under the weight of this realization. Perhaps he isn't so gullible after all. Finn suspects that on some level, he's known what Smith is really capable of, even if he hasn't wanted to believe it.

"I didn't think that he'd—" Ashworth starts, but then he breaks off. "Maybe I did." He buries his face in his hands. His voice is a half-decipherable mumble. "God. I can't think. I can't . . ."

He's swaying slightly on his feet.

Finn should have placed the signs earlier. Twice now she's witnessed Cas fall into a vision. Twice, she's watched Cas come untethered from the present world and lose himself in a glimpse of something yet to come. The headache, the paleness, the faraway look on his face.

Finn has no idea how or why it's happening to Henry Ashworth now. But she knows what this is.

The two Order members waiting by the ladder seem to have

realized something is wrong. One of them starts toward them. "Ashworth," he calls down the passageway. "Are you all right?"

"I'm sorry," Ashworth says after a pause that's several beats too long. "I'm afraid . . . I'm afraid I don't feel well."

"Water," one of the men says. "We'll fetch you some water. And—"

Ashworth's knees give out. He scrabbles at the wall to catch himself, hand tensed into a claw, his jacket sleeve sliding back to show a pale stretch of arm. Finn's eyes lock on the fine, narrow bones of his wrist.

Perhaps I'll need to craft a new reaper's glass, Smith had said. But the reaper's glass isn't something that's crafted intentionally, Finn thinks—because a new one has emerged either way.

Finn lunges at Ashworth. She wraps her fingers around his wrist and hangs on tight.

"Show me," she says.

He doesn't fight her. They hurtle into the vision.

Finn doesn't feel her body collapse, though she knows, distantly, that it must. She and Ashworth are standing on the main deck of a ship, just as they stood a few minutes ago. But this isn't the *Mori*; the details are all wrong. The ship is larger, and the layout is different, and the men on the deck aren't the sailors Finn has come to know so well. Most of them she doesn't recognize—but Smith and Pastor Dekker are among them.

None of them acknowledge Finn and Ashworth's appearance. The scene is perfectly silent.

Two of Smith's men are holding Remy by the arms, pinning her against the mast, like an insect pinned to a terrible display in a museum. Remy struggles to escape their grasp, but it's no use.

Finn's chest has seized up. Is this scene happening *now*? Surely not; this must be aboard the *White Swallow*, and even if Smith and his men dragged Remy into their boat the moment Finn was taken belowdecks, they can't have reached the *Swallow* yet. This is the future—or *a* future. The plan Smith envisions.

Remy is speaking, but there's no sound in this vision. No rumble of the ocean waves. No voices arguing. Finn can see Smith's mouth moving, forming words she can't hear. He's reciting something, his eyes half closed, as if he's in a trance.

The world around him is blurry, and at first, Finn thinks this is just how the vision is. But it isn't the *whole* world that's blurry, she realizes. There's a sort of wall, and Finn thinks of Díaz's talk of the Veil, of a barrier between the material world and . . . something.

Smith turns to Remy. He draws a small silver knife from his pocket.

He approaches Remy, slowly and with intention. Remy says something, though Finn can only read her lips on the final words: "you monster."

Finn tries to lunge for Remy. Before she can reach her, Smith plunges the blade into Remy's heart.

Remy's face screws up in a silent scream. An impossible amount of blood pours from her chest. It soaks her shirt in seconds. Finn tries to scream, too, but she can't. There's no sound. This is a pantomime, a play, a terrible prophecy. It isn't real. It can't be. It *won't* be. Finn doesn't have lungs, but her chest and throat burn from the need to cry out, to let this primal rage and grief escape her.

When Finn wakes from this, she's going to murder Smith with her bare hands.

Remy stops struggling. Her body goes limp. The life leaves her tea-dark eyes.

The scene ripples like the surface of a pond, and Remy's lifeless body is gone. Finn waits to wake up.

She doesn't.

She and Ashworth stand once again on the deck of the *Mori*. But the world of this vision feels even less substantial than before, faded at the edges. If the scene of Remy's death was a play, the scene now is a *dream* of a play—something strange and fluid, with logic that doesn't quite hold up after you wake.

Remy is nowhere in sight this time. Now, it's Cas who the two men hold against the mast. His jaw is tightly clenched, his face screwed up, but he can't hide his shaking.

Smith finishes his recitation and turns to Cas with the knife in his hand.

At Finn's side, Ashworth—the real Ashworth, the one who's having this vision—twitches and strains, trying to intervene. But he and Finn are silent audience members, helpless observers. Finn can't make out Ashworth's face clearly, but she can feel the terror rolling off him as he realizes what's about to happen.

Smith stabs Cas through the heart—his original, intended sacrifice. Cas collapses on the deck in a growing pool of blood.

The scene ripples once more.

Remy is alive again, on the *Swallow* again, as Smith continues his recitation and the world around him blurs. The knife is in his hand. Finn blinks, and it's Cas. She blinks again, and it's Remy.

This isn't how Cas has described *his* visions of deaths. Cas had been surprised to see Finn's death more than once—and those visions happened days or weeks apart. Not one right after the other. And even as Finn and Ashworth watch, the vision keeps changing, faltering. It's as if the future is still in flux, a too-wet ball of clay that can't hold its shape.

Cas's visions showed him the fates of those on the reaper's list—the people who were Marked for Death. But Smith doesn't care who's been Marked. He said it himself. He has no intention of following some predetermined list from a mysterious source.

Smith has decided he *is* the source now. He's writing a list all his own.

And now the glass to Smith's reaper is catching glimpses of that list. Ashworth's visions are showing Smith's plan, however fluid that plan may be.

In agonizing silence, Finn and Henry Ashworth watch Remy and Cas die again and again. Finn's throat feels as if it's tearing from the effort of a scream that can't release.

The vision lingers. A girl stands in the blurry space of the Veil, hazy and indistinct. But as Remy's blood—Cas's blood—Remy's blood—seeps across the planks of the *White Swallow*'s deck, the girl becomes more solid. She looks down at her own hand, confused. She brushes the blurred air before her as if clearing away a spiderweb.

The girl steps through the hazy wall and stands, solid and real, on the deck.

Finn slams back into her own body. The vision has ended at last. She's sprawled on the floor of the passageway, shaking and wrung out, and someone is shouting, and it's too much. Finn rolls onto her side and vomits. It's a relief, in a way, to have a body again, to have some physical means of releasing the horror of what she's just seen. If only she could rid herself of the images in her mind so easily.

Smith believes his sacrifice will resurrect someone who's long dead. But the vision isn't real yet. It can't be. This is only Smith's intention.

Smith has imagined in gory detail his plan to murder Finn's friends.

When Finn's stomach is empty, one of the Order members drags her upright by the collar. The world comes back into focus around her in pieces. Ashworth is still on the floor, trembling. The Order member shakes Finn violently. Her head feels broken and rattling.

"What the hell was that?" the man snarls at her. "What did you do to him?"

But that vision wasn't Finn's doing, and Ashworth knows it. Finn recognizes the look in his eyes: the fear, the regret. The self-disgust as you're forced to face the consequences of your own choices at last.

It's the realization that you've given your soul to a demon. No, Ashworth bargained with something worse than a demon: a man who believes the rules of morality apply to other people, but not to him. A man who wields the power to make his vision a reality.

As one of the other Order members helps Ashworth to his feet, Ashworth's eyes, wide and terrified, find Finn's.

"How do we save him?" he whispers. "How do we keep him safe?"

It's that little "we" that does it. She's not sure Ashworth even realizes what he's said. For no good goddamn reason, that little "we" wriggles in through a crevice in Finn's armor.

Finn has never been quick to trust people, but she trusts her own instincts. Her instinct is telling her that Ashworth does love Cas, in his own way. And that love is a powerful thing. Something in Ashworth has shifted. The sails have set at a new angle. A change of course.

Ashworth wants out of his bargain.

"I'll tell you where he is," Finn says. "Get us out of this, and I'll take you to him."

Ashworth rounds on the guards.

XXXII.

CAS

The fear has caught Cas and won't let him go. After he's shut himself inside the dark, cramped space of the hidden smugglers' compartment, he waits for his eyes to adjust. They don't. The world remains perfectly black. On the other side of the panel door, the water that leaked inside while the crew rushed to patch the hull sloshes as the ship rolls on the waves. Or are those footsteps splashing through the cargo hold? Maybe it's Finn coming back for him. Maybe it's Smith and his men. At any moment, the panel is going to be flung aside, and some Order member will drag Cas out of here and present him to Smith like a lamb for the slaughter—

Cas braces himself. The panel doesn't open. He stays braced. He can't make his muscles unclench. There's a stabbing pain in his chest, a knife pressing under his ribs. The body isn't made to hold this much tension inside it. Sound has turned fuzzy in his ears. He can't hear the footsteps in the cargo hold anymore—but that doesn't mean the footsteps aren't there.

It's only when his head starts to feel as if it's floating away that Cas realizes he isn't breathing. He forces his lungs to draw air. Shaky, but his head clears a little. He just has to breathe. How had Leo shown him? Long inhale through the nose. Longer exhale through the mouth. Something about the nervous system, about physiological connections. Where is Leo now? Cas lost track of him in the confusion after the cannon fire. Did he take little Nessa to hide out with her and the ship's cat belowdecks? Are they safe?

The breathing isn't enough. Cas's ears are still filled with a rushing sound. This isn't some irrational surge of panic he can talk himself out of—this fear is founded. The threat now is real.

He *should* be trying to meditate. He's alone in the dark and the quiet, and what else is there for him to do? If he could just focus his thoughts, if he could connect with Death in his mind again, at least he'd know what was happening with the others back on the deck. The idea is almost laughable, though. How the hell is he supposed to meditate right now? He tries to settle himself in his body. It's so dark that he can't see his fingers when he wiggles them in front of his face. It's as if he's stopped having fingers at all. As if he doesn't *have* a body. He's a formless ball of nerves. He feels like he's dying. Maybe he's already dead. Maybe everyone he cares about is already dead, too.

Stop. Just breathe. Just think about breathing. Think about Death, and the river, and connecting with Death in your mind. The tension in your chest is real. It hurts because you're still here. You're still breathing and kicking and trying to stay afloat. Your muscles burn with the effort. You're too exhausted to swim. You swim anyway. You struggle in the waves. The sky above you is a swirl of dark storm clouds, and the ocean around you churns. You're completely alone in the water. As the waves rise, you see the distant line of the shore, and then you drop, and it's nothing but stormy sea in any direction.

Sky above you.

Ocean around you.

Cas is aware, on some level, that this isn't real. It isn't quite a dream, though. It isn't even a vision. When he's in a vision, he's drifting and weightless, but now his body feels terribly heavy.

And there's *sound*: a roll of thunder, the roaring sea. He can taste salt water on his tongue. He spits it out.

Some part of him knows he's still huddled in the cargo hold aboard the *Memento Mori*. He must be, because he would have remembered leaving, wouldn't he? Or maybe he fell asleep, or maybe his pounding heart finally gave out, or maybe this is a vast hallucination he's having. What he's seeing now can't be *real.*

It feels very, very real, though. Cas doesn't feel like he's in the cargo hold. He's outside, alone, set adrift in a wild storm. When the storm clouds above him begin to pour, he can feel the very real rain pelting his very real face.

A dangerous thought: Can he really drown out here?

He treads water, kicking valiantly to stay afloat as the icy waves toss him around. The shore he'd spotted is impossibly far away. He tries to swim toward it anyway. The tide is working against him. The waves keep knocking him back. He isn't strong enough for this. He's going to drown, or freeze, or both.

If only this rain would break. If only the tide would change directions and stop fighting him. If this *were* a dream, maybe Cas would have some control over these elements. Maybe he does. He closes his eyes and wills the storm to end. All he gets for it is a mouthful of salt water.

"You can't just calm the sea," a voice says, as if this is obvious.

Cas recognizes the voice at once, though he can't see Death anywhere. He's not even sure if Death is speaking aloud or in his head. His throat stings from the salt water, and the only response he can manage is a strangled, "What?"

"The storm isn't *trying* to hurt you," Death says. "It's only being a storm."

"Where are we? Is this real?"

"Does it feel real?"

It does.

"So stop trying to will the storm into stopping," Death says. "You don't control the weather."

Cas is well aware that he doesn't control the weather. That's the whole issue. "So I should just let myself drown, then?"

"Of course not. But you're focusing on what you can't change, instead of what you can. You can sail through a storm without drowning. People do it all the time. *You've* done it."

Cas doesn't have time for this. He's exhausted, and sooner or later, his legs are going to give out. "Not like this," he rasps. "Not without a ship, or a boat, or—"

"Exactly," Death says.

Which is damn typical. Cas would glare at Death if there was something to glare at instead of a disembodied voice. "I don't have any of those!"

"No," Death says. "You don't. So what do you need?"

Another wave crashes over him, and Cas has to kick back to the surface with all his might. Damn him. Cas doesn't need Death or his cryptic advice. He needs the waves to calm down for two goddamn minutes so he can *think*.

"Fair," Death's voice says, as if he can hear Cas's thoughts. Because of course he can. "But as I said: Calming the sea isn't an option. What do you *need*?"

It doesn't matter what Cas needs, because none of it is here. He doesn't have a ship or a boat. He doesn't even have a buoy. He and Finn *would* have drowned in that storm off Cape Cod if

Remy hadn't turned up in the jolly boat to save them. There's no one here to save him now. Remy could probably solve this strange riddle in a second, but Cas doesn't have a mind for—

"Enough of that," Death cuts in. "I've been in your head, too, you know, when you were poking around in mine. You're far more capable than you think you are."

Cas's limbs feel so heavy. "I don't know what answer you want me to give!"

Death has the audacity to snort at that. "There's no one right answer. What's the answer for *you*? What do you need?"

He needs *help* instead of questions. He needs his friends—a jolly boat appearing on the waves, with Remy and Finn reaching out an oar to him, tugging him aboard. He can't do this alone. He knows it's too simple, but his mind feels wrung out, and he says the first and only thing he can think of: "I don't know—a boat!"

Cas is in a boat.

The hull is shockingly solid beneath him. For a long moment, he clings to the bench in front of him, marveling at the wood. The boat is small and rickety, and it tosses wildly on the waves, but it doesn't capsize.

Death lounges on one of the benches and waits while Cas catches his breath.

"Well, this is something," Death says, drumming his fingers against the boat's weathered gunwale.

Cas gives him the glare he's been saving. "What the hell is this? Where are we?"

"We're in a boat," Death says.

"That isn't—" Cas shakes his head. The storm hasn't relented, but Death seems completely unbothered by the rain or the wind whipping through his hair. "How are you here?"

"I'm not," Death says. "Or I am, but not only. I'm sorry to say that at this present moment, I'm locked inside a cursed brass casket at the bottom of the sea somewhere."

Cas thinks for a moment that he's joking, but his face is deadly serious. "Smith caught you?" he asks.

"I let him," Death says. "Though if I'm honest, I didn't think it would turn out like this."

He's frightened, Cas realizes. He's trying to hide it, keeping his tone light and airy, but Cas can still feel the fear rolling off him. Even the single brass panel they found at Georges Bank had given Cas a bad feeling. He can't imagine being trapped inside a box made from that cursed metal.

He doesn't have to imagine it. Death is experiencing it, and the cold of it is spreading over Cas's skin even as their boat tosses on the stormy sea.

"We're connected, you and I," Death says. "The reaper, and the reaper's glass. I'm at the bottom of the ocean. And I'm here now, talking with you, while *you*—let's see"—Death squints at Cas—"you're tucked away in some hidey-hole aboard the *Mori*, aren't you?"

Cas settles onto the bench across from him, trying to shake off the chill, though the rain hasn't stopped. "Am I . . . dreaming, then?"

"No. Yes. Something like that. You're still on the *Mori*, yes. And you're also here. On the sea, in a storm, in a boat you just *imagined into being.*" He raises his eyebrows, as if making sure Cas appreciates the impressiveness of this.

Cas doesn't feel very impressive right now. He feels exhausted, and the storm is still raging. "If this is a dream," he says, "why can't we just snap our fingers and appear on shore? Why all of . . . this?"

Death shrugs. "You work with what you've got."

Death studies Cas for a moment.

"I've always had a head full of storms, too, you know," Death says. "I think you and I are alike in some ways. Perhaps that had a hand in why *you* became the reaper's glass, after Charles DeWindt, may he rest in peace. I'm not sure how the reaper's glass is passed on, to be honest. Could've just been bad luck on your part."

Cas has resented the visions for so long, but he's also coming to accept them. "Not *bad* luck," he says.

Something about the way Death looks at Cas then—sad and almost apologetic—makes Cas feel very young. "You should never have been burdened with this," Death says. He pauses, then asks, "Do you know why the reaper's glass exists?"

"No," Cas says. He expects Death to go on, but he doesn't, so Cas asks, "Why does the reaper's glass exist?"

"Oh, *I* don't know," Death says. "I can only speculate, same as you."

"You've had a lot more time to speculate, though."

Death tips an invisible cap at him as if to say, *Fair enough.* "All right. Here's my theory. There are different names, right? The reaper's glass. Death's looking-glass. I used to think it was a sort of mirror. But I think you're more like a lens. A window into . . ."

He studies Cas with a wryness, and Cas again feels very young, though it's different this time. Not because Cas has only lived for eighteen years, but because Death has lived for centuries.

"It wears on you, this job. Being *death*. Walking people through their final moments, over and over. All the fear and the pain. All the regret. You stop feeling it, after a while. You *have* to stop feeling it. It'll drive you mad. But . . . I think you're meant to feel it, sometimes. I think it's meant to hurt."

Death's long, dark hair is tangling in the wind. He's tied back the top layer of it to keep it from his eyes, but the rest whips around his face. It's dashing, in an old-fashioned epic hero sort of way. God, should Cas grow his hair back out?

"I've been feeling the distance more and more lately," Death says. "I'm not really human anymore. But *you* are. The visions you've had, the deaths you've seen . . . I've felt those. They hurt."

Cas thinks about all the visions he's had over the years. They've always been the most painful deaths, the most shocking, the ones that felt like they happened before the person's time. Smith had tried to tell him that this was because the reaper was causing these deaths, and that the reaper was deliberately causing pain. But Cas has only been seeing a tiny fraction of the souls Death has to gather. He's only been seeing whatever leaks through.

"Death is natural," Death is saying, "and it's inevitable, and that doesn't make it hurt less. And seeing it through your eyes, through the eyes of a human . . . it helps me remember."

I've been in your head, too, you know, Death had said. And that ought to be terrifying. Cas has tried so hard to hide how badly he's been drowning—but Death has seen it up close.

And still, Death is the one to see what Cas might be capable of.

"I'm sorry that you've been burdened with this," Death tells him.

"It's all right," Cas says automatically.

"It isn't." A simple statement of fact.

The storm quiets. Everything goes dark.

At first, Cas thinks he's back in the smugglers' compartment.

Back in his own body. But this cold is deeper, and he's lying down, not sitting, and the texture under his hands is cold and metallic instead of wood.

He's inside the casket.

It's like when he found the grotto, when he was sharing Death's memories, except these memories are happening in real time. Because Cas is in Death's mind, he knows how he got here: He climbed into the metal casket, and the casket was devoured by the sea. His love was meant to come find him, and he'll try—he'll probably dredge the whole harbor if he has to—but it's possible that even those efforts won't be enough. Everything has gone wrong.

"Cas."

He—Cas—Death—feels the chill of the box around him. The sense of dread is mounting. It's terrible and ancient, self-righteous, unholy. A beast growing in size and gnashing its teeth. He almost can't blame the ocean for wanting to destroy this thing, or, barring that, to hide it away where it can never be found. To bury it.

Cas doesn't know whether it's himself panicking, or Death. Probably both.

Cas startles back into his own body to find Finn shaking him by both shoulders. He gasps and grabs for her, clinging to her sweater, heart racing. He's back in the smuggler's compartment. Finn is crouched in front of him. Behind her, someone holds a lantern and is peering through the opening.

"You're all right," Finn whispers. "Just breathe. You weren't breathing."

Cas assumed it was Remy holding the lantern. But as his eyes adjust to the light, his heart nearly leaps out of his chest all over again.

"Finn, behind you—"

"He's helping us," Finn says quickly, before Cas can do anything more than try to pull her away from Henry in the opening. "He helped take out the other Order members belowdecks. Kit and Striker and the others are getting everyone free."

Cas can't wrap his mind around any of this. He can't deal with Henry standing five feet away, peering in at him, face pinched with concern. Henry takes a few steps back, disappearing from view, and Cas appreciates this much, at least. Finn gently pries Cas's fingers from her sweater and clasps them in her own hands, trying to warm them.

"Christ, you're ice-cold," Finn tells him. "What happened?"

"I honestly don't know," Cas says. His throat feels raspy, as if he really was coughing up salt water just minutes ago. "Did they . . . drown . . . Death?"

Finn stares at him. "They did. How did you—?"

"Where's Remy?"

"He took her," Finn says. "Smith took her."

Her voice trembles as she gives a brief account of everything that's happened: Smith's transformation, Remy being taken to the *White Swallow*, and the vision—or visions—she and Henry just had. Henry has retreated farther out into the cargo hold. He doesn't say a word.

"We have to stop Smith," Finn says. "But I don't know *how* we can stop him, now that he's . . . whatever he is. Remy tried to shoot him, and he just . . . didn't die."

"We can't kill him," Cas says. He racks his mind, trying to remember the specific language in the new contract Finn made with Marbas. "We just have to finish him, somehow?"

"*Just*," Finn echoes, incredulous.

"Death might know what to do."

"We don't have time to go scouring the bottom of the sea for him, though. Smith has Remy *now*. He's going to use her as the sacrifice. And the ocean could've taken Death anywhere."

"He isn't *anywhere*," Cas says. "He's nearby."

Finn's eyes widen. She's staring at him again the same way she had when Cas told her the Latin name for the tiny golden flowers they found in the woods. "Are you saying you know where he is?"

Not exactly where; Cas couldn't point to it on a map. But when he closes his eyes, when he lets his mind drift on the waves for a moment, he can sense the direction of Death in his casket. He can't explain the instinct, exactly, but he trusts it. It's the same sense of knowing he had when he dived off the ship to rescue Finn during the storm.

"I can find him," Cas says. "I can find Death."

XXXIII.

REMY

As Smith and his men lower their boat and start rowing across the water toward the *White Swallow*, Remy tries and fails to make a plan. The fog descended swiftly after Smith's men threw Death in his casket into the sea, and the *Memento Mori* looks like a ghost, hazy and indistinct behind them. Smith seems to be finished making his speeches for the moment. Remy can't say she's saddened by this, though his sermonizing might be helpful. She needs to work out what exactly he's doing so she can find a way to counter it.

If Smith is going to kill her in his attempt to bring back his daughter, Remy isn't sure why he hasn't done it yet. Maybe there are elements of the ritual he's planning that he left back aboard the *White Swallow.*

When the crew of the *Swallow* has pulled up the boat, Pastor Dekker reaches for Remy and tries to help her out. Remy jerks away from him. She climbs onto the deck herself.

The man who chased Cas from outside the Boston customhouse—the man whose coat they stole—strides across the deck to meet Smith.

"Make for open water," Smith tells him, and the captain goes to direct his crew.

"Where are we going?" Remy asks.

"Not far," Smith says.

Remy wonders if she can stall whatever's about to happen by getting Smith talking. "I thought you were Death now. Why do you have to go anywhere?"

Smith doesn't answer. Remy recalls something he said back at the Chapel this evening—something about a pilgrimage.

"Are we going to the place where she died?" she asks.

Smith turns to her with cold eyes, and Remy understands. He's planning to reach through the Veil—and he'll need a tether to find the specific spirit he's looking for. Death said that Viola Smith was no longer in that in-between dream space. But Smith himself is surely one tether to his daughter's spirit, and according to Díaz, the place where she died would be another. Will this be enough to truly reach her, wherever her spirit has moved on to?

"My daughter was taken from this earth in a shipwreck," Smith says quietly. "She died at sea. I thought, in the beginning, that I would need to return to the site of the wreck to find her through the Veil." He gazes out at the foggy water around them. "But the sea is all connected. Once we've reached the open water, the ritual can begin."

It's a relief to realize he isn't taking Remy hundreds of miles away, to wherever the ship had wrecked. But this also means Remy is running out of time. She fights down her panic.

Death had seemed skeptical that Smith's plan was even possible—but he'd warned that Smith might just do it anyway. Whether or not Smith can truly bring his daughter back to life, Remy won't survive his attempt.

The *Swallow* slides across the water. The sea is unnervingly calm after the brief, violent uprising that swallowed Death in his casket. It's as if something has been placated, though the fog still hangs heavy in the air.

When Smith steps forward to begin his ritual, the *White Swallow* has just passed the curves of the shore on either side. The sea before them stretches to the horizon. Remy squints through the fog in the other direction. She can still make out the *Mori*'s sails. She wonders if she's imagining it, that the ship is inching closer to them.

She told Finn she'd figure something out. But Remy was lying to Finn, or lying to herself.

She has no idea what to do.

Smith stands at the prow of the ship. He's murmuring something.

He doesn't use a book this time. And the language he's speaking isn't Latin. It's something Remy doesn't recognize. Remy thinks of the way Death described the understanding that came when he became a reaper: *You know what you need to know when you need it.* Smith has unlocked a deep knowledge that Remy fears will make him all the more powerful.

The air before him begins to shimmer. The fog becomes almost solid. And maybe it's because Remy has heard it described as a Veil, but that's all her mind can compare it to: It's as if she can suddenly see a gauzy sheet hanging in front of him, a piece of fabric laid atop the fog.

Smith draws out his knife.

Remy instinctively moves to back away. One of Smith's men blocks her retreat. But Smith doesn't even look at her. He's focused on the sheer film spreading through the air before him.

He slides the knife cleanly through the Veil.

Remy's gut is roiling awfully. Maybe it's her own fear, but she thinks this is something larger: None of them are meant to witness this. No one is.

Only Smith—Death—can look directly at the gash he's cut through the Veil. He reaches a hand toward it.

"Viola," he says.

Remy thinks, at first, that he's said this in greeting. But no one is there. It isn't a greeting—it's a summoning. A question.

"Viola," Smith says again through the rift. His voice sounds so different from his usual coolly distant tone. This is sad and terrifyingly human. "Viola, darling. Are you there?"

What does it take to bring someone back through the Veil? Sacrifice.

Remy feels a hand on her shoulder, and she braces herself to fight. She thinks it's one of Smith's men.

She turns.

The young man standing beside her is wiry and thin. There's a scholarly air about him, and Remy can't make out the details of his face. His outline is hazy and indistinct—as if Remy is staring at him through fog, or through gauzy fabric.

Remy has never seen this man before. But she knows him. She understands at last who's been haunting her.

She reaches instinctively for her carpetbag before realizing she left it back in Windover with her mother. She doesn't have her research journal with her, or the letters this young man wrote to her from the Eden seminary when he was a student there. When he was alive.

He doesn't need those letters to reach through the Veil to Remy now. Smith has cut an opening.

Remy thought Daniel Stevens graduated from the seminary. She thought he was off living his life somewhere, that he'd probably forgotten all about the twenty-five-year-old private detective he once helped investigate the people who had disappeared from Eden.

But Daniel Stevens became one of them—one of the people Smith murdered in his attempts to bring back his daughter. The souls he's left trapped beyond the Veil, unable to move on. More figures are emerging alongside Stevens on the deck. They're shrouded in fog, but very real.

Smith's daughter hasn't appeared here tonight. Smith is reaching through the Veil, and she hasn't reached back.

But the others have.

XXXIV.

FINN

The sailors of the *Memento Mori* have taken back the lower deck of their ship. The two young men who Smith sent belowdecks with Ashworth are now tied up and locked inside one of the cabins; Kit and Striker are watching them, while the rest of the crew quickly gathers around the large dining table. Finn isn't sure how many other Order members Smith left behind on the *Mori* when he returned to the *White Swallow* with Remy in his boat. Sooner or later, whoever is left on the main deck is going to realize their captives have broken loose.

They need to have a plan for when that happens.

"Do we have another of those whale balls?" Cas asks.

"Only one," Striker tells him.

"One is enough. I can dive for him. I can find the casket and break Death free."

"You're going to *dive*?" Ashworth says, eyebrows raised. "Underwater?"

Cas rounds on him in an instant. "*You're* not a part of this conversation."

"Are you certain it's safe to—"

"It's a little late for you to be worried about my safety," Cas cuts in, physically turning away from Ashworth so he doesn't have to look at him. Finn appreciates Ashworth's change of heart; she can also appreciate that this alone isn't enough to win back Cas's good opinion. "The fog will help, right?" Cas gestures at the stern windows, which are still clouded over with the thick gray mist outside. "They won't be able to see me from the main deck while I'm swimming out."

"You're not going alone," Mita says firmly. Cas opens his mouth to argue, but she cuts him off. "We'll take a boat. You can direct me where to row, to get as close as we can from the surface before you dive."

Cas closes his mouth. He nods, jaw set.

"I'd like to come with you," Leo says quietly, and Cas nods again.

Leo goes to fetch the last whale ball in its tin while the others discuss what to do about the men up on deck.

"The fog should be enough to conceal the boat as we're rowing out," Mita says. "But if we are spotted, we're going to need cover."

She's eyeing Captain Hobbes, who's been even quieter than usual as they've all been making plans. He doesn't push to join the group going to rescue his partner; he must know he's needed here, aboard his own ship. But Finn suspects the decision isn't an easy one for him.

"We'll cover you," Captain Hobbes says. "We'll be prepared. If we hear raised voices—if anyone on the main deck starts to raise an alarm—we'll storm out and give them something else to focus on."

Kieran circles the table to stand with Finn as they talk. It's odd, Finn thinks, seeing him moving so easily through this crew. Or perhaps the odd part is how normal it is.

"Remy will be all right," Kieran murmurs. "She's a tough one, your girl."

Finn feels her cheeks growing warm. "I know she is."

She suspected Kieran knew her relationship with Remy was not entirely platonic. It's possible Kieran knew about Finn's feelings longer than Remy did.

"If this goes badly," Finn says, "if it does come to a fight . . ."

She isn't entirely sure what she's planning to tell him: To stay out of it? To leave Finn and the rest of the *Mori*'s crew to do the fighting while Kieran runs to safety somewhere? But Kieran is no longer the boy on the packet ship who needed Finn to stand up to his bully in his place. Both of them have grown since then.

"I know how to hold my own," Kieran tells her. "We'll keep each other out of trouble, yeah?"

All of their guns have been left abovedeck, but the sailors gather kitchen knives from the galley and anything else they can find on the lower deck to use as makeshift weapons. The boat that Mita, Cas, and Leo will use is hanging in its usual storage place off the back of the ship, just above the wide stern windows, where Kieran and Immortal Gabe can hook it and pull the boat down without alerting the men on the main deck. The two of them are speaking in sailors' parlance as they slacken the lines; Finn can barely follow what they're saying. She's been at sea for less than two weeks; she's still a greenhand by every measure. But Kieran has been sailing for years, and he's more in his element here than Finn has ever seen him before.

This is something else she and her brother have been avoiding, isn't it? Finn had been so angry when Kieran told her he was taking to the sea. She'd heard plenty about the dangers of the sailor's life. After what she'd done to save her brother, his choice had felt like a betrayal, even though Kieran could have no idea why.

Finn didn't *want* Kieran to need her; it still hurt that he didn't.

This isn't the life Finn would've chosen for him, no. But it's what he's chosen for himself. And he's good at it. That much is obvious already.

Together, Kieran and Gabe lower the boat until it's hanging just below the windows, where Cas, Mita, and Leo can climb aboard.

Ashworth looks like he wants to say something to Cas, but Cas brushes past him to talk to Finn.

"Stay safe, all right?" Cas tells her.

Finn allows herself a pained smile. "Bit late for that, isn't it?" She gave up on "safe" six years ago when she sold her soul to a demon.

"Stay alive, then," Cas says. "When all of this is over . . . be alive."

Finn nods, suddenly shaky. "I'll do my best."

He crawls out through the window behind Leo and Mita, all of them careful and quiet. The fog is still thick as Kieran and Gabe lower the boat to the water. Finn clutches the handle of her knife. As Cas's group rows the boat out, Finn stands with the other sailors, braced, ready to rush up onto the main deck if anyone there calls out.

Her knife isn't her only weapon. If she needs to, tonight, she's going to use her fire. Marbas told her to wait for her moment; he warned her that if she's going to burn out in a glorious blaze, she should make it count.

And Finn intends to.

Finn wants to live to see the other side of this—but she has to protect the people she loves, too. She runs through the possibilities in her mind. If the *White Swallow* has cannons, there's likely a powder magazine somewhere aboard the ship stocked with gunpowder. Fire is the best enemy of a ship like that. If Finn needs to, she can destroy Smith and his men in just the sort of glorious blaze Marbas talked about.

Remy is probably aboard the *Swallow* by now. But Finn thinks back to the fire parting before them at the Chapel in Boston—even as Finn's senses failed her. She's always been able to protect Remy from her own fire. She has to trust that she can keep Remy safe.

When her moment comes, Finn is ready to give everything.

XXXV.

CAS

The whale ball is working. Cas knows it is, because his mind is predictably spiraling into panic, but his heart is pumping slowly and steadily. *Too* slowly. More slowly than a human heart is meant to pump. The realization sets his mind panicking even more, and his pulse picks up slightly, fighting against the effects of the magic.

"Breathe," Leo reminds him. "Or . . . I suppose you don't *need* to breathe much, do you? That's the whole idea. But it might help. While you're adjusting."

Cas draws in a long breath, and he holds it, and then he holds it a while longer. The whale ball is *definitely* working. This knowledge doesn't make him feel any calmer. Leo is still watching him, and Cas tries to focus on the rhythm of inhaling and exhaling even though he doesn't need to. Breathing does help a little.

At least they were able to row away from the *Mori* without being spotted. Cas is still braced to hear shouts coming from the ship, but the *Mori* is far enough behind them that it's invisible in the fog. Cas does his best to direct their boat as he helps Mita and Leo row. He doesn't *think* they're heading toward the *White Swallow*, either; they've set off at an angle, not back toward the beach, but not toward the open ocean, either. It's impossible to maintain his sense of direction in the fog, though. The world around them is the same eerie gray.

All Cas can do is follow that vague instinct that connects him with Death. It's a strange, tenuous thread—the slightest pull that tells him where to direct the boat. He knows he must look odd, pausing every few moments to close his eyes and feel for that connection again. His confidence is wavering. He can't tell if he's actually following anything or just making wild guesses.

"Take your time," Mita tells him. "You're doing well."

"We don't *have* time," Cas reminds her.

"We have enough," she says. "And trying to rush isn't going to help. It takes the time that it takes."

A low stretch of beach floats into view through the fog. Long Beach, Cas realizes suddenly. The same stretch of shore where he accidentally pulled Henry into a vision and set these pieces into motion. Something is drawing him here, and he swears it isn't just memory. The beach is long and low, but it ends in a high, rocky cliffside, a jutting piece of land at the edge of the harbor.

"There," Cas says, pointing their little boat toward the cliffs. "I think we're close."

At least the whale magic has loosened the tension in Cas's chest a little. His fear and panic haven't gone anywhere, but they're not so physical now. His muscles are tingling, as if his whole body is filled with clean air instead of only his lungs.

They stop rowing when their boat is a dozen yards away from the wall of rock. Cas's stomach sinks as he realizes.

"There's a cave," he says.

Of *course* Death would be trapped in an underwater cave. The ocean didn't have to drag the cursed casket far to hide it; it only had to drag it to the back of a cavern submerged under the waterline where no one in their right mind would ever dare to go looking for it.

"All right," Mita says. "We need a new plan."

"We don't have time for another plan," Cas says.

"This is not what we had in mind when you said you were going to go diving," Leo says. His voice is too level; Cas suspects this is his effort at keeping himself calm. Cas peers through the murky water. He can just make out the top of the cave entrance, where the darkness grows impossibly darker.

Leo is right; this isn't what Cas envisioned at all. He figured he'd be diving straight down from the boat when they were directly above Death's casket, which would have been bad enough. What he's proposing now is another matter entirely.

"We're too close to give up now," Cas says. "I can still do this."

"Even with the whale magic, you can't stay underwater forever," Mita reminds him.

"Five minutes, right?" Cas tries to remember what Striker had said when they were diving the wreck at Georges Bank. "Or ten if I can stay calm. I'll be quick."

Cas has no idea how he's going to stay calm while swimming through a pitch-black cave to find Death.

"Remember that when you start running out of air, you won't be able to just instantly resurface," Mita says. "And you won't be able to see anything. Not once you're beyond the entrance."

"I got us this far without being able to see Death, didn't I?" Cas points out.

He can feel that pull in his chest, stronger than ever. He swears he can almost hear Death's voice in his mind again.

He starts unlacing his boots. Leo is watching him very closely.

"I don't think this is a good idea," Leo says.

Cas starts to reassure him that it's fine, he'll be fine—but he remembers their conversation during Cas's birthday celebration.

Cas could try to brush this off, but Leo will see straight through him. He wants Leo to be able to believe him when Cas tells him how he's feeling. He wants to be someone who is honest with the people he cares about.

"I don't think it's a good idea, either," Cas says. "I'm still going to do it. But to be honest, I'm terrified. And I'm probably going to completely fall to pieces when it's over."

Leo blinks at him, taking this in.

"Can I come find you?" Cas asks. "When I'm falling to pieces?"

"Please do," Leo says.

"I can do this," Cas tells them both. "Really."

When Cas folds up his father's hunting jacket and holds it out, Mita accepts it. "We'll be here," she says.

Cas plunges into the water. The ocean is ice-cold, though the whale magic takes the edge off it. By the time he's swimming through the cave entrance, he barely feels the cold anymore. His mind is clear, even under the water, even as he holds his breath and swims into total darkness, keeping a hand on one of the rocky walls to guide him. His body doesn't feel the lack of air.

When he's far enough inside that the last glimmer of moonlight behind him vanishes, the fear catches up with him.

This is the manifestation of all his most recent nightmares. He's trapped under the water. He's going to drown. It doesn't matter that he doesn't need to breathe yet; it doesn't matter that he was bracing for this, or that this plan was of his own making. The plan is terrible.

It isn't a terrible plan, a voice in his mind says. *It's a risky one. There's a difference.*

The voice is Irish. Cas feels the thread now, more solid than ever. He nudges back at Death with his thoughts. *You can . . . hear me?*

Yes. Yes, I can hear you. Your plan isn't nearly as terrible as mine was. I got myself into this mess willingly. Having some regrets over that now.

Cas feels his way along the rocks, swimming through the blackness. He can sense Death somewhere ahead of him, but if there are fish in this cave, or snakes, or anything else, he won't be able to sense those. This is so much worse than the darkness in the smugglers' compartment. Cas isn't staying calm at all. Even with the whale magic, his heart is starting to beat too fast. He can feel his pulse pounding in his chest, in his ears, louder than ever with the rest of the world muffled by water.

He isn't even sure if he's the one panicking, or if Death is. It's as if the silence and the darkness have sharpened his thoughts; his emotions are tangling with Death's again. Cas is wrapped in that cold sense of dread he remembers from the cursed piece of brass.

Talk about something, Cas thinks at Death. *Please.*

Cas can barely handle his own fear at the moment; he doesn't need Death's fear added on top. He can't focus on his breathing the way Leo showed him. But he remembers sitting side by side in the surgeon's cabin while Leo told him about the nervous system.

What do you want to talk about? Death asks.

Anything! It doesn't matter. Just distract me, please, so we both stop losing our minds. Jesus Christ.

You want me to talk about Jesus Christ?

That almost makes Cas snort, though he catches himself before he inhales any water. He isn't sure how long he's been down here; there's no way to keep track of the time. The passageway through the rocks narrows a little, and Cas has to feel around to find which direction it continues.

Then Death says, *Did he tell you about the night we met?*

Who? The captain?

Yes. The ship he was on had already wrecked by the time I saw him, hanging on a scrap of a raft. He and his crewmates were trying to swim for shore. But the sea was frigid, and the waves were too strong.

It's a terrible scene he's describing, but his voice gives Cas something else to focus on besides the fear and anything unseen that might be lurking.

I took so many that night, Death continues. *One by one, their bodies gave out, and I took their souls and led them away. I don't even remember what I said to them. Or if I said anything. I'd been alone for so long, and I didn't want to do it anymore. It was easier to just feel . . . nothing.*

The darkness in the cave is all-consuming as Cas pulls himself forward.

He was speaking to them, though. Death's voice is so gentle, so fond, as he remembers. *That's Edward Hobbes for you. On the verge of drowning himself, and there he was, comforting his crewmates as they died in the sea around him. It's what I was meant to be doing. I'd nearly forgotten how.*

Cas thinks of the garden back at Dungeon Rock, and Thomas Veal's crewmates, and the way Death talked about loss. They're close enough now that Cas can feel their memories tangling again. He's felt Death's love for his own crew, who he hadn't been able to comfort in their final moments. He feels, now, what had stirred in Death's weary heart when he saw Captain Hobbes offering the comfort to his crewmates that Death hadn't been able to offer for his own.

God, I love that man, Death's voice says in his head.

There's a glimmer of light through the darkness just ahead of Cas. The cold water grows even colder.

The casket is buried under rocks at the very back of this narrow underwater cavern. If it weren't for this thread of connection with Death, Cas never would have found him. No one would have.

As Cas scrambles to move the rocks wedging the casket's lid closed, his chest starts to feel tight. A haze is settling over his mind. He has no idea how much time has passed since he last breathed, but the air his body had stored is running out.

He's too close to turn back now. He moves one of the rocks. The metal underneath is glowing, so faintly that it wouldn't be perceptible if it weren't for the total blackness of the cave around it. Cas's hand brushes against the bare metal of the casket as he tugs another rock away.

The touch sends a jolt running up his arm, like an icicle prodding an exposed nerve. It nearly startles a gasp out of him. He bites it down. If he isn't careful, he's going to drown sooner rather than later.

I can't touch it, Cas thinks. *I can't get it open.*

There's a faint thudding sound from inside the metal box. There's no denying it—Cas is very lightheaded now. He manages to push away the last of the rocks, but the casket is latched shut, and when he tries to open the latch, that jolt of energy pushes him away again.

There's a terrible weight to this casket Smith has forged.

And maybe it's the magic of the whale ball running through his system, or the countless unbelievable things he's experienced over the course of his life, or sheer, foolhardy desperation, but he doesn't speak to Death now. He speaks to the ocean itself. To the curse.

He isn't the one you want. It's the box. Let him go, and let it stay buried here forever.

Even if Cas gets the casket open, he doesn't have enough air left to swim back.

He thinks, *Help me. Please.*

There's a shift in the current. Something stirring. Something listening.

Something that trusts.

When Cas reaches for the latches, this time the metal doesn't hurt him. He can open the latches and pry the casket's lid back on its hinges.

Death is there inside the casket, eyes closed, barely visible in the dark, illuminated only by the glow of the metal box around him.

His eyes open, and he grins a roguish grin.

Then the water is pushing them, the surge of a fierce current, hurling both of them back through the winding cave.

When they burst free of the cave, into the moonlight and the clear air above the surface, Cas gasps it in and lets his head clear. Death is still grinning even as they bob there in the water.

"How did you do that?" Cas asks, marveling at the current that carried them, which has subsided just as quickly as it started.

Death shakes his head. "That wasn't me," he says, eyes shooting to Cas with something like admiration.

Mita and Leo are already rowing toward them.

"I see you've got a boat."

"You need to go," Cas says. "Help Remy. Stop Smith."

"You're all right?" Death asks him.

"I'll be fine." It isn't even a lie, Cas realizes. He *will* be fine. "Go!"

"Thank you," Death says, and he's gone.

Cas swims for the rowboat, where Mita and Leo haul him

from the waves, where Mita bundles him into his dry jacket and Leo buries his face in Cas's shoulder and whispers, "That was incredible. Do you know that? You're incredible."

Together, they row for the *Memento Mori*.

XXXVI.
REMY

When the ghost of Daniel Stevens touches Remy's arm, her mind flashes with an image of herself, seen from the outside: She and Finn are standing before Pastor Dekker, back at the Eden seminary. Remy holds Striker's rifle in her hands. Flames consume the room around them.

Remy's memory of that night is a blur of rage and grief. But Daniel Stevens remembers what she said to Dekker, when she chose to let him live: *Now you can watch while I take down your Order.* A promise to make Smith pay for killing Remy's father.

Daniel Stevens wants revenge, too. Remy knows it as his hand passes through hers, the same way she knows that the other figures that have appeared around her are Smith's other victims. The spirits Death spoke of, trapped beyond the Veil. Trapped by this man who's so focused on his own aims that even now, he's unaware of the ghosts surrounding him. He's still calling his daughter's name through the wound he's cut through the Veil.

His men can see these apparitions, though. Pastor Dekker's face has gone slack; he backs away. The shouts of the other Order members are distant in Remy's ears.

When Remy and Captain Hobbes prepared to break into the seminary, when they attempted to save a petulant Henry Ashworth who didn't want to be saved, Remy's notes from Daniel

Stevens's letters were invaluable. They were her map. In a sense, he's been beside her for some time now. Remy felt him on the ship, and when she sat on the beach in Provincetown and read the letters he'd written. He's been clinging to the points of connection he could, trying to reach her. Trying to help her make Smith pay for everything he's taken.

"Viola," Smith says again, very softly.

"She isn't there."

Death—the real Death—is on the ship with them.

Smith whirls around, furious. "What have you done? Where did you take her?"

"I didn't take her anywhere," Death says. "I showed her the door, and she moved on, as all souls should. You should be glad for that. It's a far better fate than what you've condemned *them* to."

He gestures at the spirits who've joined them on the ship, and finally, Smith's eyes widen. Does he recognize their faces, Remy wonders? Does he remember them at all?

"You trapped them," Death says. "Tampering with forces you had no business with, touching things that shouldn't be touched. You can't bring her back."

He turns to the spirits of Smith's victims.

"I'm sorry," Death tells them. "You deserved so much better."

Smith's eyes land on Remy. He seizes her by the arm. He pulls a silver knife from his coat.

"I'll summon her with blood," he says.

A column of flames erupts on the deck of the *White Swallow.* The fire that engulfs the ship is so sudden and so unnatural that Remy knows it can only come from one source. Smith has flinched back from the sudden heat; his grip on Remy's arm loosens, and she shoves him away, pushing him toward the rift in the Veil. Even Death himself looks startled by the ferocity of the blaze.

But the flames don't touch Remy. They lick around her harmlessly—just as Finn's fire always has.

Remy runs to the ship's railing. The fog is already starting to lift; however Death managed to escape from the casket, it seems to have settled something in the air. Remy can see the *Memento Mori* clearly.

Finn is standing at the bow, eyes fixed on the *White Swallow* across the water. She's watching the flames she's conjured through sheer willpower. The look of determination in her eyes is like nothing Remy has ever seen before. It takes her breath away.

But Finn is beginning to sway. She's pushing herself too far. With a stab of panic, Remy realizes what Finn's determination might cost her.

Smith's men on the *Swallow* are shouting at each other, trying and failing to smother the flames. Smith himself still stands by the rift in the Veil. Daniel Stevens and the spirits around him are unaffected by the fire.

Across the water, on the *Memento Mori*, fighting has broken out—the crew tries to take back their ship. Finn is clinging to the rail with both hands. The flames are still growing. Finn doesn't realize that Remy isn't alone here; from across the water, she must not see Death or realize that the spirits standing here are ready to fight at Remy's side.

Finn has always been too willing to sacrifice herself.

Remy wants to fight alongside Daniel Stevens and all these other wronged souls to the bitter, well-deserved end. She wants to tear apart the Order of Lazarus—to avenge her father, yes, and to stop Smith from hurting the people Remy cares about, and to fulfill the terms of Finn's deal with Marbas and free her from her contract.

More than anything, she wants Finn to live through this.

"Take him," Remy tells the spirits. "You don't need me."

She turns away as the spirits descend on the Reverend John Smith.

Remy climbs up onto the railing. She eyes the distance between the two ships. It probably isn't much farther than the length of Cedar Pond.

She can't overthink this. She dives into the sea.

XXXVII.

FINN

Finn pushes her fire to her limit, and then she pushes it further.

The fight to take back the *Mori*'s deck feels like it's happening in a dream, even as Kieran and the others rush around her. Finn keeps her focus on the *White Swallow*, on the flames consuming the ship. Remy is still aboard it, but Finn can protect her. The fire won't hurt her, and perhaps it will distract Smith and his men long enough for Remy to break away. Remy will find a boat, or Death himself will pull her to safety. Remy will survive this.

Finn is determined that Smith and his Order of Lazarus won't.

Finn doesn't *want* to burn out in a glorious blaze—but she saw Smith draw his knife, and she can't let Ashworth's vision of Smith's plan come true. At least Finn's death will mean something. She can give Remy the justice she's sought ever since she learned the truth about her father. Finn can do this for her. And for Cas, and for Kieran, and for everyone else on this crew. The Order has to be stopped.

Finn's vision is narrowing to a single point. She can't see what's happening on the *Swallow*'s deck through the fire. The flames will find the powder magazine soon. The whole ship will go down in a fiery explosion. Marbas told her to wait for her moment, and she has.

She pushes the flames out of her.

As the world fades, she feels only water.

No. That isn't right. She feels *arms.* A familiar embrace.

Finn must be falling into some sort of dream as Remy's arms wrap around her. Remy is soaked to the skin, her dark, tangled hair dripping in her eyes. Finn imagines the sensation of the water droplets landing on her own face.

"You don't have to do this!" Remy says as she shakes Finn, still clutching her tightly. "*Please.*"

Finn can't get the words out. How is Remy here, on the *Mori*, holding her? Smith had been about to use her as his sacrifice; Finn is certain. Finn was going to save her. She *needs* to save her.

She doesn't realize she's saying this aloud until Remy takes her face in her hands.

"You don't need to save me!" Remy says. "I'm trying to save *you*!"

Finn can taste salt water. The cold drops of water on her face are real. Remy is really here.

Finn feels something in her release. She surrenders her hold on the fire on the other ship. The flames can sputter out; they can run their natural course. Finn stands down.

She lets herself live.

She doesn't know how long Remy holds her there as Finn comes back to herself. Her vision is still swimming. Voices are speaking; people pass. Remy is drenched and shivering. Kieran is there, offering her a blanket, kneeling at Finn's side and telling her they've done it. They've taken back the *Mori*. Everyone is all right.

"Smith is gone," a voice says, and Finn looks up to find Death standing over them—freed from the casket and on the *Mori* again, where he belongs. "Trapped beyond the Veil. He can't come back.

He can't move on, either." He must see that Remy is about to ask him a dozen questions, because he says bluntly, "Daniel Stevens stole his train ticket."

There will be business to deal with; even without Smith, there are still Order members left alive who believed in his mission. When Finn leans up to peer over the rail, she can see the *White Swallow* across the harbor, badly damaged but still afloat. Several Order members are still here aboard the *Mori*, tied at the base of one of the masts while Captain Hobbes decides what to do about them.

"He's . . . dead?" one of them says, staring up at Death.

"No," Death says. "But he's finished."

Death can't know the significance of this word choice. But Finn feels dazed. It's over, she realizes. *Finish John Smith, the would-be usurper of Death. Maintain the present Death in his post.* Finn is terrified to believe it. But Remy is gazing down at her with tears in her eyes—tears of joy.

Smith is gone. The present Death is here, freed from the cursed casket. Could it be possible that they really fulfilled the contract's terms?

Finn's head has cleared enough for her to push herself upright. Remy helps her to her feet. The young man by the mast who had spoken is still staring at Death open-mouthed. Then his gaze falls on Finn. His face shifts to anger.

"You did that," he says. "Didn't you? *You* started that fire. You're a *devil*."

Finn doesn't know, exactly, how it happens. The man wriggles free of his bonds and lunges for one of the rifles on the deck. Kieran is on his feet. Immortal Gabe and Henry Ashworth both run toward him, too, but Kieran is faster. He dives at the man, wrestling the gun from his hands.

A gunshot cuts the night.

The gun clatters to the deck at the man's feet as Gabe and Ashworth both shove him away. Kieran sways for a moment.

When he turns, the blood is already soaking his shirt.

Finn runs to him. Her world shatters as Kieran falls to the deck, and she falls along with him.

Remy is beside Finn as she cradles his head in her arms. There's too much blood. A searing pain wrenches through Finn's sternum, as if *she* were the one shot through the chest, instead of her gentle brother, who never wanted to fight anyone. She remembers the sick baby bird he brought home when they were young, the way he nursed it through its final hours and was devastated when it died. She remembers those awful days when Kieran was ill, when he was dying, when Finn sat at his bedside and watched him fade and couldn't do anything about it.

Except she *did* do something, back then. She saved him. And she can't save him now.

He fades, and he fades, and he's gone.

XXXVIII.

CAS

When Cas, Leo, and Mita make it back to the *Mori* in their boat, the fog has lifted. The morning sun hasn't quite crested the horizon, but the sky is growing lighter.

And Kieran Robinson is dead.

Cas can't process the whiplash, their victory followed by this immediate and crushing loss. Finn is still clutching her brother's body. As soon as their boat is pulled up, Leo runs to help, but there's nothing to be done. Remy holds Finn as she cries.

Cas lingers in an out-of-the-way spot near the stern, giving them space. He listens as Immortal Gabe tells him quietly what happened. He feels utterly wrung out. Smith and his Order did too much damage long before last night, and now they've done this.

Death and Captain Hobbes have disappeared to one of the cabins belowdecks. Leo is moving through the crew, patching up the small bumps and scrapes from the night's events. Cas watches it all from a remove.

He startles as someone comes to join him. It's Henry.

Gabe told him how Henry helped the crew take down the Order members on the *Mori*'s main deck. How he attempted to stop the man who tried to attack Finn. Maybe Henry really has seen the error of his ways; maybe he can change for the better. Cas can't bring himself to care anymore.

Henry moves as if to touch Cas's arm, then seems to think better of it and stops. He looks so entirely out of place here aboard the *Mori*, a character in the wrong story. Maybe he could have fit in this story, once, if he'd chosen a different path. Instead he's an outsider here.

"Are you all right?" Henry asks.

Cas isn't, but he is. He *will* be all right, he thinks. He nods.

"Good," Henry says. "I'm . . ." It isn't like Henry to fumble like this, but even he seems aware of what unfamiliar territory he's standing in. "I'm glad," he says. "And I'm sorry."

Cas is so tired. "What are you sorry for?"

Henry holds up his arms, as if to gesture at everything—but Cas needs him to say it. He waits.

"I should have listened to you," Henry says quietly. "About Smith, about the danger . . . about everything."

Cas studies him. "Yes," Cas says. "You should have."

"I should have stood by you. I should have been at your side the whole time, through all of this."

Yes, Henry should have done that, too. Cas has been carrying it like a hot coal in his chest—the anger, and then trying not to feel the anger because it hurt too much. It was burning him even while he pretended it wasn't there. He lets out a long breath.

"Thank you," he says, and it doesn't feel like an act, accepting this apology. The apology doesn't fix anything, but it helps anyway. "And thank you, for helping us now."

He and Henry won't see each other again. Cas knows this in his gut, or in the truest part of his heart. Once Henry returns to shore, he'll go off and live his life, and Cas will live his own, and their paths won't intersect again. Maybe Henry will campaign with his dream senator in Boston. Maybe they'll make the world a better place, and Henry will create a legacy, and Cas will see his name in the papers and appreciate, logically, that people can change.

But Cas is done with him.

He wishes Henry well. And then he goes to sit beside Remy and Finn.

Finn is still holding Kieran's dead body when Death and the captain emerge from belowdecks.

"It's time," Death says quietly.

"No," Finn says. Her head has jerked up. Her face is red and splotchy from crying.

Cas understands her protest—and yet he understands, now more than ever, that Kieran is gone already. Death is the natural end, and it still hurts. It's meant to. It's time for Death to lead Kieran's soul to wherever he's going next.

But Captain Hobbes is standing at Death's side, and he's crying.

Cas can't fathom it. He doesn't know what to make of this anguish on the usually stoic captain's face. He feels like he should look away, like they should all look away, but he doesn't. A question is stirring in his chest.

"It's time," Death says again, "for me to pass on the mantle. I understand now."

Cas realizes very suddenly what he means.

Death takes his partner's hands. Quietly, he says, "Did you know there's a species of agave plant that grows for over eighty years?"

The captain stares at him. "What?"

"Could be even longer than that," Death says. "It grows and grows for decades before it ever produces a flower. And then it only flowers once, in its final days. A sort of death bloom. Out of nowhere, they produce this massive stalk, and they bloom gloriously, and then they die."

Captain Hobbes presses his forehead to Death's, quietly and gently. "My love," he says, "you have been blooming gloriously for a long, long time."

Death smiles. "I know," he says.

The captain laughs wetly.

"And I lived a long time before that, too," Death says. "I've had centuries. And I've done what I need to do." He takes the captain's hands in his. "And now it's time."

The captain doesn't argue with him. Cas feels something shifting in the wind. Only last night, Death told them he didn't know *how* the reaper before him passed on the role. Death knows, now, what to do.

The ship is very quiet. Cas realizes Death is looking at *him*. He studies Cas for a moment, sizing him up, but not in a way that makes Cas want to hide.

"I suspect you'll still be the reaper's glass," Death tells him. "Can't say for sure, but . . ." He nods, as if confirming something for himself, and his mouth twists. "I have a feeling. If you are . . ." Now he looks down at Kieran's limp form. "Help him, will you? He's going to need someone, as he adjusts. And long after, probably. He'll need someone who can be a lens."

"You're leaving," Cas says. A question, but not a question.

"I'm leaving."

"Do you know where you'll . . . go?"

Death cocks an eyebrow at him. "Do any of us?"

He turns to the captain and cups a hand to his cheek.

"I love you."

And he's gone. The scene has reset. Death is nowhere to be seen, and Kieran isn't a limp, empty body on the deck. Kieran is standing at the base of the mainmast, blinking in the pale light. His expression turns to confusion as he realizes they can see him.

Finn is on her feet.

"What . . . ?" she says. "How . . . ?"

Her hands and shirt are still stained with her brother's blood. And yet her brother is standing here. Unharmed, but not quite alive.

Finn runs to hug him. The cool morning air feels hopeful but heavy. Death seemed at peace with his decision, and still Cas feels a weight in his chest. Remy catches his eye, and he knows she feels it, too. She comes to stand beside him, an arm around his shoulders.

A chilly breeze sweeps across the deck. Cas tries not to shiver. The cold is settling over him, seeping into his bones.

A shadow has formed on the deck behind Finn. Something with arms. Tentacles. Something Cas has seen in his visions.

"Finn, *run!*" he shouts.

He isn't trapped in a vision this time, and still it doesn't matter, because Cas can't do anything to stop what happens.

In one swift motion, the demon reaches a shadowy hand straight through Finn's chest and snuffs out her heart.

XXXIX.

FINN

Finn finds herself, very abruptly, in a sort of void. An in-between. A dream space. Face-to-face with the demon. This isn't the human form of the demon; this is the same shadowy monster that appeared in the church, and that Cas has described from his visions. The form she saw from a distance on Mount Desert Island.

Perhaps this *is* a dream. Finn knows Marbas has spoken with her in her dreams before. Or perhaps this is somewhere beyond the Veil. Perhaps Finn is dead.

Perhaps this is hell.

The injustice of this realization is what helps her find words at last.

"We had a deal," Finn says, angry.

The demon only stands there, watching her.

"I did my part," she says. "Smith is gone. We've dealt with the—what did you call him?—the *would-be usurper of Death.*"

The shadow says nothing.

"We had a deal!" Finn says again, and she feels the rage building up in her. "Smith is finished, just like we agreed! And we've restored the original Death to his post, and—"

But she realizes her mistake even as she says it. Marbas's loophole.

They finished Smith, just as the deal required. But the original Death, Thomas Veal, is no longer at his post.

"No," Finn says. *That isn't fair*, she almost says, but she stops herself. When has the world ever been fair? *That isn't right*. But the world has never been righteous, either. Finn should have known better; she should have accepted her fate like she tried for all those years. She should have known there was no way for her story to end except like this. Of course Marbas would find a loophole, and of course Marbas would exploit it. It's been so obvious all along. Finn was a fool to believe she might ever stand a chance.

Never trust a demon.

And still the shadowy figure stands there, watching her. As if waiting to see what she'll do. Because what's the hurry? The demon has waited this long already, hasn't he? Finn was ready to die when she was twelve years old, and instead she's spent years in limbo, and it's now, of course, when she finally, *finally* has a future she can see, a life she's ready to fight for, that it's all snatched away from her.

She feels the fire stirring inside her. She thought she'd used it all on the *Swallow*. She's surprised to find that not only is it still there inside her, but she can still bring it to the surface with ease, even here in this dream space that Marbas has dragged her to. She holds out one hand and reaches for that fire. A flame starts to burn in the palm of her hand.

You're an odd one, aren't you? Marbas said when she summoned him as a child. *You're so young, and yet you're powerful. You ask audacious things, and yet you feel no entitlement.* It's not entitlement she feels now, but she does have something to fight for, something she couldn't access six years ago. She wants to live. Is that such an audacious ask after all?

"You were never going to let me out of the deal," Finn says to the demon, "were you? You were only going to keep me around for as long as I was useful to you. Because I *intrigue* you. Is that it?"

The demon doesn't disagree.

Finn pushes the flame in her hand a little larger. She waits for that weakness to take her again as she pushes herself too far, but it doesn't. She feels, somehow, that she could keep pushing now, and the fire won't burn out.

Out there, on the deck of the *Mori*, it was Finn's own life force that was being used up. *Vitalis vis.* The flame's fuel. In this dream space with Marbas, she no longer has her earthly limitations.

She lets the flame grow, hot and searing on her face, though her own skin doesn't burn. She's in control. The demon gave her the knowledge, showed her how to bring the flames to the surface, but it wasn't the demon who gave her the fire. It was hers all along. And he made a mistake in teaching her how to use it.

The flame in her hand has turned into a fiery pillar. In the orange glow, she thinks she sees Marbas shifting. Shying away from the glare of what he unlocked all those years ago. For all Finn's nightmares about the fires of hell, the demon is a creature of cold.

"I will burn you," Finn says.

The demon watches her through a wall of fire now.

"Do you hear me? I will *burn you.* I'll burn everything. I'll burn it all to the ground, and then I'll burn it again."

She pushes the wall of flame forward. She isn't certain the inferno will truly hurt the demon until she hears the piercing, screaming sound. The demon burns.

Remy and Cas had both accused her of trying to use her fire as the solution to everything.

And it isn't the answer to everything. But it's the answer to this.

When Finn wakes, she's going to tell them both so.

EPILOGUE
REMY

When she was eighteen years old, Remy DeWindt accepted a placement as a lighthouse keeper on the North Shore of Massachusetts. She was an unconventional candidate for the position; a handful of other women had become lighthouse keepers, yes, but only because they'd succeeded their husbands after illness or death. Remy was not only a woman, but a very young one, and she had no prior experience managing a light.

Still, the official responsible for her nomination swore Remy was the ideal choice. He was high up in the Treasury Department, and he approved Remy's even more unconventional request for her two assistant keepers, too. If blackmail played a role in these appointments—if the man at the Treasury had ties to a secret society now embroiled in several murder charges, and if the new appointees knew it—there was no paper trail. Remy, Finn, and Cas were offered a post at a light station just outside Marblehead Harbor.

The October fog was thick through the night, but it lifts with the dawn. Remy props her logbook on the rail at the top of the tower, watching the last silvery wisps fading over the sea. As the first beams of sunlight crest the horizon, she turns and signals to Finn in the lantern room just above her. Finn snuffs out the lamps, right on time. It's been a long night. They've made it through.

None of them slept much during the night. Usually they take the work in shifts, but with the fog, it felt safer with all three of them on watch. They spent the summer training—first with one of the captain's acquaintances, Gilly, at his lighthouse in Maine, and then with Mr. Spencer and Mr. Ambrose on Cape Cod. Remy has studied the rules and regulations for lighthouse keepers so thoroughly she nearly has them memorized by now. But reading the guidelines and actually putting them into practice are two separate matters. She isn't proud of the means by which she and her friends were appointed to this post. She's determined to do the job correctly.

Finn climbs down from the lantern room and joins Remy outside. She stands by her at the rail, quietly watching Remy finish her notes for the night. Remy wipes her eyes, crusty with lack of sleep, and closes the book.

"Any ships crushed upon the rocks?" Finn asks as Remy tucks her logbook in the pocket of her coat.

"Not a single one," Remy tells her.

"A success, then. I'd say you're getting rather good at this."

She stands on her toes to kiss Remy. Finn is warm; when she realizes how chilled Remy's cheeks are, she cups Remy's face in her hands and kisses her again. The touch does thaw Remy's cold skin a little, but not nearly as much as the happy glow in Remy's chest as she marvels, for the millionth time, that they can do this. Finn can kiss her, simply and easily. Remy can kiss her back.

Finn cut her hair recently, just to her shoulders. She described it as a practical decision—said that she was tired of working out the tangles from the sea-salt wind—but Remy has caught her studying her own reflection in the glass. She tugs on a lock of Finn's hair where it tumbles out beneath her knit cap. The change suits her.

There's a clatter of a metal pail from inside the tall brick tower, then a lot of swearing echoing up the staircase. Remy and Finn duck inside the service room to find Cas grunting as he heaves a bucket up the last few steps. He nudges it into its usual position and wipes his hands on his trousers.

"All right," he says, out of breath. "Oil levels are good. Water buckets are refilled for tonight. I spilled some water on the stairs. Don't step in it."

"I think we're meant to clean that up," Remy tells him.

"It's water. It'll dry."

Remy is almost certain there's a regulation about keeping the walkways clean and free of spills. Cas must see the look on her face. He shakes out his arms like a bird preparing for a first flight.

"Yes, fine, I'll go mop it up in a minute," he says. "Just wait until I can feel my arms again. We need to get a pump. Or a pulley system, or *something.* I can't keep hauling buckets up and down the stairs."

"I offered to help with the buckets—" Remy starts.

"No, you offered to *swap.* I'd rather do this than paperwork."

"If you weren't hauling buckets up and down the stairs, how on earth would you ever get your arms good and muscled?" Finn asks him.

Cas blinks down at his arms, as if muscles might have suddenly become apparent beneath his shirtsleeves. "That's a good point, actually. Never mind. We don't need a pump."

Remy laughs. "Where is Kieran this morning?"

Cas's eyes turn glassy for a moment, gazing into the middle distance. "Near Gloucester, maybe? Or a little farther north. He's somewhere near the sea, anyway."

Finn leans against him, arm to arm. "And the *Mori*?" she asks.

“That’s near the sea, too.”

Finn jabs him in the shoulder. “You know what I mean.”

It’s been a while since Cas has fallen into a vision, though his bond with this new Death is stronger than ever. He and Kieran stay in regular communication these days. The reaper, and the reaper’s glass. Whatever channel of connection Cas has been learning to navigate extends to the *Memento Mori*, too, with the Mark of Death still carved into the ship’s skeletal figurehead.

Cas is quiet, breathing deeply. He’s still Cas, Remy thinks, with his constant movement and fidgeting, but something in him seems more settled these days. More balanced. In contrast to Finn’s newly trimmed hair, Cas has let his grow out a little—just enough that he has to tie back the top layer of it to keep it from his eyes. It makes him look older. All of them are older.

“They’ve left Boston,” he says finally. “I think they’re sailing this way. They’ll probably be here by the afternoon.”

They climb down the spiraling stairs, and Remy helps Cas mop up the spilled water. Through the tower’s window, Remy can see the line of lights of the town across the water. Her mother and sisters have been quickly settling into their new townhome there. Remy will row over today or tomorrow to pay them a visit when she picks up supplies. The house is small and cramped, and the roof started leaking barely a month after they moved in. But Remy’s mother says it already feels like home. A fresh start.

Once they’ve put away their cleaning supplies, all three of them button their coats and trail outside to the beach. They’ll go to bed soon. But Finn had asked, when they were moving into their new home here, if they could all watch the sunrise together each morning. Finn asks for things so rarely that Remy and Cas agreed immediately. It’s become a ritual, sitting on the beach, or in the lantern room of the tower when the weather is foul. Taking this new future day by day. This future is a good one.

"I was thinking I might sail out with the *Mori*'s crew, when they stop by," Cas says.

They're sprawled on the rocks, watching the morning sun paint the ocean gold. Remy is leaning against Finn's shoulder, their fingers intertwined. Cas is stacking pebbles into a tiny tower by his feet.

"Penelope's coming up on the train next month," Finn reminds him.

"I know," Cas says. "I would only be gone for a week or two. Cruise up to the coast and back. Just long enough to catch up with everyone, and then remember why I don't like sailing."

"I imagine Leo would be happy for you to spend a bit more time together," Remy says.

Cas throws a pebble at her. "Yes," he says, "he would, and I'd be happy for it, too. Leo's a delight. I don't know why you look so smug."

"I think it's a grand idea," Finn tells him. "And we'll be here when you return."

The lighthouse has become a regular stop on the *Memento Mori*'s journeys up and down the northeast coast. The captain always has news to gather and news to share, for Remy and the others to pass on to any other ships in their network that pause here.

Finn takes Remy's cold fingers and rubs them between her hands to warm them. Maybe the three of them will take it in turns, sailing out with the *Mori*. Or maybe, when the ship passes through today, the captain will moor for the night, and Immortal Gabe will build a bonfire, and Cas and Leo will end up sitting quietly on the other end of the beach for a while, and Mita will teach Remy and Finn how to repair the siding of their little house where it's starting to come loose. And they'll revel on the beach the same way they did months ago when they were just beginning to see what was possible. When all of this was so new.

For now, the three of them just sit here, watching the waves. The sea stretches out before them, infinite and wild and full of possibility.

The day will be a warm one, Remy thinks, despite everything. Even now, if she squints, she can almost make out the familiar white sails on the horizon.

ACKNOWLEDGMENTS

I've been carrying this story and these characters around in my head for nearly a decade. Thank you, truly, to all the librarians, booksellers, and readers who've supported *Devils Like Us* as it ventured out into the world. It's been an honor and a joy to get to finish telling Cas, Remy, and Finn's story and share it with you.

Thank you as always to my outstanding agent, Beth Phelan, as well as Marietta Zacker and the entire team at Gallt & Zacker.

Thank you to my editor, Meghan McCullough, who was incredibly patient with me along this journey and who solved several plot problems that had stumped me for months. It feels serendipitous in the best way that I got to work with you on this book.

Thank you to the whole Bloomsbury team, especially: Rebecca McGlynn, Laura Phillips, Nicholas Church, Faye Bi, Briana Williams, Phoebe Dyer, Tiffany Coelho, Beth Eller, Erica Barmash, Alona Fryman, Ashleigh James, Leah Robert Packer, Jennifer Choi, Andrew Nguyen, Daniel O'Connor, Emelyn Ehrlich, Sarah Rucker, Valentina Rice, Sarah Shumway, and Mary Kate Castellani. Thank you to Marisa Aragón Ware for creating yet another beautiful cover illustration, and to Jeanette Levy for the cover design. Thank you to Cameron Kellogg for all your help in building this duology into what it is.

An enormous thank you to my writing community, especially

Sacha Lamb, Jas Hammonds, Avery Mead, Kirt Ethridge, Octavia Saenz, JD Scott, Lakshya, Katherine Ouellette, and Natalie Morgan. Extra thanks to Jen St. Jude, who cheered, commiserated, brainstormed, read, and cheered some more. Here's hoping for calmer seas ahead, but if we had to weather the storm, I'm glad we could weather it together.

Thank you to Molly, Al, Megan, Kate, Kevin, and Tricia, for all your support and for indulging me when I had to point out every single landmark from *Devils Like Us* we encountered in Acadia.

Finally, thank you to Cara, who's been with me through it all. You listened, read, problem-solved, figured out character motivations, filled plot holes, and fixed the church attic scene. You celebrated with me when I was excited and talked me through when I was losing my mind. Let's go sit by the water somewhere and watch the sunrise.

Return to the beginning with **Cas**, **Remy**, and **Finn** in the Stonewall Honor–winning *Devils Like Us*,

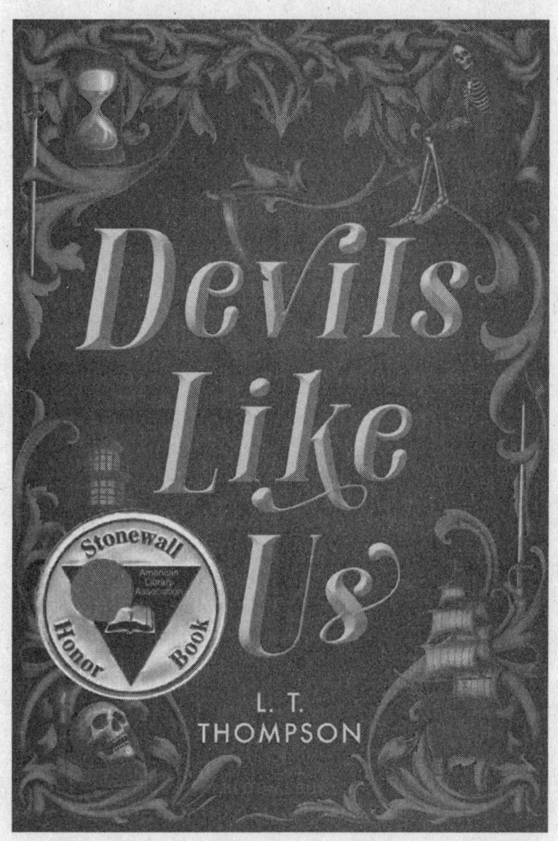

when a prophetic vision sets the three of them on a collision course . . .